PASSAGE TO TOKYO

Book Two of the Ancestor Memories series

POPPY KUROKI

MAGPIE
BOOKS

A MAGPIE BOOK

First published in Great Britain, the Republic of Ireland and Australia
by Magpie, an imprint of Oneworld Publications Ltd, 2026

ISBN 978-0-86154-763-0
eISBN 978-0-86154-765-4

Tokyo map © Duits Collection / MeijiShowa

Typeset by Geethik Technologies
Printed and bound in Great Britain by Clays Ltd, Elcograf S.p.A.

The authorised representative in the EEA is eucomply OÜ,
Pärnu mnt 139b–14, 11317 Tallinn, Estonia
(email: hello@eucompliancepartner.com / phone: +33757690241)

Oneworld Publications Ltd
10 Bloomsbury Street
London WC1B 3SR
England

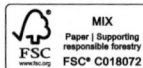

For my children, whom I love more than anything,
And for Declan, one in a million.

TŌKYŌ

SCALE

KOISHIKAWA - KU

USHIGOME - KU

YOTSUYA - KU

HONGŌ - KU

AKASAKA - KU

KŌJIMACHI - KU

KANDA-KU

SHITAYA - KU

ASAKUSA - KU

AZABU - KU

NIHOMBASHI - KU

KYOBASHI - KU

HONJŌ - KU

FUKAGAWA - KU

SHIBA - KU

TŌKYŌ BAY

PART 1

'There was silence, like the world had stopped.'
Earthquake survivor

CHAPTER 1

Early dawn always had a heavy, grey filter over it in the summertime. Nothing felt real, especially after a night shift under the bright lights of the convenience store. Sanada Yui's body wanted to be awake even as she craved sleep. Stepping outside was like walking into a sauna, even at this early hour. The summer of 1995 was proving to be blazing.

Yui debated whether the price of a Tokyo Metro ticket was worth avoiding the heat. She decided it wasn't and slipped through an alley that led through the grounds of Sensō-ji Temple, the jingle of the shop's entryway still jangling in her ears.

There were many tourists around Sensō-ji Temple, even at this early hour. How could they have been voluntarily out facing this humidity? Yui slipped through a throng of chattering Chinese tourists, glancing only briefly at the stone steps leading to the enormous red temple. Then her gaze slid to the five-storey pagoda. Even though she walked past it almost every day, the building still made her breath catch a little. She always had a hundred things on her mind, but in this place, she could relax for a moment.

Some nights, this road would be full of stalls selling grilled noodles and fried squid, but in the morning it was mostly tourists and the occasional student or businessman, dabbing their foreheads with hand towels. Yui was sweating by the time she had passed the Hanayashiki Theme Park and entered the quieter residential district that served as her neighbourhood.

Asakusa itself wasn't so bad. It was one of the oldest neighbourhoods in Tokyo, and of course home to some pleasant places. But Yui's mood soured, like it always did, the closer she drew to the narrow streets that led to her home. She passed a building where men liked to bet on the horses. A loud cheer rose as she passed it. A man marched past, holding his young son's hand, an eager look on his face as he held a paper betting ticket.

Yui wished she could hold her breath all the way past the building, and the Pachinko parlour opposite. Both stank of tobacco, sweat and despair.

The rickety stairs that led up to her family's flat on the third floor always wobbled precariously when she climbed them, as though one wrong step would snap the cheap metal and send them collapsing. She was pretty sure if an earthquake hit, the whole shabby building would crumble to dust.

Had she beaten her mother home today? The inside of the small, one-bedroom flat wasn't any cooler than outside, though a fan hummed in the living space. Hiro was already up, the low buzz of the TV and the clack of controller buttons reaching her from the *genkan* entryway, where she kicked off her trainers. Mother's heels were there, one of them knocked over, alongside Hiro's school shoes. She straightened them all then stepped through the narrow hallway.

'*Tadaima,*' she said by way of announcing her return.

'*Okaeri,*' grunted Hiro to welcome her home.

Piles of papers, books, bags, storage boxes, and more sat around Yui's younger brother, who sat cross-legged in the living room. A half-empty bowl of cereal was beside him, and he was playing on their Famicom console. Yui had saved up for weeks to buy it for him.

'It's nearly eight o'clock.' She held out a rice ball from the convenience store that had been on discount. He didn't reach for it, so she put it before him. There was a hole in one of the socks he was wearing, but at least they matched today.

'Thanks.' Hiro's large eyes didn't leave the screen.

'C'mon, Hiro, or your teacher will give me grief again.'

'It's the last day of term.'

'You need to go to school, Hiro. So you can get a good job and be able to afford things. Like living somewhere nice. Not working minimum wage like me.'

He glanced up at her, pausing his game. 'Welcome!' he said in a mocking tone, pretending to bow at her.

'Ha, ha.' She leaned in. His smooth chin was pebbled with greyish purple. 'You have a bruise on your jaw.'

Hiro scowled, turning back to his screen as he pressed his hair against his cheek, hiding the birthmark he was so self-conscious of. 'Tamura was annoying me. He was teasing me for not having a dad.'

Yui swallowed a sigh. 'Then he deserved it. But you still need to go.'

She managed to get him out of the house by eight-twenty, under the promise that he would go to straight to school. 'It's too hot to hang around anywhere,' she reminded him. 'And the school will ring me if you don't show up.'

'I know, Yui-chan,' he said. 'You mother me too much.'

Yui kept her mouth shut, thinking privately that Hiro was lucky to have someone to mother him.

She waved as he left her alone in the apartment, bouncing his way down the rickety stairs into the hot summer morning. Yui counted the money in her purse. There were still eleven days to payday, and one of the big letters Hiro had torn open notified them their rent was overdue. Again.

She ate the rest of Hiro's soggy cereal then checked the drawers. Her mother hadn't gone to the supermarket. She didn't know why she'd hoped she would.

They had only one bedroom in the apartment, but the fug of tobacco and old booze lingered in the thick air even when Mother wasn't around, so Yui gathered some blankets in the living room to get some sleep. It was past noon when she snorted awake and rubbed the drool from her chin.

The fan did little to help the heat. It was just hot air blowing on her. What she wouldn't give for air conditioning! That was one good thing about working in the convenience store: the steady blast of cold air.

Yui knocked on the sliding door of the bedroom. 'Mum?'

She slowly slid it open. A fan blew on the far futon, her mother's arm thrown over her face. Her sequinned dress and matching bag lay on the floor, looking cheap and garish in the faint noon light.

'Mum,' Yui whispered again.

Her mother grunted, finally moving. Her lipstick was smudged, her hair spread on the yellowing pillow. 'What?'

'The rent's overdue. Do you have it?'

'You woke me up for that?' Mother turned over. 'You know I don't. If you stopped buying sweets for Hiro all the time, you'd have it.'

Yui had expected this response, but Mother's attitude still set Yui's teeth on edge. 'I have a job to save money.' She didn't add, 'So I can move out.'

Mother muttered something and pulled a sheet over her head. Yui leaned her forehead against the wall, struggling to rein in her temper. Her job at the convenience store didn't pay much, and every spare yen went into her bank account. Once she had enough money, she wanted to move out of here and take Hiro with her.

But when Mother pulled shit like this, it meant Yui had to empty her meagre savings to make sure they didn't all end up homeless.

'It's your job to pay the rent on this place,' she said. 'Since you're our mother and all.'

Mother threw off the sheet, glaring at Yui with bleary eyes. 'You're an adult too. I'm a single mother. I work hard. All you do is give me grief.'

Yui's temper flared. 'How you manage to work every night and still be broke is beyond me. Maybe if you stopped smoking and buying gifts for those losers at the club.'

Mother scrambled to her feet, the sheet falling off her body. She pushed Yui against the wall and slapped her across the face. Yui's cheek stung, but she barely flinched, glaring at her mother.

'You're an ungrateful brat,' her mother snarled. 'If you're so much better than I am, why not leave? You're, what, twenty? Most of your friends are out there with real careers.'

'I'm twenty-two, not that you care. And I *want* to move out,' Yui shouted back, shoving her mother away from her. 'I would, if I didn't have to keep paying for the rent and for food for Hiro.' She pushed past the older woman and headed for the door. Had it been lost on her that Yui hadn't gone to university because she hadn't been able to afford it? Did her mother really think Yui still wanted to be here when her friends were enjoying studying abroad and planning their future careers?

Yui's head pounded. She wanted to go back to sleep, but she was too angry. She fumed as she shoved on her shoes, feeling her mother's glare on the back of her neck.

This was why she hated the night shift, even though it paid more. Mother worked at a *kabakura,* a hostess club a few streets down. Night-time was the best time to be home, where she could help Hiro with his homework and play games with him.

Now, though, home was the last place she wanted to be, and Hiro was at school. Yui grabbed her bag as she heard the bedroom door slide shut.

The sun beat down, the July heat sweltering on the Tokyo streets. Yui marched past the rundown apartment buildings and along the main road, where box-like Kei cars chugged past, until she found an alleyway sporting a karaoke box. It was a scruffy place, but at least it was cheap. She paid for two hours, which cost almost nothing at noon on a weekday, filled a large cup with water and slipped into a tiny room that smelled vaguely of smoke, a bright screen advertising a new Masaharu Fukuyama song. Yui dozed off dreaming of a fancy two-bedroom apartment in central Tokyo, of taking the train to her high-paying office job, to Hiro smiling broadly as he graduated high school …

She awoke with a crick in her neck and her throat dry, but a little more alert. She chugged her water and left a minute before her time was up.

She almost wished she'd had a double shift, but her manager wouldn't let workers do a night and a day shift in a row. She already felt bad for spending the money on the karaoke place.

She wandered to Sensō-ji Temple. Walking around the grounds was free. Distant screams of delight from Hanayashiki Park and cicadas' pulsing cries echoed around the square. She headed to the small bridge between the temple and the pagoda, where a statue smiled down at her. She leaned against the bridge, looking at the koi carp swimming in the small river.

When she'd been younger, she had dealt with her mother by going out, smoking, drinking and hanging around at friends' houses. To say she was over it now would be a lie. It was more that she had just accepted her mother wouldn't get any better. Looking after Hiro had given Yui a purpose that dragged her away from trouble, but she'd lost some of her friends along the way. If you could call them friends.

Now she worked towards her goal of moving out. She'd give Hiro a better childhood. Get another job if she had to.

The sun was burning her neck. She sighed, stepping into the temple's shadow and looking at the carvings in the red wood like she had a dozen times before. Tourists waved incense around their heads or sought their fortunes in the booths, their laughter echoing around the square as they shook out long sticks with numbers painted on them or slid open the corresponding drawers to find a good or bad fortune. Yui watched two women, possibly mother and daughter, reading out their fortunes. The older woman locked eyes with Yui for a moment. She gasped, a hand covering her mouth, and the fortune slipped from her fingers. The younger woman gave a cry and chased the tiny slip of paper as it blew off in the breeze. Yui left them to it and walked towards her home.

Near a convenience store on the way back, she spotted a poster for a festival at Ueno Park tomorrow afternoon.

It might be nice to take Hiro. The summer holidays would be starting from tomorrow, and it was always a challenge finding things to do that didn't cost money. At least now, at twelve, he had his own friends to hang out with. Yui didn't blame him when he stayed for dinner at their houses or hung around school clubs. She did the same when she was his age, until her mother started forgetting to make his meals.

'I'll get us out of here, Hiro,' she murmured to herself as she memorised the details of the festival. She scowled as she withdrew the money for the rent, feeling the precious ten-thousand-yen notes in her fingers.

Yui had been looking after Hiro since he was a toddler. It wasn't his fault he'd been born. And no father had ever shown up to meet him, any more than Yui's father had. She strongly suspected both their fathers were regulars at the hostess club, but how would she ever prove it? No one would care.

Yui had asked once, and all she'd been able to glean was that he'd been half-American. Or was it Canadian? 'He was tall,' her mother had said vaguely when Yui, a small child at the time, had pressed the issue.

'So I'm a quarter American?' Yui had chirped.

A shrug. 'I suppose so.'

Her mother hadn't cared to tell her more. Maybe she hadn't known much more than that, not even giving up his name. No one cared about them at all, so it was important for her and Hiro to stick together. Yui couldn't imagine moving out and leaving Hiro with *her*.

Mother would be out of the apartment by the early afternoon. Yui still had some time, so she wandered to the supermarket to check the discount section. She managed to find some sandwiches and vegetables, and she was in a marginally better mood by the time four o'clock rolled around. Sure enough, her mother was gone when Yui arrived home, her futon still sprawled across the tatami mat floor.

The flat was quiet, but Hiro came home at just after six, and she greeted him with as much cheer as she could muster. He grunted in response, sliding his bag off his shoulder.

'Got a lot of summer homework?' she asked brightly. 'C'mon, let's play something.'

Cicadas buzzed outside, filling the air with their trilling cries. When the sun set hours later, Yui's eyes stung from staring at the TV. Hiro had fallen asleep, his head on her lap. Yui's stomach rumbled as she leaned her head against the precarious pile of crap Mother had never bothered sorting out properly. Hiro's school term had finished, so now what? Yui tried to time her shifts for when Hiro was at school, asleep or out with his friends. Mother barely noticed him, and when she did it was to snap at him to get out of her way. Yui wondered what she was doing now. Complimenting some businessman, pouring him drinks and lighting his cigarette? Was she as popular as she used to be, or were the younger, fresher hostesses getting all the best clients?

Yui could sometimes hear the chime of the convenience store in her sleep. Stocking shelves and murmuring *'irasshaimase'* to welcome a customer weren't the most mentally stimulating things she had ever done, but there were worse jobs. And there were times when they were about to throw out some expired produce that she could sneak home.

She wondered if she should try becoming an office worker, get more consistent hours and a stable salary. But that was something she had imagined doing when she and Hiro already had a place. Maybe a two-bedroom apartment in an upscale neighbourhood. She had often drifted off to sleep lost in fantasies like that. They'd buy all their own furniture, and Hiro would have his own room with a huge TV and all the games consoles he wanted.

But Yui hadn't graduated high school. She had missed most of her final year and exams to look after Hiro. Most offices wanted a university degree. Still, it was fun to dream about it.

She would do worse jobs if it meant more money. She switched on the news, idly stroking Hiro's hair. Kobe, five hundred kilometres to the west, was still recovering after the huge earthquake back in January. She grimaced at the awful sight of the cracked roads and broken bridges as a serious-faced newscaster reported on the hundreds of people still missing, even after all these months. It made her think of their rickety apartment building and whether it would survive a big earthquake.

'This is the worst natural disaster Japan has seen since the Great Kantō Earthquake in September seventy-two years ago,' the newscaster droned, 'where fires killed over a hundred thousand—'

Yui switched off the TV, rubbing her face. The ten-thousand-yen notes sat in her wallet. It felt like dead money.

Hours and hours working in the convenience store being flushed down the toilet.

She wondered how much her mother made, how much she had wasted on presents for her favourite clients and cheap perfume. Or how much she was secretly keeping to herself, hidden in an old shoebox among the sea of crap in their bedroom.

Wouldn't that be great? If she and Hiro came across a treasure hoard of stashed money. Maybe a couple of jewels and expensive watches while they were at it. Enough to put a deposit down on a house.

Yeah, right.

Yui didn't feel like crawling under the old sheets in their room, so she lay beside Hiro. A siren wailed in the distance. Yui felt the tatami mat beneath her, imagining everything shaking in an earthquake, imagining herself and Hiro buried under clothes and boxes and the apartment roof, unable to escape.

CHAPTER 2

It was some time in the night when Yui and Hiro rose from the tatami mat, each agreeing the beds were more comfortable. They fell onto their futons, Hiro's in the middle, Yui's closest to the door. Yui dragged the fan as close to them as she could. It rattled when she switched it on, and she dearly hoped it wouldn't break. Hiro scowled in bed, scratching his arm where a mosquito had bitten him.

'Don't scratch it, it'll swell up,' she whispered into the dark. A pause. 'Want to go to the summer festival tomorrow?'

Hiro gave his arm one final scratch, then shoved it under the blanket before she could scold him. 'Sure.'

'Even if it's with me?'

Hiro laughed. Or it might have been a scoff. 'Even if it's with you, *onee-chan.*'

'Still not too cool to go with your sister?'

She thought he might say she embarrassed him, but he said in a small voice, 'No.'

The next morning, Yui felt like she hadn't slept at all as she washed in their sputtering shower. They could reach Ueno by train, but it would save them money to walk.

'You want a *GariGari-Kun* ice pop?' she asked as they passed the Lawson convenience store on the way to the district of Ueno.

'*GariGari-Kun* is for kids.'

'Exactly.' She stopped, swallowing. 'C'mon, let me buy you one.'

He didn't realise how much this meant to her. An ice pop just cost a couple of yen. It wasn't an apartment, or a new school uniform, but it was something she could do.

A middle-aged man in a suit deposited a dark umbrella in the holder outside the convenience store. They followed him inside, sighing with relief at the cool interior. The welcome chime filled their ears, and Hiro headed straight for the ice-cream section.

They were lining up, *GariGari-Kun* in hand, when the man turned a corner, almost colliding with a woman pushing a pram.

'Watch where you're going!' he roared.

'I'm sorry.' The woman's eyes widened as she gave a hasty bow, looking like she'd gladly melt through the floor.

'You almost crashed right into me.' The guy stared at the mother like she was something foul he'd found on his polished shoes.

The woman apologised again, dipping her head.

'What an arsehole,' Yui muttered, poking Hiro's back when the cashier called for them. 'Go on.'

When they stepped outside, the man's black umbrella was still there, stuffed haphazardly into the stand. Yui snatched it up.

Hiro giggled, unwrapping his ice lolly. 'You said it was wrong to steal.'

'It's not wrong if they deserve it.' Yui glanced back at the shop. 'Quick, come on.'

Giggling, they fled the store, the stolen umbrella in Yui's hand. When they'd mingled with a crowd heading for Ueno Park, they slowed and Hiro was soon slurping on his ice lolly, trying to eat it all before it melted. Yui glanced at him now and then, warmth fuzzing in her chest. He used to do that as a kid. He would beg her to buy him an ice lolly whenever they passed a shop. Back then, he couldn't eat it fast enough, and the sticky blue liquid would run all over his fingers. She'd pretend to lick it off, and he would squeal and laugh.

As they neared Ueno Park, they passed a cicada on the ground. Yui thought the bug was dead at first, but it twitched in the hot morning sunlight.

'Look.' Hiro stopped. He moved his shoe on top of it.

'Don't do that,' said Yui, but there was a crunch as Hiro crushed the bug with his foot.

'*Yada,*' remarked Yui in protest. 'What did you do that for?'

The bug was flat on the concrete. 'It was going to die anyway.'

'Still.'

People were heading for Ueno in droves. Echoing in the distance were the drumbeats of festival music, and as they passed the bustling Ueno Train Station, they joined the crowd up the stone steps towards the park. 'There are so many people,' said Yui needlessly. She wiped sweat off her brow and put down the umbrella.

'Let's take a break here.' She stopped at the statue of Saigō Takamori, a famous samurai, at the top of the stone steps.

There was a memorial about the last samurai of Kagoshima and some information written about him. Hiro stopped to eat his ice lolly, looking up at the broad-shouldered, beefy man and his dog. Yui watched him, daring to allow herself to once again fantasise about a time sometime in the future, where she would get an apartment somewhere in Tokyo, maybe the nearby Chiba Prefecture, with a decent job. Hiro would have his own room, would be able to join the baseball team or the football team or whatever he wanted to do. She would always have time for him, always have spare money to buy him what he needed. They'd go travelling. She went to ruffle his hair, hesitated, then lowered her hand. He didn't like her doing that anymore.

She sniffled.

'What's up?' he asked, strolling alongside her.

'I've got hay fever,' she lied.

'Hay fever season's over.'

'Then it sucks I still have it.'

She wiped her eyes then pointed ahead to where a line of cherry blossom trees flanked the long path up to the main park area. Right now, the branches were full of green leaves, shielding passersby from the worst of the sunlight. There were hundreds of people here, but Yui put the umbrella back up, and in the shade it was nearly bearable, though the air was thick with humidity. More drums and laughter reached them, and aside from the complaints about the heat, people sounded mostly jovial.

Yui liked the atmosphere here. There was a point in the long summer days when you accepted you were going to be sweaty and just went with it. A group of workmen, towels tied around their heads like bandannas, laughed together as they sat holding cans of beer. Groups of teenagers ate delicious-smelling meat on sticks. Men in *happi* robes chanted, welcoming in a floating shrine and shouting at the tops of their voices, keeping alive some tradition or other Yui had never learned. Hiro glanced around, and though his expression said he was thoroughly unimpressed, Yui could tell he was enjoying the flurry of activity.

'Yui-chan!'

The excited shout startled Yui, and she spotted a friend from high school, Ayano, who grabbed Yui's arms and jumped with excitement. 'I didn't know you'd be here.'

Yui couldn't help grinning. They used to greet each other like that at school, even if it had only been a day since they'd seen each other.

'It's been so long!' Ayano sang. 'How are you?'

'Nothing much to report.' Yui knew anecdotes of her job at the convenience store weren't very interesting compared to Ayano's life at university. She pushed down the envy as Ayano introduced Yui to her friends, and they exchanged bows and smiles before Ayano said, 'Are you having a drink, Yui? Let's *kanpai* to celebrate seeing each other again.'

Shouting men and women at stalls were selling lemon sours and beer from boxes of ice water. Yui dug out some change.

'Kanpai.' They toasted, jostled by other festivalgoers as they tapped their cans together.

'Who are you here with?' Ayano took a big gulp of her lemon sour.

'My brother.' Yui looked around for him, expecting him to be beside her. But he wasn't. She glanced over her shoulder, seeing people crowding around the stalls, standing and talking, but Hiro wasn't anywhere.

'Hiro?' Yui licked her suddenly dry lips. She mustn't panic. Hiro wasn't a little kid. He'd probably seen someone from school and gone to say hi.

Her gaze swept over the dozens of heads. People wiped their brows with hand towels, frowning at the heat. A little kid cried at her spilled ice cream. Friends laughed together, too loudly, at some unknown joke. A stall worker bellowed to passersby, asking them if they wanted ice-cold beer. It was too hot here, too many bodies pressed together.

'I'll catch up with you later.' Yui handed her drink to Ayano. Her friend was laughing with the others. Yui looked around for Hiro, hoping to see him in the crowd.

'Hiro!' she shouted, startling some nearby schoolkids. An older man with receding grey hair smiled at her, raising his hand to wave. A woman next to him shushed him. Yui averted her gaze. Where had her brother got to?

Fresh sweat coated her now. He couldn't have gone far in that minute she was talking to Ayano. She was furious with herself for taking her eyes off him for even a moment.

What colour shirt was he wearing? She couldn't remember. She looked around, gripping the umbrella. It hit someone's shoulder. She muttered an apology then folded it.

'Hiro,' she called, slipping through the crowd. She was going to tell him off when she found him. He'd laugh and say she worried too much, but Yui had a horrible feeling she couldn't shake off. Something wasn't right. Maybe it was lack of sleep, or stress, but she wanted to grab Hiro and leave. Why had she allowed herself to get distracted? Hiro must have been annoyed with her and wandered off.

The drums were too loud. The sound of her gasping breaths was strong in her ears, the lemony tang of the drink sticky on her tongue.

She was close to panicking when she spotted him. Was he looking for her, too?

'Hiro.' She shoved past someone to reach him. Being smaller, he slipped through the crowd with more ease. The umbrella got caught between some people's legs. She abandoned it, not bothering to be polite.

'Hiro!' she bellowed. A nearby man grunted in annoyance, covering his ear. Yui glared at him and ran after Hiro.

He was heading away from the festival, towards the train station and the steps back to the samurai statue. She finally found some breathing room as she left the crowd behind, stumbling onto the walkway. A stitch prickled in Yui's side as she climbed the stairs past Kiyomizu Temple.

'Hiro!' she called again, relief mingling with annoyance. 'Hiro, wait.'

She expected him to be waiting at the top of the steps, but she had lost sight of him again. She stopped, clutching her ribs. A crow cawed above her head. She glanced up the temple steps, saw no one, and sighed, turning round and blowing air up her forehead.

She walked until she could see the statue up ahead. Hiro was standing near it. Relief and annoyance flashed through her. What was he doing there? Was he ready to go home already?

She marched towards the statue, hating the slippery feeling of sweat running down her back, the burning sun on her forehead. She wiped it, thoroughly cross now. She approached the statue, ready to scold him for running off.

But Hiro was gone.

'What the hell!' She threw up her hands. He was *just here*. Her hands cupping her mouth, no longer caring about disturbing people, she yelled his name. Her shout echoed across the square. Worry crawled along her skin again. 'Come on, stop ignoring me. This isn't funny.'

She half-ran to the statue of the samurai, wondering if Hiro was hiding around there. Maybe he was waiting behind it, ready to jump out and scare her.

Then she saw it.

The statue's base should have been a pillar of stone. But now there was something else there. An arched space, as if the stone samurai stood on a bridge.

She stepped towards it, curious. How had she not noticed this before? It looked like a tunnel. Had that always been there? She had been here only half an hour before and not noticed something so ... out of place.

She climbed over the fence around the statue and peered down it. She couldn't see anything. When she called for Hiro again, her voice echoed, like she was shouting into a cave. It looked so long she couldn't see the other side. Wait, how was that possible? The statue was barely a metre wide. An optical illusion, maybe? Part of the festival?

She reached inside, expecting to feel her fingertips touch cold stone on the other side. But her arm stretched out to nothing.

Something whispered by her ear, like someone had leaned in to murmur something. Jumping, she whipped round, wondering what creep had come over to whisper at her. But nobody was here. Not even Hiro, sneaking up to prank her.

Were other people seeing this? This was impossible. The other side of the statue was just … the other side. 'Hiro!' she called again, but there was no answer.

She looked around, willing someone else to join her, to agree that this was impossible. But a strange hush had fallen over the park.

A shiver ran across Yui's shoulders, instinct prodding at her that something was terribly wrong. The park was too quiet. The background noise of passing trains and walking people had muted, like she was encased in a bubble. Even the birds were silent.

Then another whisper, this one full of urgency, rippled across her mind. Maybe she was losing her grip on reality. She couldn't make out what they were saying. Yui shook her head, confused. Everything felt wrong. She had to get Hiro and go home.

More whispers echoed all around her, always too quiet to make out. She felt like they were … encouraging her to take a step into the tunnel. Something was telling her to go inside and look around.

He wasn't anywhere else, not even when she circled the entire statue and checked behind nearby trees. She couldn't waste time. Hiro had gone down here; she was sure of it. Yui looked into the tunnel again that had hollowed out beneath the stone samurai's feet. She stepped cautiously into it, the light from behind her blocked by her body, her shadow on the ground before her. It was cool in here, like a cave.

Another whisper. *Go on*, it seemed to say.

'Hiro?' She wondered if she really was losing her mind. 'Stop messing around. We need to go.'

She glanced behind, to where the heat and light of the park awaited. This didn't make sense, either. It was still summer, still humid. But stepping here, beneath the statue, felt like she had walked into an air-conditioned room. The sweat on her face cooled, her fatigue fading. She reached out, still expecting to find a wall on the other side. But her fingertips touched nothing but air.

'Hiro?'

Her voice echoed all around, and then the darkness whispered back. It sounded like a boy this time. Right, so Hiro was hiding.

'You're in so much trouble when I find you,' said Yui. She took a step forward, hands outstretched, fully expecting to touch a solid wall, maybe find Hiro crouching, laughing at her expense.

Another whisper. Louder this time, right by her ear.

Yui swivelled, swiping at nothing, thoroughly freaked out. Where was she? Where was Hiro?

Darkness swallowed her. One moment the entrance was there, the next, she was plunged into blackness.

'*Kuso!*' she swore, groping in the dark for something, anything, to lean on. The entrance, if that was what you could call it, had disappeared. The door to Ueno Park was gone.

'Hiro! Now's a good time to let me know you're actually in here!' Yui cried. She wasn't afraid of the dark, but she didn't like this at all. Her voice echoed around the strange passage. It took several heart-pounding moments of groping before she finally found a wall, and she slid her hand along the rough stone. Her breathing mixed with the whispers that had returned. Hundreds of them, encouraging or mocking, it was difficult to tell.

23

Then a glimmer of hope. Daylight! She stepped towards it. As she got nearer so did the humid summer air, coming back to press in on her. Shielding her eyes from the light, she stepped outside.

She was back in Ueno Park.

Yui let out a breath. This was so confusing. She was sure she had been stepping forward through a passage. Unless she just did a full circle? She couldn't quite remember. She held her head, a wave of dizziness and fatigue washing over her. She felt like she had just run several kilometres then spun in place. Somehow drunk and hung-over at the same time.

She groaned, holding her head. *Hiro* ... She needed to find her brother.

She turned to see the Saigō Takamori statue, but the passage or hole or whatever it was had gone, leaving in its place the familiar stone and etching. Yui touched it, wondering if the heat was getting to her. Just a moment ago there had been a tunnel here. She had got lost in it, called out for her brother, those strange whispers had followed her ...

There weren't any whispers now.

Hiro had better be here, she thought, expecting he would jump out from behind the statue or a tree, laughing. She hoped that would happen. She hoped it more than anything.

She stood, her gaze on the statue. The samurai's little dog, frozen in stone. But nothing happened.

A warm breeze touched her face. Was it her imagination, or were there more trees here than before? And as she turned, she spotted a wooden building. It looked old-fashioned, nothing like the restaurant that had been standing there a moment ago.

Hadn't it?

CHAPTER 3

Everything felt different. Even the weather. It wasn't as humid, the smell more like nature and grass than the industry of eastern Tokyo.

Yui's first thought was that, somehow, this was a different statue. There must have been some kind of tunnel that connected them. But that didn't make any sense because she was still in Ueno Park … right?

'Hiro.' It came out a weak croak. There was only a man and a woman in the distance. The man wore a coat and hat, the woman a *yukata* robe. Yui staggered, dizzy again. She was sick with anxiety for Hiro.

Calm down, she commanded herself. She straightened and wiped her cheeks, putting on a cool, unbothered look even as her insides writhed with anxiety.

She walked along, but the dizziness was still there, making her stumble. Blowing out a breath, she grabbed hold of the nearest thing she could see. It was cool against her hand, thin and tall. She looked up.

It was an old-fashioned lantern, the kind lit with oil. It looked stark against the grey sky, cool beneath her touch. This didn't belong here, either. What was happening?

A weird dream, or a complicated trick. Part of the festival, maybe? Yes, that had to be it. They were running a theme of the Taishō era or something. She had been too busy to hear about it. *Why* had she become so distracted? The taste of the lemon sour was still sticky on her tongue. It tasted like regret.

Yui pushed off from the lantern. Her head felt a little clearer now. She didn't feel so much like she'd just spun in place. She didn't know what to do. Hiro knew the way home from here, but she didn't know if he would go all the way home by himself without telling her. Still, he was rebellious lately, and he often got annoyed if she was overprotective. Maybe he had met up with some friends and thought being seen with his big sister would be embarrassing?

The thought made her feel lonely, but she'd been like that at his age, too.

'All right.' Yui sighed, glancing around. She was tired. It was hot and she didn't feel like wandering through the crowds. Even though she couldn't hear the festival or see that many people anymore, they were surely still drinking and hanging around over there. And she had *seen* Hiro here.

Hiro was a junior high school student, and he rode the train by himself. He'd never got into much trouble before, except the occasional fight. Yui had been in a few fights during her school days, too, so she couldn't blame him. She would just have to tell him off when she got back. He'd probably be there already, playing their Famicom console with the fan blowing at full blast.

She approached the steps that led down to Ueno Station. Why did everything look so different? Where were the skyscrapers, the vending machines? Tokyo looked so … open and empty. The few buildings she could see were either wooden constructions or a strange mishmash of Western-style architecture.

Yui closed her eyes, massaging her temples. Was she lost? In a different place? How long had she wandered in that weird tunnel? She wasn't dreaming. Dreams were never this vivid. She could feel the warm air on her skin, the hardness of the ground beneath her feet, the sweat rolling down her back. Her heart fluttered, panic rearing its head again.

The couple from before wandered past, giving her a strange look. She straightened and said, 'What are you looking at?'

Ignoring their surprised mutterings, Yui started to walk. She had to get home, then she'd smack Hiro around the head before hugging him and telling him not to run away from her again.

She glanced around again for good measure. Those trees weren't there before. The vending machines had gone, though she wasn't fully sure they had been there to begin with. She was doubting her own memory now.

Maybe it didn't matter. Until she was home and Hiro was found, nothing else mattered at all.

Her trainers smacked the stone steps down towards Ueno Station. She expected to see the lines of shops, the crowded street leading to the market, the bustling train station.

Well, there was the station, though it looked weird. Duller, older. But where was everything else? People walked around, yes, but many of them were in summer *yukatas* and hats, looking so old-fashioned Yui wondered if the festival had found its way down here. People gave her strange looks; a woman with red lipstick and her hair in a complicated bun stared after Yui as she walked, trying to find a landmark she knew.

Was that Ueno Station? It was much smaller, a sloped roof and beams holding it up. Yui felt she was going insane. Was this her reality?

She just walked. She had a good sense of direction and felt like home was this way. But nothing looked how she remembered it. Everything was so … visible. She could have sworn she could see the red roof of Sensō-ji Temple. But that was impossible. There were usually too many buildings to see landmarks so far away.

A newspaper stand stood nearby, an old man running it. He looked her up and down as she approached, her heart hammering.

He said something she didn't understand. It was Japanese, her native tongue, but it was such a low growl she didn't catch what he said.

'What?' she asked.

He said something again, gesturing towards the newspapers.

'Oh.' She pulled out her wallet, her head spinning. She rifled through the coins and pulled out a silver hundred-yen coin. She pressed it into his grubby hand.

He held the silver coin to the light, squinting at it. She watched, bemused, as he turned it over in his hand, from the '100' printed on one side to the cherry blossom motif on the other.

He glared at her and barked something. It sounded like he was saying *sen*, or one thousand.

'I just want a newspaper.' She drew herself to her full height, which turned out to be a few centimetres taller than his. 'What, is it two hundred? It can't be a thousand. That's way too much.'

He yelled, shaking the coin at her. Yui didn't have time for this. It was his own fault he didn't have the price written down somewhere.

She snatched the nearest newspaper off the rack and ran into a crowd of people. A hundred yen was more than enough. Besides, there was only one thing she wanted to know.

She ran through a street and turned a corner until she was sure she hadn't been followed. Sighing, hot and sweaty, she unfolded the paper. It was the *Tokyo Nichi Nichi Shimbun*. Black and white looked back at her, the pictures unclear and slightly smudged-looking.

Her eyes sought the date. Summer, obviously. July, yes. But the year ... the year was wrong.

It said it was *July 1923*.

The newspaper shook in Yui's hands. She stumbled, almost bumping into someone. No. That was a newspaper stand selling ... old newspapers, or something. Never mind that copies like these would be long gone by now.

But the way he had stared in confusion at her coin ... the old clothes ... and Ueno Station was so different.

Yui glanced around, then sank to her knees next to a wall. People passed her, taking no notice. Yui clamped her lips together as she scanned the story in her hands. She read until her vision blurred. No, this was impossible. He was selling old newspapers as some sort of history-themed event.

She started walking. To where, she didn't know. Because none of this made sense. She was dreaming, or delusional. Anytime now she'd blink and be back on familiar roads, with markets and bars and karaoke.

This wasn't today's news she held in her hand. It wasn't July 1923. That weird tunnel had not somehow led her here.

She was still *here*, in Tokyo. Things were different, but also still the same. The people, though dressed differently, could have been any of the thousands of strangers she passed every day. And Ueno Station was still in the same place. Even if it was *wrong*.

She clutched the paper, disbelief pressing down on her. She had to look at the facts.

A strange tunnel, a passage, that should not have been there.

Finding Ueno Park with more trees and fewer buildings.

Tokyo, so unlike the city she knew.

And the man's confusion at her hundred-yen coin.

Yui pressed her hand over her chest, felt her rapid heartbeat. She couldn't deny what was plainly in front of her, as impossible as all this was.

Hiro had come here, too. She had to find him. They could work out the rest later.

Yui didn't know what to do now. She supposed she should still try to head home. Maybe somehow there'd be another tunnel. That was it. This was a temporary glitch. Any moment now she'd spot a landmark, something familiar. Maybe this was all part of the festival, and she was being drawn into an elaborate performance. It's just that everyone was in on it.

Everyone in Tokyo? the logical side of her mind demanded.

Should she head back to the park or for home? Yui loitered as people passed her. A man in a Western top hat shook his head in impatience. It was like tradition and modernity competed for space. Restaurants with fluttering *noren* curtains stood alongside brickwork with iron gates. Yui breathed in the humid air. It smelled different. Of bodies and fabric and brick. A hint of sewage.

30

Shouting sounded behind her. She couldn't linger here.

Abandoning the newspaper, Yui slipped through the crowd, trying to navigate the streets that were familiar yet so different. Men in straw hats pulled rickshaws, women in fancy *yukatas* sitting in the back. A horse pulled along a carriage. A man on a bicycle grumbled to himself as he tried to get through the crowd, brakes squeaking.

Yui's clothes clung to her sweaty skin. Crowds didn't usually bother her, but there were so many people, all dressed wrong. She glanced behind her, wondering if the newspaper salesman would be after her.

She glimpsed a red roof in the far distance. Yes. Sensō-ji Temple would still be here in the 1920s. Even though being in the 1920s was impossible.

It was a long walk, and Yui ignored the stares, the muttered questions about her short hair and her strange clothes. She slid her hand into her pocket and felt the reassuring weight of her wallet. She still had those ten-thousand-yen notes for the rent.

She arrived at Sensō-ji Temple. It was undoubtedly the temple, but it was different. More traditional, and a lot more wood. And the pagoda building ... it was in a different place from where it should have been. Yui looked up at it, at the architecture she had walked past a hundred times. Several people stood around the ornate incense burner, waving smoke around their heads to ward off bad spirits.

This was not the temple she knew. It wasn't the Tokyo she knew.

Yui wavered. The world swam about her. She sank onto a stone wall. This couldn't be true, could it? Had she somehow stepped through time? Was this 1923? Her instincts screamed no, but the facts around her couldn't be denied.

Hiro, beat in her mind over and over again. She had to find her brother. He would be as confused as she was.

Where was her home? She followed the path she had taken the other day, past where the Hanayashiki Theme Park should have been. Now it was a … zoo? Some animal brayed from across the fence.

Yui walked as though in a dream. All of this was impossible, yet here she was. Once she found Hiro, she would be able to face the rest of this crazy day.

The streets held wooden houses and old lanterns. A bicycle bell rang. Women shuffled along in summer *yukatas*, men in either robes or old-fashioned Western clothing. Though would they be old-fashioned now?

Was Yui really in July 1923?

She knew what she would find at home. Or, she knew what she would *not* find. The apartment building where she lived was old, but it wasn't this old. But she had to know for sure. She had to find out for herself. What else could she do, surrounded by strangers in an unfamiliar place, without a clue where to start looking for Hiro?

The temple grounds lay behind her now. Without the tall buildings, Yui could see ahead the silhouette of the mountains. It was starting to get dark, the sun setting in the cloud-strewn sky towards the silhouette of Mount Fuji.

It was the same. The perfectly shaped mountain, the flat peak, a guardian of the capital. It calmed her.

Yui couldn't locate her home exactly, everything looked too different. But there were rows of wooden constructs built into narrow neighbourhoods. Many of them stank of waste, and in a shadowy corner she spotted a rat sniffing among some discarded fabrics.

Yui rubbed her eyes, trying not to panic. Oil lamps were lit, the skies darkening. What could she do now? She had nowhere to sleep. The newspaper salesman had responded in anger when she'd tried to use money. What had he meant by *sen*? She'd assumed he meant a thousand, but was he possibly asking her to pay in sen, the older currency? That would explain his anger and confusion when she handed him the hundred.

It was more evidence to back up the truth she wasn't yet ready to face.

She closed her eyes, weighing her options. She could go back to Ueno Park and try to find clues there, but it would take hours to get back there now. Her stomach rumbled. She needed somewhere to sleep. Going to bed hungry wasn't strange to her, but she needed somewhere safe to lay down her head.

'Hiro,' Yui whispered, hugging herself. Her brother would be frightened. He might put on a brave face and pretend he was fine, but he would be as scared and confused as she was.

A group of young men were gathering at the other end of the street, their laughter high-pitched and echoing. Yui backed away, turning a corner. A horse and carriage clopped past, the driver glancing at her clothes with a bored expression before turning his eyes back to the road.

Eventually she found a small park. By now the crickets were buzzing, and Tokyo's lights were familiar but alien, like an ill-fitting shirt. Yui curled up, hoping she would wake up on her futon, her mother grumping at her to wake up, Hiro's Famicom blaring from the living room.

CHAPTER 4

Yui awoke to itchy mosquito bites on her arms and the sun shining through the canopy directly into her eyes. It took a moment to work out where she was, why she wasn't in her apartment amid Mother's complaining and Hiro's snores.

Still here.

Yui found a bush in which to pass her water, dizzy with hunger. It would be another hot day. She wanted a bath, some food. But she still wasn't any closer to getting home.

She rolled her shoulder, working out a crick, feeling disgusting in the same clothes she'd been wearing since yesterday. Wooden buildings with sloping roofs stood around her, the air thick and hot.

She decided to go back to Ueno Park. What else could she do? Her neighbourhood didn't exist. Brushing grass off her skirt and checking she still had her wallet, Yui traipsed miserably through the streets, desperate for water. What was the point in having cash if no one would accept it?

She kept a hopeful eye out, in any case. Maybe she'd blink and be back among familiarity. Maybe somehow, she'd come across a vending machine selling ice-cold water and soda. She wanted to groan aloud at the thought.

It took ages to get through the odd streets and back up to Ueno Park. Yui felt calmer when she beheld the statue of Saigō Takamori. He was identical to how she remembered him. At least that was the same, and the road leading up to Kiyomizu Temple.

But there was no tunnel at the base of the statue, no strange passage that had brought her here.

Her brother was nowhere to be seen.

She watched people go by. There was no doubt about it now. Somehow, she had travelled through time. It was unbelievable, but there was no other explanation. The buildings were different, the clothes were old-fashioned, there wasn't a single modern thing in sight.

Yui clenched and unclenched her hands, desperately hungry and thirsty. There was no convenience store she could walk into. Her money was useless. She circled the statue again, searching for the strange tunnel. What did she have to do to get back? Had Hiro even come here at all?

She had to find something to drink. It was approaching noon, and it was the height of summer. To her surprise, there was a public fountain where she spotted a mother and a child drinking some water. She loitered until they had finished, wanting to scream as the little boy played with the water for ages until finally skipping off. The water wasn't cold, but it was glorious down her parched throat.

She sighed, sinking to the ground, miserable and afraid. What was she supposed to do now?

*

Aoki Chiyo never felt she could breathe properly while she was in the Nakamura household. Even though the scent of cedarwood and incense and clean sheets mostly masked the stink of industry from outside, Chiyo was conscious of the sound of her breathing or the occasional gripe of her hungry stomach. Heaven forbid if she came to work with a sniffle. Still, things weren't so bad when her boss, Mrs Nakamura, was safely out at work herself.

'Do you think they'll have to cut it off, Chiyo-san?'

The boy's question made Chiyo glance up. Jirō was five years old, tall for his age, cheeks round from good food and comfort. She finished bandaging his leg, which he had scraped while running around outside.

'No, of course they won't.' She resisted the urge to stroke his cheek. 'You'll be fine.'

'My uncle said that his friend got stabbed in the leg, and they had to chop it off.'

Chiyo sat with Jirō on the floor near the open window. It always amazed Chiyo to see such a large garden in the middle of the city, with its tiny koi carp pond and stone walkways. They watched as a butterfly flitted around the bushes.

'Your uncle's friend's leg was probably infected.'

'What does that mean?' asked Jirō.

Chiyo hesitated. 'It means you don't have to worry about it, because yours *isn't* infected. Okay? Listen, there's your brother.' A baby's wails filled the house. 'He's ready for lunch. Are you hungry?'

Jirō vigorously shook his head, snatching up his kendama toy, a wooden mallet with a ball attached by string. The player had to try to swing the ball and position the mallet the right way to catch it. He messed with it as Chiyo rose to fetch his little brother.

Minoru was a rosy-cheeked, healthy boy, so different from the skinny and dirty kids in Chiyo's neighbourhood. He quietened as she lifted him, exclaiming, 'You're getting so big, Minoru-kun.'

Minoru liked putting things in his mouth, and Chiyo often had to remind Jirō to keep his smaller toys away from his little brother's chubby, lightning-quick hands. She held him on her lap as she fed him rice gruel. Jirō's lunch was an array of dishes provided by the household's cook: steamed fish in soy sauce, pickled vegetables and fluffy rice. She watched Jirō pick at his food; she was so hungry she could easily have snatched it all up and stuffed it into her mouth. Mrs Nakamura always assumed Chiyo brought her own lunch. Sometimes she did, when she could.

Jirō and Minoru's mother returned as Chiyo was mopping the mess from the baby's chest and the floor. He often insisted on feeding himself and made a grand mess whenever he did. Mrs Nakamura's sharp face appeared round the corner of the open door.

'Oh! Nakamura-san. You're back early.' Chiyo bowed to her, Minoru burbling in her arms.

A stiff nod in return. 'You can go now, Aoki-san.' She took Minoru from Chiyo, who pretended not to notice that Minoru's little arms reached for Chiyo still.

'Bye, Chiyo-san.' Jirō hugged Chiyo around the waist.

'Jirō, let her go,' his mother snapped. 'She has to go home now. I will pay you next time you come, Aoki-san.'

'Thank you, Nakamura-san,' said Chiyo, wondering if the older woman thought that being poor was contagious. 'See you.'

Chiyo waved goodbye to the children. Behind his mother's back, Jirō stuck out his tongue, making her laugh. She hastily disguised it as a cough and let herself out.

The summer heat was brutal. Perspiration beaded on Chiyo's forehead as she left the wealthy neighbourhood of Azabu behind and headed towards her home in Asakusa. She didn't believe Mrs Nakamura had ever crossed the bridge to the poorer neighbourhoods. The room where the children had eaten was larger than Chiyo's whole house.

As the nanny crossed the city, she walked along a wide road filled with men on bicycles, tracks of a one-carriage tram, and women in summer *yukatas* holding parasols as they chatted and laughed in the backs of rickshaws. She even spotted an automobile, chugging softly along the road, and risked a glance inside to see a woman wearing pink lipstick. What must it be like, to ride in a car? It sounded like luxury.

A serious-looking policeman, in his buttoned jacket and hat, glanced at her. She kept her gaze ahead, aware her shabby robe and old sandals did not belong here. Soon she crossed the Nihonbashi Bridge, and her surroundings changed.

She passed workers with bandannas around their heads hauling carts of goods, sandal-clad children in groups sword-fighting with sticks, and the brick Western-style homes were replaced by wooden houses packed closely together.

It felt like home, and there was a bounce to Chiyo's step. She would get paid on Sunday. Two weeks' worth of nannying would bring in some much-needed money to her parents.

She was not due back yet for another hour or so. Mrs Nakamura had let her leave early. She hesitated. Was there time?

Before she could talk herself out of it, she headed towards the Asakusa red-light district. Ahead, the Twelve-Storey Tower stood like a sentinel against the orange sky. Chiyo slipped through an alleyway and into the red-light district, where already courtesans were strolling towards their places of work, smiling coyly at passing men or talking quietly to each other.

Chiyo's eyes scanned the many young faces. Some were familiar, some not. Her heart leapt when she found who she was looking for.

'Riko.' She shuffled over to a group of courtesans. They were so beautiful. Fancy kimonos, elaborate hairstyles, perfume that filled Chiyo's nose with the heady scent of cherry blossoms or jasmine.

Riko gave an excited, open-mouthed smile to see her friend, and slipped away from the others to meet Chiyo in a shadowy corner.

'Are you working soon?' Chiyo asked.

'Well, fairly soon. I've heard there are some Americans here, and they always pay well.' Riko gave a small giggle. 'How are you, Chiyo-chan?'

Chiyo liked the way Riko said her name, with the affectionate honorific 'chan'. 'Another shift at the Nakamuras',' she said, and Riko rolled her eyes knowingly.

'I hope you didn't get dirt on their precious tatami mats.'

Chiyo giggled guiltily. Riko knew all about Mrs Nakamura.

'I tell you, these rich people. They look down on us, yet they couldn't live without our services. Guess how many poor working men came to see me this week? None!' she cried, before Chiyo could guess. 'No, it's always politicians and foreign expats and surgeons' sons. Sneaking into downtown

Asakusa for a bit of fun with *real* people.' Riko blew onto her forehead, blowing some errant hairs from her face. 'Don't let her get you down, Chiyo-chan.'

'Thanks, Riko-chan. I don't.' She shifted on her feet. 'Hey, can I ask you about your work? Do you ever get female clients?'

She thought Riko would be surprised. But she simply tilted her head. 'Rarely,' she said. 'You know, I grew up around here. Whenever I saw a woman who didn't work here, I always thought she was here to talk to our manager or to clean or something. But when I was a kid, I saw a woman leaving one of the rooms, and my *senpai* taught me all about that. Some are just curious. And it's safer because you can't get pregnant from a girl.'

Chiyo wondered what it would be like to step into one of the perfumed rooms, concealed by curtains, to enjoy a courtesan for an hour with no one else looking.

Not with Riko, though. She was her friend.

'I have to go,' Riko said apologetically. She gave Chiyo a quick hug, her sweet perfume filling Chiyo's senses. 'Let's get tea sometime. Come through the backdoor.'

Chiyo waved goodbye to her friend, hoping Riko had taken her question as sheer curiosity and nothing else.

The glowing red lanterns and tightly packed buildings gave the street a sense of intimacy, but Chiyo knew not to linger. It would be dark soon, and on this Saturday many men (and a few women, apparently) flocked to the red-light district to seek pleasures of the night. Trying to push away thoughts of sneaking into a private room with a faceless courtesan, Chiyo slipped through several alleyways until she was in her residential neighbourhood.

She glanced backwards only once, spotting the glowing lights in the Twelve-Storey Tower, Asakusa's pride. Maybe she was wrong. Maybe the Nakamuras *had* come here, if only to see the skyscraper with its many floors and shops. It was Chiyo's dream to visit one day. Maybe she and Riko could go there sometime on their day off.

She sighed happily at the daydream. She hoped Eomma had cooked something good. Maybe kimchi rice or grilled fish.

A young woman stood in the middle of the street. Everyone around here had somewhere to go or a job to do. People walked with purpose, carried buckets of water from the communal well or beat towels and futons.

This girl just stood there. She didn't have Riko's confidence, nor Mrs Nakamura's sense of superiority. She looked ... confused. And alone.

She stood a little away from everybody else, people flowing round her like water. She looked dazed. Pity and curiosity winning over caution, Chiyo approached her.

'Are you all right?'

The girl started, then blinked at her in confusion. She looked a lot cleaner than most people who were from around here. Her hair, cut short, was shiny, though there were a few leaves in it. She had a button nose, a strong jawline, and her clothes were unlike anything Chiyo had seen before: a skirt that reached her knees and a short-sleeved garment that ended where the skirt began. Black charcoal, or at least that was what it looked like, shadowed the young woman's eyes. Chiyo found it enchanting.

'Is this Yanagi Street?' the girl asked, with some desperation.

'Yanagi Street?' Chiyo hadn't heard of it. 'This is the Asakusa district. Are you lost?'

'But … it should be here!' Confusion and anger crossed the girl's face. 'It should be right here. I've been wandering around for hours. Everything's different, the shop is gone, but it can't be right, it can't be true. I'm dreaming.'

Concern spiked in Chiyo for the woman. 'Are you okay? Have you been attacked?' The girl had nothing with her, no bag or anything. Had she been robbed and hit her head?

'No,' said the girl weakly. 'I don't know where I am, and I've lost my brother.' She blinked at Chiyo. 'What year is it?'

Chiyo was seriously concerned now. 'Do you need to sit down? Here, my house is just this way. You can have some tea; my mother won't mind.'

'But what *year* is it?' the girl almost screamed. Some passersby glanced at them.

'It's Taishō 12,' said Chiyo in alarm. 'Remember?'

Maybe taking the girl to her home wasn't a good idea. She could be ill and possibly dangerous. But she surely couldn't leave her out here on her own. This neighbourhood could get dangerous after dark, especially for young women. Besides, her father would be home soon. He'd know what to do.

'I'm Aoki Chiyo,' she said, gently taking the woman's warm arm.

'Sanada Yui,' said the girl, letting Chiyo lead her home. At least she remembered her own name.

'Tadaima.' Chiyo announced her return as she opened the sliding door of her home. There was a warm, starchy scent of cooking rice that made Chiyo's stomach gurgle. She slipped off her sandals and Yui did the same beside her, looking around with apprehension.

'Welcome home, Chiyo-chan.' Eomma smiled warmly at her. For a lot of Chiyo's childhood, her Korean mother had insisted she use the Japanese word *okaasan* to address her as Mother. Calling her the Korean Eomma, she'd said, would only draw attention to the fact that Chiyo was half-Korean. Mrs Nakamura had sniffed loudly at that fact. Koreans, after all, were considered second-class citizens.

But Chiyo didn't care. Eomma was from Korea, and that's what she wanted to call her. She tried to ignore the spike of anxiety when she realised Yui would have heard her use the Korean word, but the young woman didn't seem to have noticed.

'I'm sorry to disturb you,' Yui mumbled.

'Eomma, this is Yui. She's lost and can't find her brother. Since it'll be dark soon, is it all right if she stays for some tea?'

Eomma looked surprised, taking in Yui's clothes and her bare feet, which were almost spotlessly clean. Chiyo found herself staring, too. Yui had some kind of colour on her toenails. Seeing them looking, Yui turned away with an annoyed look on her face.

'Yui, did you say?' Eomma said, fiddling with the bun that kept up her long hair. 'Yes, you can stay for a bit. Are you all right? Where are you staying?'

'I think she hit her head,' Chiyo said in apology. 'She, um, doesn't seem to remember much.'

'I can speak for myself,' Yui snapped, making both Chiyo and Eomma blink in surprise. Yui swallowed. 'I'm sorry. That was rude. Just, the last few days have been awful. I've lost my little brother. I slept in the park last night.'

Eomma made a sympathetic noise. 'You poor thing. Have you been to the police?'

Yui's look of distaste told them she hadn't. Chiyo couldn't believe a young woman had slept in the park all by herself.

Her father had told her how dangerous it could get at night. Indeed, Yui had big pink mosquito bites on her arms and her neck, one of which she absent-mindedly scratched.

'Have some water,' Chiyo offered. But Eomma had used most of their supply for boiling for dinner, so they went to the well to get some.

Yui looked around in disbelief at their surroundings. Chiyo chanced a look at the woman's hands. Her fingernails were neat, with only a little dirt beneath them. Her hands didn't look calloused from work. 'Are you from the west side of Tokyo?' Chiyo asked, wondering if the woman was lost. 'This is the east, you see.'

'I'm from …' Yui hesitated. 'You could say it takes years to get there.' She snorted, startling Chiyo. Was that a laugh or a cry?

Chiyo puzzled over her answer as they collected water from the communal well. Some of it splashed on the dirt at their feet, making it run brown. 'What do you mean, it takes years to get there? You're Japanese, right? That doesn't make much sense to me.'

'What I was looking for isn't here, anyway.' Yui helped Chiyo pull the bucket up the rest of the way, the contents sloshing and threatening to spill again. 'Thanks for the help.'

They drank some of the water together from clay jars Chiyo had brought, then dunked the bucket back in to refill it. Yui made to leave, but Chiyo didn't like to see her go off alone. She didn't have any way to contact her. How would she know if she found her brother or got home, wherever that was, safely?

'Yui, wait!' Chiyo called after her. 'Don't be like that. Come on, you can stay at my family's place tonight. They won't mind.'

'Are you sure?' Yui sounded uncertain. Chiyo pressed a jar of fresh water into Yui's hands, then sipped some herself. It was wonderfully fresh and cold on this humid night.

'Yes, I'm sure.' Well, she wasn't entirely. But Eomma had shown sympathy. Father would, too, she was sure.

It was fully dark by the time they returned to Chiyo's house, another of the many tightly packed wooden houses in this dark street, lit by a single oil lantern. A tram rattled somewhere nearby. Groups of youths shouted on the next road, their laughter bouncing around the street.

'It's a wonder you're able to find your house in the dark,' said Yui. A cricket chirped nearby, falling silent when Chiyo slid open the door.

'Katsuro, is that you?' Eomma called in Korean. She looked startled when she saw Yui.

'We got water.' Chiyo raised the bucket. They both glanced at Yui, who swallowed and said, 'Sorry to be a disturbance. Again.'

'Oh.' Eomma blinked, relief on her face when Yui said nothing about her speaking Korean.

'Please, Eomma, can Yui stay tonight? It's dark already. I don't want her wandering around on her own.'

'Yes, of course.' Eomma took the bucket from Chiyo. 'I'll make some wheat tea while you get out the spare futon.'

It took a while for Chiyo to find it. They had last used the spare futon when Chiyo's father had helped a neighbour when he'd hurt his leg. She soured at the memory; the man had been happy to lie on their bed and eat their food while he recovered, but he had left quickly when he'd overheard Eomma speaking Korean.

'Here it is,' said Chiyo, pleased, and laid the futon out beside her own. Chiyo's sleeping space was divided from her parents' by a curtain. After sipping tea together, Yui staring worriedly at the corner, Chiyo offered Yui a spare under-kimono robe for sleeping.

'You'd do all this for me?' Yui's light brown eyes went glassy, and she quickly blinked, looking away from Chiyo. 'Why?'

'Well, because you need help,' said Chiyo.

'Just relax tonight,' said her mother. 'Tomorrow, you can get your bearings and find your way home. Are you hungry? There might still be soup left.'

Yui nodded gratefully and ate the miso soup slowly, like she savoured every mouthful. She was a mystery, but Chiyo felt a powerful urge to look after her. Maybe it was foolish to trust her, but what would Yui do? It wasn't like Chiyo and her family had anything valuable to steal. Besides, it seemed like Yui had some secrets, ones Chiyo hoped to uncover.

CHAPTER 5

The heat was oppressive tonight. Yui reached to switch on the fan, but her hand ran across the rough straw of a tatami mat, then something warm and soft. The girl beside her grunted and turned over, making Yui stop, her heart thumping. Then it all came back to her in an instant. She was in Chiyo's home.

She threw off the sweaty blanket. She didn't feel like she'd slept long. Somewhere on the other side of the curtain, an oil lamp burned. The front door slid open, startling Yui.

'Tadaima.'

'Katsuro.' The soft sound of a kiss on a cheek. Chiyo's mother and father – Eomma, Chiyo had called her mother – talked quietly. Yui had closed her eyes again when she heard Mrs Aoki say her name.

'She's staying with us tonight. She seemed confused, so we decided to help her.'

Yui tensed. Would Chiyo's father be angry at the unexpected newcomer in their house? But after a brief silence, she heard a concerned, 'A woman, all by herself? Is she all right?'

'I gave her something to eat and she's sleeping now. Here's some for you.' The soft sound of a plate being set onto the table.

'Thank you, my love. It looks delicious.'

After some whispering, the oil lantern went out and Yui stared at the cracks in the ceiling until she finally drifted off. When Tokyo came awake in the early hours, footsteps and voices outside, Yui opened her eyes, her head heavy with tiredness.

'Good morning,' said Chiyo brightly. She sat up and stretched, her eyes squeezing shut. It was strangely cute, and Yui didn't realise she was grinning until Chiyo asked 'What?' through a yawn.

'Nothing. Thanks for letting me stay.' Yui rose, wishing she could take a shower. Daylight glowed on the square washi paper walls, and it promised to be another hot July day.

The curtain opened. Eomma was already wearing a light robe, her long hair resting on one shoulder. 'Good morning, Yui-chan,' she said warmly. 'Did you sleep well?'

A question her own mother had never asked her. She nodded. 'I'll be out of your hair soon.'

'What are you going to do today?' Chiyo asked. 'Go to the police?'

Yui supposed it was a start. It beat wandering aimlessly through Tokyo. A Tokyo that was vastly different from the one she knew. She dressed in yesterday's clothes in silence. It felt strange to dress in a shirt and skirt, and she self-consciously tugged it over her knees.

Chiyo's father was up, drinking miso soup. He had thick, greying hair and creases around his eyes that told her he was fond of jokes and laughter. 'You must be Yui,' he said as Yui sat before him. 'It's lovely to meet you.'

'Thank you for letting me stay in your house.' Yui bowed her head.

'What exactly happened?' Chiyo asked, sitting beside her. 'It seemed like you were looking for something.'

'She got separated from her brother, poor thing,' said Eomma. She brought both girls small bowls of rice and some fish. They both thanked her.

All three of the Aokis looked at her expectantly. Yui knew she owed them an explanation, seeing as they had welcomed her into their home. But what explanation could she possibly give? She had barely come to terms with the truth herself.

'Maybe we shouldn't pry,' said Chiyo anxiously. 'But are you in danger, Yui-chan? Are you in trouble?'

Yui didn't answer at first, letting the sense of dread wash over her. Was this all really happening?

Yui had dealt with many kinds of situations in her short life, most involving thinking on her feet with Hiro. Pushing away the panic and disbelief, she decided she had to think rationally.

'No, I'm not all right.' Yui sighed, accepting a steaming cup of barley tea. 'I can't find my brother anywhere.' That was the least strange truth she could stick to right now.

She told Chiyo and her parents what he looked like. Longish hair, the birthmark on his cheek he always tried to hide. 'And he's twelve years old, small for his age,' she said. She felt bad, sitting here drinking tea when he was still missing, but she couldn't think of what to do. She had checked Ueno Park, and where she sat right now was where her own home used to be.

Will be, she reminded herself. That was still unbelievable, but she had to go with what was happening before her eyes.

'You really should tell the police,' said Chiyo's mother. She hesitated. 'Take Chiyo's father with you. He's Japanese, so they're more likely to listen to him.'

Yui grimaced at that. But she was right. If Hiro had been taken in somewhere, the police would be able to find him. The thought cheered her up. Once she found Hiro, she could get them out of Tokyo and figure out how to get back to their own time.

'I can take you to the police station before work, if you hurry,' said Mr Aoki. He had a round, friendly face, and one of those smiles that made you feel at ease. Yui didn't much like or trust men, but it wasn't like she'd be able to find the police station by herself.

She felt a little awkward as she pulled on her shoes. They stepped onto the morning street, already hot and crowded, past rickshaw pullers and men going about their trade, squinting in the sunshine as their sandals hit the hard-packed dirt.

'Your brother is missing?' Mr Aoki asked with sympathy. 'What about your mother and father? Do you have a husband?'

Yui almost laughed but managed to keep her face straight. 'I'm not married. My parents ...' She hesitated. 'I don't know my father. My mother is ... she works a lot. I don't see her much.'

'Your brother won't be with your mother?'

That'd be a trick, Yui thought glumly. If her situation was to be believed, her mother hadn't been born yet. 'No, definitely not. He was with me until the other day. We got separated in Ueno.'

The police officers' outfits were so different from what Yui was used to that she couldn't help but stare. They wore buttoned-up jackets and smart hats. Some even had swords at their hips. What would Hiro make of this?

A middle-aged man looked bored as they told him of Hiro. Anxiety squeezed Yui's chest as she thought of him, out there and lost, all on his own. 'He has a birthmark on his left cheek. He's always trying to hide it under his hair.'

'We'll check some orphanages,' promised the officer. 'Don't worry, we'll find him.'

Yui wondered how Hiro would've responded to everything. Maybe he'd have made friends with some local boys and got up to mischief with them. He'd be missing his Famicom console, no doubt. Despite everything, Yui was amused to think of her brother trying to explain *Super Mario* to other kids.

Oh, this was all too insane.

They walked along the noisy Tokyo street. Bikes rang, people talked, a bell gonged somewhere, a train rattled over some tracks. It smelled of industry and body odour and steel and smoke. Some things looked familiar, others not.

'What's that?' She pointed to a tall red tower. She had never seen it before.

'The Ryōnkaku,' said Mr Aoki. 'Locals call it the Twelve-Storey Tower. Isn't it magnificent?'

The fat stone tower marred the familiar landscape. Then again, nothing looked right here. Everyone was dressed wrong. It was like some huge, expensive elaborate prank where she was the butt of the joke.

But it wasn't. This was real. *She* was the unusual one. She wished she was wearing one of Chiyo's plain robes. Her skirt was too short, her T-shirt garish and grubby. It was a wonder none of the Aokis had remarked on her trainers.

'Can you get yourself back to our house?' asked Chiyo's father. 'I'd walk you home, but I have to be getting to work. And Yui, stay as long as you like. I mean it.'

'I'll help Chiyo and her mother with work,' Yui promised. She knew poor when she saw it. She had to pull her weight while she was here. There was no guarantee she'd find Hiro today, or even tomorrow. She could only hope he had somewhere safe to stay until she tracked him down.

This version of Tokyo looked different in the daylight, and she found herself watching people as they passed. Some talked loudly, smelling of tobacco, dressed in ragged robes. A group of kids not much older than Hiro wandered past, loudly chatting and laughing. Apart from their clothes, they didn't look very different from a group of friends in her time.

She quickly headed back to Chiyo's, the only place that felt safe right now. It took her a few moments of panic when she rushed through crowded streets before finally recognising Chiyo's door.

'Excuse me,' she said with relief, and slipped her shoes off.

'Those are so unusual,' remarked Chiyo's mother, spotting Yui's ragged old trainers.

'Yeah.' She didn't know what else to say.

'Where are you from?' Yui knew Chiyo's mother was trying to make conversation as she joined her inside. Mrs Aoki was frying some fish on a small grill, the window open to let out the smoke. The scent made Yui's stomach groan with hunger.

'Far away from here,' Yui said weakly. She didn't want to lie to Mrs Aoki, but how could she possibly tell her the truth?

Mrs Aoki gave an understanding nod, even though she might have thought Yui was being secretive on purpose.

'You're from Korea, right?' Yui asked, eager to change the subject.

Mrs Aoki's shoulders stiffened just a fraction. 'Yes. I came from Korea when I met Katsuro, Chiyo's father.'

The place was small and cramped like Yui's apartment back home, only one room with a curtain separating the places where Chiyo and her parents slept, but there was a homely feel in the lacy tablecloth, the folded futons in the corner, the few ragged books on a dusty shelf. Where Yui's apartment had felt crowded and stale, Chiyo's house was lighter. Simple and drab, the wood peeling and the occasional scurry of mice's feet on the roof, but Mrs Aoki quietly hummed as she turned over fish, gracing Yui with a reassuring smile when she caught her looking.

'Sit down, Yui-chan. Are you hungry?'

The fish was unlike anything Yui had tasted before. She tried to imagine it in a little plastic box, shipped and sold at a convenience store, but she couldn't manage it. She was still hungry when she'd finished, but she was used to that.

Chiyo returned soon after, her face lighting up. 'You're still here,' she said warmly. 'I just got back from work. They only needed me in the morning.'

'What do you do?'

Chiyo settled at the table, thanking her mother for the fish and rice. 'I'm a nanny in west Tokyo.'

'Yes,' said Mrs Aoki proudly. 'You love children, don't you, Chiyo?'

Chiyo nodded, then started eating with delicate precision Yui could never have managed. Yui helped Mrs Aoki clean the dishes, feeling that was the least she could do. It was weird not using a sink and tap; they used water from a communal well. Yui resolved to always appreciate clean, running water from now on as she carefully dried the plates and chopsticks.

Yui felt restless now she'd eaten, wanting to go and search for her brother even without a clue where to start. The police officer had mentioned an orphanage. She could start there.

She stepped outside, groaning in frustration. She squinted at everyone Hiro's size, hoping to see his face among the dozens moving through the neighbourhood. Guilt squirmed in her for losing him. He had definitely gone through the passage, right? How did she know whether he was here in the 1920s at all?

The door rasped behind her and Chiyo stepped out. Yui wiped her face, annoyed with herself for getting emotional, and raised her chin.

'When did you last see him?' Chiyo was soft-spoken, pity on her face as she witnessed Yui's pain. She could tell she was upset, even if she tried not to show it.

'Ueno Park.'

'Then let's go there.' Chiyo beamed at her.

'Right now?'

'Yes! We might find a clue as to where he went.'

Chiyo called to her mother that they were going out, and soon Chiyo and Yui were walking side by side along the busy, dirt-packed road.

As they headed for Ueno Park, the sun hidden today by a haze of cloud but nevertheless hot and humid, Chiyo asked her about her parents. 'Surely your mother and father will be looking for you?'

Yui wondered how to answer. 'My mother works a lot,' she said finally. 'We were out together at the park, and he disappeared. That was two days ago.' She swallowed. 'I don't think he'll still be there.'

'It's worth a try,' Chiyo encouraged her.

'Where do you work?' Yui asked, trying to steer the conversation away from her family. She still hadn't come to terms with the truth herself.

'Over in the Azabu district.' Yui let Chiyo chirp happily about her job looking after five-year-old Jirō and baby Minoru. The route from Asakusa to Ueno held some familiarities Yui hadn't noticed before, like the bridge she *thought* might be in the same place. The river was unchanged, but instead of the Asahi Beer Hall overlooking the mostly clear river, the water was filled with fishermen's boats. Factories lined the horizon, belching smoke. In one of those, Chiyo's father worked.

Yui wondered how she could make herself useful while she was staying with the Aokis. What use was her knowledge of the future? She knew a little more about medicine, but not much.

'I got paid this morning, so Eomma will be able to make something nice for dinner tonight. I asked her to buy lots,' said Chiyo brightly.

'I won't intrude much longer,' Yui said. It was painful that Chiyo's family were willing to share so much when they were so poor. It wasn't fair to rely on them so much.

'Oh.' Chiyo looked a little crestfallen. 'Well, okay. But at least stay another night if …' She hesitated, then said, 'Well, I do hope you find your brother.'

'Me, too,' said Yui, sighing.

She kept hoping they would turn a corner and she'd suddenly find herself back in 1995, with roads she recognised, brightly lit shops, and convenience stores. But the surroundings remained hot and dusty, with things that were familiar but alien: *noren* curtains above doorways, painted red lanterns, a Western-style lamppost on a corner.

'Your mother must be worried about him, too,' said Chiyo. 'Do you live with her?'

Yui had once heard that the best way to lie was to keep close to the truth. She didn't like lying to Chiyo, but the Aokis' was the only shelter she had, and she couldn't start talking about time travel now. 'We live together, yes, but we work at different times, so I don't see her much,' she said. 'I've pretty much been the one to look after Hiro since he was a baby.'

'Oh,' said Chiyo, with sympathy. 'I can't imagine having to look after a little child *all* the time. You're very strong, Yui-chan.'

Yui blinked, surprised to feel tears welling up at Chiyo's kind words. She cleared her throat. 'You must be good at looking after kids, too.'

'I do like it,' said Chiyo. 'Though, you know, the lady I work for often makes mean remarks.' She fiddled with a corner of her robe sleeve.

'Mean remarks? About what?'

'The fact my mother is Korean. I had to tell her when I was reporting my family history.'

Yui stared at her, then shook her head. She would never understand the prejudice against Koreans. There were plenty of them living in Tokyo in her time, and they weren't any different from the Japanese.

'You don't mind, Yui-chan, do you?'

'Mind what?' Yui asked. 'I think your mother's lovely.'

Chiyo gave a delighted sigh and reached to squeeze Yui's fingers.

'Father has been hassled by our neighbours and people who know us for marrying a Korean,' Chiyo said, her glee fading. 'But they love each other.'

'Then I don't think he regrets it,' said Yui. 'True love's hard to find.' Not that Yui knew much about love. Her own mother had certainly never shown it. Maybe she had never even experienced it.

'I'm a quarter American, too,' Yui said, remembering. 'At least, I think I am. That's all my mother knows about my father, that he was half-foreign.'

'Wow,' said Chiyo, nodding. 'So you'll know what it's like.'

Yui didn't. She didn't look like she was a quarter Caucasian. But she said nothing as they ascended the steps to Ueno Park. A group of *yukata*-clad courtesans passed them, their lips red and their hair tied in complicated styles. A man passed them, glancing at the girls before continuing, fingers clasped around the handle of a briefcase.

Despite Yui's doubts they would find Hiro here, anticipation rose as they crested the top of the steps to the statue of Saigō Takamori, the place Yui had found herself two days ago. She scanned the grounds as her excitement mounted. Would Hiro be here, maybe sitting against a tree, hugging his legs as he waited? She ran to the statue, peering at it, wondering if the passage would be back, those strange voices that had whispered to her beckoning again.

But as the warm summer wind washed over her, she knew she'd see nothing. Not even Hiro.

'Ueno Park is big,' Chiyo encouraged her. 'Let's search near the lotus pond.'

In Yui's time, the homeless and their makeshift tents and tarp populated a lot of Ueno Park, as well as museums and memorials of the Second World War. Some parts felt familiar, but it still wasn't a place she knew. Chiyo led the way, her slender frame moving with purpose, as Yui glanced around for Hiro.

She could feel he was here in Tokyo somewhere. If only she could home in on him, pinpoint his exact location. When she found him, she would hug him so hard. She'd kiss his face as he protested, grumpily telling her to stop, that he was embarrassed. But she wouldn't mind. She'd never mind any of that again.

They circled the entirety of Shinobazu Pond. The lotuses with their pink flowers were so thick they could hardly see the water. 'He's not here.' Yui's heart sank. 'It's hopeless.'

It had been two days since they'd emerged from the passage. She was kidding herself, no matter how much she thought she could feel him. That was wishful thinking.

She lowered into a squat. Even in this open space, with the sound of footfall and twittering birds, the reality of her situation crushed down on her. Everything else aside, her little brother was missing. He was *her* responsibility, and she had lost him.

'Where are you, Hiro?' She knuckled her eyes.

A gentle hand touched her shoulder. 'Hey, Yui-chan. It's going to be okay, I promise.'

Such empty words. 'What do you know?' she snapped at Chiyo. The young woman stood before her now, silhouetted with the sun shining behind her. 'You don't have any brothers.'

Chiyo flinched, snatching her hand away. 'I did,' she said, her voice cold. 'They died.'

The words knocked into Yui like bricks. 'I'm sorry, Chiyo. That wasn't right for me to say.'

'I'm trying to help you,' Chiyo reminded her as Yui rose. At their full height, Chiyo was a hair shorter than Yui. Her eyes, large and black as a new moon, rose to hers.

'I know,' Yui assured her. 'And you're doing an amazing job.' A warm wind rustled the leaves above them. 'Maybe we should get back. It's a long walk.'

Chiyo nodded, friendly again. They walked side by side, passing the lotus pond and through a path in the trees up past Kiyomizu Temple.

Already here in the 1920s. Yui glimpsed at its sloped roof and stone lanterns.

Chiyo saw her looking. 'Strange to think this used to all be temple grounds, isn't it?'

'Yeah,' said Yui. 'Things change so quickly. And we're all swept along with it.'

That evening, Eomma proudly showed them the Chinese pork she had bought. It was *chashu*, often seen on top of ramen noodles. Chiyo and her father gazed at it in wonder as though they were admiring a rare baby animal.

It is rare to them, Yui reminded herself, and smiled with enthusiasm, too.

'And some sake for Father,' said Eomma when they sat at the table. Rice and beansprouts accompanied their meal. Chiyo's father happily took the ceramic bottle. When he poured out a small cup for himself, the familiar, slightly fruity scent hit Yui's nose.

'Would you like to try some?' he asked.

Chiyo nodded, but Yui said, 'It's yours, Aoki-san. Enjoy it.'

Chiyo took a tentative sip, then wrinkled her nose. 'It's so strong.'

They laughed and talked as they ate. For once, there was enough for everybody, and Yui felt properly full for the first time in forever. She wondered if Mr Aoki would turn nasty as he drank his sake, but he only grew rosy-cheeked and laughed louder. When he planted a big, sloppy kiss on his wife's cheek, Mrs Aoki loudly exclaimed, 'It's getting late! Time for bed, everyone.'

CHAPTER 6

Mrs Aoki had prepared Chiyo and Yui's futons, and they lay side by side. Her husband was already snoring on the other side of the curtain.

'Thank you for letting me stay again,' said Yui. 'I promise I won't for much longer.'

'Until you have somewhere else to go, you're welcome here,' said Chiyo's mother. She seemed to truly mean it, too. It made Yui uncomfortable, how nice everyone was being. She half-expected them to turn on her and decide she wasn't wanted after all. Being here felt wrong, like trying to put on a glove that was too small. But right now, she was too tired to argue.

Chiyo fell asleep quickly, but Yui lay awake, listening to the sounds of the city. She let it finally sink into her that she really had, somehow, travelled to the 1920s. There was no doubting it now. As she rubbed her sore calves, she contemplated everything she had seen.

It wasn't something that happened every day. But somehow, it had happened to her. And now Yui was in a tiny tatami room in the neighbourhood where *her* apartment building should be, no closer to finding Hiro.

Yui didn't have much faith in the police. She wondered if they'd bother trying to find one boy. Tokyo was a decent city, like it was in the nineties, right? Maybe Hiro had been picked up by a kindly adult who gave him some food and a bed to sleep in. Hiro could turn on the charm when he wanted to, and surely no one would turn away a little boy. She imagined him lying awake somewhere in Tokyo, pressing his hair over his cheek to hide his birthmark, curled into a ball and wondering when his sister was going to come and get him.

She would search for him again as soon as it was morning. Hiro was Yui's responsibility. All she had was time. The alternative was sitting here doing nothing.

Time ... She had never imagined it to be so malleable, something that could be bent and shifted by simply walking through a passage.

Yui watched a fly buzz around, bumping into walls as it tried to escape. Beyond the house's walls, the city was alive with activity, people returning home late after work or searching for pleasures of the night.

Chiyo sighed in her sleep, shifting closer to Yui. Her arm moved and landed on Yui's stomach.

Yui didn't move. It felt nice.

Would anyone notice her and Hiro's absence? Her manager and a few of her coworkers were probably the only people who would notice she was missing when she didn't show up for her shift. Maybe her mother would, but only when the landlord came to kick her out for not paying the rent.

She was almost surprised that ancient apartment building wasn't already here. It was so rickety by the nineties it would collapse in an earthquake.

... *Earthquake.*

Yui gently moved Chiyo's arm as sweat broke out across her forehead. She had watched the news just a few days ago, hadn't she? Everything that had transpired in the last few days had wiped it from her mind.

Think, Yui. Yui recalled sitting with Hiro, half-listening as the TV blared on in the background, talking about the earthquake in Kobe.

The newscaster had talked about the Great Kantō Earthquake. What year had it been?

September seventy-two years ago, the newscaster had said. 1995 minus seventy-two was …

1923.

Yui sucked in a breath, hugging her knees. She wanted to punch something, if only to ease the growing dark pit in her chest.

If her situation was to be believed, there would be an enormous earthquake here soon. In September.

Oh no. What date?

Yui tried to remember. She had never thought much about the past, not the wars nor the era of samurai and castles. History had not much interested her when she had been trying to make sure she and Hiro had food to eat and a roof over their heads. Besides, she hadn't finished school. Classes were a blur, a world away.

She let the truth wash through her mind, dissecting it. *There will be an earthquake, a huge one that'll kill thousands, in September.*

It was July now, presuming the day was the same as she had left it before stepping through that damn passage. Only a matter of weeks until it would happen. And Hiro was nowhere to be found.

That red tower they'd seen; Yui had never heard of it. Was it one of the many structures that would cease to exist? It must be. Could an earthquake really bring a tower like that to the ground?

Yui placed a hand on the tatami mat, hearing Chiyo's soft breathing, the scuttle of a rat somewhere in the rafters above. She had felt earthquakes, of course. Small ones that were occasionally frightening, but would soon end after maybe knocking some things from shelves. Yui had never felt a huge one. Had never given them much thought beyond emergency drills at school and making sure the emergency supplies at work were up to date.

But if a mega earthquake was coming, thousands of people would die.

Yui had cried in silence many times. Now she hugged her legs, rocking herself back and forth. None of this could be real. The Great Kantō Earthquake happened over *seventy years ago*. She was Sanada Yui, it was 1995, and this was all one long, horrific dream.

But dreams didn't present themselves with such startling clarity. They didn't feel humid, smell like old cloth and the lingering remnants of dinner. They didn't sigh awake and softly say, 'Yui-chan? Are you all right?'

For a moment, Yui was at home, despairing over how hungry she felt and how she couldn't afford a school uniform, and it was Hiro behind her, whispering into the dark.

But it wasn't Hiro. It was Chiyo, her hair in a tussle, her eyes still half-closed with sleepiness.

Yui didn't know what to do. She couldn't tell Chiyo the truth, however much she wanted to. She would sound demented.

'Hay fever,' she grunted, rubbing her eyes.

Chiyo said, 'My mother cries sometimes, too.'

Yui turned away, embarrassed for some reason. 'Why does your mother cry?'

A rustling of sheets. 'Well, maybe because my father can't get a promotion at work. She thinks it's her fault. She's Korean, after all, and a lot of Japanese people don't like Koreans.'

Yui scoffed. 'Why would you hate someone just because they're from a different country? That's the dumbest thing I've ever heard.'

Chiyo made a noise. At first Yui thought Chiyo had dissolved into tears, too. Then she glanced over to see Chiyo covering her mouth, her shoulders shaking in silent giggles. 'Oh, Yui. You're so cool.'

Yui's lips tugged into a reluctant smile. 'Your mother is wonderful. Both your parents are. I always wondered what it would be like to have nice parents.'

Chiyo shifted over and wrapped her arms around Yui, holding her close. Yui stiffened. She never got hugged. Chiyo's arms, firm from labour, and her soft scent, her hair tickling Yui's neck, was all alarming but also … nice.

They stayed like that for a while, listening to the night sounds of the city. Yui needed a plan, both to find her brother and to somehow see if there was a way to confirm – stop? Warn about? – this upcoming earthquake.

*

Chiyo wasn't quite sure what to make of Sanada Yui.

The young woman often scowled and stared into space, but always jumped to offer help around the house. She seemed to feel bad about staying and wanted to make herself useful. Chiyo and Eomma had shouted down her suggestions of leaving. Eomma said Yui wasn't going to leave until she had somewhere safe to stay, a sentiment with which Chiyo heartily agreed.

Yui went to the police station every day to ask for updates about her brother, always coming back with a glum look and a shake of her head. 'They mentioned they had a missing boy, and I got excited, then they mentioned it was years ago. Well, why mention it then?' she grumbled.

One evening after work, Chiyo found Riko, the courtesan in the red-light district, and mentioned the situation. 'You came from an orphanage, right?' Chiyo asked, sipping the tea Riko had given her. 'Do you remember which one? My friend Yui has lost her brother, and he might be there.'

Riko always looked like she was thinking deeply about something. 'Yes,' she said. 'It was a Christian one, not far from here.' She gave a soft laugh. 'They baptised us as Christians, you know. Old Mother Tamura would have a heart attack if she saw what I was doing now.'

She wrote down the name of the place. Riko's boss soon came to shoo Chiyo out, some male clientele arriving to be entertained. Chiyo hugged Riko goodbye, her flowery perfume tickling her nose.

'Yui is a nice name,' Riko remarked dreamily.

'Yes, it is.' Chiyo left with a final wave.

She stepped outside, eager to tell Yui about the orphanage. Maybe Hiro was there. She couldn't wait to see Yui's face when she finally reunited with him. Even if it meant Yui would leave.

The following day was Chiyo's day off, so she offered to accompany her. 'They might be in touch with other orphanages,' she pointed out. Yui just gave a tired nod.

The orphanage wasn't difficult to find. It was a wooden building with a battered Christian cross above the entrance. It looked like it had once been a temple, but repurposed by evangelists.

'At least they're doing something good with the building,' Chiyo said, her heart swelling with pity to see the children looking out at them with big eyes through the windows. She gave them a little wave, and they scattered. She wished she could take care of all the orphans in the world. Whenever it came to children and babies, her heart melted.

They stepped inside to find a sour-faced woman wearing a cross around her neck. 'Please, have you had any new children join your orphanage in the past few days?' Yui looked so desperate and vulnerable that Chiyo wanted to take her hand. 'Sanada Hiro, twelve years old?'

'Not that I know of.' Despite her scowling face, the woman was soft-spoken, and she flicked through a file. Chiyo glanced up to see another woman in an apron ushering some toddlers along, chirping that it was time to eat before their nap. At least they seemed well taken care of. Some of the littler ones only wore underrobes, maybe too hot for a full outfit. Their chubby little legs were so cute.

'We haven't had any new children for several months,' said the woman finally, tucking away the file. 'Certainly no Sanada Hiro here.'

Yui deflated. 'Okay. Thank you.'

Chiyo's anxiety matched Yui's. Tokyo was no place for a child by himself. 'What do I do?' Yui asked, her voice cracking when they stepped outside.

Chiyo didn't know. She hugged Yui, breathing in her clean smell. It was a scent Chiyo couldn't place, not quite floral, not quite soap. She could feel Yui's heartbeat against her chest. Yui's breathing slowed as she wrapped her arms around Chiyo, too. When they parted, their faces were close. Yui's eyes were a light brown, her eyebrows thin and neat. She had that expression on her face – the slightly sulky look that meant she was in pain and trying to hide it.

She had a freckle near her lip. Chiyo hadn't noticed that before.

Chiyo swallowed, stepping away. 'Maybe we should head home,' she said. 'Eomma might need help.'

As they walked back in silence, they spotted men carrying bundles of straw, bags of incense and wooden animals.

'What's going on there?' Yui asked.

'They're preparing for the Obon festival.' Chiyo supposed Yui was too stressed to have remembered. 'Eomma might be cooking some special dishes. We go and clean graves usually.' She hesitated. Her mother's relatives were back in Korea, and her father's parents didn't live in Tokyo. They didn't have a proper family grave for Chiyo's brothers, who had died as babies before she was born. 'We've been washing an honorary grave for my uncle. He died a few years ago. I never met him, but we got a letter from my grandmother about it.'

Aware she was rambling, Chiyo fell quiet, and the young women concentrated on making it through the crowd preparing for the festival. Chiyo always enjoyed the *bon odori* dance and taiko drums, but it felt almost perverse to get excited when Yui had not yet found her brother.

She knew it wasn't her problem, but Chiyo couldn't help feeling responsible for Yui. Besides, she liked her company. Chiyo didn't have any living siblings, and it was nice having someone around who was her own age, to talk to and laugh with.

She recalled the letter her father had received, the tears he'd shed to learn that his brother had succumbed to a bad flu. 'Should we go and visit them?' her mother had whispered to her father that night. Chiyo had been eighteen then.

'You know what they said last time we met. I'm surprised she even bothered writing a letter.' A rustle of paper. 'She just wanted to emphasise how much better he was than me, I suppose. She probably wishes it was me who had died instead.'

Chiyo hated how her father's voice had cracked. She had clamped her hands over her ears after that, refusing to listen to any more.

'Chiyo?'

Yui's voice stopped Chiyo in her tracks as she blinked out of her memory.

'You almost walked past the house.' Yui's voice held a tone of laughter. Chiyo swivelled round and grinned.

'Oops. I was daydreaming.'

Chiyo's mother was in a good mood, reporting that she had sold a lot of kimchi at the market today. 'How wonderful it would be if kimchi became popular and we all ended up rich merchants,' she said, half to herself, before shooing Chiyo and Yui out of the house to wash clothes. 'Come back before it gets dark,' she called after them as Chiyo slid the door closed.

'You'd think I was a child,' Chiyo remarked. Then she saw Yui's face. 'Oh, Yui. I'm sorry. I know I'm privileged to have a mother who cares.'

'Don't be sorry,' Yui said with a shake of her head. 'Are we going to use well water?'

'It won't be long until it's dark, so we'll use the river. Don't you wash your clothes in the river where you're from, Yui?'

Yui's nose wrinkled. 'The well water is cleaner.'

Chiyo thought about it. Yui was right; sometimes the river could get nasty from industrial excess or other waste. So they headed for the communal well, Chiyo wondering where Yui had grown up to be so meticulous and clean.

A thought occurred to her.

'Um. Yui-chan,' she said as they used the cold well water to wash robes and a futon blanket. She glanced at Yui, who was struggling with washing a heavy sheet. Chiyo watched her, feeling more and more like she was right. 'I won't tell anyone, but have you run away?'

Yui glanced at her. 'Run away?'

'Yes, from … from your family. Your mother works hard, right? And you looked after your brother? Are you from a wealthy family where you were going through a hardship?'

Yui stared at her for a moment, then snorted with laughter. 'Trust me, I'm not wealthy. And no, I didn't run away. I came here by accident.'

Chiyo was confused. 'Came to Tokyo by accident?'

'No …' Yui squeezed some water from the sheet. Nearby, more families lined up to collect water from the well. 'I mean, yes. It's difficult to explain.'

'I can try to understand,' said Chiyo in earnest.

Yui gave her a hard look. It was like a wall had shot up between them. 'Stop asking me questions I can't answer. Once I find Hiro, we'll both be out of your hair.'

Chiyo's eyes narrowed. She was *worried* for Yui, not that Yui seemed to much care. 'Fine.'

'Good.'

They finished their work in silence and trudged home in the dying daylight, the clothes damp in their baskets.

CHAPTER 7

Yui felt bad for snapping at Chiyo, but she couldn't go around shouting that she was from seventy years in the future. She had nowhere else to go. She didn't know much about this period of history, but even she knew being alone outside in the city at night was a horrible idea. She'd been lucky enough to find a family kind enough to take her in. She just hoped her brother had, too.

'Chiyo-chan, *okaeri*,' welcomed back her father. He smiled warmly at Yui, too. '*Okaeri nasai*, Yui-chan.'

Yui gave him an awkward bow and helped Chiyo hang up the clothes and sheets they had washed. Then they gathered around the table to eat as Mr Aoki said, 'The Obon festival celebrations are on tonight. Let's all go!'

Yui was unsure. Was it right, given the circumstances? But lying awake here worrying about Hiro might be worse.

'Yes, let's go,' said Chiyo with enthusiasm. She nudged Yui with her shoulder, a friendly gesture that made Yui soften. 'C'mon, Yui-chan. Maybe we'll see Hiro there.'

'All right,' said Yui, making Chiyo grin broadly.

The four of them walked down the brightly lit Tokyo street, lights on all around them, people dressed in summer *yukata* robes, the atmosphere electric. The Aokis strolled hand in hand as they headed to the river. Chanting and taiko drums pounded through the air. Groups of dancers in identical bright robes swayed to the music, hands in the air.

'Wow!' Chiyo exclaimed. Passersby joined in, laughing as they moved along to the simple dance. A reluctant smile tugged at Yui's lips as she raised her hands with Chiyo, copying the dance moves, the drumbeats pounding in her chest.

They followed the crowds to the river, where people lit lanterns to float on the water to help guide their ancestors to the afterlife.

It made Yui consider her own ancestors. Her grandparents, whoever they were, would be young now, somewhere in Japan, maybe in Tokyo. Maybe her American grandfather would be here already, one of the nameless Western men she sometimes spotted on the streets.

The thought was strange. Her mother had always said she didn't know much about where she'd come from. 'I don't remember my childhood,' she'd recalled once. 'Found myself in Tokyo as a young woman, so, I did what I was good at.'

Yui found she was glancing at Chiyo a lot, the girl's joy more attractive than the bobbing red lanterns. Simple, innocent happiness that made her ache.

Mr and Mrs Aoki still held hands, and soon Chiyo's father's hand slid to his wife's shoulder, holding her close. Yui had never seen affection like this before. It was tender and … that ache grew.

*

Chiyo loved the Obon festival. Though she had no ancestors she knew of in Tokyo, there was something magical about sending off the spirits and bidding them goodbye at the end of the season.

Eomma and Chiyo's father shared tender looks, like there was no place they would rather be. Yui's face had crumpled up. 'Yui-chan,' said Chiyo. 'What is it?'

The girl swallowed. 'It's all so beautiful.' She looked at her. 'Sorry for snapping at you today. I'm trying to work things out.'

Chiyo softened, the last bit of tension between them melting away. 'That's all right. We're all going through things. I shouldn't have been so nosy.'

'You can be nosy. It's nice having someone who cares.'

Those words hurt to hear. How could someone as cool and fearless as Yui be unwanted by her own mother? It must have been horrible to have only yourself to rely on. Chiyo didn't have any living siblings, but she was grateful to have a caring mother and father.

She wanted to share them with Yui.

Chiyo had not forgotten her suggestion to look for Yui's brother at the festival, but there were so many people here. Yui's eyes scanned the crowd, maybe looking for a boy pouting in the shadows, or maybe with a group of youths causing mischief. But there were hundreds of people here.

Chiyo's father bought them both some dorayaki, pancakes with a sweet bean filling. It was warm in Chiyo's hands, and one bite was so sharp and sweet it almost made her forget where she was.

Yui's eyes rolled and closed. 'Mmm,' she groaned, making Chiyo laugh.

'You've got a crumb on your chin,' said Yui, her light brown eyes flicking to the lower part of Chiyo's face. She reached and gently wiped it off.

The touch of her soft thumb on Chiyo's chin made goosebumps spring up on her arms despite the hot night. Chiyo stiffened, watching Yui as she slowly chewed. Such a simple gesture, and yet she felt like birds had taken wing in her chest.

Yui, unfazed, took another bite of her dorayaki, her gaze sweeping the crowds. Chiyo had no idea how they would come across Hiro unless they were incredibly lucky.

'I keep getting hopeful whenever I see a young boy with longish hair or a sulky expression,' Yui sighed. 'But it's never him.'

'Shall we look for him?' Chiyo asked. 'Eomma, can we meet you and Father at home later?'

Her parents agreed, and Chiyo linked her arm with Yui's. The dancing was still going on by the river. Families clapped or danced along, some with small children on their shoulders. The scent of sweet treats wafted past them, the sweet bean flavour lingering on Chiyo's tongue. If only they could find Yui's brother, they could relax and enjoy the evening. Yui beside her was like an anchor. She couldn't help feeling safe with her.

'I don't know how we'll find him,' Yui said eventually.

After some persuading, Yui allowed Chiyo to lead her home. She must have been desperate about her brother. Chiyo wished she could make her feel better. She was disappointed, too, that Hiro hadn't shown up at the festival. It had been a slim chance anyway, but Yui had seemed more buoyant at the hope. Her shoulders sagged as she walked.

'Are you tired?' Chiyo asked. 'You can talk to me.'

'Yeah, I'm a bit tired. What's that? Your father said it was called the Twelve-Storey Tower or something.' Yui pointed across the river to the tower Chiyo had often admired whenever she was around Asakusa.

A smile spread on Chiyo's face. 'Isn't it amazing? They call it the Cloud-Surpassing Pavilion. It has shops selling goods from all over the world and it has an electric elevator. Imagine! I'd like to go there one day.' Chiyo had often imagined herself browsing the expensive imported goods or sipping tea in the lounge, wearing a fancy kimono robe or even a Western-style dress. She had always admired the pretty hats and cotton frocks brought in from lands far away.

They left the crowds and the festivities behind and were nearing her neighbourhood, but it was still noisy with shouting people and far-off music.

'I'd be lost if you weren't here,' Yui remarked.

Chiyo knew she meant lost in the neighbourhood, but the words still made her flush. The streets were not very well lit, and the sun had already set. Chiyo thought back to their conversation, where Yui had become defensive. Chiyo wasn't certain why she felt she could trust Yui. She hadn't known her for long, and she clammed up when it came to certain topics. But somehow, she felt she *could* trust her. There was vulnerability beneath all the toughness. She had glimpsed it, like catching sight of a koi carp in a river before it darted away. Chiyo wanted to protect it. Even though she was scared for her brother, Yui could still be strong and make decisions. Something Chiyo had always struggled with. She never seemed to know what to do unless someone told her.

'It's still kind of early, right?' said Yui. 'Why don't we go somewhere?'

'Like where?' Chiyo asked in surprise.

'The wind feels nice,' Yui said. 'Isn't there anywhere you like to go at night?'

Chiyo's mind wandered to the red-light district, to where Riko worked among dim lights and soft laughter. She hadn't told her mother and father about Riko; they wouldn't understand her fascination with the ladies of the night. But she felt a surge of mischief at the thought of telling Yui, of sharing this secret with her.

'I do know a place.'

The young women slipped through the shadows and headed down some side streets to the heart of Asakusa, where the city was still active, glowing with lanterns. Men stood outside bars, calling out to passersby to try their sake and exotic Western drinks.

'Father likes sake,' Chiyo mused. 'I don't know if he's ever been here, though.'

They soon arrived at the little place on the corner where Riko worked. 'I'm not sure my friend will be here,' she admitted.

A middle-aged balding man in a Western-style suit shuffled past, bowing his head as he passed through the red curtains. Chiyo stood on her tiptoes, wondering if it was wise to go round to the backdoor like she usually did.

'Never expected you'd be into this sort of thing,' Yui remarked.

'Someone I know works here. But no! It's not like that. She's my friend,' said Chiyo, panicking. *Is that what Yui meant?* 'I mean, I find it all so …' She couldn't put it into words. She had never managed to articulate it because it seemed like something she *shouldn't* feel. 'Aren't women just beautiful?' she blurted.

She thought Yui might demand to know what she meant. But Yui gave her a crooked, knowing smile. 'Yeah.' Her gaze lingered for a heartbeat longer than was comfortable before she glanced at the establishment. Another man passed, clearing his throat as he stepped into the red glow of the interior.

'I usually go this way.' It would be nice to introduce her friend. She wondered what Riko and Yui would make of each other.

But the proprietor appeared almost as soon as Chiyo had stepped through. Chiyo swallowed, recognising the middle-aged woman at once. 'No, no. I turn a blind eye when you come in the daytime, when it's quiet, but it's a busy evening tonight. Go on, off with you.'

Chiyo had no choice but to step outside. 'Why not say you're looking for Riko?' asked Yui.

'I don't want to get her into trouble,' said Chiyo. The truth was she'd floundered when the stern-looking woman had appeared. Riko must be busy tending to a customer.

'That's fair.' Yui glanced around. 'Shall we go back?'

Chiyo didn't say it aloud, but she thought of Yui's crooked grin after Chiyo's outburst. Her agreement. Chiyo didn't know if that meant what she thought, but she didn't want to ruin things by asking.

'Don't mention this to Eomma and Father,' Chiyo begged. 'They don't know.'

'Course I won't.' Yui linked arms with her, giving her a reassuring squeeze.

They arrived at the house shortly before Chiyo's parents did. They were hand in hand, Eomma giggling at something Father had said. Yui had a wistful look on her face as they readied for bed.

'Oh, he's singing,' Chiyo whispered later, and clamped her hand over her mouth to swallow her laughter. Chiyo and Yui grinned at each other as Chiyo's father, on the other side of the curtain, sang a song Yui didn't recognise, occasionally going off-key. Eomma giggled next to him, giving a half-hearted 'Shh!'

'Goodnight, Yui-chan,' said Chiyo as her eyelids grew heavy. She had often fallen asleep to her parents' whispers, and it was a great comfort to her.

CHAPTER 8

Chiyo was like a shield. A protective layer of calm and serenity. Yui felt halfway between her life here and her old life in the nineties – sometimes she saw bits that were familiar, a mirror between her worlds. A shrine gate that might still exist in her time, a familiar street corner. Now she had to seriously ask herself: would she go back to her old life, if she was given the choice? She had been here for weeks now, settling into a routine of helping Chiyo and her mother with chores and sometimes helping to cook. She had joined Eomma at the clustered, crowded market to help sell kimchi, where people haggled over a couple of sen. It was smelly, unpleasant work, but Eomma appreciated the help. Yui did as much as she could to pull her weight while staying with the Aokis.

She went to the police station every morning to ask if they had news on Hiro. Today she pushed open the door only to be greeted by the shaking head of the constable. Frustration ran through Yui. How could Hiro have disappeared? Had he looked for her too? Or had he not time travelled at all?

Her stomach lurched at that. It was somehow worse, to think he might have been left in 1995, all alone and thinking she had abandoned him. He would have searched for her all over the park, then back home eventually, with no one to make sure he ate or did his homework.

No. She shook herself. He was here. She could feel him, somewhere in this city.

The west side of Tokyo brought cleaner, wider streets, buildings of brick instead of wood, and upmarket shops and stalls. Yui felt shabby in Chiyo's borrowed robe, but it didn't matter. She was an alien in this world.

She wasn't sure when she had accepted her situation. Maybe it was Chiyo's calming presence. Her parents' kindness. They always made sure she had food, and last night they had played *sugoroku*, a traditional board game, together. Yui couldn't put into words how much it all meant to her.

They strolled down the bank of the Sumida River, the lush green leaves shielding them from the harshest of the sunlight.

Soon summer would be over, and the earthquake would come. The men going to work, women here for shopping, children and babies who'd never done anything wrong. How many of them would die?

Yui could hardly imagine this city in flames, buildings levelled by the quake. If she was a fool, which she wasn't, she could convince herself it wouldn't happen.

She had been carrying this knowledge for weeks now, a dark secret locked in the valleys of her heart. She had tried to deal with one problem at a time: find Hiro, then worry about the future. But she hadn't managed step one yet, and the timebomb was ticking.

Chiyo handed her a clay jar of water. As always, it felt like the world was brighter with her here. Yui didn't think she was imagining the lingering looks between them, nor the way Chiyo's breath hitched adorably when their fingers brushed. It was a wonderful, exciting feeling, but one that made everything more complicated.

No one was around now. The trees swayed in the summer breeze. Water lapped the sides of the river. Yui wanted to tell Chiyo everything. That she had travelled through time, that thousands would soon die in an upcoming earthquake. It all sounded unbelievable.

But all Yui could do was take in Chiyo's delicate features, the brown eyes that crinkled when she smiled, the adorable way her lips turned up at the corners when she was thinking of something funny or mischievous. Every logical and serious thought fled her mind when Chiyo looked back at her.

Oh no. This complicates things.

Yui had never banked on liking this girl. Hiro's absence was a constant worry, but the spiky anxiety smoothed to flat stones when Chiyo was around.

Did she feel the same? Or was Yui kidding herself?

Her pulse quickened. Hadn't Chiyo said she liked women? Yui was sure that was what she'd been getting at that night in the red-light district. A rush of impulsiveness seized her. Life was short. Bad things were going to happen. But Chiyo was here, she was real, solid, warm …

Yui leaned in.

Chiyo jerked back, startled. 'Eh? What are you doing?'

Yui froze. She wasn't expecting that. Had she misread everything?

'Uh.' Embarrassment swept through her. This was torture. *Say something!* Her brain screamed.

Yui reached up and plucked a leaf from Chiyo's hair. 'You had a leaf on your head.'

She busied herself with throwing away the leaf, which really was tiny, mortified. She had tried to kiss Chiyo, in public no less, and Chiyo had recoiled. It made Yui's stomach writhe with embarrassment. She'd read it all wrong. She was an idiot.

They sat in silence. Yui tried to think of something to say. Chiyo wasn't stupid; she knew exactly what Yui had tried to do. *You've just made a massive fool of yourself.*

She handed the jar back, not meeting Chiyo's eyes. Yui didn't deserve someone as pure and sweet as Chiyo. She had to treasure their friendship and focus on her problems, not pine after a girl who felt nothing for her but platonic, sisterly affection.

The sun went behind a cloud. Chiyo drank from the repurposed jar and Yui stared at it, wondering where that jar would be in a couple of weeks' time when disaster struck.

'We have to save metal cans,' she said.

'Hm?'

She might not be able to prevent the upcoming earthquake, but she could make sure the Aoki family was as prepared as possible. 'Save everything,' she said. 'Water, blankets, food.' She rose and paced, anxiety thrumming through her. Chiyo might look at her differently if she thought she was lying or making things up. But how could she say nothing?

'I have something to tell you,' she said, breathless now. She could hardly stand seeing Chiyo sit there, content with her simple life, knowing nothing about the coming danger.

'Okay.' Chiyo set down the jar, giving Yui her full attention. Why was it that Chiyo could make Yui feel like the only person in the room? In the world? She tried to shake off her complicated feelings and started talking. She told Chiyo about the earthquake, but not about the time travel. Of all the revelations, she didn't think she could take it all at once.

'No one can predict earthquakes,' said Chiyo wisely, picking up her jar. 'My father always says so. People try to, and sometimes animals get panicky if a tsunami is coming and run for higher ground. How are you so certain?'

Yui expected this response, but it still set her teeth on edge. 'I promise you, Chiyo. In September, I don't know what day, a huge earthquake will hit Tokyo. Thousands will die. All this ...' she gestured around them, 'will be gone. Buildings levelled, and fires like you've never seen.'

'You're scaring me.' Chiyo had risen while Yui had talked, and now she took a step back from her. 'You shouldn't say things like that.'

Yui wanted to scream that she was telling the truth, but overreacting wouldn't get her anywhere. She breathed long and slow, feeling her heart pound against her ribs. It was almost painful. Frustration battled desperation.

'You have to trust me,' she said.

'I do,' Chiyo said. 'I believe that *you* believe you're right. I just think you're wrong.' She lowered her head, and Yui saw a flicker of fear in her eyes.

Denial.

Well, who wouldn't deny it? 'We should leave the city, just in case,' Yui said. 'For safety. If I'm wrong, we'll just come back.'

She wouldn't be able to help everyone. And the thought of leaving without trying to help Chiyo's family was an impossibility.

'And go where?' They walked along the riverbank now, the awkwardness of the failed kiss forgotten. 'My family doesn't have any money. Trains and rickshaws are expensive, and there's nowhere for us to go.'

'Don't you have family anywhere else?' A brief thought of heading over to Korea crossed Yui's mind, but she pushed that away. She had no idea of the state of Korea in 1923, but it couldn't be great. Didn't Japan occupy Korea right now? She wished she had paid more attention in history class.

'I have grandparents in Nagano Prefecture, but …' Chiyo hesitated, her cheeks pinking. 'They weren't very happy with my father for marrying a Korean. I've never even met them.'

Yui said nothing as gravel crunched beneath her shoes. How could she possibly get Chiyo to believe her? She couldn't claim to see the future, but was the truth any more believable?

How would she have felt, before that day in Ueno Park, if someone had come over to her and said 'I'm from the future, and a huge earthquake is coming'?

Things seemed hopeless. Despair fell on Yui, weighing down her shoulders. That evening, as the family ate at the small table, Chiyo said to her father, 'Have you heard anything about an earthquake that might happen in the future?'

Yui stared at her rice.

Mr Aoki chewed slowly, frowning at the wall. 'Now you mention it, there was a professor who published a paper on it. Imamura, I think his name was. He said there was going to be a big earthquake in the next fifty years, and we should be prepared.'

Chiyo shuddered beside her. 'When did he write the paper?'

'Not sure. The beginning of the century, I think.'

'Is he still alive?' Yui asked at once. If there was even one person who would agree with her and believe her, she should track them down.

'I think so. Maybe you should check the library for his paper. Or the university, perhaps.'

Yui was determined to find this Imamura. It finally felt like a step in the right direction. She was tired of hanging around and waiting for things to happen.

The next morning, wearing a simple robe bought with some local currency Mrs Aoki had given her for helping with chores, Yui set off to catch the tram to Tokyo Imperial University. Yui recalled looking at universities when she was in high school, back when she was naive enough to think she'd be able to go. She had never ridden a tram, so she copied what other people were doing, boarding the squeaky tram when it rattled up to them. She ended up with a pregnant woman sitting in front of her, a gloved hand on her stomach. Where would she be during the earthquake?

Stop it, she scolded herself.

The journey was long and arduous, and she was missing Chiyo by the time she arrived on a long, tree-flanked street that led to the university. It all seemed so big, and she was just one shabbily dressed woman in a sea of men, some wearing navy imperial suits she supposed must be the university uniform. Many of them glanced at her.

She couldn't let her resolve crumble. Her back straight, she marched to the heavy double doors of the university.

'Good morning. I'm looking for a paper on earthquakes by Imamura.'

She tried to look like she was supposed to be there, but as soon as the male receptionist, if that was what he was, looked up, she knew she'd made a mistake.

His eyes went from her hair to her robe, which seemed shabby and dirty in this building with its polished floors and brick walls. 'What is this regarding?' he asked.

She shifted. 'I'm looking for the one about there being a big earthquake in the next fifty years. It was written around the turn of the century.'

The man cleared his throat and set down his pen. He looked to be in his thirties, with clean hands and pristine nails cut short. He wore a Western suit with gold buttons down the front. He wrinkled his nose slightly, as though Yui had brought in a bad smell. To be fair, perhaps she had. 'Who let you in? Women aren't permitted in the university.'

Oh. Of course. 'Well, that's stupid.' She thought fast as the man blinked behind his glasses. 'I'm here on behalf of a scholar. Uh … Watanabe Ken. From the University of … Ahh … Aichi.'

She winced inwardly. She doubted there was a university named after the far-northern prefecture.

'Never heard of him.' The man picked up his pen.

'Of course you haven't,' she said. 'He specialises in seismology. I've come a long way, so I'll just have the paper and be on my way.'

The man scoffed. 'If you have a letter from Professor Watanabe, kindly present it.'

I'm so stupid. I should've thought this through. 'All right. I'll go and get it.' She turned and marched out of the building before the snooty man at his desk could say anything else. As she stepped into the humidity, she decided to look for the paper herself. She didn't much want to return to the Aokis' empty-handed.

She followed a group of students through clean, grassy grounds towards a building marked LIBRARY in kanji characters. Nobody paid them any notice as they slipped inside. Yui loitered by a tree, glancing around, then stepped inside, too.

The smell of paper and books tickled her nose. The inside was cool and dark, and she wiped her damp brow. Shelves and shelves of books and scrolls and papers. Where to start?

Some of the books looked ancient. What would become of the library during the earthquake? Would any of these books and scrolls be saved, or would they burn down with half the city? It was a miserable thought, but one that spurred her on.

More history. Archaeology. Geography. And …

'Yes!'

Yui clamped a hand over her mouth. Her outburst echoed up and down the aisle.

'What was that?' said a voice.

Clenching her teeth, Yui tiptoed backwards into a shadowy corner.

Footsteps approached, then passed. A man said something, and a hoot of laughter followed. Yui slowly exhaled, her pulse slowing. Time to find that research paper and get out of here.

There was already a lot of research on earthquakes, papers and books by various scientists taking up the shelves. Yui searched for Imamura. Most of the kanji she could recognise, but some words, complicated scientific vocabulary she'd never learned, were lost on her.

She finally found Imamura Akitsune, only a few papers of his on the shelf. She pulled out one, then another, both of which were about physics. The third, however, was written in printed kanji that was difficult to follow. At the times Yui should have been drilling the complicated characters at home, she was working or making sure Hiro was doing his homework.

Her heart ached for her brother, but she couldn't focus on him right now. The gist she could glean from the paper was that an earthquake and tsunami that hit Iwate Prefecture in 1896 was caused by movements of the Earth's crust.

Obvious to Yui, revolutionary in this time.

The paper had been published in 1905, nearly twenty years ago. The sweat on Yui's skin turned cold as she read his prediction: in the next fifty years, a huge earthquake would devastate the Kantō region and kill over a hundred thousand people.

Chillingly accurate.

She had to talk to Professor Imamura. Maybe he was still teaching at the university.

Satisfied, Yui carefully placed the papers back before heading outside.

'What's she doing here?'

'A woman?'

Yui stiffened, realising she had walked into a group of students. Three young men, all wearing caps and navy uniforms, stared at her in surprise.

'Oh, good.' She straightened, looking the tallest in the eye. 'I'm looking for Professor Imamura. Is he here?'

A shorter student snickered. The other two glanced at each other.

'He isn't here right now. He's on a trip to Kyoto.'

'When's he coming back?'

Yui knew that feigning authority was the best way to seem like you belonged. She pretended she was where she should be. Maybe knowing one of the professors by name had blindsided them.

'Next week,' said a student finally.

'Thanks.' Yui swept away from them before they could ask her any questions.

CHAPTER 9

'You went there by yourself?'

Yui's eyebrows raised at Mr Aoki's question. 'Yeah. The receptionist wasn't very helpful.'

Chiyo's father guffawed around a mouthful of food. 'Yui-chan, you're more daring than I thought.'

'I could never do that,' said Chiyo. 'What was it like? A real university!'

'Full of rich idiots.' Yui scooped some of the soy-sauce-soaked potato into her mouth. It was a little bitter, but a delight to her empty stomach. 'You should've seen how he looked at me when I asked for Imamura's paper.'

She sensed it wouldn't be wise to tell Chiyo's parents of her sneaking into the library, so she whispered it to Chiyo that night.

Chiyo laughed into her hand. 'You're so funny, Yui-chan. What if they'd caught you?'

'They'd probably have fainted at the thought of a girl wandering the shelves and poisoning it with her femininity. Anyway, I'm going again on Monday. That's when the professor's back.'

Chiyo went sombre, reaching for Yui's hand. Her fingers stopped a few centimetres away. Maybe she was remembering the awkward moment of Yui leaning in for a kiss. Yui was glad it was dark; her cheeks heated at the memory, too. 'You want to talk to him about an earthquake, right?' Chiyo whispered.

Yui nodded. 'It was like your dad said. He predicted it.'

'In the next fifty years.'

'It's coming this September, Chiyo.' Yui sat up, fresh fear flooding through her.

Chiyo shivered despite the oppressive heat. 'How do you know?'

Yui picked a hangnail. This wasn't the time to tell Chiyo everything. In this tiny, hot space late in the evening, her parents only a metre or so away. But it felt lame to say, 'Just trust me.'

Instead, she said, 'I'll let you know what he says.' It stung, but maybe Chiyo would take her seriously if they had the backing of a professor.

She lay down, turning her back to her friend. She tried to think of anything besides Chiyo's midnight-dark eyes, and how her breathing suggested she was lying awake, too.

When Monday came, Yui could hardly wait to go back to the university. But would Professor Imamura be back? Was he returning from Kyoto today, or back in his office that day? Surely the latter.

'I'll come with you, if you can wait for the afternoon,' said Chiyo's father as he readied for work. He wore brown slacks and a plain shirt for his work at the factory. The armpits and collar were yellowed with use. 'I'll come back at lunchtime and we'll both go.'

Yui wanted to protest, but what if Professor Imamura could convince Mr Aoki of the coming disaster? It would be much easier to get the family to leave Tokyo if Chiyo's father agreed.

She decided to wait. She spent the morning at the market with Chiyo's mother, after her usual trip to the police station for news about Hiro.

Time was running out to find him. It was running out for everyone. The anxiety made Yui so sick sometimes that she wanted to empty her guts out on the dirty, mud-stained road. Eomma said with sympathy, 'What is it, Yui-chan? Are you not feeling well?'

Yui supposed she must look pale. Eomma herself always looked tired, and when she thought no one was looking, she sometimes winced as she touched her lower back. She never complained, though.

'Just my monthly flow,' Yui mumbled, busying herself with dividing portions of kimchi.

'What is that? It's stinky!' exclaimed a little boy clutching a woman's hand. 'Smells Korean.'

'How can something *smell* Korean?' Yui grumbled as the embarrassed mother dragged the little boy off.

'Maybe it's our delicious seasonings,' said Eomma. She smiled at an approaching customer. 'People can hate us all they like; they still eat our food. *Irasshaimase!* Delicious homemade kimchi sold here!'

'Cook it with meat or top it on your rice,' Yui called out. It was easier to throw herself into this job. Pocketing a couple of sen from work with Eomma was easier than agonising over things she couldn't control.

It felt like several years before noon came. Sweating and tired, Yui and Eomma headed home, listening to a leaving train at Ueno Station. A teenage boy strolled past, looking so like Hiro that Yui stopped dead. She stared at him and he frowned back, no recognition on his face.

Of course it wasn't him. Sighing, Yui hurried after Eomma.

Mr Aoki was waiting for them when they got back. Yui thankfully dumped the remaining bag of kimchi on the floor. 'Can we go now?'

'Yui-chan,' Eomma gently admonished, indicating the discarded bag. Yui blinked for a moment. She was about to retort when it occurred to her that this felt … motherly.

Like a daughter being reminded by her mother.

'Sorry, Eomma.' She picked up the bag. 'Where do these go?'

It wasn't until she'd stepped outside with Chiyo's father that she realised she had automatically said 'Eomma,' the Korean word for mother. Not 'Aoki-san.' She wondered if Chiyo's parents had noticed.

'There's a breeze on the air today,' said Mr Aoki cheerfully. 'Shall we walk?'

The university was a stone's throw away from Ueno Park. A tram ran by, squeaking slightly on its metal tracks, and Yui watched it go, thinking about how they didn't have as many trams in her time. All this would be gone soon. The thought made her stomach squeeze. She hoped beyond hope Professor Imamura would be able to convince Mr Aoki of what was coming.

'Wow.' Chiyo's father looked around at the neat, trimmed grass of the university grounds and the brick buildings. 'It's beautiful here. Where to first? Reception?'

'Maybe not,' said Yui in alarm, remembering the man who worked there. Mr Aoki was wearing his dirty factory overalls;

no one would believe he was the fictional professor. 'Let's ask someone.'

It was a Monday afternoon and plenty of students were about. All young men, some glancing at Mr Aoki's grubby work outfit or Yui's plain robe.

'There's an entrance here.' Mr Aoki walked ahead to an ajar door. 'It might be a good place to start if we don't want to, ah, disturb the receptionist.'

They exchanged guilty grins and slipped inside the cool interior. The low thrum of professors' voices reached them from behind heavy doors, and the corridors smelt of paper and ink. Yui felt an ache at the academic lifestyle she would never have.

'Look.' She nodded to a sign that indicated upstairs was where they needed to go. They hurried up, and to Yui's relief, a corridor of doors greeted them with professors' names engraved on each.

'Imamura,' said Mr Aoki with satisfaction. 'It doesn't say his first name, though. Let's hope it's the same person.'

They waited around until a bell rang and students filed from their classrooms. Yui crossed her arms, trying to look like she belonged as suit-clad professors, all men, talked quietly as they approached. Some glanced at Yui and Mr Aoki. Finally, a man in his fifties with a moustache and thinning hair stopped in front of his doorway.

'It's all right, we've got a meeting,' said Yui loudly to a staring professor down the corridor. 'After you, Professor.'

The bewildered academic entered his own office at Yui's invitation, and after Mr Aoki was inside, she closed the door behind them, letting out a small breath.

Professor Imamura held a slightly sad look. He blinked slowly as he regarded them both. 'May I help you?'

Yui strode to a chair in front of his desk. 'You're a bitch to find.'

'Yui-chan,' said Mr Aoki in shock. He cleared his throat. 'I'm sorry to disturb you, Imamura-sensei. We have questions about your paper on earthquakes. You're Imamura Akitsune, right?'

'Oh.' The professor looked harried. 'Well, yes. I suppose you'd better sit down.'

Professor Imamura's office held all the pomp Yui had expected of a university professor: an enormous oak desk, framed paintings of various locations in Tokyo and beyond, including a giant Buddha statue. A wooden clock ticked on the wall.

Yui perched on a chair in front of the professor's desk.

'What is it you wanted to talk to me about?'

She detected a southern accent, masked, perhaps, by trying to speak the standard dialect in years of academia.

There was no point wasting time with niceties. 'I read your paper,' she said. 'I'd like to know more about it.'

'It is true that twenty years ago, I published a paper on an upcoming quake,' said the professor. 'I've worked in seismology for most of my life.' He rummaged in a file and brought out some old newspapers. 'Two years later, I was heavily criticised.'

Yui and Mr Aoki examined the newspapers. A scientist called Omori Fusakichi had downplayed Imamura's predictions, accusing him of fearmongering.

'He's a clever man,' said Professor Imamura. 'Very accomplished. But he always ridiculed my ideas. There's a big earthquake every hundred years or so, but it is only recently we have been able to properly measure them and tried to understand them.'

'So this Omori, he disagreed with you?' Yui could almost see the tension deflate from Mr Aoki. The relief.

Yui didn't see the point in sugarcoating it. They'd worked hard to get here. She inhaled a steeling breath. 'There is another one coming. Very soon.'

Now she was here, sitting in the professor's office surrounded by certificates and books, she knew she must look a bit ridiculous, a shabby young woman with no academic background. Mr Aoki cleared his throat, leaning back in his chair as though he secretly wished it would swallow him. Professor Imamura listened carefully as Yui told him what she knew.

'There'll be fires, too.' She strained to remember. 'That's what'll kill a lot of people.'

'You seem to know a lot of details,' said Professor Imamura. 'Sanada-san, I work with science. You seem to work with ...' He gestured vaguely at her.

'It doesn't matter how I know, surely?' she said, fighting to keep her voice level. 'All that matters is that you're right, and Mr Omori is wrong.'

It worked to appeal to people's – especially men's – egos, and as she'd hoped, Professor Imamura gave a satisfied nod.

'So, what are we going to do?' She glanced between the professor and Chiyo's father, hoping that somehow, they could come up with a plan. She had been sent back in time for a reason. Maybe this was it. To save people.

It was an encouraging thought. She gripped the arms of the chair, taking in Professor Imamura's grim look and Mr Aoki, who was examining his fingernails.

'It depends on whether people want to believe,' said the scientist finally. 'Most people don't. If you tell them there

97

might be a disaster up to fifty years from now, they don't care. They would rather ignore it and focus on the here and now.'

'What if it wasn't years away?' Yui pressed. 'What if it was weeks?'

Professor Imamura shifted the newspapers on his desk. 'I published this paper with evidence I gleaned from science, but even I admit it's an estimation. Tell people if you like, Sanada-san. It won't work.'

She blinked, annoyed by his defeatism. 'It might. What if we asked the newspapers?' The idea was already forming in her head. Get the press to print it, a warning of an upcoming mega-earthquake that would destroy most of the city and bring tsunami waves all across the Kantō region. 'People might listen if it's in a newspaper.'

'And who will print it?' the professor scoffed.

'Aoki-san,' said Yui, with increasing desperation. 'You believe me, don't you?'

'I believe you,' said Mr Aoki, to Yui's surprise and disbelief. 'But Professor Imamura is right. People won't believe us, and no newspaper is going to listen. No one can predict earthquakes. Right?' he asked the professor.

The scientist nodded. 'That's why they're so dangerous. We have tried to predict them, but right now we can only measure them as they're happening. There is no way to know *when* the plates will shift beneath our feet.'

'We have to try. We can't just give up.' Annoyance flashed through Yui at the dismissal. 'Come on. You know it'll happen, and I know it'll happen. September. If we can warn people—'

'No one can predict earthquakes.' He tilted his head as though analysing her. 'I don't even know if you're telling the truth.'

'If you think I came here for fun, you're out of your mind,' Yui snarled.

Professor Imamura made a 'hmmph' noise. 'You can go now, Sanada-san.'

Yui stood, her chair scraping. 'Fine. But you'd better make sure you're out of Tokyo in September, Professor Imamura. You and anyone who'll listen.'

She heard Mr Aoki apologising behind her as she swept to the door, her last bubble of hope gone.

CHAPTER 10

Professor Imamura had been useless. Chiyo's father had remained grim and quiet all the tram ride home, and when she had prodded him about the professor's prediction, he gave her a sad, sympathetic smile. It was so *fatherly* that she'd wanted to snap at him. Instead, she had drawn the curtains to the little space she and Chiyo shared and screeched into a pillow.

Now Yui abandoned her work to search for Hiro again. The police weren't doing anything, and she knew he was here, somewhere in the city. Whatever instinct that drove love and hunger urged her to keep searching for her little brother. There were only days left until September, and from there it was a mystery. The newscaster had never said what day the earthquake struck. All Yui knew was she needed to find Hiro before the thirty-first of August.

It was infuriating to know and be unable to do anything about it. She wandered the city, stopping only to draw water at communal wells. She asked for Sanada Hiro at schools, only to be sent away with wrinkled-nosed disdain. She found a hospital holding the sad scent of disinfectant and old bandages. Everyone insisted there was no twelve-year-old boy with a birthmark on his cheek. Like he'd vanished.

Maybe he hadn't come to 1923. Yui had no idea how any of this worked. Whether the passage only led here or if it had sent Hiro somewhere else. Or if he was even here at all.

She arrived at Chiyo's after another tiring day. *'Tadaima,'* she called dully.

The others were already sitting down to eat. Yui slipped next to Chiyo onto a cushion, thanking Eomma for cooking. Meals made with love and care. It didn't matter to her that they were simple and sometimes bland. Eomma cooked for everyone because she loved them. Yui chewed slowly, enjoying each mouthful as she listened to Chiyo talk about her day.

'Jirō has almost mastered his kendama game. He gets the ball in almost every time now,' she said, pride in her voice. 'He even shared some of his dessert with me today.'

How strange it must be for Chiyo, to be so close to luxury and then come back to the slums. Mrs Nakamura sounded like a handful. But Chiyo always returned home bright-eyed and eager to talk about the children she looked after.

What fate awaited them?

After they cleared away the plates, Mr Aoki said, 'Look what my boss gave me today.' He brought out a battered pack of cards.

'What are they, Father?' chirped Chiyo.

Yui played cards in junior high school, making bets for cigarettes and sweets. She listened while Chiyo's father tried to explain a pack of fifty-two cards, though he clearly didn't understand it himself. When he laid them out and looked at them, puzzled, Yui gently asked, 'Can I try?'

She recalled the games she knew. 'Make up a new rule each time,' she said as they played a fast-paced game that involved putting one card down each round. Each one meant something, whether it was skipping a turn, changing direction, or setting down a matching card.

The rules got sillier and sillier, and at one point Mr Aoki sat bewildered as Yui, Chiyo and Eomma all slapped down cards, their laughter bouncing on the walls. 'Wait, I'm confused,' he said. 'What does four mean again?'

Yui made a rule where if someone put down a seven, everyone had to raise their hand. Mr Aoki forgot the rule and groaned as he picked up all the cards. 'I'm too old for this game,' he said, struggling to hold twenty or so cards in his weathered hands.

They ended up with so many silly rules that they shouted, slapped down cards, threw their hands into the air and loudly pointed out when someone forgot a rule and had to suffer a penalty. They ended up laughing in a heap on the floor. Chiyo giggled at her side, the sound like merry music.

Later, Chiyo snuggled into her futon, closer to Yui than normal. Heat rose in her at Chiyo's closeness. She hadn't forgotten the awful look she'd given her when Yui had foolishly leaned in for a kiss.

Chiyo fell asleep quickly, making contented sounds in her sleep. Yui smiled fondly. She was so grateful to the Aokis for taking her in these past few weeks. They had welcomed her into their home and treated her like a daughter. In that moment, lying in the futon with Chiyo softly snoring beside her, she loved everyone in this ramshackle little house.

Hiro. If only you were here, too.

Her anxiety spiked as she thought of September. She had hardly mentioned the earthquake again, not wanting to upset the family. But wasn't it Yui's responsibility to do something about it?

Yui didn't know what day of September would bring the earthquake, but she didn't want to be here when it happened. As Professor Imamura had predicted, no one was interested in her warning of the upcoming earthquake. Some people, such as the staff at the hospitals and orphanages, listened with worry, before assuring her that no one could know these things for sure.

She wanted to scream. Why was she brought back here? Why couldn't she have just caught up to Hiro that day at the festival and taken him home?

Would that be better? Yui peered down at Chiyo's peaceful, sleeping face. Well, things here weren't all bad.

She turned over, ignoring the heat that flared at Chiyo being so close. Yui still needed a roof over her head and chose not to pursue the subject. As much as she loved the Aokis, she couldn't force them to leave. Especially as they had nowhere to go. They weren't much better off than Yui herself had been in her old life.

The thirty-first of August was another fruitless day of searching. Yui looked around at the noisy city, its factories belching smoke, the people around her clueless of the coming disaster.

'Chiyo,' she whispered after dinner. 'Want to go for a walk?'

Chiyo nodded, and after finishing folding clothes, they sneaked outside. Beyond the sounds of the city, crickets chirped in the long grass between houses. It was still so hot, and Yui longed for a cool bath.

People used to say earthquakes were caused by a restless catfish, rolling and churning the seas and earth. As they headed towards the Sumida River, Yui thought about the tectonic plates beneath their feet. Next month, they would move and rock the earth on its axis.

They clambered up a grassy bank beneath the branches of a cherry blossom tree. Right now, it had thick green leaves, the pink buds not due for months. A mosquito buzzed by her ear; Yui waved it away. People crossed the bridge above where the city lights gleamed in the river, maybe going home from work or heading to the red-light district. They had no idea Tokyo was about to fall. Yui wished she didn't know either.

'Chiyo.' Her name on Yui's lips brought something calmer, warmer to the turmoil roiling in her mind. 'It's happening soon.'

Chiyo didn't ask what she meant, but the side of her mouth drew inwards, like she had toothache. 'Yui-chan …'

'Please.' They sat together on the grass. Yui pulled her wallet from her robe and pressed it into Chiyo's hand. 'Look at this.'

Chiyo took out the ten-thousand-yen notes, then poured out the silver hundred-yen and fifty-yen coins. She held them up, squinting. 'What is all this?'

'It's money.' Yui paused. 'From where I'm from.'

'And where is that?' Chiyo rifled through the notes. 'You said you were from far away. And this money, it's … how is it a thousand yen at a time? Ten thousand?' That amount of money was astronomical by 1923 standards.

'When you and I first met, I had come from a … tunnel of some kind. A passage.' She waited, somehow hoping that if Chiyo said it, it would make it easier to believe. 'I think that's why I haven't been able to find my brother. Maybe he never stepped through the passage at all. He never came here.'

'What do you mean?' Chiyo asked, shifting closer, resting her head on Yui's shoulder. But Yui couldn't, or wouldn't, answer. With Chiyo so close, her sweet-smelling hair tickling her nose, it was difficult to think. She was content to stay here, looking at the city view, her pulse quickening as Chiyo shifted, her warmth pressing against her.

Somehow, with all this mess coming and Yui's insides wound tight, she was calmer with Chiyo at her side. Chiyo was … happiness. Her soft voice, her kindness, the way she heated Yui's skin in ways she tried to suppress.

'You come from a different place,' Chiyo said quietly. 'A place that's Japan but … different.'

Yui nodded. 'Where you live now … that's where I live. In my time.'

'Your *time* …' Chiyo sighed softly. Yui swallowed. She couldn't give in to the wild thoughts in her head. It was hard enough sleeping beside her. Chiyo's head turned, and Yui looked down at her. Their foreheads were almost touching. A hot flush crept over Yui, her heartbeat fluttering to a quick hammer.

She could get lost in Chiyo's midnight eyes. They were so big, and the city lights made them sparkle. 'Yui-chan,' she whispered, her breath warm on Yui's lips. 'I think I believe you. Nothing else makes sense.'

'It doesn't make sense at all.' Yui touched Chiyo's arm, feeling the rough fabric of her robe. She just wanted to feel her near. 'You believe me?'

'You wouldn't lie to me.'

'Never,' Yui breathed. 'I could never.'

Things were going to change for them fast. They might not find another quiet moment like this. Yui had told Chiyo everything, and now she wanted to lie bare before her, in every possible way. She had never felt so close to anyone. And despite a childhood of disappointment and abandonment, Yui could trust Chiyo, too.

Now Chiyo took Yui's cheek in her palm. She leaned in the rest of the way, the sweetest little groan escaping her as she pressed her lips to Yui's.

Warmth flooded her. Their lips moved, every movement igniting fire inside Yui. Her instincts had been right. Chiyo had not been disgusted at her advances – just surprised. Maybe not ready to face this truth about herself but now … now she was.

Chiyo's lips were impossibly soft, and Yui wanted more. But all too soon Chiyo pulled away, slightly breathless. They laughed, foreheads pressing together.

Happiness ran through Yui, like rivers calming and exciting her all at the same time. She held Chiyo to her, savouring the feeling. She was everything. The rest of the world melted away as she kissed her again.

Soft lips, her heady scent, the rustle of fabric, their groans and giggles as they kissed … if there was a heaven, Yui was close to it. She didn't want it to end. They were shy and hesitant, and Chiyo tensed when Yui's hand started to move aside Chiyo's robe. Her fingers fell away at once. They ended up lying on the grass, fingers entwined. Like lovers. They had been living like sisters, but Yui wanted so much more.

'I didn't know you liked me, too,' said Yui. She sounded lame, but she didn't want to hide anything from Chiyo. She wanted to tell her everything and see how it went. All those lingering looks, the small smiles, the electricity she felt between them. It hadn't been like that only for her. She hadn't imagined it.

'I've liked you for a long time, Yui-chan.' Chiyo's cheeks were flushed, her eyes narrowed with desire. She was shy and bold all at once, and it was positively endearing. 'Maybe since I first met you. Just ... when you tried to kiss me that time, I wasn't ready. I felt so bad, but ... I didn't know it was okay for women to kiss women.'

'Of course it's okay, so long as they both want it.'

Chiyo kissed her again, a soft caress full of promise. Now the sounds of the city came back to Yui, it was a sharp reminder of their situation and what was coming. But it was so hard to care right now. She danced on happy clouds, her heart fulfilled. Chiyo was here. Was this what happiness could feel like? Even when a dark cloud threatened to take it all away?

She hugged Chiyo close. Those three words rose, and she badly wanted to say them, but she held her tongue. Not too much at once. Right now, she revelled in just being here with her, the shy kisses still hot on her lips.

Chiyo's mouth found Yui's neck, making her gasp. 'Sorry.' Chiyo giggled. 'I just wanted to try it. Did you like it?'

'You've no idea,' groaned Yui. Chiyo's lips on her throat had sent a jolt of lust through her. She longed to do more, but she forced herself to say, 'We'd best get home.'

'Yeah.' They rose. Chiyo gently brushed away some grass that had stuck to Yui's robe, looking shy as Yui grinned at her.

She managed to calm down on the walk home, and she could no longer deny the danger. 'It's September tomorrow.'

'Yes.'

Yui hesitated. 'I'm not lying. About what I said. It's going to happen, and it's going to be devastating. I know you have nowhere to go, but let's at least gather supplies, make a safety plan.'

Chiyo took her hand. Only for a moment, as there were people around, but she lightly squeezed Yui's fingers. 'I believe you, Yui-chan. It's not something you'd lie about.'

'You can trust me.' They stopped by the river, the gentle sway of whispering leaves above them. 'I'd never lie to you. Especially not about something as important as this. I'm … from the future, Chiyo.' It was her first time saying it aloud. 'And by some magic, or holy intervention, I found myself in 1923. Here before the earthquake. Whatever happens, it brought me to you.' She pulled Chiyo close. Tears choked Yui, which horrified her, and her voice went strangely high-pitched and shaking. 'This city will be destroyed by quakes and fires. I wanted to help, but no one would listen. At least I want to help you and your parents.'

She trembled as she held Chiyo. All the tension flooded out of her. She was desperate to cling on to this evening forever, to never let summer end. But the passage of time flows whether we like it or not, and soon Yui's tears had dried, Chiyo gently rubbing them away with her thumbs.

'Let's tell Eomma and Father,' she said. 'We have to try.'

Yui had already tried. Maybe it was too late and they should have run away while they could. But she had clung to the hope that she would find Hiro again, so they could all be together to try and weather the coming disaster. In the past few weeks, she had achieved so little.

'What year are you from?' Chiyo asked in a careful tone.

'1995. Heisei 7.' She used the Japanese calendar. Future eras of emperors' reigns, Shōwa and Heisei, did not yet exist in Chiyo's time. For her, it was still the twelfth year of the Taishō era. 'Seventy-two years in the future,' Yui added.

Chiyo remained quiet as they hurried home, noise from the red-light district reaching them. This Friday night, men were off work, enjoying cabarets and drinking. Chiyo glanced in the direction of the district, wistfulness on her face. Yui thought of her mother, a lifelong worker at hostess clubs, and wondered if their timeline still existed. Yui and Hiro had been gone for over a month now. Did their mother care? Or was she relieved?

'Tomorrow,' Chiyo whispered, and Yui nodded, knowing what she meant. They couldn't tiptoe around the subject any longer. They had to pack supplies, prepare to leave. Warn her parents and anyone else they could.

'Blankets,' she said. They'd need those to lie on. 'Extra water. Clothes, too.'

'What are you two doing?' asked Eomma the next morning.

Chiyo nervously glanced at Yui. Maybe together, they could convince her.

'Eomma.' They sat with her in the living space, where the scent of last night's dinner lingered. In the corner, a caterpillar struggled to squeeze through a rotting gap in the wall. Yui watched it, her stomach churning.

Chiyo said, 'A big earthquake is coming, Eomma. We have to prepare.'

Eomma sniffed. 'It's always good to be prepared, but don't let tales of disasters scare you. People predict the end of the world all the time.'

'It's not the end of the world, but it's the end of Tokyo as we know it,' Yui said, abandoning watching the caterpillar.

Chiyo's mother looked so tired, and they piled more onto her shoulders now, but she had to know the truth. 'It's happening sometime this month, I don't know when.' She wished she did. Did they have weeks or days? 'Please, we need to leave. Pack some supplies and get out of the city. You'll be glad when we do.'

'And then do what?' Eomma demanded. 'What will your father do for work? Where will we go? How will we live?'

Chiyo looked around at the mention of her father. 'Where is Father, Eomma?'

'He's at the factory. His boss promised extra pay if they came in on Saturday.'

'Come on,' Yui muttered. The best they could do was to make sure they had supplies ready.

The fear made Yui's insides turn to water. Somehow, knowing the disaster was coming and being unable to do a thing about it was far worse than not knowing at all. The news report she had seen all those weeks ago played in her mind. *The worst natural disaster Japan has ever seen … over a hundred thousand people killed …* She wished she'd left the TV on and listened to the rest.

A hundred thousand people. The number was unfathomable. Would Chiyo's family be included in that number? Would Yui? Hiro?

Eomma started cooking lunch while Yui and Chiyo checked their meagre supplies. Yui wished for water bottles, for a simple tap they could use to get as much fresh, clean water as they wanted, a luxury she had taken for granted. Instead, they had to travel to the local well or a public water tap.

It was a warm, dry day, the sun shining as it neared noon. A pleasant breeze washed over them. 'I would love to go to a bathhouse,' Chiyo said with a sigh. 'Bathe the day away. Wouldn't that be wonderful?'

The remark was so normal it relaxed Yui. 'I'd love to take a bath with you.'

That made Chiyo giggle, and a smile spread on Yui's lips to see her getting flustered. The thought of Chiyo's slender body, glistening with bathwater, made her clear her throat. *One day, maybe.*

People waited in line for water, and Yui and Chiyo managed to get some after drinking their fill from their jugs. A flock of birds flew off, squawking. Yui watched them go, wretchedness suddenly washing over her.

She looked around. An old woman yanked up a bucket. A sigh of dry wind swept over the ground, blowing leaves and dust.

Then in an eyeblink, the world ended.

PART 2

'Tokyo … at the zenith of its prosperity, burned down and melted away over two days and three nights.'
Beiho Takashima

CHAPTER 11

The sound of thunder came first. A great roar, like an approaching freight train. Smiles vanished, and slowly, horror dawned on them. The earth rumbled and growled. Chiyo turned to Yui, her eyes widening. 'Yui-chan?'

The world lurched.

It threw Yui and Chiyo onto their backs. Gasps and screams rose. Timber creaked. Ground cracked. The earth heaved. Yui felt like someone had grabbed her and shaken her hard. And it wasn't stopping.

She grabbed Chiyo and they lay thrown around, the ground shaking so hard it felt they would fall off the Earth. Hot, dry air washed over them. Yui crouched low on her stomach, tucking her legs beneath her. All around them was a terrible roaring, the crashing of buildings, people screaming and sobbing. Yui buried her face into Chiyo's shoulder. She just had to hold on. The world was ending, but if she held on to Chiyo, it would be okay.

It lasted an eternity. Roaring smashed into Yui's ears, as loud as a plane engine, as a freight train. A crying woman ran past and was thrown to the ground.

'The building's falling!' someone screamed.

Crash. Smash. Crumble. Yui clutched Chiyo, squeezing her eyes shut. This was it. She hadn't saved anyone. They had waited too long.

I'm dying I'm dying I'm dying I'm

It finally ended. Yui lay there panting, Chiyo in her arms. She didn't want to look up. Didn't want to see it.

Movement around her. 'Is it over?' said someone.

Wails of despair rang around them. Chiyo and Yui rose, trembling.

Tokyo was gone.

Thick, yellow dust rose from the debris of what used to be their district. Just rubble, everywhere. The sky had darkened. Ash covered everything. In moments, everything had disappeared. A dark wind howled over them, dry and thick, making them cough.

Then for a moment, there was silence. People around them struggled to rise, choking on smoke or nursing sore arms or heads.

'Eomma.' Chiyo ran back towards her house. The street was unrecognisable, a pile of broken wood. Somewhere to Yui's left, the unmistakable sound of crackling flames rose from a knocked-over outdoor cooker. Heat and dust washed over her. People backed away as smoke filled the air. Yui ran after Chiyo, wondering if she even knew where the house was.

How did this happen? Just a few seconds ago, we were getting water.

'Eomma!' Chiyo screamed, running for her mother.

Half the house was gone, collapsed to the side. Chiyo slid open the door, which stopped halfway. Her mother appeared, ashen-faced and clutching a bag.

'Are you hurt?' Eomma grabbed her daughter, looking at her.

'No,' Chiyo sobbed. 'Are you?'

'I'm fine, I'm all right. Oh Yui-chan, come here …'

Chiyo stood dazed in her mother's embrace as Eomma's slender arm clutched Yui tight, too. 'It isn't over,' Yui whispered. It was just beginning.

The first of September. She felt she had barely tried.

Another violent tremor shook the earth. Chiyo whimpered. The three of them bolted from the house, collapsing to the heaving ground littered with loose wood. Something sharp dug into Yui's palm.

Shrieks erupted around them as the earth trembled and heaved. More buildings crunched and collapsed. Terror pounded through Yui. The roaring came back, and she clamped her hands over her ears. It was like the whole world screamed.

'One day, Hiro, we'll move somewhere, you and me.' The memory blocked out the screams and bedlam. *'As soon as I have enough money.'*

Hiro …

'Yui-chan? Yui. You have to get up. Come on.'

Yui unfolded herself and rose on trembling legs. Dust coated their hair. The Aokis' house was gone, little more than a pile of debris. Memories, gone forever.

But they were alive … for now.

Dark smoke blackened the horizon. Fires had sprung up everywhere. People had been cooking their lunch, and wooden homes … wood couldn't withstand fire. Behind them, the neighbourhood burned. It was hot on their backs.

People screamed and wailed, running into destroyed homes to grab supplies or search for parents, children, siblings, grandparents. Chiyo's mother held in a bag the

117

supplies that they had gathered – a few cans and jugs of water, some food, blankets and bandages. Better than nothing.

A fissure had erupted in the road, a great crack in the shape of a lightning bolt. People stepped carefully over it, calling into the ash-filled, smoky air.

'You were right, Yui-chan,' Chiyo whimpered.

The words brought her no joy. She desperately wished she *hadn't* been right.

'What do we do?' Chiyo gripped Yui and Eomma's wrists. 'Where do we go?'

A splinter had cut into Yui's hand. She fidgeted with it. They couldn't go running off in random directions. They needed a plan.

'Avoid the fire for now,' Yui croaked. She wished she could switch off her ears. It was chaos. Sobs and wails filled the air, battling the horrible crackling of burning wood. When Yui glimpsed up the street, she spotted a bonfire and a black, charred road. She lurched her gaze away, swallowing the horror. Were there bodies? She didn't dare look again.

Another violent quake sent them to the ground, and more chaos erupted. The people around them screamed for loved ones, dragging sacks or wheelbarrows of supplies. Flames roared, buildings still falling to fires. When the aftershock finally stopped, a loud screech of wood sounded as more buildings fell with a clatter.

'We need to get out of the district. Find somewhere the fires can't reach,' said Yui. Crowds of people were appearing as though from nowhere, some calling for help. A woman knelt sobbing by a broken-down house, and Yui's stomach lurched. An old woman lay motionless, half buried beneath a collapsed house.

The Twelve-Storey Tower's black silhouette lay against the smoke-filled sky. Half of it was gone, crumbled by the quakes. People around them, covered in ash and dirt, all walked or ran in the same direction. The yellow dust was so thick they could barely see where they were going.

'We need to find Father,' said Chiyo. 'Please, Eomma! Isn't he at the factory?'

Eomma stood in a daze, looking around at the destruction with glazed eyes. She looked like she had aged twenty years.

They had to reunite with Father. This was one of the poorest districts in Tokyo, and the fires were getting closer.

Flames bellowed behind them, spurring on the panicking crowd. Someone shouted for water. One man carried a bucket, the contents sloshing on the road, but it was hopeless expecting to fight the fires. Black smoke washed over the crowd, the wind blowing it over them. Burning filled Yui's nose and throat. They coughed violently until it passed.

'Your father is on the other side of the river,' Chiyo's mother panted as she carried the sack. Yui grabbed it, and they carried it between them. Yui took Chiyo's hand with her free one, and they headed for the river in a tightly packed group.

So different from the crowd at the festival. Many people were injured, bleeding from heads or arms, carrying children who sobbed, faces buried in parents' shoulders. They half-jogged along, risking looks behind them or to the sides. Black smoke snaked into the air. An abandoned rickshaw lay collapsed. The horizon glowed with flames.

People crowded the bridge. More boats than Yui had ever seen were on the river, men calling to each other. The boats were laden with so many bags it was a wonder they didn't sink.

'Don't go down there!' Yui cried, taking Eomma's arm. 'Please.'

Something nagged at her. Only death awaited them down there. Following the crowds wouldn't end well.

People behind them pushed them forward. 'Wait!' Yui cried, bodies crushing her. Her hand slipped from Chiyo's. 'Stop! Don't!'

The nightmare dragged her farther towards the bridge. Hundreds tried to cross, cowering and pointing at the flames blowing across Tokyo. People were so tightly packed on the bridge they looked crushed, desperately trying to cross in both directions. The crowd swept them farther towards it like water, feet stamping on Yui's toes. It was chaos, everyone trying to escape the crush.

This was hell.

A great roaring rose as fire swept towards them, the sky painted black and red. Flames closed in from all directions.

'Go back!' Yui bellowed, but it was like trying to push a mountain. 'GO BACK!'

She ducked between people's legs, surrounded by screaming. She had to find Chiyo and Eomma. Palms sweating, blood burning her throat, Yui squeezed through the crowd and found a tree. She climbed, straining to reach the high branches. Dry leaves scratched her face, a hint of green filling her nose. She peered into the sea of heads.

'Don't cross the bridge!' she screamed. The flames crackled closer, panic breaking out. 'Stop!'

It was impossible to control a crowd like this. It was pandemonium. Some people tried to scramble back away from the river, others shoving their way towards the bridge. There was no politeness or niceties here, just the fight for survival. Those in the middle screamed, crushed by the force of bodies closing in from all sides.

Wind howled, black smoke sweeping across them, blinding her. Yui coughed and choked, heat pressing in. There was no escape. She would die here. She clung to the tree, pressing her face against the bark, what remained of leaves. The only remnant of yesterday.

Horrible screams rose from the river. People jumped into the water, trying to escape the fires sweeping across. The bridge heaved with too many people on it. Cracks splintered the air, screaming *DOOM*.

'CHIYO!' Yui screamed, spotting her.

By some miracle, Chiyo looked round, panic on her face. Yui reached out a hand and struggled to pull her up. Chiyo screamed in pain and Yui was horrified, but then Chiyo scrambled up the tree.

'I'm okay,' she panted, clutching the bag of supplies.

'Where's Eomma?'

Licking her dry lips, Chiyo pointed. 'She managed to go back, I think.'

Another terrible crunch dragged their gazes back to the river. Yui couldn't look away. People were jumping or falling into the water, trying to swim or clamber onto passing boats, but there were so many people. Many of them in the water weren't moving.

'It's collapsing!' Yui screamed.

Wood split in half, stones fell. The screech of breaking wood and terrible splashes made Chiyo bury her face into Yui's chest. Yui couldn't tear her gaze away as the bridge collapsed into the water. Bodies fell like stones down a mountainside. Some of them splashed, fighting for the surface. Others didn't.

People still on the ground scrambled away from the wreckage, shouting for people to go back. People scattered, leaving the ruined bridge behind. Some carried futon mattresses, trying to shield themselves from the flames. The river rocked and frothed, washing waves over the swimmers.

Yui didn't know how long she sat there in the tree, holding Chiyo close, numb with the horrors of what had transpired.

She should have done more. She should have tried harder.

When it grew quiet, she glanced up at the river.

So many floating corpses.

'Give me that,' a man snarled, reaching for their bag. Chiyo gasped, holding it close. The man grabbed her ankle.

Yui kicked out, hitting him in the face. He growled, more animal than man, baring yellowed teeth.

'Get off her,' Yui roared, kicking out again. Her shoe hit the man in the nose. He yelled and let go of Chiyo, then disappeared into a crowd of people.

Survivors wandered in a daze, the panic dulled to numb acceptance. Newcomers arrived, stopping to stare at the crowded river. Yui watched a man in a boat with his family, dipping his oars into the water, staring straight ahead.

Yui muttered every curse she knew, holding Chiyo close. Burning wood splashed into the water. A baby wailed somewhere. Yui stared at the dead, who looked more like dolls. A few moments ago, they'd been trying to reach safety in this new hell.

Another violent quake shook the earth, and Chiyo gasped, clinging to Yui. The tremor sloshed the river, bending and cracking the tree. They clung to the bark until it stopped. Chiyo sobbed, tear tracks down her dirty cheeks.

'Let's find Eomma.' Yui kissed her forehead. 'Try not to cry. Keep the water in your body.'

An abandoned ladder and bits of clothes were scattered on the road, fallen from wagons or dragged from houses. They wandered past what might have been a restaurant, a torn flag flapping in the weak breeze. A remnant. A man stumbled from the broken building, food in his arms. He gave them a haunted look then ran off.

They left the river behind, trying to find a path that wasn't devastated by debris or burning wood. Many buildings were on fire now. People ignored them, unable to do anything as their homes burned.

Yui's throat was parched, but they needed to save their water. That was if someone didn't try and steal it from them again.

'Chiyo! Yui! Thank goodness.'

Chiyo cried with relief as her mother ran to them, wrapping her arms around them. 'I'm so sorry we got separated. Come on, everyone is going to this patch of open land. It's safe from the fires.'

People were calling out, directing people towards Honjo. 'There's an army depot there,' a passing man explained. His clothes were filthy, the bandanna around his head torn and dirty. A rickshaw driver. 'It's that way. Get there as quickly as you can. And be safe.'

They headed there, so much more of the burning city visible now that buildings were gone. People wandered around, dazed and haunted. Some people dug desperately at what remained of their homes, calling out for their family members. A child in dirty clothes staggered past them, crying for his mother.

'We need to help him,' said Chiyo. He couldn't have been more than four or five years old.

'We can't help everyone,' said Yui dully. Maybe it was cruel of her, but she couldn't find it in herself to help the boy.

'Not everyone,' said Chiyo. 'Just him.'

Eomma made to go to him, but then a woman ran over. 'Fumi! Fumi! Oh, I found you.'

'Thank goodness.' Chiyo sniffled as Fumi's mother scooped him up.

Every howl of dry wind blew flames across the city. They found a path where people had dug through the debris. As they passed a still-standing building, Eomma groaned. A man was trapped beneath some fallen bricks. Three more men dug at them to help him, scrambling to free his body. He was bleeding from his head.

Conscious, but for how much longer?

'Come on,' muttered Yui. 'He's getting help.'

More than once, their path was blocked by angry flames. A cooker burned inside a house, people having been in the middle of cooking their lunch when the earthquake hit. Yui's palm still stung, and she squeezed and prodded it as they walked, thankful that was all that had happened to them. The house could have collapsed on Eomma, or they could have been caught in one of the terrible fires.

She took Chiyo's hand, Chiyo taking Eomma's. The three walked together, all silently worrying about Father. Had he made it? Was he one of the many wandering the burning streets of Tokyo?

'None of this feels real,' Chiyo murmured. People pulled wagons of supplies, and more than one fight broke out over blankets. And the disaster had struck only hours ago. 'It all feels like a nightmare.'

Yui just wished she knew more. She had been sent to 1923 for a reason. Or had she? Was she just doomed to watch some of Japan's darkest history unfold without any power to stop it? Who would ever want to experience something like that?

The skies were grey, the air hot and dry to breathe. Would they survive?

The army depot, an open plain, held thousands of people seeking refuge. They stood with supplies packed into wheelbarrows, starting to build makeshift shelters. Many of them sat, staring into space or quietly talking, all of them wearing what they had pulled on that morning. How long had it been since Yui and Chiyo had been waiting at the well? Hours? Longer?

They settled at the edge of the plain. Yui's hands were scratched, red and brown smeared together. Her splinter throbbed. It did feel safer here, an open field where the flames wouldn't reach.

The air burned their eyes, embers floating around like fireflies. The horizon glowed. Chiyo's district was on fire; did their house even exist anymore? It was a heavy feeling, weighing down Yui's chest. She had known this would happen, and her feeble attempts at warning the Aokis now felt terribly pathetic.

She made herself look around at the destruction. The sky was dark, choked by smoke. Had they all died and gone to the underworld? Surely this couldn't be real life.

That TV presentation she had seen about the quake had been delivered in such a matter-of-fact, cold way. They hadn't captured being here, in this nightmare. Choked by smoke, surrounded by crying, injured people. Trapped and surrounded by death.

There was no water, and there were too many black trails of smoke to count. People walked past burning buildings, looking almost like they were going for a stroll or on their way to work, dazed by it all. The panic had died out a little; now people wandered, many carrying supplies, just trying to find somewhere to wait it all out.

More people arrived, word of the safe open space flying around the city. They drifted around with towels or rags wrapped around their heads. They stood vigil by wheelbarrows of supplies. Some nursed injuries. Parents held children, shellshocked looks on their faces.

'Do we have any water?' croaked Eomma.

Chiyo rummaged inside the bag and brought out a sealed jar. Yui's throat was parched, but she just licked her lips. They had to save what they could. Eomma's hands shook as she took a sip, hiding it from view.

'Hello,' a kind voice said. An older woman had come to them. 'Are you all right? My name is Kiyoko. Let's find you somewhere to sit.'

She was acting like they'd joined her for tea, not sheltering for their lives. They let the kindly Kiyoko guide them to an open spot. Eomma sat on their sack of meagre belongings, looking exhausted.

A woman sat with a child, stroking his hair and singing to him in a cracked voice. A group of boys around Hiro's age sat together. One of them must have cracked a joke, because they gave guilty grins. To smile even on the darkest of days ... to Yui, it reminded her that people were resilient. She met Chiyo's eyes and forced a smile. They *would* get out of this alive.

There must be hundreds of people here. Yui was unsure what this open space was. Someone had said army depot, but that didn't mean anything to her. They sat together and talked about Chiyo's father, hoping he was all right. Yui wondered for the millionth time where Hiro could be.

Then all at once, the world went dark. Like a shadow had descended over Tokyo.

A roar rose, and a wash of heat ripped at them. Chiyo screamed, grabbing Yui.

Shrieks erupted as a great wind blew up, snatching the air from Yui's lungs.

'A tornado!' a woman with a baby on her back cried.

'A whirlwind,' shouted someone else.

Fire, fire everywhere. A great tower of it, sweeping across the crowded plain like a burning serpent. People screamed as their clothes burned. Bodies crushed into Yui, fleeing for their lives. Yui clutched Eomma and Chiyo, running the way they'd come.

She was blind. Heat ripped behind her, searing her skin. She wanted to shut off her ears to the sounds of death and screaming behind her.

Chiyo's free hand smacked at Yui's back, putting out a flame on her robe. Jostled by panicking, fleeing people, they ran as the fire tornado screeched behind them.

Yui fell to her knees, feet kicking at her, people scrambling over her. People yelled for their children. A baby cried. Yui wrapped her arms over her head, enduring the heat and chaos until she passed out.

CHAPTER 12

'Eomma, Eomma! Where's Yui?'

Eomma either didn't hear Chiyo or ignored her, clutching tightly to her hand as they ran. Chiyo's foot caught on someone lying down, and her heart grew cold. She glanced back. To her horror, people were being thrown through the air by the powerful winds. Grabbed right off their feet and tossed around like dolls.

'Chiyo!' Eomma cried, pulling her downwards. Hot wind ripped at Chiyo's robe, trying to pull her into the sky. She and her mother held each other, her face buried into the dry grass. She wished everyone would stop screaming. Wished the smell of cooking flesh would stop burning her nose.

Then the screaming did stop. And that was worse.

*

Yui's mouth was full of ash. Her burning eyes slowly opened.

The smoke lingered, the crackle of flames still burning forever. She was on her back, dry eyelids peeling open, to behold a sky of brown clouds. She groaned, knowing she had to move. She had to, otherwise she wouldn't move again.

She sat up, nausea washing over her.

She beheld a sea of corpses.

She'd fainted on one. The nice old lady who'd welcomed them. Kiyoko's body was limp, a scream frozen on her face. When Yui gently turned her over, her entire back was burned away. She'd protected Yui in her final moments. Yui choked on a sob, clamping a dirty hand over her mouth.

Piles of bodies. Their clothes burnt off, flesh black and red. Skeletons of wagons. Many crushed. The fire tornado had wreaked its havoc.

Why was Yui still alive when all these people had gone? Why had Kiyoko chosen to save her?

If her throat hadn't been scorched, she would've screamed. Instead, Yui shuffled from Kiyoko's corpse, her body like lead. She half-crawled over the dead's charred remains. Some bodies were far too small. She hurt almost more than she could bear. Her head pounded.

Despair crushed her. She couldn't do this. She wanted to lie down and join them. Everywhere she looked was more death.

'Chiyo?' she croaked.

She looked at faces, moved aside burnt hair with trembling fingers. Chiyo's body wasn't here. Neither was Eomma's.

Hope, a tiny beam of sunshine over a dark mountainside, rose within her.

*

'Help!' a voice croaked.

'Don't look, Chiyo.'

'Someone needs help.'

Chiyo ignored her mother, turning to a collapsed wheelbarrow. She wouldn't ignore a cry for help again. People wandered around in shock. Those were the ones who had survived, looking in confusion at their burnt clothes, their reddened or blackened skin. A woman sobbed, clutching a ruined arm. A man searched corpses, looking for a wife or a child, his voice growing shaky and desperate.

Chiyo couldn't help them, but she could follow the cry for help.

'Please,' croaked a man stuck under a wheelbarrow.

'Chiyo,' Eomma moaned behind her, but Chiyo went to him, stumbling over fallen people. *They've just fallen over, they're not dead, they're not dead …*

A man struggled, pinned beneath the wheelbarrow. 'Are you hurt?' she asked.

'I don't think so.' He was middle-aged, his face contorted in fear. 'Please help me. Please … there's a kid under here.'

A child cried out from behind the man.

Chiyo pushed at the wheelbarrow, grunting. 'Help me,' she called to a nearby woman.

Another survivor hurried over, throwing her weight against the wheelbarrow. Eomma came, too, pushing with all her might. More people came, and a dozen or so joined them.

'It's moving!' Chiyo cried.

They all pushed and heaved, and the wheelbarrow tilted, the man scrambling out from beneath.

Eomma joined them, pulling the child's hands to help him out. Soon they were both out, panting but unhurt. The people cheered and clapped.

The noise was strange to Chiyo. A woman picked up the little boy, asking him if he was hurt.

'Where's my daddy?' The boy sniffled.

'Thank you.' The man bowed to them. 'I didn't know what would happen. When it went dark I … I covered the kid, and that fell on us. I …' He glanced around. 'Are we the only ones left?'

The blackened bodies, the destroyed city, the flames still burning on the horizon … this was their new reality. They had survived so far, but for how much longer?

'Where's Yui?' Chiyo asked. She felt so lost without her. She was worried for her father, too. Surely this couldn't be the end for them.

They had to leave this place behind. They had thought this open plain would be safe, but now a sea of bodies lay where survivors had stood only minutes before. A flaming tornado, that was what it looked like, had surged through the area. The air stank of charred flesh and smoke. Chiyo wanted to be anywhere but here. She wished she was home.

'Look,' whispered Eomma, pointing. Chiyo didn't want to look, but her curiosity won. 'Just ashes …'

Beyond the bodies, in the centre of the open plain, were piles of grey ash. The people in the middle had had no chance even to run. Not even their bodies were left.

Chiyo dry-heaved. If she'd had anything in her stomach, she would have thrown up. She clapped a hand over her mouth, her eyes burning. 'I can't,' she said through her fingers. 'Let's go. Please.'

'It was the winds from the passing typhoon,' someone said, a young man with broken glasses on his face. The group staggered away from the pile of death without aim or focus. 'They must have spread the flames.'

An explosion behind them startled them all. 'Bombs?' someone exclaimed.

'Who would be bombing the place?' Eomma asked, clutching Chiyo's wrist.

A sharp look from a nearby woman. 'Are you Korean?'

Yui's words echoed in Chiyo's mind. 'Who cares if she's Korean?' she asked fiercely. She couldn't bring herself to feel fear. Not after everything.

Another explosion in the distance made them jump. It did indeed sound like bombs. 'Let's go,' mumbled Eomma. 'We can't stay here.'

Chiyo glanced around, her vision full of the terrible sight. People here were alive just moments ago. How many had perished in the last few minutes? It seemed like millions.

And Yui ... where was she? Was she dead, too? Her remains among the pile of ash?

No! Chiyo refused to believe it.

They wandered through the city, drinking sparingly from their can of water. It was warm and tasted like dust, but it was better than nothing. The injured sat, staring into space or in bewilderment at burning structures. Groups of youths broke into destroyed buildings, maybe looting. Whoops of laughter echoed along with loud crashing, the voices sounding so alien. 'Where is everyone?' whispered Chiyo.

It felt like a lifetime had passed before they came to Ueno Park, where thousands of people were waiting among the temple grounds. Businessmen huddled beside the homeless. Families settled beside groups of teenagers. Small children wrapped in bandages sat around a teary-eyed woman who might have been a care worker, her dirty arms wrapped around the nearest.

Some people had taken refuge near the lake. The lily pads were still there, somehow. A man knelt by the edge, drinking noisily from the lake like a dog. A family sat together, passing around a can of water. The father glanced up at them as they passed, assessing them for danger. Satisfied they weren't a threat, he turned his attention back to his children. The youngest, a little boy, sat with his chubby legs stretched out in front of him, dirt on his face and an exhausted look in his eyes that no child should ever have.

They came to Saigō Takamori's statue. 'Look.' Chiyo approached it. 'There are pieces of paper on it.'

Chiyo looked at them as Eomma sat down nearby. Embers and pieces of paper floated along the grass and stone ground. Many people were around this square, too, sitting on the dirt and leaning against bags of supplies, talking quietly, swapping stories of survival as they tried to tend wounds.

'They're notes for loved ones,' exclaimed Chiyo. Her heart broke at each one, the desperate, scribbled notes looking for spouses, siblings, friends, children. Then one caught her eye. It was posted on Saigō Takamori's dog.

'It's from Yui!' Chiyo clutched her mother, her heart lifting. The note was written in bold, simple writing, like a child's. 'Look,' she said, and read: '*To the Aokis. Go to Asakusa Kannon Temple. It's safe there. Love, Yui.*'

Eomma gave an exhausted nod. Chiyo hauled her to her feet. 'All right. If it's safe, let's go there.'

Yui had been here. The thought brought light into this new, drab world. Chiyo glanced back at the skeletal trees, hoping Ueno Park wouldn't meet the same fate as the army depot. *I wish it would rain.*

The panic seemed to have died down, though now and then there were violent aftershocks that sent Chiyo and her mother to the ground, holding each other, as wood cracked and splintered. They stepped carefully over fissures in the ground. Everywhere they looked, entire streets had been reduced to rubble and piles of wood. Farther along were huge buildings that had collapsed on themselves. Who knew what was going on inside.

As Chiyo took a step, she gasped as sharp pain burned on the back of her leg. Her robe had been singed, the skin beneath bright red and raw.

Eomma made a sympathetic sound as Chiyo gently pressed on the skin. It stung at her touch. 'Here,' said her mother, and tore her sleeve to wrap Chiyo's calf.

'Thanks, Eomma.' They carefully wrapped it. Chiyo couldn't complain about a small burn on her leg.

Chiyo's thoughts went back to her father, working hard that day for extra pay. She missed him so much. She clung to her mother as they made their way back towards Asakusa. Would the temple really be safe? Their neighbourhood had burned to the ground.

But she trusted Yui. More than ever, now. She had been right about a huge earthquake in September, but no one had listened. And her poor brother, Hiro. She must be worried sick.

Chiyo wanted to see her. Wanted to hug her and tell her how sorry she was that she hadn't taken her seriously. She really must be from the future, then, exactly as she'd claimed.

Paper fell around them as they walked, some torn scraps of money. A few people around them half-heartedly reached for whole notes, but to Chiyo they were worthless.

Some people had gathered around a broken well, wondering aloud if it was safe to use. A man and a woman pulled a rope, bringing up a bucket of clean water. Cheers rose.

'All right, one at a time. There's plenty for everybody,' a man shouted as a half-dozen people clamoured to grab at the bucket. 'Everyone stay calm.'

'Should we line up?' Chiyo asked. She wanted Eomma to tell her what to do, and she looked expectantly at her.

Eomma's tired gaze ran over the people forming a hasty line. A few men snapped at each other, grumbling that they had got there first. 'We still have some water left,' Eomma said finally. 'It'll take hours. And Yui is waiting.'

Chiyo hoped against hope that her father was waiting, too. She kept her eyes on the ground as they walked, trying to pull energy and motivation from *somewhere*. She tried to encourage herself and her mother.

'Lots of people have survived,' she said, attempting to force some cheer into her tone. It didn't really work. 'And we can rebuild. The worst is over. We will get past this.'

Eomma merely nodded, taking care to step around bits of shattered wood, the remains of broken wagons and rickshaws. At every gust of wind, they tensed, scared more flames would reach them. It felt like the destruction would last forever, would stretch all over Japan and beyond.

But Yui had said that it wasn't the world's end. Tokyo would rebuild, would have a future. 'This will be in history books,' Chiyo said. 'But it won't last forever.'

Her forced positivity was starting to annoy even herself, but she was worried about her mother. Even before this had all happened, she always seemed so sad. Now she walked as though the world had already broken her, as though if it weren't for Chiyo being at her side, she would easily lie on the ground and give up.

'It's going to be okay, Eomma,' she said, somewhat lamely. 'Look, there's the temple.'

What remained of the Twelve-Storey Tower of Asakusa was there, too, cracked almost in half. Chiyo had looked at the mammoth, red-brick structure many times, hoping to visit it one day. Now it was crumbled to pieces. She was glad she'd been nowhere near it when the earthquake struck.

A woman scooped hopefully at a pond with her hands, examined the dirty water and let it fall miserably back into the pond. A nearby man was not so pessimistic; he was scrubbing his face and shoulders with the pond water, grimacing at his leg, where he had suffered a nasty cut.

Courtesans and entertainers in pretty robes covered in soot and dust wandered in a daze, clutching each other.

'There was no time,' a woman murmured. 'No time to do anything. I was talking to her only this morning.'

'We were lucky to get out.'

'I lent her my best *yukata* just yesterday.'

Chiyo's heart leapt. With all the worry about her father and Yui, she had almost forgotten about Riko. She scanned the group of women, but none of them was her friend. 'Have you seen Riko?' she asked a woman she had seen around a few times. 'Is she here?'

'Riko?' The exhausted woman's eyes were red, her robe charred black at the edges like she'd narrowly avoided being caught in the flames. 'No, we're all that's left.'

'Riko's gone,' said another girl dully. 'Just … gone.'

Chiyo's chest constricted. A strange sobbing sound filled the air. It wasn't until Eomma's thin arms wrapped around her that she realised the noise was coming from her.

No tears fell; there wasn't enough water in her body. But she clung to her mother, remembering Riko's dreamy smile. There was nothing left of her now. Eomma didn't ask who Riko was, but she held her daughter until she'd stopped shaking.

Poor, poor Riko. She would miss her so much. Chiyo could only hope her friend had died quickly and without pain.

'Come on, Chiyo-chan,' said Eomma gently. 'The temple's this way.'

Chiyo forced herself to walk. Riko may be dead, but there was still hope for the others. Yui was waiting for them. It was hard to navigate, the city looked so different, but Chiyo could already see the red roof of the Kaminari-mon gate that led to Asakusa Kannon Temple.

Eomma was panting now, a hand on her chest.

'Are you all right?' Chiyo asked in alarm. 'Maybe we should rest.'

The pair sank onto the ruined road. The flames and the black smoke ... had they always been here? Had Tokyo always burned? Had the air always tasted like ash and death? How was it only a few hours ago that she was collecting water at the well with Yui and all was right in the world?

Yui ... Yui from the *future*.

'Maybe we're already dead,' murmured Chiyo, looking down at her feet. The sandals she had been wearing since this morning were ready to fall apart, her toes stained black. 'And this is our punishment.'

'Punishment?' Eomma asked. 'For what? We never did anything wrong.'

Chiyo hung her head. 'Not praying enough. Being Korean. I don't know.'

Eomma sighed. 'Chiyo-chan, all my life since I met your father, people have hated me for being Korean. I gave you and your brothers Japanese names. I want you to pretend you're Japanese when you can. It'll make your life easier.'

'But I'm Korean, too.' She took Eomma's hand, felt the familiar roughness on her palm. She leaned into her. 'I don't want to hide it.'

'But you should. You sound and look Japanese. Don't waste that.'

'Did you hear that?' asked Chiyo. A noise had sounded from the temple. It wasn't the crackle of flames or screaming. It sounded like … an elephant.

'Let's go.' Chiyo pulled up her mother. They leaned on each other, heading for Asakusa Kannon Temple. Chiyo hoped so much she would see Yui again, that they hadn't left her charred corpse behind at the open plain. No, the note had been from her, she was sure of it. The sight of the dead flashed before her eyes, and she sniffled.

It *was* an elephant.

Chiyo stopped in shock. Asakusa Kannon Temple was almost intact, the fires somehow not reaching here. Many people had found shelter, sitting or standing protectively near their supplies. And in the centre, a man with a straw hat on his head stood before an elephant that was just a bit taller than he was. It nudged him with its long trunk.

'He's from Hanayashiki Zoo,' the man explained, patting the elephant's head as children and adults alike gathered around, tired smiles on their faces. 'Maybe it's silly of me, but when the fires started … I couldn't leave him. We had to kill some of the other animals so they wouldn't go on a rampage, but this little guy followed me. I just wanted to get him to safety.'

There was something bizarrely sweet about the creature, standing here among the survivors.

'Chiyo?'

Yui. Her hair was a mess, smoke on her robe. And she had never looked more beautiful.

Chiyo screamed, but it came out as a croak. She threw her arms around Yui. 'I thought you were dead.'

'Not yet.' Yui's voice was hard as she held Chiyo's face in her hands. Her eyes roamed her face. 'Let's never, ever separate again.'

'We won't. I promise.'

Yui hugged Eomma, too. 'I'm so glad you're all right.' She glanced around. 'I'm not sure, but I think we'll be safe here.' Her face screwed up. 'Though we thought that about the plain, as well.'

The guilt flashing across Yui's face bruised Chiyo's heart. She knew what she was thinking. She should have known more, should have been able to warn them all.

It was getting late, though it was difficult to tell. The fires still raged, but it was a background noise now.

'The gods will protect this place,' said a woman as she passed. It made Chiyo think of Kiyoko, the kind woman at the army depot. 'We're safe here. Get some rest. Help will come tomorrow.'

CHAPTER 13

Yui had been here before. In her time, it was called Sensō-ji Temple, and it was a place of tourism and festivals. The pagoda tower was in a different part of the grounds than in her time, but other than that, it didn't look so different from her memories. That was a comfort. While she had waited for Chiyo and her mother, clinging to the hope that they would come, she had gazed up at the temple. Damaged, but still standing. A testament to Japan's endurance.

'How did we get separated?' Chiyo asked her.

'I ran when the fire tornado came.' Yui shivered at the memory. 'I fell, and I passed out … then when I arrived, I just ran some more. I ended up in Ueno Park and saw that people were leaving messages on the statue.'

Chiyo frowned slightly, like she recalled that Yui said it was the same statue that had brought her here.

Had Yui hoped to find a passage to her own time? Maybe part of her had. Anything would have been better than this hellscape. She didn't know if she would have gone back if the passage had manifested. She supposed she would never know.

'Anyway, a man let me use his paper and pen, and I hoped you might find yourself there, too,' she said.

'We saw your note, Yui-chan,' said Eomma. 'That was good thinking.'

Yui gave her a weak smile.

Oddly, the thousands of people who had found refuge here reminded Yui a bit of the commuters in the early morning weekdays, or even tourists who came to see the temple grounds. Not speaking to each other, each with their own task in mind. They pulled blankets from bags and wagons, finding a spot near the back of the temple where they could create their own shelter. Ash and embers still fell from the sky with each gust of wind.

'Is the blanket to keep off the rain?' Chiyo asked, looking skyward.

'I *wish* there'd be rain.' Yui sighed. 'A big downpour that puts out all the fires and clears the smoke.'

Eomma pushed the supplies to the back of the 'tent' they'd made using a blanket. The three of them curled up, Chiyo in the middle, on the hard ground, only one thin blanket beneath them. In the distance, they could still sometimes hear the occasional shout or the strange explosions they'd heard before. Yui didn't think she would get much sleep.

And Hiro … did his corpse lie among the thousands dead? Or by some miracle, had he escaped? Or was he here at all?

Not knowing was torture.

Eomma fell asleep first. Chiyo wrapped her arm around Yui until their foreheads touched. Yui gently kissed her, her lips dry. 'I'm so glad you're all right,' she whispered against her chin.

In that moment, lying on the hard ground with Chiyo in her arms, she could reach for a thread of peace.

She was just drifting off when a commotion outside the tent jerked her back to consciousness. It sounded like a group of children shouting at each other. Not playing, but angry.

Curious, she carefully climbed over Chiyo and Eomma. She crawled out of their tent and saw several little boys, four of them pushing and shouting at the fifth.

'But you don't *look* Japanese,' barked the tallest. He held a stick in his hand, pointed upwards, like some sort of vigilante. 'You sure you're not Korean? Huh?'

'I'm Japanese!' The boy cowered, his robe filthy. 'I swear. My father is a businessman from Osaka. My mother's from Tokyo.' He screamed when the older boy smacked him in the leg with his stick.

'Korean pig!' jeered the others. The boy sniffled, wiping his dirty cheek.

Yui marched over. 'You little shits. Get lost.'

The boys scattered, except the tall one with the stick. 'What's your problem?'

'What's *yours*?' Yui asked. 'Haven't you seen enough misery? What are you bullying other kids for? Where are your parents?'

'Dead.' The boy gripped his stick. 'I'm on my own now.'

Yui felt for the boy. He reminded her a little of Hiro, and pain lanced her heart to see his determined, dirty face. She glanced behind her; the boy they'd been bullying had run off somewhere.

'Look, I know this is awful.' She knelt to his level. Up close, he was younger than she'd thought, maybe not yet eight. 'But we all have to band together and save who we can. Your mum and dad wouldn't want you, er, wasting your energy like this.'

The boy rubbed his eyes. 'Don't tell me what to do.' He marched off, swinging his stick like a sword.

Yui sighed. It was dark now, many makeshift tents around. Other people had curled up where they sat. The horizon still burned, almost like the glow of a far-off village. There was no water to try and put it out.

Maybe there was a well around here. Now it was night, there would be fewer people there. The thought of some fresh, cold water made her want to groan. By the light of sparse starlight and far-off fires, she searched the temple grounds. Surely, they had a well.

A man was wandering around. Was he trying to steal supplies? Desperation was at its peak, and society's rules fell apart when disaster struck. Yui waited in a shadowy corner of the temple, watching the man go from group to group, looking at them before swiftly moving on.

It wasn't until some moonlight shone through the clouds and illuminated his dirty face that Yui recognised him.

Mr Aoki. Chiyo's father.

'Aoki-san,' she said, quietly so not to startle him. He jumped anyway and turned to her, his eyes widening.

'Yui-chan! You're all right.'

She managed a smile, her cracked lips stinging as her heart flooded with warmth. He looked terrible – everyone did – but unhurt.

'My wife and daughter, are they … ?' He looked like he hardly dared to hope.

'They're fine.' The relief made him sag. 'Come on.'

She took Father to their tent and gently shook Chiyo. She gasped awake, fear on her face. 'What?'

'It's all right,' Yui whispered. 'Look who's here.'

Chiyo and Eomma squealed and hugged Father, sobbing and whispering their tale of survival. Yui hugged her knees in the corner of the tent, watching them. For the first time since this horribleness began, happiness welled up inside her. Something good had finally happened.

'Are you hurt?' Father asked, looking over his wife and daughter. He took Eomma's cheeks in his hands, searching every detail of her face.

'I'm fine, my sweet,' said Eomma.

'I hurt my leg a bit, but we're fine,' said Chiyo.

After hugging his daughter, Father asked, 'Yui-chan, did you find your brother?'

Yui clenched her jaw, shaking her head.

Father nodded, looking sympathetic. 'When things calm down, there'll be a roundup of survivors, you'll see. He might be with a family who've been looking after him. Maybe he's here at the temple, right now.'

Yui nodded along, knowing he meant well.

'How did you make it?' Eomma asked.

'I was at the factory when the shaking started.' Father settled at the mouth of the tent. 'A lot of the workers were told to stay where they were but ... I remembered what you said, Yui-chan. Then that awful sound, like thunder ...'

They all exhaled shakily at the memory of the roar of the plates shifting beneath their feet.

'I ran outside as the building collapsed. I managed to help some of the workers, but ... I had to leave. I went home, but the whole neighbourhood was gone.' He let out a shaky breath. 'Oh, I nearly forgot. I have these.'

He pulled out some bottles that sloshed with water. Eomma and Chiyo cried out with relief, grabbing the nearest ones. 'I kept these on me, Yui-chan, just in case.'

So he had believed her. Or, at least, taken precautions. She accepted a bottle with thanks. The water, though warm, was divine in her parched throat. Already, her thoughts felt sharper.

'There are some people who are bullying Koreans,' she whispered. 'Just ... be careful, all right? Maybe only speak Japanese for a while.' She glanced apologetically at Eomma.

Eomma looked determined. 'I understand.'

Father fell asleep with them, and Yui caught snatches of slumber, though every time she closed her eyes, all she could see was a wall of fire, people burning, parents screaming for their children, and collapsing buildings.

All night long, the ground shook and trembled.

*

'Is help coming, like that lady said?' Chiyo asked, like they'd know any more than she did.

'They'll bring supplies. Food,' said Father, looking determined. In the wan morning light, Chiyo could see a cut on his forehead. She couldn't stop staring at him. So many people had died, yet they all had managed to get through this. She wanted to crawl into Father's lap and be held by him like she had as a child.

'Here's another one.' Father gathered them together under the tent and held them close as an aftershock rocked the temple grounds. Screams erupted, others sobbing, some shouting for people to get somewhere safe. The elephant gave an alarmed trumpet.

'It's almost as big as the first one,' exclaimed Eomma. Chiyo clung to her parents and to Yui, closing her eyes as the world rocked beneath them. Something exploded nearby.

Finally, it came to an end. They sat there, panting, wondering if it would continue. If the world would keep shaking and trembling until the sea swallowed all of Japan.

'What if there are other countries like this?' Chiyo said. 'What if the whole world is burning?'

'It isn't.'

They all looked at Yui. Beautiful, mysterious Yui. Her short hair had grown since Chiyo had first met her, brushing her shoulders. Dirt smeared her face, the same haunted look in her eyes Chiyo had seen on everyone since this whole disaster had begun.

'You knew it would happen, Yui-chan,' Chiyo said. 'You tried to warn us.'

Yui rubbed her face with her sleeve. 'I should've tried harder,' she said. 'I should've got you out of Tokyo. But it's not the whole world. Not the whole of Japan. There are safe places, and Tokyo will rebuild.'

'How do you know all this?' Eomma asked. She spoke in whispers now, scared her Korean accent would bring vigilantes upon them.

Chiyo watched Yui. She hadn't forgotten her showing her the money, the little paper card she claimed was from the future. But that was ridiculous.

Was it, though? She hadn't believed she would watch hundreds of people burn to death, watch a bridge collapse, or see the town she loved in flames until yesterday. Yet here they were, exactly as Yui had predicted.

But it wasn't her secret to tell. Yui had trusted her, and it wasn't something people would just believe without proof.

'Trust her,' she told Eomma. 'I do. What else do you know, Yui-chan?'

'Not much,' Yui admitted. 'I saw it on … well, I read about it. All this. I didn't know I was coming here, otherwise I'd have read more about it. I feel like I've failed you all.'

Eomma hugged her. 'You couldn't fail us, Yui-chan. You couldn't have stopped any of this. And all of us are safe, which is more than can be said for a lot of people.' She shivered at that, and Father put his arm around her.

'What do we do today?' Chiyo asked. She hadn't eaten anything since yesterday morning, and she felt hollowed out. Father looked inside their sack of supplies, but there wasn't much. Still, he pulled out a can of kimchi and they all ate some. The sweet and spicy flavour perked Chiyo up. They had a sip of water each, too, rationing their limited supply as much as they could.

They ventured outside. Asakusa Kannon Temple was still standing. Now without the buildings, they could see so far. Chiyo glanced to where she thought west was, where Mount Fuji stood.

'Will it erupt?' she whispered to Yui.

Yui shook her head. 'Don't worry. The worst is over.' She swallowed. 'We just have to get out of the city.'

The baby elephant was still here, the man they'd seen yesterday standing vigil over the creature.

'Fukui-san! What's his name?'

'What kind of elephant is he?'

147

'How did you rescue him?'

'What about the other animals?'

It was bizarre seeing children cluster around the man who had rescued the elephant, Mr Fukui, shouting their questions and laughing in delight at the elephant, who was lying beside the temple steps, his trunk curled up on his head.

'Easy. Don't frighten him,' said Mr Fukui. 'He's an Indian elephant named Johnny.'

A screech of laughter. 'That's a funny name.'

'Like an American.'

A man ran through the groups of people. 'Did you hear? The Koreans are poisoning the wells! They're setting off bombs!'

Yui's head snapped up, looking at the breathless young man shouting his lies. 'What is he talking about?'

As though on cue, another violent explosion sounded a few streets away. 'See!' The man thrust his finger in its direction. 'They set the fires on purpose. They're stealing from survivors. Don't drink any well water, okay? And if you see any Koreans, send them to us. We'll sort them out.'

The man ran back through the streets, yelling to anyone who would listen. Cold fear flooded Chiyo. If they found Eomma ...

'Is it true what they said, Fukui-san?' asked a little girl. She was wearing sandals, her hair a matted mess, pants rolled up to reveal chubby legs. Chiyo watched her, wondering what horrors she had seen.

'I don't know, little one.' Mr Fukui sat beside Johnny the elephant.

'Of course it isn't true,' said Yui through clenched teeth, taking Chiyo gently by her elbow and guiding her back to the tent. 'We have to get out of here.'

Crouched in the tent, Yui spoke quietly to them. 'It's not safe to stay here. Didn't you say your grandparents live in Nagano? Can't we go there?'

Chiyo met her father's gaze. His mouth was in a straight line. 'They haven't spoken to me since ... since I married. I only got that letter from my mother.'

'They'll know what happened in Tokyo by now. Or they will soon.' The Tokyoites were nothing if not efficient. Already, printed presses were probably publishing stories on the earthquake, on the fires and the bridge collapse. 'Millions are homeless. If we have somewhere to go, we should take it.'

The first question was *how* to leave. Tokyo was enormous, and there were only a few, expensive trains. Even if one was in service, it would be overwhelmed.

Yui glanced upwards, something she did when she was thinking. 'Ueno Station?' she suggested. Chiyo nodded. When she and Eomma had gone to Ueno Park, they had seen the train station mostly intact.

'Where do the trains go?' asked Chiyo.

'There are thousands of people leaving by train,' murmured Father. 'I suppose we could wait in line. It's better than being here.'

They packed up what little they had, their bellies still groaning with hunger. The spice of the kimchi Chiyo had eaten still lingered on her tongue. It was much better than the taste of ash.

It was a cold, scary feeling, wondering if help was coming at all. When she asked Yui, the young woman gave a helpless shrug. The four clung to each other, stumbling over broken buildings, averting their eyes from charred bodies.

Suddenly, Father threw out an arm to stop them. Ahead, marching men, many of them young, carried weapons. Chunks of wood torn from houses. Sticks or even police batons. They had tied towels or other fabrics around their heads.

'They look like a mob,' whispered Chiyo. They disappeared round a corner and someone screamed.

'You're Korean, aren't you? Answer me!'

'This again?' Yui groaned. 'Why are they fighting among themselves at a time like this?'

They turned the corner, staying out of sight. Seven or eight men in police uniforms were beating up two others. The victims cowered as the men hit them with their weapons, their screams and begging filling the air. Meaty thunks sounded as the attackers jeered and yelled slurs.

'We've got to help them!' Chiyo tried to dart forward, but Father grabbed her and pulled her back.

'You can't do anything, Chiyo-chan.'

'But—'

A bloody, gurgling cry. One of the victims slumped on the ground, bleeding from his head. His death rattle filled the air.

The man beside him, bleeding from his eye, crawled over to the man. His fingers were bent horribly as he struggled to move. Bile rose in Chiyo's throat.

The man whimpered in Korean, shaking his dead friend. 'Sung-ki? Sung-ki? My brother! You killed him!' The man sobbed, his whole body trembling. He swiped at the legs of his nearest attacker. 'Bastard!'

His next word was cut off by a crunching blow from a baton. Chiyo screamed, muffling the sound with her fingers, and buried her head in her father's chest. The man flopped like a fish on top of his brother.

'Why?' Yui whispered. The police officer spat on the dead Koreans, said something to his friends – his tone jovial, like they were on a casual day out – and off they went, swaggering and striding over broken rubble and burning bits of wood as if murder and violence was a normal part of their day.

The two men didn't get up.

'They're dead,' said Yui dully.

Chiyo was silent, her gaze moving over each of the bloody corpses. They hadn't helped.

'You wouldn't have been able to make a difference, Chiyo-chan.' Her father took her shoulders and looked her in the eyes. The cut above his eyebrow had scabbed over, the purple and yellow of a bruise around it. 'They would have killed you, too.'

'Come on, Chiyo.' Yui tugged at her arm.

Avoiding the horribleness of the dead Koreans, they headed west, along the river. As expected, the remaining bridge was full, though the news of the collapse of the other one seemed to have spread; an exhausted-looking man in a dark uniform was waving people over, using a whistle to get people to stop and wait their turn. People pulled wheelbarrows and carts full of supplies. Everyone looked displaced. No one glanced up to see the burning ruins or stopped to exchange news. They focused on the path ahead.

On the road down, they passed more bodies. Some charred and half-hidden by rubble. Yui turned her gaze away from a child, crushed by a falling lamppost and left to lie where he was.

And more bodies. Fresher. Not burned or crushed, but beaten to death. Eomma's shoulders shook with dry sobs as they staggered through a sea of bodies. Cracked skulls, bleeding heads, broken limbs. Some had their wrists tied together. One woman had her head caved in, her arms still clinging around an old lady.

'People need someone to blame,' Father said dully. 'They're trying to take back a sense of control.'

'There are ways of doing that without violence,' Yui snarled.

Chiyo wanted to tear her gaze away, but she couldn't. Somehow, the sight of the murder victims was even worse than the earthquake's destruction. The fact that these people had survived the horrors of the collapsing buildings and fires only to then be killed later …

'Come on,' said Father. 'Let's head to the train station. There'll be news, if nothing else.'

Those who had somewhere to go would go. Those who had friends and family in Tokyo would stay and try to reclaim some sense into their lives.

They walked beside a woman who had a baby on her back. Chiyo looked at the baby, who lay limp with her eyes closed. An elderly man followed her gaze, then he said something to the woman.

The woman looked startled. 'No. No, no. She's just sleeping.'

Chiyo's heart cracked into pieces as the old man touched the baby's cheek, then sadly shook his head.

'She's *asleep!*' the woman cried, scrambling to take off the sling. 'She's just asleep … she's fine …'

They carried on their stumbling march through hell as the mother's grief cracked the air.

CHAPTER 14

The journey to Ueno Station was slow work. Yui was exhausted. Her lungs hurt, she was weak and dehydrated, and every time they encountered a corpse, it drained a little more life from her.

They came upon a quieter district, what was a street only a few days ago, now little more than piles of broken wood. Ueno was just on the other side. Yui thought of the thousands waiting in the park. They and those at Asakusa Kannon Temple were the safest. If only she'd realised that before.

Eomma started coughing, hacking into her fist. Chiyo patted her back, worry on her face. 'Are you okay?'

Father held his wife until the coughing fit had passed. 'I'm all right,' she said finally. 'I must have inhaled some dust.'

She froze, looking ahead.

Two young men were nearby. They glanced up, eyes narrowed as they fell on Eomma.

Yui's blood ran cold. They had recognised her accent.

The youths glanced at each other, then strode towards them, turning over weapons in their hands.

'Go. Go!' Yui tried to shove Eomma and Chiyo behind her, but a broken wall met their backs. More boys had surrounded them, crawling from the wreckage like insects, tapping weapons against their hands or thighs.

'Another filthy Korean,' sneered one thug. He grabbed Eomma's arm.

'Get off her,' barked Father, but they grabbed each of his arms. One punched him hard in the stomach and he wheezed, doubling over. Terror flooded Yui as Chiyo screamed.

'Stop it!' Yui pummelled the boy's back with her fists. Growling, he turned and grabbed her hair. A shriek escaped her as pain lanced through her scalp.

'Are you Korean, too?' he spat. 'Or just protecting them? I'll kill you.' His eyes looked wild. 'I'll kill all of you.'

'What the hell is wrong with you?' Rage and terror flayed Yui's soul as the boys, so many of them now, grabbed the family. 'Don't touch her!' she roared as two young men grabbed Chiyo's arms. One of them laughed and grabbed Chiyo's breast.

Blind with rage, Yui kicked out, her foot hitting the boy's thigh. She didn't see the fist flying for her face. Pain exploded across her jaw, white light flashing before her eyes. She drew in a painful, hoarse breath, shock blinking in her mind like strobe lights. Panic seized her as rough hands grabbed her arms, nails digging in. Was this how it would end? Murdered like dogs in the street?

'You do it, Hondo,' said the thug who had touched Chiyo, jerking his head to one of the men holding Father. A nearby young man, holding Eomma's arm, blinked for a moment.

'Do what?' the skinny young man said. Yui thought she saw his grip slip on Eomma's arm.

'That bitch is Korean,' said the thug. 'I heard her accent. Bash her head in, go on.'

'No! Leave her alone,' Chiyo cried. 'Please!'

'Touch her and I'll kill you,' Yui snarled through bloodied lips. Her whole face stung. She thrashed in the men's crushing grips. 'You hear me? I'll kill the lot of you.'

'She's just a woman. She didn't hurt anyone,' muttered the young man they'd called Hondo. 'I don't think she, you know, poisoned the wells or anything.'

The young thug rolled his eyes and took a step towards Eomma, who recoiled from him. Then Father lunged with a strangled cry, wrapping an arm around the thug's throat. Some of the young men backed away. Chiyo wriggled out of her assailants' arms and ran to Yui. Yui elbowed the shocked men away and grabbed her, holding her close. Father struggled with the others while the men started hauling Eomma away.

'Katsuro!' she screamed for her husband.

A man threw Father to the wood-strewn ground and kicked him in the head. His grip loosened on the leader's neck. The young man scrambled to his feet, massaging his throat, glaring as he turned over the plank of wood in his hand.

'Do it, Hondo!' snarled the leader, swivelling to face Hondo, who had blanched. 'Kill her. See how violent these Koreans are. They poisoned the wells, man. It's their fault your mum died.' He snarled at Father, 'You can watch her die. Then I'll kill you, too.'

Hondo marched over to Eomma. As he did, a gust of wind ruffled his hair. The hair blew over his face, exposing a birthmark on his cheek.

Yui froze. She knew that birthmark.

'Hiro?' she breathed.

155

The man they'd called Hondo froze in place. He turned to Yui. With his resolve fallen away, his youth came back in an instant.

There was no doubt about it. Before Yui stood her little brother Hiro. Except now he was older. Grown up.

'It's you,' she said. It was like the rest of the world had fallen away. 'Isn't it?'

'Hondo!' roared the younger man, shaking Eomma. She sobbed.

Hondo – Hiro – blinked, then stepped over to the man holding Eomma. He smacked the young man on his shoulder. 'Enough. Let her go.'

'But—'

'I said *fuck off!*' Hiro roared. 'Go on, get out of here. Or I'll fuck you all up, I swear.'

To Yui's shock, the hands fell from Chiyo's family. Eomma fell forward to her husband, cradling his bleeding head as the young men swaggered off, muttering beneath their breaths and throwing hateful glances.

'Father, are you okay?' Chiyo asked, falling at her father's side. Dirt clung to his hair where the young man had kicked him.

'I'm all right.' He coughed, then rose into a sitting position as he put his arm around Eomma. 'That was close.'

'I'm sorry. It was my fault.' Eomma rubbed her eyes. Her hands were trembling.

Yui was staring at Hiro. He was much older than the twelve-year-old boy she had lost that day at Ueno Park. He was a man now, maybe even older than she was. He was staring in shock at Chiyo's family, then down at his hands. They were marked with scratches and dirt, and he wore the remains of ragged clothing.

'Hiro?' she said, not knowing what else to say. Where to even begin. She swallowed. 'Let's find somewhere to sit.'

There were many quiet places now, areas where the flames had burnt to embers. Chiyo's family sat in shock, away from the man the others had called Hondo. Chiyo glanced at her, a question in her eyes, but Yui gave her a reassuring nod. They would feel better now that Hiro had chased away the others.

It *was* him; Yui knew it in her soul. His reaction had told her as much. She sat in front of him, taking him in. The muscles, the wiry, adult body. The way he still flattened his hair over his cheek, trying to hide his birthmark. He had matured into a man, but she could still catch hints of the young face she knew, like glimpsing a loved one through a frosted window.

She stared at him, relief and shock mingling with anger. 'Why are you attacking Koreans?'

He looked up at her, his expression sulky. 'That's the first question you ask?'

'It's an important one.' Her shock was fading, replaced quickly by disgust. 'How could you join those vigilantes? Do you have any idea how many people have been killed?'

Hiro shrugged like it wasn't any of his business. 'Some of the boys went a bit crazy, I guess. Besides, the Koreans have been setting off bombs all over the city. They capitalised on the earthquake.'

'Oh, Hiro, that's such bullshit and you know it.'

The siblings glared at each other.

'Well, how about you?' Hiro asked.

'Me?'

'You haven't aged.' He shifted closer to her now, sliding along the ruined house they had perched upon and staring at her, taking in her face. 'You look exactly the same as I remember.'

'You do remember me, then,' she said, glad.

'I was twelve years old when I stepped out of a tunnel in Ueno Park.' He turned over the wood in his hands, looking around. 'I looked all over for you. Eventually I was put in a hospital, then an orphanage. And the Hondos took me in. I told them I was looking for my sister. But no one believed me when …' He sighed. 'Wow, so you *are* real. It *is* all true.'

'Of course it's true,' Yui said, fiery indignation running through her. 'I've been looking all over for you since *I* got here.'

'When was that?' he asked. 'When I asked my mother – my adoptive mother, I mean – she said that she met me in Taishō 2.' He did a calculation in his head. The look of concentration reminded her of when he was doing his homework. '1913.'

'Ten years ago?' exhaled Yui. No wonder no one had been able to find her *younger* brother. He had arrived ten years ago and was already grown up. They had been searching for a child.

'Yeah, and I half-believed I'd made up my home, our mother. And you.' He rubbed his face. 'We really did it, didn't we? We travelled through time.'

'But I only arrived two months ago,' said Yui. 'When I woke up, it was July 1923.' Pity ran through her. 'Oh, Hiro. You've been here all alone for ten years?' *And now he's twenty-two years old. The same as me.*

'The Hondos took me in. I had a mother at last.' Hiro suddenly pressed his lips together, an expression Yui knew only too well. 'Had. She … she died when our house collapsed.'

'I'm so sorry,' she said quietly. All of this still blew her mind, and as she struggled to understand, she knew how awful it must have been for Hiro. But still being young, he had managed to find a family. 'Is there anyone else in your ... family?'

Hiro shrugged. 'My dad might be out there. But he smacked me around when I gave him lip. My brother, who lives north somewhere. I don't know how to contact him.'

'Smacked you around?' she asked in disgust.

'Well, slapped me when I was bad. Beat me around the legs once when I talked back to him.' Hiro lifted his chin in defiance. It was ... beyond surreal to see her little brother, now her own age, already gone through puberty and growth, now a man but somehow not so different from the skinny boy she'd parted ways with only two months ago.

'I'm so glad I found you,' she found herself saying. She shifted forward and hugged him, inhaling his scent of sweat and dirt. He had fallen into a terrible crowd, but he had also protected Yui and Chiyo's family.

Hiro stiffened at her embrace, not moving as she clung to him, resting her head on his shoulder.

'Yui-chan?'

Yui looked up to see Chiyo standing a bit away. 'Who is this? What's going on?'

'That boy attacked us,' said Father, holding a hand against his sore head. Yui withdrew from Hiro, swallowing.

'I managed to scare those guys off, but there are some crazy ones out there. Way worse.' He looked at Yui. 'Even the military and police are killing people. The one who was leading us, he bashed the head in of an old Korean man who looked at him funny.'

'Tell me you haven't,' Yui whispered. She didn't want to know, but she wouldn't be able to look at him until she did. 'Please. You haven't k-killed anyone, have you?'

Hiro shifted. 'No. I might have kicked a few while they were down …'

Tears burning her eyes, Yui leaned forward and slapped his face. 'Stupid kid!'

Hiro held his cheek, which reddened under his fingers. 'You don't know what it's like, Yui. You don't know what it's like here.'

'I know enough,' she said fiercely. She turned to Chiyo, who looked stunned. 'Chiyo, I know you need an explanation. This is … well, he's my brother.'

Yui knew the thoughts racing through Chiyo's head as she looked him up and down. 'Your younger brother you've been looking for?'

'Yes. It'll take some explaining.' The concept of travelling through time to 1923 had barely begun to sink into Chiyo's mind. She didn't know if Chiyo would be able to handle the thought of Hiro travelling further back into time, growing up, and them now being the same age reunited.

The thought was still insane to Yui, and she was living it.

Something sounded ahead, the crash of timber. 'Let's go.' Hiro leapt to his feet as men's voices reached them. The echoing Japanese was littered with loud, raucous laughter, so alien in this burning world.

Yui didn't need telling twice. Chiyo helped her mother to her feet and they quickly made their way through a side street between some collapsed houses. Chiyo's family threw suspicious, confused looks at Hiro, and Yui couldn't blame them. A skinny cat lapped at a puddle of dirty water from a leak somewhere; it streaked away at their approach. The voices echoed, one boy shouted something, and they went a different way.

'Why are groups of people getting together to *kill* Koreans?' Yui asked. It was all so cruel and absurd.

'We heard they'd poisoned the wells and were setting off bombs,' Hiro whispered as he glanced out of the alleyway.

'It's not true. Why would they do that?'

Hiro shrugged. 'Taking advantage of the panic.'

'They're trying to survive, just like us!' Yui hissed back. 'It's stupid rumours and people panicking, looking for someone to blame.'

'The newspapers printed it, too.'

Yui snorted. 'Because the news *never* engages in fearmongering.'

'Either way,' Father's gentle voice broke up the siblings' argument, 'we need to get out of Tokyo. I've decided. We're heading up to Nagano Prefecture. My parents are in Hirano village. It's a landlocked town. There's no … no seacoast.'

Yui knew what he was thinking. No sea meant no tsunamis. Already, reports were coming in that Yokohama and Kamakura had been decimated by high waves. 'It sounds nice,' she managed to say.

Eomma said nothing, perhaps choosing to go for silence after what happened last time.

'Are you coming with us?' Yui asked her brother.

For one frightening moment she wondered if he would refuse, if he would want to look for the people who had been his brother and his father for these past ten years. But his eyes raked over Yui's face, as though taking her in, as though accepting at last that he had found his big sister.

'I'll come with you,' he promised. He still held that piece of wood in his hand, torn from a collapsed building, maybe. 'I'll protect you. All of you,' he added, looking at Chiyo's family. 'I'm sorry for everything. I really am. I'm not with them, not really. Let me make it up to you.'

Eomma and Father glanced nervously at each other. 'Please,' Yui said. In this moment, she didn't believe Hiro would hurt them. 'I can vouch for him.'

'I trust you, Yui,' said Chiyo, glancing at her parents.

Father stepped forward, his eyes narrowed. 'You chased off those boys,' he said. 'I still don't trust you, but you can come with us. Yui-chan, if he does anything …'

Yui nodded frantically. 'He won't. But if he does, he can't come with us.'

Hiro swung the wooden plank around in his hand, fresh determination on his dirty face.

It was getting late. They headed towards Ueno Station, but as they had thought, it was overcrowded with refugees. 'Are the trains running?' Father asked a man.

'People are inside the trains, *on* the trains,' the man croaked. 'I've never seen so many people. And the tickets … not everyone can afford them.'

Father grimaced as he faced his family. 'It might be difficult for us to leave by train. I have a couple of sen in my pocket, but that's it.'

Between them, they didn't have enough even for a meal, let alone a train ticket. Eomma leaned into her husband and whispered, 'What do we do now?'

They all looked at Father expectantly, as though trusting he would have the answer. 'The richer part of Tokyo might be better,' said Hiro, and they all glanced at him. 'Someone was shouting before about help coming, but I don't know if it's true. Oh! I almost forgot,' said Hiro, pulling a satchel from beneath his robe. 'I do have some food.'

They walked a little way away from the station, avoiding the crowds. Eomma and Chiyo cried out in relief as Hiro shook the satchel he was carrying. Out poured a small bag of cold, cooked rice, some dried fish, and some strips of dried, salty meat.

'It's not much,' he said. 'But it's what I could find.'

They hadn't had anything since the kimchi this morning. Eomma and Chiyo started dividing it out equally between them while Yui stared at it. Found or stole?

Hiro wolfed down his share in two seconds, but Yui savoured each bite, her groaning stomach demanding more. They lay down, Hiro at her side like when they were kids.

They decided to go back to the temple, knowing the city centre, were it safe, would be overcrowded with refugees. Hiro at their heels, the family made their way back to the temple, where the blanket they had erected between two trees still sat. No one had bothered trying to loot it, for they had left nothing behind.

'Remember I used to bring you here when you were a kid?' Yui asked Hiro as they settled in a corner of the 'tent'. There wasn't any room to do more than sit with their legs tucked beneath their chins, but it felt safer than being exposed. Chiyo sat between her parents, her head leaning on her mother's shoulder.

'Not really.' Hiro shrugged. He glanced at the Aoki family. 'They're scared of me.'

'Of course they are,' she whispered. 'You and your friends attacked us.'

'They aren't my friends,' Hiro grumbled. 'I just joined them so I wouldn't become one of the victims. You understand, don't you? *Nee-chan?*'

The nickname for 'big sister' made her heart melt. Hiro had always used it when he wanted to wheedle something out of her. She sighed, too tired to argue, and too relieved to finally be reunited with him to pick any more fights.

'Tomorrow will be better,' she said, feeling her eyelids grow heavy. Chiyo gave her a weak smile from across the tent.

'It will,' said Chiyo's father. 'We're alive and we're safe.'

CHAPTER 15

It had been two days since the earthquake. All of them agreed that, one way another, they would get out of Tokyo today.

Already, people had constructed tents and shelters in both Asakusa Kannon Temple grounds and Ueno Park. Merchants were erecting makeshift stalls, all merrily singing a song about endurance and commerce. 'Listen to that,' said Chiyo as strong male voices reached them. 'They're surviving.'

It was heartening, listening to the merchants setting up business. 'They'll probably charge triple the usual prices,' Hiro grumbled.

Those who had nowhere else to go and no money to pay for a way out had to make do with what they had. Rumours flew around that masses of people were fleeing the city on foot, heading for nearby places like Saitama and Kanagawa.

'Nagano is far away,' said Father. 'It'll take weeks to walk there.'

'Anything's better than here,' Yui said. She didn't want the five of them to be another homeless family. 'Surely your folks won't turn us away if we go?'

A stroke of luck found them when they headed to the centre of the city, where many of the buildings were still standing. Some brick buildings were damaged, but this district had resisted most of the fires. If it weren't for the crowds of refugees, it would look almost normal.

Yui had sometimes seen news of refugees on the TV from all over the world. She had never been able to relate to the crowds of hungry people, carrying all they owned on their backs. Now she was one of them, lining up for what food the military had been able to provide. It was a comfort seeing the military hospital tents, the erected stalls offering rice balls and dried fish to the most needy. Soldiers stood around, ensuring fights didn't break out.

'Chiyo! Chiyo!'

The Aokis, Yui and Hiro all looked around, wondering whether the small voice was calling out to their Chiyo or to someone else. Chiyo herself looked confused, then she glanced down to see a well-dressed boy waving to her. He looked so clean and unblemished, like the horrors of the earthquake had not touched him.

Chiyo gasped when she saw him. 'Oh! It's Nakamura Jirō! The little boy I look after.' She stepped towards him, then hastily bowed when she spotted his parents.

'It's Chiyo!' the child insisted, waving wildly.

It took only a moment for Yui to take in the well-dressed family, shabby but unhurt, holding bags. Did their fancy house in the Azabu district still stand? Did they have a pocketful of money they could use to get a first-class train? Jirō's mother looked exactly as Yui had imagined her; like everything was beneath her and there was a nasty smell around. Yui and Hiro exchanged guilty smirks.

Mrs Nakamura held a baby in her arms. Yui wasn't sure how old he was, but he looked old enough to sit up. He was playing with his mother's dress, burbling. She was heartened to see the healthy baby's chubby cheeks. He wouldn't remember any of these horrors, though he would grow up with the stories.

Chiyo talked to the family, and to their credit, Mrs Nakamura didn't ignore or avoid her. Chiyo's family awkwardly hung back, Hiro wandering off to … Yui wasn't sure what he was doing. Yui stood out of the way, thinking perhaps Chiyo was telling them her tale of survival, was perhaps trying to glean some information only the higher-ups knew. For a moment she allowed herself to hope that the family might offer a helping hand to the Aokis, but hadn't Chiyo mentioned Mrs Nakamura's disdain for Koreans? She might not hunt them down and murder them, but she was no less capable of being racist.

She hung back, forcing a small smile when they glanced her way. Then a strange noise attracted her attention back to the Nakamuras.

Chiyo hadn't noticed. Neither had Mr Nakamura. His wife looked down in horror at the baby boy cradled in her arms. He was wheezing, his face turning purple.

'He's choking,' gasped Mrs Nakamura.

Chiyo stepped back, confusion on her face. 'I … what?'

Yui's vision tunnelled. She darted towards the family and snatched the baby from Mrs Nakamura's arms. The mother gave a wail; Yui ignored it as she turned the child almost upside down and thumped him hard on the back.

All sound muted for a moment. Nothing else mattered. A terrible gurgle came from the baby as she held him face-down and smacked his back again hard.

One more time. Her heart raced, the mother's panicked shouts echoing in her head far too loud. *One more.*

Thump. The baby coughed, something flying from his mouth and bouncing on the ruined concrete. Yui turned the baby the right way and looked at him. He sucked in harsh breaths, his red face slowly turning normal. Then he burst into tears.

'Minoru!' Mrs Nakamura sobbed, hesitantly taking her child and looking over him. Yui's gaze moved to a tiny plastic button on the ground. The baby must have plucked it off Mrs Nakamura's dress without anyone noticing. 'Minoru, you're all right.' She looked at Yui, her eyes red with tears. The haughty look had vanished. 'How did you do that? Thank you, thank you.'

She closed her eyes, holding her baby close and rocking him. Her husband, white with shock, gave Yui a strange look.

'Yui-chan.' Chiyo gently touched Yui's arm. 'You saved his life.'

'Thank you,' sobbed Mrs Nakamura. She glared at her husband. 'Well?' she snapped. 'Give them something!'

Mr Nakamura jumped, then looked guiltily around at the family. He cleared his throat, then bowed low to Yui. 'Thank you. That was close. Um, what do you need?'

What a question. Yui glanced at Chiyo's parents, her first thoughts being food and shelter. But Father said, 'It's a good thing Yui was here. We were happy to help and are glad your baby is safe. We need to get to Hirano village.' He hesitated. 'It's in Nagano Prefecture.'

Yui thought that Mr Nakamura would shake his head and say that was impossible. But just an hour later, the wealthy family had given them cash in a bag and were handing over tickets to a tired-looking carriage driver. His horses looked well, and the carriage was big enough to hold around ten people. It had a roof but was open to the elements, no glass in the windows. But it was their way out.

'You will need to change carriages in Sagamiko,' he informed them as they clambered into the carriage. 'Then get a train.'

'Thank you,' Eomma said, sighing as she leaned back in the seat. Yui looked around at the refugees by the tents, clamouring at the stalls to get food or water. She reminded herself that they couldn't help them. The danger was over for them as well. It was all about rebuilding now. And they would. In just a few short years, Tokyo would be a thriving metropolis again.

'Did we make it?' Chiyo whispered. 'Are we getting out of here?'

'Looks like it,' said Hiro. Yui could see him watching her from the corner of her eye.

It was Father who asked, though. 'How did you know what to do?'

The carriage rumbled along with the horses' steps, jolting now and then from a crack in the road. People wandered past, throwing them tired glances.

'The same thing happened to Hiro when he was little,' Yui said, running fingers through her greasy hair. 'I studied a manoeuvre for when a baby is choking.'

'When he was little?' Eomma glanced between Hiro and Yui. 'Yui, is this the same brother you've been looking for? You said he was twelve.'

'That's because he was,' Yui said. She had to tell them the truth. Now they were on their way to a new hope, it felt like the right time. 'I knew the earthquake would happen. I was looking for my brother because we came here together. To Tokyo. To 1923.'

She'd expected the stunned silence. She just didn't think it would last so long. Yui explained everything else: finding herself outside the Saigō Takamori statue in an unfamiliar time, realising she had come to the summer of 1923; trying to get home to Asakusa, only to come across Chiyo.

'When I stepped out of that passage, I was twelve years old,' Hiro said to the family. He had balanced his wooden plank on his lap, and his leg jiggled nervously. 'I came to 1913, Taishō 2. I've been living in Tokyo ever since, and I'd almost forgotten about my life before because nobody believed me. Then ...' He swallowed. 'Well, you know the rest. When Yui said my name, it all came back.'

'It's true. I was ten when Hiro was born.' Yui's chest felt lighter now she had confessed everything. 'But now we're the same age.'

Father rubbed his face. 'This seems impossible to believe. But you were so adamant about the earthquake coming ...' He put an arm around Eomma's shoulders. 'What do you think, my dear?'

Eomma looked between her husband and daughter with wide eyes. 'I think,' she said faintly, 'that we should all get some sleep.'

It would take some time for Chiyo's family to process what she'd told them. Maybe they'd want to talk about it more, maybe not. But that wasn't the most pressing issue now. A long journey lay ahead.

*

Chiyo slipped in and out of sleep, often jerking awake with a sore neck as the horses struggled over ruined roads.

Yui had her face buried in her arm, and it was impossible to tell whether she was awake or not. Her brother was slumped with his head back and his mouth wide open, looking oddly vulnerable. When she really looked at him, she could see similarities between him and his sister. They shared the same thin eyebrows, and their front teeth, especially when they smiled, could be identical.

Eomma and Father were asleep, leaning on each other. Chiyo glanced outside, not sure how long they had been travelling for. She supposed it must be a couple of hours already.

What lay ahead for them in Nagano Prefecture? She hoped her grandparents would welcome them. She imagined a kindly, smiling grandmother who made the most beautiful meals, and a strong, twinkle-eyed grandfather who would tell them funny stories. She had almost dozed off, lost in her daydream, when the carriage came to a halt.

'Toilet break,' grunted the driver, and the carriage swayed as he hauled himself off. Chiyo carefully opened the carriage door, too, and looked around. It was cooler out here, the sky darkening. When she glanced behind, she could see the ruins of Tokyo stretched out on the horizon.

Black smoke drifted across the sky like a smear of oil paint across a canvas. Many of the buildings were gone, and those that weren't leaned strangely to the sides, the foundations crumbled. Chiyo shivered and looked the other way. There were several carriages here, many looking to have stopped for the night. They had arrived at some kind of outer village, though it didn't look very active. Many of the houses here had collapsed, too.

'You need to go?' grunted a voice, making Chiyo jump. It was just the carriage driver, who clambered back on. 'We'll go in five minutes.'

Chiyo thanked him and passed her water near some nearby trees. She hadn't needed to go for ages, so it felt, so dehydrated her body had been. She wondered if she should wake the others, but before she could decide, Hiro clambered out, rubbing his eyes.

'This place looks as messed up as Tokyo,' he remarked. Chiyo wasn't sure how to talk to him, so she just said, 'There's a group of trees over there if you need to go.'

'Thanks.' He started wandering off into the gathering darkness, then he stopped. 'Chiyo, right?'

'Aoki Chiyo.' She bowed to him, reverting to basic politeness.

'Sanada Hiro.' She wasn't sure if he was making fun of her when he bowed, too. 'Look, I'm sorry about everything with your family. It was stupid of me to join those guys.'

Chiyo fidgeted. 'It's not me you should be apologising to.'

Hiro tilted his head. 'I know.'

She climbed back into the carriage, appreciating the scent of this place. It smelled so much greener and fresher. When Hiro climbed back inside, the carriage continued on until they'd found a quiet road.

Since the usual ryokan inns and stops were closed or destroyed by the earthquake, they didn't have much choice but to stay inside the carriage. They ate what was left of the food and got as comfortable as they could. Crickets chirped in the distance. A mosquito buzzed around the carriage. The carriage driver went off somewhere for a while, then came back with a paper bag clenched in his fist. Chiyo watched him feed the horses, then untie them from the carriage so they could rest.

The next day, they found more crowds of refugees. The carriage driver urged the horses on, weaving through crowds of people with bags and sacks on their backs, looking dully up at them as they fled the destruction to the cooler north.

'Hey,' shouted a man as they passed. 'Let us on.'

'Yeah,' another called. 'There's plenty of room for more!'

Chiyo recoiled as a dirty hand gripped the sill, a maddened face appearing behind it. 'C'mon, where are you going? Let us on!'

CHAPTER 16

Some people melted from their path; others joined the man, shouting to be let on to the carriage. Chiyo backed away into her father, who held her to him as people thumped the carriage, trying to open the doors. The horses whinnied in alarm.

'Oy!' Hiro roared, jumping forward as a man tried to climb through the window. 'Get out.'

The man ignored him, struggling to squeeze himself through. Chiyo whimpered, frozen with fear. Yui sat in the middle of the opposite seat, staring with wide eyes.

'Last chance!' Hiro roared. When the man ignored him, he smacked the plank of wood against the man's wrist. He howled as Hiro shoved him from the carriage.

Eomma covered her eyes. Hiro darted to the other side of the carriage. 'All of you, fuck off! Or I'll shove this wood up your ass!'

The carriage driver snapped his reins. The horses set off at a canter, the carriage rumbling over the uneven dirt path. The Aokis clutched each other as they left the refugees behind, some yelling after them.

'That was close,' said Yui as Hiro sat next to her. 'Well done.'

'I wish we could help them,' said Chiyo, unable to stop the tears slipping down her cheeks. 'I know they could have hurt us. But they're desperate.'

'It was them or us.' To her surprise, Hiro's voice was gentle. 'Sometimes you have to do bad things to survive. If they'd collapsed the carriage, we all would have ended up walking.'

After checking everyone was all right, the carriage driver told them it would be several more days before they arrived at Kōfu Station. 'That's where you get your train to Nagano,' he grunted.

The farther west they went, the ricketier and hillier the roads became. Chiyo and the others often got out to stretch their legs, matching the horses' slow pace as they passed through hills and forest. For hours at a time, they saw nobody else.

'We're going to make a stop at Sagamiko, see, and the driver's gonna change. He knows where you're going. We'll replace the horses and you can get some food. You got money?'

'Some.' The Nakamuras had assured them the cash they had given them was enough to get to Nagano, but they hadn't mentioned whether it would cover food along the way.

'It would be nice if they stopped near a hot spring,' Chiyo remarked when Hiro was walking alongside her. He still had his wooden plank, swinging it as he walked.

'And a restaurant,' said Hiro. 'With all you can eat and drink. Steaming noodles, big piles of fluffy rice, grilled meat and sausages.'

Chiyo's stomach rumbled at that. 'Oh, don't.'

At around noon, they reached civilisation. People worked in rice paddies that stretched as far as the eye could see. The driver pointed out the Sagami River, where people collected water, wiping sweat from their brows. Men pulled carts, and they trundled through a main town, passing teahouses and buildings with thatched roofs.

'It's so peaceful,' Chiyo said. She liked it here.

They stopped at an inn, where a man took the carriage's horses. 'I would love a proper bed for the night, but I'm worried about money,' said Father. 'I don't know how much the train tickets will cost.'

'Let's get some food,' said Yui. 'That's the important thing. And I want to have a look around. Maybe we can wash up in the river.'

A middle-aged woman who said her name was Ōtsuka Eriko took pity on them when they told her their story. 'We don't have much, but what we do have, we can spare,' she said firmly. 'Let me take you to the river. I know this good spot that has plenty of trees, so you won't be disturbed. Darling,' she said to her husband, 'Go and get some towels and my spare robes. Get a couple of your old things, too.'

Dazed, they followed the woman to a grassy riverside. Chiyo longed to dunk herself straight into the river, clothes and all. The woman kindly told them to take their time then went off to fetch supplies.

Emotion welled up inside Chiyo. It was the first time they had experienced any kindness in what felt like a lifetime. Even before the earthquake, their neighbours had mostly shunned them. Now a stranger wanted to make sure they were all right.

'Ōtsuka-san, how will we ever thank you?' Eomma said when the woman returned with spare robes for all of them, towels for drying themselves, and clean blankets. Mr Ōtsuka laid down another bag. Inside it were salted rice balls with *umeboshi* plums.

Chiyo couldn't help it. She burst into tears.

'Oh, you poor thing,' said Mrs Ōtsuka. Eomma put her arm around Chiyo.

'I'm just so happy.' Chiyo pressed her palms to her eyes, embarrassed to cry in front of a stranger. 'Thank you. You've no idea how much you're helping us.'

'What was it like?' whispered Mrs Ōtsuka.

Chiyo and Yui glanced at each other. Yui had some rice stuck near her lips. She had a haunted look on her face, the glee at the food gone. Chiyo knew what she was seeing. It was the same thing Chiyo saw whenever she closed her eyes.

Fire. Ruined homes. Endless smoke. Charred corpses.

'We've been getting snatches of news,' said Mrs Ōtsuka. 'The bridge collapsed?'

'We saw it happen,' said Yui as Chiyo took another bite of the rice ball. She wished Mrs Ōtsuka had waited for them to finish eating before asking them about the earthquake. Suddenly it felt less appetising.

Yui didn't go into gory details when she mentioned the bridge collapse, but Mrs Ōtsuka pressed her with questions, almost perversely enticed. 'And the army depot. The newspapers said it was like the remains of a bonfire afterwards. Just ash.'

'Yes,' said Yui blankly. 'Just ash.'

Mercifully, the Ōtsukas headed off. Eomma came back soon after, Hiro and Father at her heels. They looked like new men.

'Is that food?' Hiro snatched up one of the remaining rice balls. He tossed one to Chiyo's father then bit into his. He groaned, his eyes closed, and Chiyo giggled. He looked like Yui when he did that.

'Bath time,' she said when she'd eaten, rising. 'C'mon, Yui. I'll race you.'

Neither of them had much energy, but they giggled and ran through the overgrown grass to the river, towels and fresh robes in their arms. They stripped off, their backs to each other, and Chiyo felt suddenly shy. She hadn't seen Yui naked before. She had seen other women before, of course, at the bathhouse. But with Yui it was different. She hadn't forgotten their kisses, their murmured words of affection. It all felt so far away now, survival more pressing, but now she stood naked, the breeze warm on her skin and Yui's uneven breathing behind her, a ripple of heat washed through her.

'Let's get in before some pervert fisherman sees us,' Yui said, and warm fingers closed gently around Chiyo's wrist. Yui looked pointedly away, but Chiyo couldn't resist glancing at Yui.

Firm, round breasts, nipples pebbling in the breeze. Flat stomach. Slender thighs. Chiyo sucked in air through her teeth.

'You peeked.' There was laughter in Yui's voice. They stepped into the river. It was cold, making Chiyo gasp as goosebumps stippled her skin. When she was safely chest-deep, Chiyo shyly said, 'Yes, I peeked.'

Chiyo's cheeks burned as Yui's gaze roamed over her slender shoulders. 'I'll get you back for that.'

'I'm sure you will,' Chiyo said playfully. She didn't know where this mischievous streak had come from. Maybe it was having food at last, or being somewhere safe, but she finally felt like she could breathe again.

And bathing ... oh, it was glorious. Chiyo waded out a little, keeping close enough to the bank to avoid the strongest current, and dunked her head into the fresh, clear water. Fish darted away as she scrubbed herself, days' worth of muck washing away. What she wouldn't give for some soap ... but this was wholly better than nothing.

Eomma joined them not long after, and Chiyo stood by her, happy to see her mother enjoy the fresh water. She scooped some up in her hands. The river in Tokyo was never this clean.

It was mid-afternoon, a cloudy haze over the town. When they reunited with Hiro and Father, Chiyo felt reborn.

'Thanks for saving us some food,' said Yui, kicking her brother gently in the side.

'It was two each, wasn't it?' Hiro grumbled, half opening his eyes.

Chiyo chuckled as she lay in the grass. A dragonfly flew nearby, passing between them on translucent wings. She wanted to fall asleep right here, but when her father declared they should check on the carriage driver, she reluctantly rose.

Hiro, it turned out, had had an idea. 'Give me one of those blankets,' he said when they had reached the centre of town, a market street flanked by thatched-roof houses. Several stalls had been erected, selling various pickled vegetables and wooden bowls of miso soup.

Chiyo threw Yui a questioning look. Yui tilted her head.

'Come stand in front of me,' Hiro whispered, sitting on the blanket.

Hiro launched into a monologue. His back straightened and his usually low voice turned jovial and upbeat. Passing people stopped and glanced over with interest.

His pacing and delivery were quick and timely, and soon the crowd were chuckling. Eomma chortled next to Chiyo, who found herself smiling. Hiro gesticulated and jumped between characters, sometimes uttering phrases in a deep, manly voice, and other times as an old lady, bending his back and wheezing, or an excitable child. Yui's mouth was slightly open, staring at her brother in shock and delight.

'He's performing *rakugo*, isn't he?' Chiyo whispered to her father. She had heard of it – performers monologuing funny stories – and sometimes they performed in Tokyo. She'd had no idea Hiro had this talent.

The sulky young man had gone, different characters flashing across his face and through his body as he told a story that had people laughing out loud. When Hiro had finished, he swept to his feet and bowed to much applause.

'Look,' Chiyo said. People were offering Hiro money. One old woman pressed a wrapped parcel into his hands. They all wanted to talk to him.

'Well done, Hiro,' said Yui later, when the crowd had dispersed and Hiro stood grinning, money in one hand and food in the other.

Hope filled Chiyo. This town had been more welcoming in one day than their neighbourhood of Asakusa had been in Chiyo's entire life. 'Maybe we should stay.'

'We can't decide that after one day,' said Father gently. They found a quiet place to sit and opened the spoils. The old woman had given Hiro some dorayaki pancakes from her stall. Hiro handed them all one, looking pleased with himself.

'We still wouldn't have anywhere to live,' Yui reminded Chiyo. She took a bite of her pancake and chewed slowly, bliss crossing her face.

Hiro's glee was wearing off, adopting a grumpy look again. 'Just because they threw me some cash and food on the street doesn't mean they'd welcome us,' he said. He counted out the sen in his hand. 'Well, it's better than nothing.'

Chiyo stayed quiet. She was clean, they had food, and a pleasant breeze from the river washed over them as birds flocked overhead. It felt safe here. But maybe that was wishful thinking.

'We'll get on the carriage tomorrow,' said Father, and swallowed the rest of his dorayaki. 'Hiro, that was wonderful.'

'Anything to help,' said Hiro, looking sheepish. Chiyo felt a warmth towards Yui's brother she couldn't quite describe. She had no living brothers, but she felt she could trust him. He'd done his best to help.

'We will be safe in Nagano.' Father rose. 'Maybe they'll let us stay in the stables tonight. I don't want to spend money on the inn and not have enough for the train.'

The carriage driver woke them up the next morning. 'Rough night?' he asked, not without sympathy as the family rose, stiff and uncomfortable and covered in straw. 'We leave in ten minutes. Say your goodbyes.'

Mrs Ōtsuka was waiting for them, a bag of rice balls in her arms. Eomma offered her some of the money Hiro had earned, but she waved them away.

'Good luck with everything,' Mrs Ōtsuka said as they clambered into the carriage. 'Take care.'

Chiyo watched the little village of Sagamiko shrink behind them, the morning sun glittering on the river. She was a little sad to say goodbye to it, but her heart was full of hope.

They passed tree-covered hills as the day wore on. 'I wish we had those cards with us,' said Father. 'Remember that time we all played together?'

They talked fondly of their memories of that evening, where they had made up silly rules to made-up card games. Hiro listened with amusement.

'What kinds of things did you get up to for fun, Hiro?' Father asked. Chiyo knew he was trying to give more attention to the young man, grateful for his help and protection.

Hiro shrugged. He had abandoned his wooden plank at some point, and sat back in his seat, tapping his thighs. 'Sumo wrestling,' he said. 'My brother always beat me, though. Bug-catching in the summertime.'

'I tried taking Chiyo to catch bugs once,' said Father, looking wistful. He still grieved the baby boys they had lost.

Chiyo had done her best to mirror her father's enthusiasm. 'We did catch that cicada once,' she said, recalling. 'Remember? It screamed so loudly it scared me, and I let it go.'

Father chuckled. 'You liked reading poetry instead.'

'It helped put you to sleep,' Chiyo reminded him. 'I could get through maybe four haiku poems before you'd start snoring.'

Yui grinned at that. Chiyo looked at her. 'What about in your time?'

The atmosphere in the carriage shifted. Everyone looked at Yui.

'Sorry,' said Chiyo quickly. 'I mean, only if you want to talk about it.'

She wanted her parents to listen to Yui, to believe her. None of them had broached the subject since they had left Tokyo, and she didn't want it hanging between them, unsaid.

'Well.' Yui leaned forward. She looked … relieved. Glad to be able to talk about it. 'Hiro had this gaming device called a Famicom console …'

CHAPTER 17

It took the best part of two days of travel to reach Kōfu Station. Yui found herself glad that it was still late summer; the mosquito bites were worth the cool breeze from the surrounding hills. The carriage would have been a nightmare in mid-winter.

Nerves thrummed through Yui as rain pattered above their heads, mist clinging to tree-covered peaks around them. Eomma passed around blankets the Ōtsukas had given them. Chiyo sat close to Yui, her cold hand finding hers under the blanket. Yui squeezed back. Nerves fluttered in her belly. It was another venture into the unknown.

They ate the rest of the rice balls, which were lightly salted and tasty. Yui sent a silent thank-you to Mrs Ōtsuka. She couldn't imagine how grimy she'd feel if they were still in their same clothes from the first of September. She worked it out in her head – yes, it would be the fifth or sixth by now. Still here, in 1923.

The carriage driver grumbled at the rain, but the horses trudged on, carrying them through mountain roads and hills. When the rain had stopped and clouds hung low in the sky, the driver's voice croaked, 'Almost at Kōfu.'

Yui stuck her head out of the window to see a bustling town, bigger than Sagamiko village they had left behind and surrounded by mountainous views and farming fields. People pulled wagons or carried satchels, working hard. Smoking factories stood all around, which the carriage driver told them were for producing silk.

Chiyo's father asked about the train station, and the carriage driver pointed a dirty fingernail to the north. 'Can get your tickets there,' he grunted. 'Now, if you don't mind, I'm going to find the nearest pub.'

He gave them a bow and swept off, still grumbling. 'Friendly fellow,' remarked Hiro, jumping from the carriage. 'Do you think there's a train today?'

'Only one way to find out,' said Father, and they headed in the direction the carriage driver had led them. Kōfu seemed to be a mishmash of the modern – if the twenties counted as modern, Yui thought privately – and traditional. Narrow streets coexisted with thatched-roof houses. Men shouted as they unloaded goods from wagons. A rickshaw driver passed them, a chubby man in a suit reading a newspaper sitting behind.

'There's the station,' said Father at last. He added, cheer in his voice, 'Once we've paid for the tickets to Okaya, we'll know how much money we have left. We can get something to eat.'

This cheered them immensely, and with thoughts full of hot soba noodles and grilled meat, they headed for the station. It smelled of coal and dust, and as they approached a modest wooden building with sliding doors, they spotted men in Western suits and hats moving from the station, walking silently with purpose, almost in unison.

Inside, wooden benches lined the wall. Yui couldn't help comparing it to the train stations of her time. Vending machines, ads on bright posters, machines for tickets. This was plain and functional. Eomma and Chiyo perched on a nearby bench, looking around in awe.

'Look, Eomma! A steam train.' Chiyo almost fell over herself with excitement as she pointed outside, where an enormous black steam engine puffed smoke.

'Buy the tickets quickly, dear, that might be the train we need,' said Chiyo's mother.

A man in a buttoned-up uniform and peaked cap bowed to them in greeting. Yui sidled over to Father as he asked about ticket prices. The cash he had, together with the small bit of earnings Hiro had got, made just over twelve yen.

'First-class ticket to Okaya is ten yen for one adult,' said the man, his eyes moving from Father's robe to the others, who were exclaiming at the train like it was a baby dragon. 'Er ... perhaps ... ?'

'How much is a second-class ticket? Or third-class?' Father's voice was laced with anxiety, too. Yui wasn't sure how to try and comfort him, but when he glanced her way, she gave him a small smile.

'Second-class ticket is five, third class is two.'

'Five adults in third class, then, please,' said Father in relief. Yui grumbled to him, 'We saved their baby's life, and they could only spare enough for third-class tickets?'

'At least we're getting there in one piece,' Father whispered back. Yui nodded, her cheeks burning. He was right. How could the Aokis always be so cheerful?

'Where's Hiro?' she asked. She hadn't seen him since they'd entered the train station.

It only took a moment to look around the little room and know that Hiro was not with them. Panic seized Yui for a moment before she chided herself. Hiro was an adult. He might be waiting outside.

But he wasn't. She stepped outside, looking around for her brother. 'Damn him,' she muttered, rubbing her arms. The wind blew much colder up here in the mountains. The sky was cloudy, but the hills she could see were capped with snow, blue or black against the sky.

'Yui-chan?' Father slid open the door. 'The train leaves in thirty minutes. I've got the tickets. We can walk to Hirano village from Okaya Station.' He gently patted her shoulder, then pulled his hand away as though embarrassed. 'We're almost there. The hard part's over.'

'Great,' she said. 'There's a bit of money left over, too.'

'Two whole yen,' he said proudly. 'Come on, we might have time for some dinner.' His face fell. 'I'm just sorry we couldn't get a nicer seat. I wanted Eomma to try out first class.'

'Maybe one day.'

Yui worried for Hiro. He should be with them. He didn't even know what time the train was.

'Shouldn't we wait for him?' Chiyo asked.

Yui's stomach groaned with hunger, but she reluctantly said, 'You all go ahead. I'll wait for Hiro.'

'We'll bring you something back,' Chiyo promised, and gave her a sympathetic look as she and her parents left. Yui sat on the bench, jiggling her leg, growing more and more annoyed with Hiro. Why had he snuck off like that? Him running away without telling her was what had started everything in the first place.

Travellers filed past her, having travelled from Nagoya or the Tokyo direction. It was easy to tell who had come from the capital; refugees, tired-looking and with soot-covered bags on their backs. Yui hoped they would find the help they were looking for.

She started to drift off, well aware that their train would soon be ready for boarding and hoping Hiro wouldn't be stupid enough to stay away much longer. Would they leave him behind if he wasn't back in time?

The door slid open and footsteps reached her. She knew it was him before she opened her eyes.

'Where the hell have you been?' she demanded, jumping to her feet.

Hiro scowled and held out a bag. Inside was some wrapped food and jars of sake.

'Where did you get these?' She grabbed his elbow and pulled him out to the platform. A locomotive was there, noisily puffing smoke. It was loud enough where they wouldn't be overheard.

'I didn't know how much money we'd have left, so I … got these,' said Hiro. 'You don't have to be such a grump about it.'

Yui spluttered. 'But, you could have stayed out too long and missed the train.'

'I wouldn't have. The timetable is outside, and there's a clock on the station building. I'm not an idiot.' He folded his arms. 'I'm sick of being hungry all the time. Aren't you? I knew those Nakamuras wouldn't give us enough for food as well as train tickets.'

Yui's pulse slowed, and she gave a reluctant nod as she clutched the bag to her. 'Well, thanks,' she said finally. 'Did you do some *rakugo* performances or something?'

Hiro didn't quite meet her eyes. 'Uh, yeah. Believe I earned it, if you want to.'

'Hiro,' she moaned.

Chiyo appeared on the platform just then, her expression melting into relief when she saw the siblings. 'Thank goodness you're here. We were worried when we didn't see you inside. Come on, it's nearly time to board.'

The steam engine hissed and puffed, staff opening the doors and people clambering on. It was easy to tell who had first-class tickets; they wore Western suits or smart robes, their hair coiffed and neat. They boarded the front of the train. Yui and the others battled the smoke-filled platform to find the third-class carriages.

They clambered inside, taking in the small space with its wooden benches before the station guard slammed the door behind them, his shrill whistle filling the air. Chiyo plopped down on a bench and looked out of the grimy window, her face shining with excitement.

'Next stop, Okaya Station, then a short walk to Hirano,' said Father as he helped Eomma sit down. 'To our new home and new life.'

Chiyo handed her and Hiro small bags of tempura, saying they had brought them from the small eatery where they'd found their lunch. Yui could have cried. It was the most delicious thing she had eaten in weeks. Hiro ate with identical gusto beside her, and all too soon, the bags were empty.

It was a long, rickety ride, punctuated by the shriek of the steam train's horn, the chug-chugging of steam, and frequent stops and slowing in the mountains as they trudged farther north.

Father was excited to see the bottles of sake Hiro had conjured. Was he not going to ask where he got them? Hiro crossed his arms and stared out of the window, looking so like he had as a kid that Yui's heart gave a squeeze.

'I was only trying to help,' he grumbled. The wooden bench was firm beneath them, the carriage jolting every few moments.

'It's wrong to steal.' She felt preachy saying it, especially when he scoffed.

'It's not wrong if they deserve it,' Hiro quoted. 'Didn't you tell me that once? We've been starving ever since that damn earthquake. I took it from a wagon belonging to a merchant who was trying to overcharge a little old woman for his wares, okay? He deserved it. Besides, even if he notices, it's too late for him to do anything about it.'

Yui sighed, not having the energy to argue. Hiro offered some of the food to Eomma, who politely declined. Chiyo gave him a look of sympathy, then glanced at Yui as though asking permission.

'It's food. It'll go to waste if it isn't eaten, and then that's even worse.' Hiro shook a bag of mochi rice cakes at her. 'Go on. Wasting food is a sin.'

Chiyo started at that, then snatched the bag from him.

Yui supposed the poor in the 1920s hated wasting food even more than in her time. It felt strange, realising Hiro probably had more in common with Chiyo than with herself. Yui's stomach soon rumbled, and she reluctantly accepted some seaweed-wrapped salmon rice balls and mochi cakes, which were, admittedly, very good.

Father was getting red-faced as he drank steadily through his second bottle of sake. 'He's nervous,' Eomma said later. 'About meeting his parents.' She looked worried, too.

'It'll be good farm food and snowball fights from now on,' said Yui, forcing cheer she didn't feel. She always felt a little sorry for Eomma.

'All I have to do is not be Korean,' said Eomma flatly.

Yui drifted off for a while, though she was often jerked awake by the train's whistle or one of its many stops. When the sun was sinking, the train huffed to a stop and the train guard shouted that they had arrived at Okaya Station.

'Here we go.' Hiro jumped out first, followed by Eomma and Chiyo. Yui followed Father onto the quiet platform.

'Hirano village is just that way,' said the guard when Father asked, pointing down the hill to several slope-roofed houses near a lake that sparkled in the sun. 'You can't miss it.'

The family exchanged hopeful looks. Finally, they had arrived at Hirano. It was much colder here, the icy breeze making them shiver, but to Yui it felt like heaven. Whenever she closed her eyes these days, she saw reddened skies, trails of smoke, collapsed buildings, and piles and piles of corpses. But here … there were trees, mountains, the air smelled of grass and flowers and the lake, not of death and ash.

'My parents don't know we're coming, so I don't know if they'll be very welcoming,' said Father. Of course, he hadn't been able to send a letter in the rush to leave. He swallowed. 'Well, this should be interesting. We haven't spoken in person since, well …' He threw a guilty look at Eomma.

'We're safe now,' Chiyo encouraged her mother, putting an arm around her.

Hiro pointed. 'What lake is that?'

'Lake Suwa,' said Father. 'When I was a child, we used to skate on it when it froze over in the winter.'

The sparkling water stretched for kilometres, hills and green on the other side dotted with buildings. *Erect* buildings. They had left death behind. Tokyo and Yokohama's destruction lay kilometres and kilometres behind them now. What lay for them ahead couldn't possibly be worse.

CHAPTER 18

Chiyo was worried about Eomma.

The spark of life that had always been in her mother had vanished. They were all traumatised from the disaster, but ... it was like Eomma had left part of her soul behind in their ruined house in Tokyo. She stared into the distance. She had spent most of the train ride worried and distant. It took them several times speaking before she noticed they were talking to her.

'Soon we'll be in a nice, warm house eating delicious food,' said Chiyo, trying to act cheerful like her father always did. 'Look how beautiful this place is.'

'There's a silk factory nearby. Maybe I can find work there.' The thought seemed to perk up her father, and he took Eomma's hand as they passed green bushes.

'Ooh, look at that spider,' said Chiyo, pointing to a brilliant green and yellow spider in its web in the bushes. She shuddered, much to Hiro's amusement.

The village of Hirano was simple and quaint. People glanced at them as they walked by, probably noting that they were strangers; their clothes, though old and ragged, weren't much different from the simple clothes people wore here. Unlike in the city, people didn't seem to want to show off their wealth. Or perhaps they simply didn't have much to display. Yui wondered if the news of the earthquake had reached all the way out here. Surely it had. Maybe they had even felt the tremors this far north.

They wandered past the lake and through some narrow streets as the sun descended past the hills, the sky turning milky-blue with dusk. An old woman swept the ground outside her building, where a shovel and a bucket stood beside some sliding doors. Her little black eyes watched them as they passed.

The houses grew sparser, a cold breeze blowing over them as dry leaves blew around their ankles. They came to farmland, where fields stretched as far as the hills, kilometres away.

'This is where we lived when I was growing up. The address on their letter was the same, so they should still be here.' Father looked nervous as they came to a house on a quiet street. It had a slate roof and sliding wooden doors, a traditional home. Yui peered at him; the whites of his eyes were a little red, but he appeared to have sobered up from the sake.

Chiyo straightened with anticipation. 'I'm finally meeting my grandparents.' She grinned excitedly at Yui. In that moment, her enthusiasm almost won Yui over, and she felt a spark of hope as Father knocked on the front door.

They waited. Father wrung his hands, stepping back to squint at the windows. Yui swallowed, wondering if they had moved, or whether they were still living at all.

But soon there was movement in the house, and the sound of shuffling. The door slid open to reveal an old woman, bent from age, her greying hair cut short like a man's, practical and neat. She squinted at them all and did not smile.

'Hello, *ofukuro*.' Father used the honorific word for older mother.

His mother blinked at him. Yui could see the similarities between her and her son, the shape of her face, the cheekbones. But she lacked his smiling demeanour. 'Who are all these people?' Her gaze fell on Eomma. 'Still with the Korean, I see.'

Father's Adam's apple bobbed as he swallowed. Eomma wilted. As small as the woman was, her hateful gaze was penetrating.

'This is my wife, Mi-Ja.' Father put an arm around her. 'And my daughter, Chiyoko.'

The woman sniffed, giving Chiyo the tiniest of nods. 'And who is this young man? Another child of yours?'

'That's Hiro,' Chiyo said meekly. 'And this is Yui. They're brother and sister.'

'Hmm, right. And what are you doing here?'

This wasn't going the way anybody had hoped. 'Mother, have you not heard about the earthquake in Tokyo and Yokohama?' Father asked. 'Surely you even felt it here.'

The old woman sighed. 'I suppose you better come in. It's getting dark.'

They all took off their shoes in the *genkan*, the house's entry hall. The front hallway was bigger than Chiyo and Yui's sleeping space had been back home. The place smelled of cedarwood and something faintly cooking, perhaps soba noodles.

Yui's stomach groaned with nerves. They had been anticipating a warm welcome, not this standoffish coldness the old woman was treating them with. Maybe she was in shock?

'Is my father … ?' Father trailed off, as though afraid to ask.

'Working the fields while there's still daylight,' his mother grunted back as she lit lanterns. Her hands shook slightly as she held up the matches, but she impatiently waved away her son's offer of help. 'As usual, since there's hardly anyone here to help him after your brother passed. Well, sit down.'

The main room was of tatami mats, a small wooden table and cushions in the centre. They sat there, Hiro opting to sit by the wall.

'You're all filthy,' Chiyo's grandmother remarked.

'We just came from Tokyo, *ofukuro*. We barely escaped with our lives. Please, don't you have some food? And some clothes?'

'Clothes, no. But there might be some noodles left.' Grandmother shuffled towards the kitchen. Eomma made to get up, but Father put a gentle hand on her wrist, shaking his head.

'I'll go,' whispered Chiyo, rising elegantly to her feet. Soon she was talking quietly to Grandmother, who begrudgingly gave her directions on what to do.

Father let out a low breath. 'That could've gone better.'

Eomma nodded, a worried expression on her face. Father gave her a reassuring smile, ensuring she was comfortable on her small cushion.

What if the husband is worse? Yui thought. They had nowhere else to go. The small bubble of hope that had formed popped.

They learned that Father's family owned the farm they had seen, growing vegetables and taking care of a couple of chickens. Many people here and in the surrounding villages worked in the silk factory now, but the Aokis had stayed in agriculture. 'Everybody needs food,' said Grandmother. 'That will never change.'

Yui noted how the old woman was aged and bent, but she moved with fluid efficiency, though she set things down a little harder than was maybe necessary. She had a no-nonsense air to her that Yui might have liked if she didn't sniff disapprovingly in Eomma's direction every few minutes.

'You'll be wanting baths, I suppose,' the grandmother remarked. 'You all stink. What exactly happened in Tokyo? I saw the newspapers.' She brought a newspaper out to them and threw it onto the table, almost upsetting Eomma's cup of barley tea.

Yui hadn't seen a newspaper up close for weeks. In the black-and-white printing of the local Nagano newspaper, it said that over a hundred thousand people were suspected dead.

'A hundred thousand,' Eomma whispered. It was the first words she'd uttered all day, and her voice was raspy.

Waking up on a corpse. People screaming as they batted at the flames on their clothes and hair. Piles and piles of bodies. Yui tore her gaze away from the newspaper.

'We have nowhere else to go,' said Father. 'Can we stay here, *ofukuro*?'

'I'll work,' grunted Hiro from the corner. 'I can do farm work.'

'I'll work, too,' said Yui. Chiyo nodded vigorously.

Grandmother's narrow-eyed expression didn't change as she took in the three young adults. 'Fine. We need more hands on the farm anyway. Though we don't have spare rooms for all of you.'

The Aoki family were used to sleeping in one room, separated only by a curtain, so this wasn't a problem for them. 'We'll sleep in the barn,' said Father. He smiled at them all, a forced look. 'Everything's going to be okay.'

'Sleeping in the barn like pigs,' muttered Grandmother, shuffling about in the kitchen. 'Never thought I'd see my son marrying a Korean, now living like one.'

Yui glared at Chiyo, longing to say something. Father *had* made a good life for them in Tokyo.

To her surprise, it was Chiyo who spoke up. 'Grandmother, Father worked hard in the factory in Tokyo. We were very happy there. Now our house is rubble, and we're sorry to disturb you. Thank you very much for your hospitality.' Chiyo bowed elegantly on the tatami mat, her forehead touching the floor. 'And for your kindness when we showed up here so unexpectedly.'

'We will find a house to live in, too,' agreed Father.

Grandmother came and knelt before Chiyo. Her gnarled hand took Chiyo's chin and turned her head left and right, as though examining her. 'This one will be old enough to marry,' she remarked. 'How old are you, girl? Eighteen?'

'Twenty-one,' squeaked Chiyo.

'Widowed?'

'No, Grandmother.'

'Still unwed, then?' Grandmother tsked and rose, elegantly despite her age. 'We will have to find a husband for you. And you, I suppose.' She nodded to Yui, who would have laughed if her words hadn't been so disturbing.

Chiyo scurried to Yui's side as soon as Grandmother left the room and clutched Yui's hand beneath the table.

'Well, this turned out quite well, don't you think?' Father asked. 'We have a home, safety, food, and work. More than can be said for so many people back in the Kantō region.'

Eomma rose to her feet, wincing slightly as she did. 'I will help *ofukuro* around the house and cook meals. Chiyo-chan, Yui-chan, you can help me. Hiro, you can work on the farm. I'm sure Grandmother will show you what to do.'

Hiro grunted, fiddling with a twig in his fingers. Yui hadn't even noticed he'd picked it up.

'What about your father?' Chiyo whispered. 'Is he ...?' Yui knew what she wanted to say. *Is he even worse than Grandmother?*

The door opened just then, the strong call of '*tadaima!*' announcing his return. Chiyo looked startled, and Yui threw her what she hoped was an encouraging look as they all rose to their feet.

Chiyo's grandfather was a short-statured fellow with a good-natured, wrinkled face, darkened by the sun. He was taking off his hat when he walked in and said, 'Oh! Hello, hello. My, what a lot of visitors. You didn't tell me we were having visitors today, *Yome.*'

Yui blinked. It took her a moment to realise that he meant Chiyo's grandmother. It seemed almost strange for him to have such a cute nickname for his wife when she was ... like that.

'They showed up on the doorstep a little while ago with only the clothes on their backs,' grumbled Grandmother, appearing behind him. '*Okaeri*, husband. Welcome home.'

'Katsuro, is that you?' Grandfather stepped forward, realising who he was looking at.

'It's me, Father. How are you?' Father said warmly. When his face had been tense when seeing his mother, his expression

199

now broke out into a warm smile to see his dad. Chiyo sniffled beside Yui as Grandfather cupped his son's face.

'My, you look older. And skinnier,' he said. 'We heard about all the horribleness in Tokyo. We were so worried. Thank goodness you're all right.' He smiled around at the rest of them. 'Are you our grandchildren?'

'Just Chiyo.' Yui gently nudged Chiyo, who stepped forward.

'Hello, Grandfather,' she said respectfully.

'What a beautiful young lady.' Grandfather took her hands, and Chiyo blushed. 'And you must be her husband?'

Hiro snorted with laughter while Chiyo blushed crimson. 'I'm nobody,' Hiro said.

'You're not,' Yui said quickly. 'Sir, I've been staying with Chiyo and her family for a while. I'm Chiyo's, um, friend. This is my brother, Sanada Hiro. I'm Sanada Yui. Thank you very much for your hospitality.' She bowed low, then gave her brother a sharp look. Hiro bowed, too.

Grandfather beamed at them. 'Well, of course you're welcome to stay. We felt the earthquake even here, didn't we, *Yome?*'

Grandmother grunted at him from the kitchen. Yui wasn't sure what she was even doing in there.

'Have you eaten? Let's get you settled in.'

Grandfather was reluctant to agree that they could stay in the barn, though he nodded along when his wife reminded him there was no room for them in their house. Their home consisted of the living room and kitchen, which was really all one room, a small toilet, and the room where the grandparents slept.

The farm where they worked was large, neat rows of vegetables stretching to a fence before silhouettes of mountains. The barn's door opened with a creak, smelling of hay. It was large, though, and there were many boxes and bundles of sticks and straw, as well as barrels for storing dry food or pickling vegetables.

'Well, this will do nicely,' said Father cheerfully, stepping into the dark barn. 'Don't look so glum, Chiyo-chan. With some blankets, some oil lanterns, and maybe some shelves and books, this place will be cosy. Look, it's bigger than our house in Tokyo.'

Cosy. Yui looked around at the holes in the roof, the slits of broken wood in the sides. It would get wet when it rained. It was September now, summer's warmth still lingering, but what would this place be like in a couple of months?

'It'll be winter soon.' Eomma wrapped the shawl around herself as though the thought of it made her feel cold.

'But we're alive and we arrived safely, and that's what matters right now.' Father took her shoulders. 'Everyone, listen to me. Things ... they're going to be all right. We're together and we're safe. Everything else, we can work out as it comes. Okay?'

Father hugged them all, even Hiro, who looked embarrassed as he pulled them into his embrace.

'We always wanted more children, didn't we?' Father nuzzled into Eomma's hair, softly stroking her back. 'Our sons never made it past infancy.'

'And we always wanted a mother and a father,' mumbled Yui. Hiro had found adopted parents, but her only memories were of their mother back home, back in the nineties.

'Everything's going to be all right. You'll see.'

PART 3

'Fall seven times, stand up eight.'

Buddhist saying

CHAPTER 19

'A re you all right?' Yui asked when she managed to get some alone time with Chiyo. Father and Hiro were in the barn, discussing ways to improve it. Eomma was in the house with Grandmother, maybe being shown where everything was so she could help with the cooking.

'I hope she won't be too hard on her,' Chiyo said as they walked along the rows of rice paddies, familiarising themselves with the layout of the place. Sparse trees were dotted around the farm, the fields in neat rows. Some were unused, with previously not enough hands to tend all the land.

Yui didn't comment. The impression she'd got of the old woman in the house wasn't good, and there was nothing truthful she might say that would make Chiyo feel better.

'She'll be fine,' Yui managed to say. They went behind a tree, out of view of the barn and the house. 'But how are *you* feeling?'

She took Chiyo's slim shoulders, looking into her eyes. Chiyo leaned against the tree, a look of despair crossing her features. The features Yui loved so much.

She couldn't put into words how relieved she was that Chiyo was unhurt. After everything, they were here and safe, and with Hiro with them, too.

'I'm ... all right, I think,' Chiyo said finally. 'I mean ... but all those people ...' Her voice cracked at the last word, and tears dribbled down her cheeks.

Yui cried with her. They'd never forget the horrors they had seen in Tokyo. Now they were here, in a safe place, they could let it wash over them.

She gathered Chiyo into her arms and held her close, both the women's shoulders shaking with grief. They cried for what they had witnessed, the people who would never see another day, the injustice, the home they had lost. The uncertainty for the future.

'I'm glad you're with me, Yui-chan,' Chiyo whispered finally, kissing Yui's damp cheek. Yui turned her head slightly, kissing Chiyo back on her lips. Chiyo's palm found Yui's cheek, her mouth opening. Her tongue glided over Yui's sending a ripple of heat through her. Her fears melted away as longing rushed through her veins. God, she loved this woman. She wanted her so much.

'I'll always be here with you,' Yui promised, gently leaning Chiyo against the tree so their bodies were pressed together. Chiyo's heartbeat against hers. 'I promise. We'll be all right.'

*

Over the next few days, more news about the disaster trickled in. Millions were homeless, refugees fleeing north and west. Over three quarters of Tokyo had been decimated by fires.

Almost everyone who died had been burned alive where they stood or crushed in the panicking crowds.

Charred corpses, black ash, the stink of death, the crunch of the bridge collapsing, corpses floating in the river, lifeless as dolls.

'If only it had rained that day,' Chiyo said one evening as they gathered around the small table for dinner. At least Grandmother let them sit here when it was time to eat, the barn growing chillier as autumn marched towards winter. 'If it had rained, the fires wouldn't have killed so many people.'

'The weather was just right, wasn't it?' Yui said with a sigh. 'It was perfect for spreading the flames …'

They all sat in silence for a moment, remembering those who had been crushed, burned, suffocated, and beaten to death. Yui hated thinking about it too much, guilt clenching her heart as she thought about the Koreans and Chinese murdered by vigilantes, those she hadn't been able to save. To survive the horrors of the earthquake only to die so horribly …

'You killed him!' The Korean man swiped weakly at his attacker. *'Bastard!'*

But what could one woman do against a mass of angry men? Hiro had helped. He was wearing one of Grandfather's old shirts today, the fabric hanging off his skinny form. He ate as quickly as was polite, hungrier than ever now he was helping fix the barn. Grandfather showed him in the early mornings how each plant worked and when to harvest them. Yui and Chiyo listened, too, ready to help. They pulled radishes with Grandfather while Eomma and Grandmother stayed busy in the kitchen, pointedly ignoring each other.

'We'll cook some of these for dinner,' said Grandmother when they took a basket of fresh radishes home. 'And take these ones to the market to sell.'

Hirano village was small, and judging by the number of people who nodded and said hello to Grandfather, he was a popular man. Chiyo and Yui happily shouted, *'irasshaimase!'* to welcome passersby and get them to look at the radishes, turnips, and edamame beans they had harvested.

They went home with some money in their pockets. Yui bought some more blankets for their barn room and new matches for the oil lamps, though Chiyo didn't like using them and would never leave them lit while they slept.

Yui understood. She was terrified of starting a fire, too.

That night, a cold wind howled. The family huddled up in the middle of the barn, Eomma and Father sleeping in the middle, Hiro on the other side of them beside Father, his arm thrown over his eyes as he snored. He had slept like that as a child, too.

'Yui-chan?' Chiyo whispered, her warm hand sliding over Yui's stomach.

Heat flushed through her. Since they had settled at the farm, she and Chiyo had barely had a moment alone together. Occasional kisses when no one was around was as far as they had got. It was tough to lie next to her at night, feeling her warmth, and not being able to do anything.

Yui had always known she preferred girls, but she had never really explored it. Once, when she was in the first year of high school, she and her friend Saya had kissed. But nothing else had come of it, and they hadn't spoken of it. Saya had seemed embarrassed.

But with Chiyo … just being near her brought a sense of calm and safety, like everything would be okay because they were together. Yui held on to that. But the sight of her skin in the moonlight, her slightly parted lips, the vulnerability in

Chiyo's eyes as she looked back at her … it all stirred heat in Yui. She wanted her hands on her. Now.

In silence, they left their family sleeping on the barn ground. Yui picked up the blanket and wrapped it around both of their shoulders. Chiyo had taken a bath tonight, her hair still slightly damp, and her feminine heat pressed against Yui was driving her crazy.

Another fierce wind pelted the barn, but their parents and Hiro slept on. A thrill of nervous excitement ran through Yui as they slipped outside, closing the door behind them.

It was cold, but they found solace between some boxes, sheltered from the wind. They settled beside each other, their eyes meeting. This was the first time they had ever been truly alone for more than a moment. No one sleeping next to them, no one beside them.

Chiyo's breathing had grown heavier. Her hand slid to find Yui's, slender fingers grasping hers tight. Yui didn't want to wait, but her courage was failing her. Perhaps they would just sit here, tensions running high, her heart beating at a feverish pace. She so desperately wanted this to happen, but maybe it was better to wait for the right place and time. She wanted to be with Chiyo on a soft bed in a warm room.

But when would that ever be?

'Yui-chan?' Chiyo's perfect lips parted, so close her warm breath tickled Yui's mouth. Yui kissed her, even as nerves screamed inside her. This wasn't cold, desperate fear like everything they had been through. But it did make her stomach writhe, the sensation thrilling and terrifying all at once.

Chiyo kissed her with urgency, her mouth opening eagerly to Yui's. That tingling excitement rushed through Yui at once, pinning her in place. Another blast of wind howled above them, buffeting the strong box. It didn't budge, protecting the girls from the elements, from everything.

Yui slipped her hand beneath Chiyo's robe. Her skin was so warm and smooth beneath, it made her breath catch. She looked at Chiyo, silently asking permission.

Chiyo bit her lip, slowly nodding, her warm hands sliding beneath Yui's robe, too. Using the blanket as a cover over their shoulders, Yui and Chiyo kissed with passion, months of built-up tension melting between them as they kissed and touched, exploring each other's bodies with the shy hesitation of inexperienced youth.

This wasn't the perfect place, but it was theirs and private. The wind died down, the moon hidden behind clouds. Yui half-listened for footsteps or a voice as she straddled Chiyo, taking in her beauty, as Chiyo gasped beneath her.

Yui wanted all of her, right now, here in this imperfect place. Chiyo encouraged her with small whimpers and whispered confirmations, guiding Yui's clumsy but eager touches, gasping as their foreheads touched. Then Chiyo's slender fingertips ran over Yui's burning skin, reaching for places that made Yui gasp and cry out loud.

Chiyo changed then. She turned confident, her lip curling as she slid two fingers into the slick wetness between Yui's thighs. Pleasure radiated through Yui as she whispered in her ear, 'Do you want more?'

She wanted more. So desperately. Each thrust sent a powerful surge of pleasure through Yui. She almost forgot where she was, who she was. She crushed her lips against Chiyo's, muffling her own increasing cries of ecstasy.

They grew bolder, encouraged by the other's whispers and groans of pleasure. Chiyo lay on her back and Yui slid aside her undergarments, taking in her scent. With Chiyo's fingers entwined in her hair, she kissed and licked, slowly at first, as Chiyo spasmed and gasped beneath her.

'Yes. Yes! There!' Chiyo clapped a hand over her own mouth as Yui found her rhythm, teasing the place that made Chiyo's grip tighten in her hair and her body shudder as she orgasmed.

Both spent and sweating, Yui and Chiyo held each other against the barn.

Yui had been wrong. This was perfect.

*

Autumn turned to winter. Though Chiyo often thought about their neighbours in Tokyo, wondering what had befallen them and the Nakamura family, and what was happening with the Koreans and Chinese who had fallen prey to the angry youths, she concentrated on helping to run the farm. Each month brought more to sow and to harvest, and that governed the meals they ate. There was never enough food for all of them to eat as much as they liked, but compared to the fates that had befallen the citizens of Tokyo and Yokohama, they were positively lucky.

'Make sure you plant them with enough space in between,' said Ota Saburō, the man Grandfather employed to help around the farm. Now there were more of them to help, Grandfather had expanded the farm as promised, declaring his hopes to sow more buckwheat in the coming spring. Saburō was round-faced and good-natured, with defined muscles from working the fields as well as his job at the silk factory. He explained to Yui and Chiyo with patience the best ways to rake, plant, water and harvest the crops.

Hiro fed the chickens some distance away, glancing now and then at Saburō. Yui had noticed it, too. How Saburō's gaze lingered on Chiyo, how his smile stayed on his face when Chiyo nodded along or made some affirmative sound. Sometimes they'd go on walks, and Yui struggled to rein in her jealousy.

'He is a good friend and teacher,' Chiyo asserted when Yui mentioned him. They had extra soup – a rare treat – and after Hiro had had a second helping, the girls had brought bowls to their corner behind the barn. The family had started eating dinner in the barn more and more often, away from Grandmother's disapproving sniffs. The steaming potatoes and meat, soaked in a soy sauce dressing, warmed their bellies this cold November night. Snow drifted down in flakes. Grandfather had lamented the fact, as snow was always bad for crops.

Chiyo suddenly sniffled, and Yui glanced at her. 'What's wrong?'

'Grandmother said I should marry him,' she said. 'Saburō. She said I'm too old to be still living with my parents, and that I'm a burden.'

Yui set down her bowl, annoyed. 'You are not a burden. You work harder than that old *baba* does.'

'Yui!' Chiyo hiccupped. 'You shouldn't call her that.'

'Well, she shouldn't force you to marry someone if you don't want to.' For all the twenties had in common with her own time, there were still things Yui struggled with. Her own mother had never married, preferring to entertain men for money and drinks. Though some still said women were 'Christmas cakes', no good after their twenty-fifth, it was common for women to wait until they were older and ready.

Chiyo was only twenty-one, barely too old to not have been married, but her grandmother had been born in the mid-1800s. Ancient history to Yui, but a time of samurai and tradition and *young wives* for her.

And this was Grandmother's farm, her land.

'Well, do you think he'd make a bad husband?' Yui asked. The words were like bile in her throat.

Chiyo sniffled. 'You're from the future,' she whispered. 'In your time, is it like this?'

Yui's arms tightened around Chiyo. 'It's very different. No, people aren't really matchmade. Though sometimes people want to be, if they're lonely.'

She didn't tell her families were shrinking. Was it such a bad thing if it meant women didn't have to be with men they didn't love? She didn't know if Chiyo liked men, too. She hadn't really thought about it.

'Grandmother is always saying I'm an extra mouth to feed,' Chiyo said.

'That old grouch is always complaining,' Yui insisted, pushing down that flare of jealousy. 'She'll probably try and marry me off, too. And Hiro.'

She considered asking Hiro if he could marry Chiyo – not for love, but to get Grandmother off their backs. She imagined their reactions, maybe wrinkled noses and snorts of laughter. Hiro and Chiyo were warming up to each other in a brother and sisterly kind of way. He'd look after her.

She brought it up with Hiro the next morning. 'The old hag wants to marry Chiyo off to Ota Saburō. Why don't you marry her instead?'

As she expected, Hiro gave a snort. 'Yeah, because I'm so eligible. No house, no proper job. Besides, she'd want us to have kids, and ...' He hesitated. 'No, I'm sorry. Chiyo's like a sister.'

Yui nodded, disappointed but understanding.

CHAPTER 20

Hiro did as much work as he felt like doing on the day, sometimes completing all his chores with diligence. Other days, he did the bare minimum before disappearing until sunset.

Yui found him in the chicken coop at one point, holding one of the birds close to his chest as the others pecked at the seeds he had scattered.

'They were bullying her,' he explained before Yui had even had the chance to ask. 'They wouldn't let her eat any seeds, and if she's stressed, she won't lay eggs.'

The chicken pecked at seed in Hiro's free hand. He stared fondly down at her. 'I named her Momo.'

Yui leaned against the shed door as her brother nodded towards the other chickens. 'That's Kirin, because her neck is the longest. And Mario and Luigi.' He cooed something to the chicken he'd called Momo, then gently set her down. 'What's up?'

Yui had wanted to ask where he rushed off to, but she didn't have the heart to scold him. 'Just checking in on you. How are you finding things?'

They stepped into the cold air. It was a cloudy day, and not so windy. Father had spent the extra yen from their trip – he hadn't told his mother about it, and everyone had silently agreed not to mention it, either – on warm coats for them all. Yui wore hers now, though Hiro only wore his usual working overalls. The cold never seemed to bother him.

'It's a life,' he said. 'Do I miss Tokyo? Sometimes, I suppose.'

'Do you miss your mother?' she asked quietly. Things had happened so fast that she had barely checked in on him about his adoptive family.

'Yeah, I do.' He kicked at some soil. 'She was nice, you know? Welcomed me in. She didn't deserve …' He trailed off, then wiped his nose with the back of his hand. 'Anyway, I suppose we have a new family now.'

'We do.' Chiyo was walking with Eomma on the field, waving at them both. Yui and Hiro returned the gesture, Yui's heart filling with warmth. 'Things aren't so bad here,' she said. 'Are they?'

'Nope.' He wandered off before she could say more, whistling.

It was a day or so later when she finally asked him what he spent his time doing when he wasn't on the farm. Yesterday he had rushed off mid-morning, practically throwing down his tools. 'Just don't tell the old *baba*,' he said, when they were alone. They walked together between two ploughed fields, where birdsong reached them on the cold mountain air.

'Like I'd tell the old hag anything,' Yui scoffed. *Baba* was the word they privately used to talk about Chiyo's grandmother when she and her husband were out of earshot. They'd been here for two months and she hadn't treated them with any more warmth than when they'd first arrived. The exception was, perhaps, Chiyo, though she still mentioned marriage every moment of the day. 'Where've you been? I won't cover your jobs for you again if you don't tell me.'

'I've made a friend.'

'A friend? Or a *friend*?' Yui asked, raising her eyebrows until Hiro snorted, giving her a friendly shove.

'Not *that* sort of friend. He lives on the other side of town. He's helping me make some money on the side so we can get the hell out of here.'

Yui perked up at that. The thought of being able to live somewhere other than that drafty barn ... 'Doing what?'

'This and that. And don't get excited, it isn't much.'

'Has that good-for-nothing brother of yours shown his face yet?' called Grandmother's voice. Yui and Hiro grimaced at each other and rounded the corner of the barn. Both of Chiyo's grandparents were there, holding farmer's tools.

Grandfather smiled warmly, but his wife just glared. 'Are the day's tasks done?'

'Yes, Grandmother,' Yui said quickly. 'All of them.'

She grunted. 'Well, the fence over by the radish fields is falling apart. Fix it. We've gone through way more food than usual since you arrived, so pull your weight.'

'I'll show you how,' said Grandfather. With him there, Yui didn't ask her brother any more questions.

The days grew colder still as the year marched on to winter. Soon the earthquake in Tokyo became old news to the citizens of Hirano village, only those with family or acquaintances in Kantō still talking about it. Hiro was careful not to sneak off too often but would sometimes return with gifts for the family: blankets, chopsticks, clothes. Once, to Chiyo and Yui's amusement, he came back with small, hand-knitted coats for the chickens, since 'They won't lay good eggs if they're cold.'

Throughout their new life, Yui and Chiyo would spend time together whenever they could. They would take walks around Hirano village, visiting shops and shrines, or taking in the beauty of Lake Suwa.

A merchant told them it was sixteen kilometres all the way around. 'Not long until it freezes over, and you'll be able to see the ice pressure ridges, formed by the gods crossing the lake,' he said. Yui smiled politely, but Chiyo was intrigued.

'What kind of god?'

'A local *kami*. He crossed the lake to see his wife, Yasakatome.' He pointed between them. 'You can see Mount Fuji from over there on a clear day.'

It was partly visible today, hidden by some clouds at the top. 'To think we can still see the same mountain we saw from Tokyo,' Chiyo said. No one was around, and she rested her head on Yui's shoulder. Yui took her hand, enjoying the feel of just being with Chiyo, with nobody else here and no grandmother breathing down their necks.

'But from a different angle and an entirely different situation.' Yui kissed the top of Chiyo's head. 'Are you happy here?'

Chiyo's head shifted until their foreheads were touching. 'Here in Nagano? There are some things that are better than before. Others, not so much.' Her fingers stroked gently over Yui's hand. 'I feel happy as long as you're here.'

Yui softened. She pulled the blanket they had brought over their laps, hands stroking and exploring underneath it. Yui longed to do more. Though just being here with her, taking in the snow-speckled mountains and the calm lake, was bliss. And enough for now.

Something in the distance boomed, like a far-off drum. Chiyo sat up straight, Yui following her line of sight. 'Is that smoke?'

Sure enough, black was snaking into the clear sky. Chiyo's breaths quickened beside Yui, her face slackening to panic. 'Fire,' she whimpered.

Panic immobilised Yui, too, its claws digging deep into her. Flashes of the fire tornado cascaded through her mind. People screaming as they were lifted into the air by powerful, impossible winds. The choking, dry smoke in her throat. Charred corpses.

They held each other, Chiyo hyperventilating in her arms. Yui froze, her limbs unmoving, the screams of the dying echoing in her mind. For a moment, she thought she could see the entire village of Hirano on fire.

Then Chiyo breathed hard through her nose. 'It's okay,' she said. 'The other buildings aren't burning. It's not like Tokyo.'

Not like Tokyo ... The ground heaved and shuddered beneath Yui in her mind, collapsing buildings, ending the world.

'Yui-chan.' Chiyo's soft voice was stronger than the flashbacks, her hands gently shaking her. 'I know, I know. It's all right. Breathe.'

Yui inhaled breaths. Not of smoke and fire, but clear and clean. Calm washed through her with every breath. She clutched Chiyo. 'Thanks. I'm sorry.'

'Don't be.' Chiyo looked determined as she rose to her feet, then held out her hand. She helped Yui pull herself up, too, and they dared another look at the smoke in the town. 'What do you think happened?'

Yui was worried, but avoiding it and letting her imagination run wild was somehow worse. 'I'll go if you do.'

People were already hurrying to the scene, buckets of lake water in their hands. 'It was a blacksmithing accident,' a man reported. Sure enough, the smoke was only rising from one building, the local smithy, and by the time Yui and Chiyo had arrived, the last of the flames had been put out.

'There's Hiro,' said Chiyo, pointing.

Yui's brother had his arm around a young man, who was clutching a bleeding ear. 'Hiro.' Yui darted to him. 'What happened?'

'My fault,' groaned the young man he was helping. He was handsome in an aristocratic sort of way, his clothes finer than theirs. His brow was tightly furrowed, and when he pulled his hand from his ear, his palm was red.

'It wasn't anyone's fault,' Hiro assured him. 'Just an accident.' He quickly added, 'This is the friend I was telling you about. San-ichi, these are my sisters, Yui and Chiyo.'

Chiyo flushed with pleasure at being referred to as Hiro's sister. They were soon shooed out of the way when Doctor Tanaka arrived, a ruddy-faced man in his middle years coming to treat the young man Hiro had called San-ichi. When they went to sit down out of the way, Yui hung back to take a glance at Hiro's friend. He was lying on a stretcher now, talking to the doctor.

A man who could only be the blacksmith was marching around. 'What idiot lit a cigarette too close to the shop? I've told you before, the coal dust gets everywhere!'

'We should go,' said Hiro suddenly, a guilty look Yui knew only too well on his face. They stood and left as casually as they could muster and only breathed freely again when they were two streets away.

'Did you start the fire? Or did he?' Yui asked, raising an eyebrow. The guilt was written all over his face.

'I ... don't know. Both of us? I mean.' Hiro rubbed the back of his neck. 'He was standing closer. I stopped to take a piss, and didn't realise how close we were to the forge. He lit a cigarette, and the whole place lit up.'

'Well, it seems like he'll be all right,' said Yui, risking a glance back.

'His parents have money. He'll forgive me, I'm sure.'

'San-ichi is an unusual name,' Chiyo remarked as they sat a bit away. The smoke from the smithy was already dispersing. The street smelled strongly of coal and smoke, but it was clear the fire was under control.

'His surname is Sanada, like us,' Hiro said. 'So I call him San-ichi. San-one. He calls me San-two.'

'San-ni?' Yui snorted with laughter.

'All right, San-ni.' Chiyo nudged Hiro and he gave a reluctant grin.

'Shut up, Chiyo-chan. I shouldn't have told you.' Concern crossed his face. 'I hope he'll be all right.'

When it was clear they couldn't do anything to help, they headed home. Father and Hiro had done a good job of repairing the worst of the cracks in the barn wall, but it was still freezing. After dinner, they piled all the blankets they had in their sleeping spaces.

They had used some of the leftover money from the Nakamura family to buy dividers for where they slept. Eomma and Father had the middle space, Hiro on their other side, Yui and Chiyo on the other. Nobody questioned the young women sleeping together. Maybe it hadn't occurred to them there was any reason other than sharing body warmth.

*

A week later, snowflakes fell as Yui and Hiro sat together on a hill, looking over the farm. Winter had arrived in Nagano. The weeks of storing vegetables and miso paste, airing out winter futons, selling what they could spare, pickling vegetables, and adding insulation to the house and the barn had meant the weeks had flown by. Yui could hardly believe it was already nearly three months since they had arrived.

Yui was wearing the coat Father had bought her and some boots she'd bought with her share of the money. Hiro wore his coat, too, though with the collar open, not seeming to care that his breath fogged before him. The snow would fall on this farm and cover it in white, and they would have to hunker down and wait out the long months, surviving on what they had.

Farm food and work had filled them out, made them stronger, but Yui had never lived through a winter in these times before. Her childhood had involved chillier days in the apartment, maybe a day or two of snow, but there had always been convenience stores open, and Yui had always managed to scavenge rice balls and sandwiches for herself and Hiro.

There had even been days where their mother had cooked. Once they'd had *unagi* eel, a great treat, on Yui's fourteenth birthday. As she and Hiro had grown older, though, those days had become fewer and further between.

Hiro had told her his friend San-ichi was all right, but he would be deaf in his right ear for the rest of his life. 'He says it isn't my fault, but it is.' He shifted his booted foot on the ground, scuffing a long groove in the dirt. 'He won't be able to hear from that ear again.'

Yui gave him what comfort she could, privately thankful it had been this other man and not Hiro who was injured. And it was a miracle the fire hadn't spread.

They sat in silence for a while, taking in the peaceful darkness. The mountains were black against the inky sky, stars twinkling through the gaps in the snow clouds.

'How much do you remember of our childhood?' Yui asked him. 'Before the tunnel. Before everything.'

Hiro glanced at her. 'Not much,' he admitted. He picked up a small twig, turning it over and over in his fingers. 'I remember sleeping in one room. We had one of those things. It was made of metal, and it made cool air blow.'

'A fan,' said Yui, amused.

'Yeah. And you always said we'd get … air conditioning?'

She nodded, encouraging him to go on. 'That's right.'

'I don't remember a mother, before mine in Tokyo.' Hiro looked out now, as though something in the far-off mountains interested him. 'I remembered you, though. Spent over a year talking about you, hoping you'd show up.'

Her heart ached. In the few minutes she had groped around in the dark beneath Saigō Takamori's statue, Hiro had lived ten years without her.

'She wasn't a good mother,' Yui said, leaning back. 'It was me who looked after you. I made sure you took a bath in the evening, and made you go to school, remember?'

'School.' He sighed. 'Right. I had that uniform, and a backpack.' He looked at her again, his eyes glassy. 'You don't understand. Whenever I tried to tell people about this stuff,

223

they always shushed me. Said I was making it up or had been dreaming. I was in an orphanage for a while, while they looked for my *real* parents. They didn't listen when I told them they'd never find you or our mother.'

Yui swallowed. 'That must have been awful.'

'It was all right.' Hiro shrugged. 'The place, I mean. The carers were nice enough. The kids, not so much. Then one day I ran away, just because I was tired of being teased and called a liar all the time. And *okaasan* found me.'

'I'm sorry she died,' Yui said quietly. Hiro had clamped his lips together, rubbing fiercely at his eyes. He almost looked twelve years old again, refusing to cry even though it was only his sister here. His older sister, who would never tease him for crying.

She shifted closer to him, not sure what to do. Hiro controlled himself, elbows resting on his knees, letting out a sigh that sent a wash of white cloud from his lips. A snowflake landed in his hair and stayed there. 'She was so kind to me, and her other son was nice, too. I just stayed with them and the orphanage never bothered looking for me. I took their surname, Hondo, and just … tried to forget what I thought was a dream.'

Then ten years had gone by. Faster than an eyeblink to Yui, who had emerged in the summer of 1923. In time for the earthquake. In time to meet Chiyo.

'Do you ever wonder why we were sent here?' she asked. 'Why the passage opened for us that day and no one else?'

'I tried to forget about it, until we found each other,' Hiro said. 'But yeah, of course I do. Time travel … it's from comic books, isn't it? It's not something that happens.'

'Maybe it's happened before, and will again,' said Yui. 'Maybe there are time travellers all over the place, and no one tells each other because they're scared they won't be believed.' She leaned back on her hands, the grass icy and sharp beneath her palms. 'I wonder if Eomma and Father believe us. I tried to warn them about the earthquake.' She thought sadly of the deaths they had witnessed, how she had failed to save anyone.

Hiro looked sideways at her. 'Did it work? Warning them?'

'I couldn't leave Tokyo. I was still looking for you.'

It had been months since that terrible day on the first of September, of chaos and fire and the following bloodshed. Sometimes it seemed far away, a long-dead nightmare, and the honest labour of the farm was all that was real. But there were still nights Yui jumped awake, drenched in sweat, seeing the dead after the firestorm, the collapsing bridge, the crumbled remains of the Asakusa Twelve-Storey Tower.

Chiyo whimpered in her sleep, too. Even Hiro gasped awake at times. Yui doubted the horrors would ever fade from living memory.

'What's going on with that tree down there?' Hiro asked, pulling her from her thoughts.

There were many trees scattered about the farm, but Hiro wasn't indicating the apple tree orchard nor the small copse near the barn that shielded them somewhat from the wind. Hiro was staring at a tree not far away. The thick trunk had gone, replaced by something black.

An archway. A passage big enough for people to enter in single file.

Was that the wind, or was it a whisper? Goosebumps sprang on Yui's arms beneath the thick wool of her coat, a shiver that had nothing to do with the chill shuddering through her.

'I can hear someone whispering to me,' Hiro said, swatting near his ear as though waving away a mosquito. 'They're … talking to me. But I can't hear what they're saying.'

'It's like the last time.' The siblings looked at each other. Certainty filled her. She didn't know *how* she knew, but it was as natural as hunger or fear. 'They're telling us to go back.'

When Yui had been searching for Hiro, the weather as hot then as it was cold now, something had whispered to her, the words unintelligible, but she had been so focused on finding her lost brother she hadn't paid it much attention. Now the voices beckoned to them both, the tree offering a way … back. She couldn't hear the exact words, but she could feel them, rippling across her skin like mist.

'We'll go back to 1995?' Yui asked, as if Hiro would know any more than she would.

'I think so.' Hiro rose to his feet. 'Yes, I think that's what this means. It's a way back. Just like the statue that brought us here.'

'But …' Yui's mind was awash with possibilities. Would it take them home? Or even further into the past? And did she even want to go? How would they adjust, with Hiro going back ten years older than when he had arrived?

She thought of going back to her life in 1995. A warm room to sleep in. A fridge. TV. Convenience stores. A normal job, not manual farm labour. No grandmother.

The wind whipped around them, beckoning them forward. Yui could almost feel hands pushing at her, or were they pulling? Hiro swayed on the spot as though fighting the invisible forces, too.

'I can't leave,' Yui said, taking Hiro's hand. She knew it in her heart. It didn't matter that life in the future was more comfortable, more certain.

'I barely remember life back then,' Hiro admitted. 'Well, not *back then*, but you know what I mean. I spent so much of my life being told it was a dream or a lie. And from what you've said, it sounds hectic. Shops that are open all night with electric lights? Thousands of people? Trains?' He plonked himself on the hill. 'Nope, I'm staying here.'

'Me, too.' Yui sat beside him, and although a small part of her ached for the easier life she remembered, she felt satisfied here with Chiyo. Complete.

She would rather face the difficulties ahead with Chiyo than head back home without her. A life without Chiyo was no life worth living. And, of course, she wanted to stay with her brother.

'I think they heard us,' said Hiro.

Sure enough, the whispers were fading, the wind dying to its normal strength. The snow stopped whipping about them so much, falling in a gentle way again. Yui and Hiro turned their backs on the strange tree and its passage, and though they couldn't hear it, Yui imagined it closing, the passage leaving them here forever.

Yui didn't mind. In fact, she gave her brother a grin. Hiro gave a tired smile, too, and they watched the stars pinprick in the sky as they struggled to peek through the clouds.

CHAPTER 21

Winter was rough.

All her life, Chiyo's winters had been spent huddled with Eomma and Father in their home, feeding the fire and eating soup. It didn't snow much in Tokyo, and their terraced house had sheltered them from the worst of the wind.

Nagano's winter, though, was unbearable. Icy air stabbed Chiyo's cheeks like knives whenever she stepped outside. She felt she was never warm enough, even when she wore several layers or soaked in a rare bath. Without the usual farm work, they worked on insulating the barn and the house, washing, mending, and preparing meals. They looked after the chickens, too, making sure they were laying eggs regularly and that they were warm enough. Chiyo was growing rather attached to the little creatures, but it was Hiro who fed them. Once she even came across him singing to the chicken he had named Luigi.

'What a funny name,' she said with a giggle. She'd never heard of anyone called Luigi.

'It's Italian,' he said wisely. 'Come on, let's make sure Momo gets enough seed. She's always being bullied by the others.'

It was nice working alongside Hiro. He was always kind to her, saving his grumpiest moments for Grandmother or for Yui. She still couldn't forget that he had called her his sister. It was a bittersweet feeling that made her warm inside.

'How's your friend? San-ichi?'

'He's good. He's all right. His family are angry, but he didn't even mention me.' He pursed his lips like he was ready to kiss someone, but it was a look she knew meant he was contemplating something. 'He isn't mad at me, even though he should be.'

'It could have been way worse,' she said kindly.

'Yeah, he could've lost a limb or something. Now he can just pretend not to hear his sisters when they're shouting at him.'

Yui had been quiet after that night she had watched the stars with Hiro. Chiyo was glad Yui still had her brother. Hiro might be wild at times, but he had helped protect them during their long journey to Nagano. She was proud to think of him as her brother, too.

Grandfather, generously, provided them with a *kotatsu*, a low table with a blanket they could all sit around. It was heated with charcoal in the middle and was deliciously toasty beneath.

'Oh, this is heavenly,' said Eomma as she slipped under it. Her health had been getting worse lately, exacerbated by the cold weather. Bliss crossed her face as she settled beneath. 'Come here, children.'

They were hardly children, but no one complained as Chiyo settled in beside her mother, Yui on her other side. Hiro slipped in beside Yui.

His mouth dropped open. 'Wow, it's so warm.'

Father got in on the other side, the charcoal-powered heat in the middle providing amazing comfort. Chiyo found her eyes drooping as she cuddled up to her mother like she had when she was a little girl.

'My darling,' Eomma murmured in Korean, stroking Chiyo's hair. Delight swept through the young woman. She so wanted to tell her how she felt about Yui, but she didn't know how her parents would react. Grandmother still hadn't forgotten her plan to marry Chiyo off, though she'd admitted that survival through the cold winter came first.

She kept her mouth shut. If Eomma and Father reacted badly, Yui would have nowhere to go. They thought of her as a second daughter and of Hiro as a son. She didn't want to spoil that.

'Thank you for the gift. It's wonderful.' Chiyo bowed low to her grandparents later in their kitchen. Their own living space had a small stove connected to their chimney, and it was much warmer in here. Chiyo was glad to be helping prepare the meals so she could spend time in this warmer space.

'It was expensive,' Grandmother grumbled.

'It's worth the price if it keeps you warm. They can't work if they lose toes to frostbite,' Grandfather reminded his wife, who shuffled off, grumbling. Chiyo watched her go, noting the aged bend in her grandmother's back, and wondered if she had ever felt joy and love in her life, or whether she had always been this way.

*

Short days and snowy nights seemed to last forever, but to Yui, the snow was peaceful. Their lives here, though far from perfect, were nothing compared to the horrors they had survived in Tokyo. As the new year approached, they cleaned the house and the barn to ward off evil spirits and prepare for a fresh start in the coming year.

1924 … not 1996. Yui and Hiro hadn't spoken of the passage they had seen that star-filled night, but they both knew it had been an invitation to the future. Whatever force, magic, or spirits had sent them here to the past, it was where they both wanted to stay.

When Yui worked at Chiyo's side and held her at night, she couldn't imagine having left her and venturing back to 1995. This was her place now, every single part of it.

On the thirty-first of December, they got together in Grandmother and Grandfather's house, a rare treat, to make a *kadomatsu* decoration, temporary housing for the *kami* gods to be placed in front of their home. Grandfather had even provided the materials to create a second set to place in front of the barn.

The barn itself didn't feel much like a home, but it was a safe place to sleep, and the charcoal-powered *kotatsu* was a lifesaver. With Hiro and Father's hard work insulating it, the boxes and sacks of food stores, the many blankets and clothes, sometimes it could even be described as cosy.

'There.' Grandmother expertly bound straw rope, completing the *kadomatsu* decoration. There were twin ones, representing male and female. 'We'll set these in front of the house.'

A blanket of white covered the farm now, and Yui's breath fogged before her. Chiyo asked Grandmother if she could make something hot to drink, and soon they were all sipping steaming barley tea.

'Spring will be here in no time,' Grandfather said cheerfully. Yui could count the freckles on his wrinkled hands. 'The cherry blossoms will bloom, and it'll be time to harvest the vegetables.' His expression darkened. 'It's always a difficult time, you know. Winter.'

'Shigeru died around New Year,' said Grandmother. It was the first time Yui had heard her say Chiyo's uncle's name aloud. 'That damn fever.'

The atmosphere frosted over, and no one said anything for a while, everyone finding something to do to keep busy. Had Grandmother's bitterness been born from Shigeru's death? Chiyo had told her about the letter they had sent to Tokyo, lamenting the fact their *better* son had died young and unwed.

'We are very grateful you've let us stay so long,' Eomma said, speaking in front of Grandmother, which was rare. Yui risked a glance at the old woman, who gave a disapproving sniff, as though Eomma had let slip a horrible swear word.

Eomma looked more and more exhausted these days, often complaining of stomach aches and heartburn. She didn't eat much, even the small portions they had to share.

'We should take her to a doctor, Father,' Chiyo whispered one evening. Eomma was already asleep, her face pale. The air outside was still but freezing. Father rubbed his hands together, casting a worried look at Eomma. He tucked the blanket up to her chin and she mumbled something in her sleep, the line between her brows deepening as she shifted.

'There's a doctor in town,' said Hiro. 'Tanaka-sensei. The one who helped after the accident.'

'Doctors cost money,' Father said quietly. 'But if she gets worse, I will.'

Father had found a job at the local silk factory, bringing in some extra income that even Grandmother couldn't sniff at. He mostly used it to spruce up the barn and buy food, though he said he was putting some of it aside and saving it up. Every now and then he treated himself to a bottle of sake, which the family agreed he thoroughly deserved.

'I'll go and get some water from the well.' Yui rose out of the *kotatsu* and winced; without the blanket's delicious warmth, it was like jumping into the lake. A shiver ran through her, but the thought of fresh water to heat up for a bath kept her from snuggling back beneath the heated table.

'I'll come with you,' Chiyo said, sending a wave of happiness through Yui.

The walk from the barn to the house was a short one, the air dry and cold. The *kadomatsu* decorations greeted them outside the quiet house. Chiyo slowly slid open the door and they both stood in the entranceway, bending to remove their shoes.

'He's a good man, and he'll look after Chiyo-chan.'

They froze, listening.

'I suppose,' Grandfather grunted.

'She can't keep staying in that barn with her parents and a man who isn't her husband. They've been here for months now, sleeping there like animals. It's embarrassing. The neighbours talk.'

Grandfather mumbled something they couldn't hear.

'When the spring comes, I'll talk to Saburō's family,' said Grandmother in a finalistic tone. 'Saburō has already spent a lot of time with Chiyo-chan. He will look after her.'

Yui and Chiyo exchanged grimaces. Grandmother wasn't going to let this go.

Chiyo put a reassuring hand on Yui's shoulder, then called out, 'Sorry to disturb you,' and slid open and closed the front door, as though they had only just arrived.

Her grandparents acted the same as usual, Grandfather kind and welcoming, Grandmother stony-faced and judgemental. They said nothing about what they'd heard, but Yui felt Grandmother's stare on the back of her neck like two red-hot pokers.

*

Winter was endless, snow falling even in March. They had to be stricter than usual with their food portions, but it also brought thick stews and soups. Father had bought a pot, and after heating it on the house's fire, brought in a terrific feast that they ate together at the *kotatsu* table. It was a rare thing to see Eomma smile so much.

Yui lost count of the days, instead taking each snowy, biting cold day as a new challenge, a mission to feed her family's bellies and keep them warm. When she and Chiyo walked the length of the farm, snow crunching beneath the Western-style boots Father had bought for them, Yui told Chiyo about the passageway that had opened for her and Hiro.

'A passage?' Chiyo gasped.

Yui nodded. 'Hiro saw it, too. I think it was a way for us to get home, but we decided to stay. I'd never leave you behind.' She glanced towards the farm, and seeing no one, pecked Chiyo on the lips.

Chiyo eagerly returned the kiss, and warmth swept through her. 'I wish we could go somewhere,' Yui groaned against her. 'Just you and me.'

'Hiro talked about a hot spring a couple of kilometres from here,' said Chiyo. 'A natural one. Where we can see monkeys. They bathe in the water like humans.'

It sounded nice, but it sounded more like something Eomma needed. The thought of Chiyo's glistening form inside a steaming hot spring sent a different kind of heat rippling through her.

Their trysts were few and far between, but Yui cherished them. In the moment where she and Chiyo united, their bodies pressed together as they tasted each other, all worries were swept away. When Chiyo's scent lingered on her lips, or her body writhed beneath hers, in that moment of ecstasy between life and beyond, Yui felt immortal.

And in the times when they could do nothing but walk the fields or work hard together, Chiyo's very presence was a gift she was determined never to underappreciate.

*

Winter yielded to spring, and Chiyo's mother only grew sicker.

The snow melted and work began on the farm again, but by now Eomma struggled to get up in the morning. When she did manage to get outside and do work, her movements were sluggish, she tired easily, and often she would hold her stomach when she thought no one was looking, pain on her face.

'Just stay here today.' Chiyo kissed Eomma's brow, trying to hide her worry. 'Under the *kotatsu* blanket. That's right. Me and Yui will take care of everything.'

It was back-breaking work, but it brought Chiyo satisfaction to know the farm would soon be flourishing again as spring thrived. 'Look,' she said to Yui. 'The cherry blossoms are starting to bloom.'

They were just tiny buds right now, but delight swept through Chiyo at the sight of the little pink flowers. Winter was beautiful, in its way, but it was also cold and dark and unforgiving. It felt like such a long time since Chiyo had last seen cherry blossoms. On the Sumida River back in Tokyo, they bloomed all down the riverside in early spring. That had been before everything had happened. Before she had met Yui.

Worry for Eomma wormed through her, but she put her negative emotions into working hard, rolling up her sleeves and tilling the fields like Grandfather showed her.

'Good morning, Chiyo-san,' said Saburō, morning frost crunching beneath his boots as he approached. With the cold winter, there hadn't been much to do on the farm, and Chiyo smiled as he walked up to her. They worked together, the three of them, Yui strangely quiet. Chiyo wondered if Grandmother had brought up the matchmaking idea to Saburō's family yet. As they walked, his fingers lightly brushed hers. It was a gentle gesture, but she felt none of the heat that came from Yui's touch. When Saburō caught her eye, she smiled uncomfortably and tucked her hand into her coat pocket, looking at the mountains on the horizon.

That night, Chiyo woke up to a strange sound. She sat up, frowning into the dark, not sure what she was hearing. It was just outside.

Again. Retching.

Chiyo left the warmth of her bed and found Eomma outside, bent over and spitting into the grass.

'Eomma,' said Chiyo, her heart breaking as she rubbed her mother's back.

Eomma wiped her mouth. 'Chiyo-chan, I'm sorry for waking you up.'

'No, no.' Chiyo held her mother carefully, hugging her close. She felt so thin now. She wrapped the shawl tighter around Eomma's shoulders. She glanced down and saw there was blood in her vomit. Her stomach sank.

The next morning, she told her father in the early hours to get a doctor to come. 'Eomma isn't getting any better,' she whispered to him as he got his jacket.

'I will today,' he promised.

That afternoon, a rickshaw pulled by a man in a straw hat arrived on the farm, a serious-looking older man with glasses clambering off. Chiyo recognised him as the doctor who had helped Hiro's friend that day of the accident at the smithy. 'I'm here for Aoki-san.'

If Doctor Tanaka was disturbed by their lodgings, he said nothing about it. Eomma sat up a little at the sight of him.

Chiyo and Yui sat by her side as the doctor pressed on her stomach. Eomma's face twitched in pain sometimes and he asked about her symptoms.

'I feel sick and weak,' she said, then hesitated, looking at Chiyo.

'I'm already worried,' she said. 'It's okay. Tell him everything.'

'I vomit a lot, and sometimes there's blood in it.' Eomma winced when Doctor Tanaka prodded harder at her stomach.

Chiyo couldn't help glancing at Yui. Was medicine further along in her time? Might she know what was wrong with Eomma?

She isn't a doctor, Chiyo reminded herself.

'What's the matter with her, sensei?' Chiyo asked. 'What will make her better?'

Father came home just then, announcing his arrival with a forced cheerful *'tadaima'*. He bowed to the doctor when they saw each other.

'Might I speak to you outside for a moment, Aoki-san?' said Doctor Tanaka.

'Stay here,' Yui whispered, rising. Needing to speak to him alone couldn't be good news.

Chiyo stroked Eomma's brow, her heart tight with worry.

CHAPTER 22

Yui stepped into the cold early spring air and edged around the barn until she heard lowered men's voices.

'It is hard to pinpoint the problem myself,' the doctor was saying. 'But I suspect it's serious. You said it's been getting worse?'

'For months now.' Father sounded stressed and tired. Yui couldn't see him, but she imagined him closing his eyes, fighting to control his emotions. 'Is she going to ... to be all right?'

Doctor Tanaka said nothing. 'I can't tell,' he said finally. 'But you might want to go to Nagano City for treatment at a hospital. They can do more tests.'

Father sighed. They didn't have the money for a hospital, and Eomma didn't want to move. Nagano City was days and days from here.

'Will it help?' Father asked.

The doctor went quiet again.

'What can you do for her?' Father pleaded. 'Right now, today, to take away her pain? I'll pay. I have some money. Not a lot, but, just make her better. Please.'

'I can prescribe her morphine to take away the pain, though I don't have that with me today,' said Doctor Tanaka. 'What I do have with me is *kampo*. Chinese powdered medicine. Have her take it with water or tea. It won't cure her, but it might help a little.'

'And the morphine?' Father asked. 'How much is it?'

Yui leaned in, but she couldn't hear what the doctor said. She thought of Father's nest egg, what little he had managed to save while buying them clothes and blankets. Of course he should spend it on getting her better.

She sighed, watching the fields of the farm, the leaves fluttering in the trees. Then she crept back to the barn. Eomma had fallen asleep, her face peaceful at last. Chiyo looked up, a question in her eyes, but just then Father came back with some of the *kampo* medicine.

'This will help,' Father promised as he gave Eomma tea later, the medicine mixed in.

Yui looked at him, knowing he was lying.

'The doctor is going to bring morphine next week,' Father said as Eomma sipped. Every one of her movements was stiff, as though moving at all caused her pain.

'Will that make her better?' asked Chiyo.

Father's smile was full of pain. 'I hope so.'

Yui said nothing. Chiyo might not know what morphine was, but she did. It was a painkiller, nothing more.

She didn't know much about medicine, but she was sure she knew what was wrong with Eomma. In her time, they would have X-rays, surgery, ways to detect it faster. But she couldn't say it aloud. Saying she knew it was stomach cancer wouldn't help anybody.

All they could do was make Eomma as comfortable as possible.

*

Chiyo lay awake, Yui sleeping beside her. She could hear Father whispering.

'We can go to a hospital in Nagano City or Matsumoto,' he said. 'They'll be able to do more, find out what the problem is.'

'It'll be expensive,' Eomma murmured back. 'And it probably won't work.'

'It's worth a try, isn't it?' Father asked. The desperation in his voice broke Chiyo's heart.

'I want to stay here, with you and Chiyo-chan. I can't face a long journey. Let me stay. Please? I can't … I don't want to go to a city. What if there's an earthquake?'

Chiyo swallowed, tears running down her temple and into her pillow. When she was sure her parents were asleep, she slipped past the divider separating their sleeping spaces and lay next to her mother. She listened to her slow breathing, the occasional twitch or murmur, and her eyelids grew heavy. She let herself float off in that old feeling of comfort and safety, feeling her parents nearby. Two adults who loved her. Before all this pain and sorrow.

She blinked awake next to Eomma the next morning, Father having already gone to work.

A fist thumped on the barn door, Eomma stirring beside her. 'Hurry up,' Grandmother hissed through the door. 'There's work to be done.'

'Grumpy old *baba*,' murmured Yui.

'Yui!' Chiyo gasped as they quickly dressed. She glanced back at Eomma, who moaned slightly in her sleep, turning over. 'You can't say that.'

'I just did,' Yui said darkly. They stepped into the morning sunshine. This was the first real warm day for months, and Chiyo breathed in the scent of grass and flowers. Despite her worries, a small smile spread on her face.

'Come on, let's finish the work quickly,' she said. Grandmother glared at them as they hurried past to fetch the farmer's tools.

They worked hard, the exercise making them sweat, muscled arms browning in the sun. The cherry blossoms were now close to blooming. Grandfather and Saburō worked a little way away, planting cabbages and spinach to be harvested in a couple of months' time. Even Hiro was here today, the three men working hard to take advantage of the spring sunshine.

The mountains in the distance were still speckled with snow, a beautiful sight. 'Yui, tell me more about the future,' said Chiyo as they worked. She needed something, anything, to take her mind off Eomma.

Between laboured breaths, Yui told her of a Tokyo with skyscrapers, gift shops, and vending machines. A world where people flew between countries in commercial aeroplanes and played electronic games, and food was easy to come by cheaply.

It sounded like a whole other universe, a future thousands of years away, not mere decades. Chiyo listened to Yui, enjoying the lilt of her voice, her mind's eye filling with utopian fantasies.

Hiro helped them on the farm most days, though often he disappeared for the day, sometimes overnight. Chiyo supposed she couldn't blame him for not wanting to sleep with them in the barn, but she wished he would stop getting into trouble with Grandmother. If he didn't work hard, he could be sent away.

'She won't kick me out,' Hiro reassured her when she tentatively mentioned it to him in the chicken coop. 'I gave her some money today.'

Chiyo blinked a few times. 'Oh. Really?'

'Yep. The old bat can't complain when I'm bringing in cash. I didn't give all of it to her, though.' As he spoke, he pulled out an envelope thick with notes. Chiyo stared at it, wanting to ask where he got it, but decided not to. Yui would interrogate him.

It was Eomma, though, who asked when they went to see her in the barn. 'Hiro? Where did you get that money?'

'I earned it, Eomma.' He knelt in front of her.

'You earned it?' Doubt crept onto Eomma's face. 'You didn't … ?'

'I promise I didn't steal it,' said Hiro, looking hurt. He looked suddenly younger. 'I'm going to buy you some medicine with it, all right?'

Eomma sniffled, Chiyo cuddling into her and putting her arm around her. She understood. She was touched, too.

True to his word, Hiro gave Father some of the money so he could get some morphine. Eomma still refused to travel to a city hospital, though. It was wonderful to see how the new medicine put her at ease, the stress melting from her face as the pain faded. The evenings when they sat together, a hearty stew on the table and a pack of cards or board game between them, Yui laughing at her side, were pockets of heaven Chiyo clung to.

*

Eomma ventured outside one morning while the frost was still melting, remnants of it glittering on the grass. Her movements were slow, and she winced in the sunlight. 'Are you girls almost finished? I'm sorry I couldn't help.'

'How are you feeling, Eomma?' Chiyo asked.

Eomma was pale, the bones in her face more prominent than before. But she glanced around in delight. 'Look at the cherry blossoms, Chiyo-chan. They're blooming.'

'It's your favourite time of year, isn't it?' said Chiyo, remembering. 'We used to walk along the Sumida River, and the petals fell onto our hair.'

'Let's go for a walk.' Eomma took her hand. 'You, me and Yui-chan.'

The three of them walked, one woman on each side of Eomma, helping her along. They wandered past the chicken coop, where the birds' clucking reached them, then away from the fields and fences and a little way up a hill, where more cherry blossom trees waited. The pink-white ceiling shielded a space of grass, the flowers' scent perfuming the air. Yui laid out a blanket and they helped Eomma lie down. Her face twinged in pain.

'How does it feel?' Yui asked when Chiyo went off to get Eomma some *kampo* medicine.

'Yui-chan, it's like knives in my stomach,' Eomma whispered back. 'I … I don't think I have much time left.'

'Don't say that,' said Yui, her words making her feel cold and lonely. 'Please. Chiyo-chan needs you. So does Father.

I do, too. You're like the mother I never had.' Her voice cracked at that, and she tried to swallow the tears that burned the corners of her eyes.

Eomma's eyes were glassy, too. 'I need to tell you both something.'

Chiyo came back with *kampo* medicine mixed with water, since Grandmother was the one who had the tea. They both settled either side of Eomma.

'Cherry blossoms are like life, you know,' said Chiyo's mother. 'Beautiful, fleeting, and all too soon, they're gone.'

The women looked at each other over Eomma's head. Chiyo's brow was creased with worry.

'I know,' said Eomma softly. Her hand took Yui's, her other Chiyo's. 'I know about you two.'

Chiyo's breath hitched. Yui tensed, but Eomma didn't look angry. A soft smile was on her face as she gazed at her daughter with maternal love.

'I want you to know that you should find happiness, even in a world that might not accept you. Your father, Chiyo-chan, he has made me so happy. Even when his parents kicked him out, even when he could never get a promotion at work, he still stood by me and married me, because we were in love. I still love him, more every day.' She closed her eyes. 'I'm just sorry I have to leave you.'

'No, Eomma, don't say things like that,' Chiyo begged. 'You're going to get better.'

'The morphine will help, Chiyo-chan, but it won't cure me.' Eomma squeezed her daughter's hand as Chiyo sniffled. 'I'm only a burden to you now. Listen to me, please. The world might not accept you, but you have to stick together. Find love and happiness in this wretched world. Me and your father, we struggled a lot, never had much money, and we lost so many babies. But then we had you, Chiyo, and you're our treasure. I wouldn't change a thing.' She turned her head. 'Look after her, Yui-chan. You make her happy. Chiyo has never smiled so much since you came into our lives. I love you like a daughter, too.' She brought their hands together until they touched, resting them on her chest. 'All I want is for you to be happy.'

Chiyo kissed her mother's cheek. 'I love you, Eomma.'

Eomma's eyes slowly opened. 'The cherry blossoms, they're so beautiful. Let's stay here and watch them for a while.'

It happened sometime in the night. When Yui and Chiyo rose with the sun, Chiyo let out a hoarse cry that sent cold darkness rushing through Yui.

Father lay in a daze, staring unseeing at the wall. Eomma lay pale and lifeless in his arms.

CHAPTER 23

The cheapest casket and forgoing a formal service was, according to Grandmother, still more than was necessary for Eomma. Yui helped Chiyo clean her mother's skin and dressed her in the nicest robe they had.

It was morbid work. Eomma's cold, greying body reminded Yui of the corpses in Tokyo after the earthquake. Chiyo cried the whole time, barely able to see through her tears, but worked with vigilance, and by the time they had finished, she looked respectable.

'She's Korean. She doesn't need any Shinto rites,' Grandmother said to a priest.

Yui's fists curled. Even in death, the old crone couldn't give Eomma the respect she deserved.

'I'd like her to stay on the family land,' Father said. 'Please, Mother. There's plenty of space. Let's put her next to Shigeru and my grandparents.'

Grandmother sniffed and scowled, but eventually relented. As the body burned in the local crematorium, the flames roared on the other side of the door, invisible to them. Yui felt Chiyo tense beside her. She hated fire, now, she knew.

The urn was simple and made of clay. Chiyo and her father made a shrine inside the barn, keeping her ashes for the customary forty-nine days before a remembrance ceremony would lay her remains to rest at the family grave.

'She deserves so much more than this,' Father murmured.

The cherry blossom petals were falling now, already bloomed and gone. They fell like rain, covering the ground outside the barn in pink and white. Some landed in Chiyo's hair. Her eyes were red-rimmed.

'I can't believe she's gone. I keep expecting her to be there, under the *kotatsu*. We didn't give her any Korean funeral rites. I don't even know what they do there. Why did I never ask her?'

Her voice cracked. Yui put an arm around her, holding her close. Her heart was broken for Eomma, too. She wanted to say to Chiyo that Eomma's pain was gone now, but they felt like empty, nothing words.

'One less mouth to feed,' Grandmother said as she ambled past. 'That woman never did any work.'

Yui's arm slipped from Chiyo's shoulders as blind anger overtook her. She marched over to the old woman.

'Wait, Yui-chan!' Chiyo cried.

'Listen, you old bitch,' Yui snarled.

Grandmother was smaller than Yui, her iron-grey hair cut short, a glint in her eye. 'Go on, say what you want to say,' she sneered. 'Hit me, if you like. Then you'll have nowhere to go. Your worthless father spent all his money on useless medicine instead of saving up and getting a house. You're still living in a barn like pigs. Korean pigs!'

Yui dearly wanted to slap the smirk from Grandmother's face. Wanted to shake her and scream at her what the hell was wrong with her to have such little empathy for the woman who had brought up her grandchild and made her son happy. But she turned to look at Chiyo, whose shoulders shook with silent tears. She'd been through enough.

Yui exhaled, trying to blow away her anger. She said nothing, stepping back and glaring at the ground.

Grandmother scoffed and marched away. 'There's still work to be done. Work on the farm never ends, even when someone dies. Make yourselves useful.'

*

'Let me tell you about karaoke,' said Yui. Her hair was still too short to tie back, and the locks stuck against her sweaty skin. Chiyo tucked some of it behind her ear, her heartbreak for Eomma mingling with love.

'What's karaoke?' she asked.

'*Kara* as in "empty", like in *karate*. *Oke* is from the English word "orchestra". Music plays and you sing a song you know to it, providing the vocals.'

Chiyo giggled. 'That sounds a bit scary. Do people watch you and listen?'

'Well, the music plays out of a machine. A small box that uses electricity. And yes, people do watch and listen. But if you've all had a few drinks and everyone knows the song, it's just fun.'

'What was your favourite song to sing?'

Yui had a few. It was insane that Yui was naming songs that had not been written yet, by people who had not yet been born. 'Sing one for me,' Chiyo begged.

'I'm not much of a singer,' said Yui, her cheeks pinking.

249

'I don't mind. Teach it to me.'

She grinned. 'All right.'

Chiyo followed along as best she could, singing a song about an island with blue seas and sending love on a riding wind. Yui's voice was surprisingly sweet.

'It's about Okinawa,' said Yui. 'You know, the tropical islands in the south, near Taiwan.'

Chiyo nodded, images of a vast ocean and green hills filling her mind. 'I'd like to go there one day.'

'We will,' said Yui, setting down her rake. 'I promise. One day, we'll leave this farm behind, make money on our own, and we'll go to Okinawa. Swim in the sea with the sun on our skin. And we'll eat spam.' Her brow furrowed. 'Er, if it exists there yet.'

It was a nice dream. Yui told Chiyo that she had only seen pictures of the tropical islands, of white-sand beaches and sparkling blue seas.

'Maybe we could get a little place on the beach,' said Chiyo dreamily. 'Away from Grandmother.' She whispered the last few words, glancing fearfully around in case they were overheard.

'I would love that.' Yui stepped up to her, taking Chiyo's face in her fingers. Chiyo smiled into Yui's palm, savouring her touch. She kissed her, the sweet-smelling breeze and the sensation of Yui's soft lips on hers bringing a rush of love.

Yui broke the kiss, smiling, then glanced over Chiyo's shoulder. Her smile melted to a slackened look of horror.

Chiyo whipped round. There stood Grandmother, her jaw open in shock.

'Oh,' Chiyo squeaked.

Grandmother glared at them both, then turned and marched away. Chiyo looked at Yui, who had fear on her face. 'What should we do?' she whispered.

Chiyo's mind was in a rush. Grandmother had definitely seen what she thought she had seen. Eomma had said she knew, but Yui and Chiyo had always been careful around the old woman. And that had been no chaste kiss on the cheek that could be explained away.

Chiyo threw down her rake and ran after her grandmother.

*

Yui watched Chiyo stumble over the neatly raked dirt fields, knowing her presence wouldn't help. Grandmother was not exactly best friends with Yui, but she might show some kindness to her granddaughter.

She tilled the field for a bit, throwing her anxiety into her work, but Chiyo didn't come back. Finally, Yui threw down her tool and ran across the field too, worried about her.

She came up to the house and slid open the door as quietly as she could. The living room door was open, and Yui could just see from the entranceway that Chiyo was kneeling on the ground, fists clenched in her lap.

'I refuse to put up with this any longer,' Grandmother was saying. 'You've all been useless since you arrived to darken our doorstep, and now you won't even marry and fulfil your duty as a woman!'

'Please, Grandmother. Please don't send her away,' Chiyo begged, and lowered herself to the ground, forehead touching the tatami mat. 'Please, I'll do anything. She and her brother have nowhere to go.'

Grandmother scoffed. 'Don't speak to me of that thug. He's nothing but trouble. At least his sister works the field. But now I understand why you never married.'

Grandmother paced. Yui tensed, but a small glimmer of hope rose in her. If Grandmother kicked them out, they'd have no choice but to leave. Maybe they could head to Okinawa …

With what money? whispered through her mind.

'All right,' Chiyo whispered. 'All right, I'll do it.'

Yui blinked. Grandmother stopped her pacing, and for a moment all she could hear was the old woman's breathing and Chiyo's occasional sniffle.

'Things will be better, Chiyo-chan.' Grandmother showed a rare display of affection, taking Chiyo's chin in her gnarled hand. 'Life is difficult, especially for women. But when you hold your own child in your arms, you will understand. You're young and not bad to look at. Life can be pleasant. But it's time to stop messing around and to grow up. You have a duty to fulfil.'

'What do you mean, you agreed?' Yui demanded as soon as Grandmother was out of earshot.

'She would have forced you to leave otherwise,' Chiyo said. She looked sadly around the barn that had been their home for nearly a year. 'This is for the best, Yui-chan.'

Yui hated it, but she knew it to be true. This wasn't the nineties. Women needed … as much as she hated it, needed men. Father was drinking more nowadays, often missing work, or coming back from his shift dead-eyed with bottles of sake clinking in his bag. The farm work fed them well enough, but they weren't making money that allowed them to do more than break even. There wasn't any other work Yui could do. All she had was convenience store experience, and what use was that in the 1920s?

Had she made a mistake, staying here?

Chiyo was as torn up about it as Yui was, she could tell. Sighing, and with the privacy of the barn to shield them, she gathered her lover in a hug.

'I'll always be here for you,' she murmured into Chiyo's hair. 'No matter what happens.'

Chiyo wrapped her slender, toned arms around Yui, her shoulders shaking. Her lips found Yui's neck, small sobs bursting from her between kisses.

Despair crushed through Yui as she kissed her back, wanting to merge with Chiyo. She felt she couldn't get close enough to her.

'Yui-chan,' Chiyo murmured as they backed into the space between the divider, their small sleeping space. Yui pulled it across, concealing them, her hands shaking as she pulled at Chiyo's robe. 'Yui, they'll hear.'

'Let them hear,' Yui murmured against her lips.

Yui had stopped wondering at the *why* a long time ago, but now the question burned in her mind again as hers and Chiyo's bodies pressed against each other's. As Chiyo's sighs filled the barn, Yui supposed this was as close to heaven as she would ever get.

'If he ever hurts you,' Yui whispered to her later, 'you tell me right away.'

Chiyo nodded against her chest. 'I will.'

Yui swallowed, wanting to be supportive of Chiyo's selfless decision, but a selfish part of her wanted to throw a tantrum about it. 'I'm going to miss you so much.'

'I'm always yours, Yui-chan,' Chiyo murmured, then planted a kiss on Yui's bare breast. 'Now and forever.'

CHAPTER 24

Chiyo and Saburō were married on an early summer evening of 1924.

Yui was exhausted, and had spent the last several, nauseating days away from the house and barn when she could, hating that the only thing that brought the old hag joy was her granddaughter marrying someone she didn't even love. Yui had so much pent-up rage and ugly feelings that all she had been able to do was throw herself into farm work. Sweat had poured down her back and her forehead in the cool, early summer day as she'd tilled and planted and raked and dug, growls escaping her, flashes of Chiyo in Saburō's arms only fuelling her work. Everyone had left her alone.

Now the muscles in her arms burned, her back aching. Hiro had finally dragged her up the hillside and now they sat together, playing with a pack of cards Hiro had borrowed from one of his friends. He said he'd borrowed them, anyway.

It was rare to see him nowadays, and Yui savoured their time on the hill, even when the love of her life was marrying someone else. She understood why Chiyo had agreed, and Saburō seemed nice enough. Yui couldn't give her babies, nor the social acceptance that came with marriage.

As if having a husband made you worth more as a person.

It still made her heart ache. Part of her was worried that Chiyo would eventually prefer Saburō over her.

'She's going to go for you next, you know,' Hiro said, slapping down a card. They weren't sure how to play, so they sort of made the rules up as they went along. 'She's going to find you a husband.'

'She can try,' said Yui with a scoff. She didn't like men at the best of times, except Hiro and Father. She couldn't imagine one pawing at her in the marriage bed.

Chiyo will have to go through that tonight. Yui resisted the urge to throw all her cards down the hillside and watch them scatter.

'I got a job, *onee-chan.*' He still called her big sister, even after all this time of them being the same age. 'I'll get us some money together and we can go away.'

'I can't leave her.' The wedding would be over by now, such as it was. The sun was setting. Chiyo would be frightened, but Yui couldn't be there for her. She could only hope that Saburō would be gentle.

It made her want to throw up, even though she knew sulking about it wouldn't help. She knew Chiyo loved her. It was *because* she loved her she had agreed. Chiyo, who struggled to make decisions on her own, had jumped at the chance to make sure Yui still had her meagre home.

'What kind of job did you get?' she forced herself to say, blinking away flashing images of the two of them together. It still made jealousy writhe in her guts.

Hiro shifted. 'Just, you know. Working the stalls at the upcoming festival. And, um, making sure people repay their loans.'

She looked at him flatly. 'You're working for the *yakuza*.'

Hiro recoiled as though she'd slapped him. 'H-How do you know?'

'We're from the future, Hiro,' she snapped. 'The *yakuza* are still a thing in the nineties. How did you even fall into something like that? Are you stupid?'

'It's just some regular work that isn't farming under that bitch's control,' Hiro grumbled. 'Besides, I want to make money. Lots of it. You said we'd go away together, didn't you? When I was little?'

She looked at him, her eyes filling with tears. Anxiety and hopelessness had pummelled her for days, and now Hiro had admitted he *did* remember things from their time together in the nineties, before they had time travelled and he had grown up in the downtown poor areas of East Tokyo.

'You promised we'd find somewhere together,' he said, suddenly seeming like a little kid again.

Yui scooted up to Hiro and put her arm around him. It wasn't something she did often, and his skinny shoulders tensed a bit. After all, he was a couple of months older than her now, not her kid brother anymore.

She glanced down to the road that led to the small streets of homes that included the Ota house. It was still a little cold at night, but she felt Hiro's warmth as a breeze blew loose grass over them.

'The mafia are scary,' she said at last. 'Don't … do anything stupid. Why not work at the silk factory?'

'Let's stop talking about it.'

Yui opened her mouth, then closed it. Hiro was stubborn. She couldn't blame him for not wanting to work at the farm with Grandmother, nor toil for hours for a pittance at the factory. Besides, his work had helped pay for Eomma's morphine. 'So what do they get you to do?'

'Mostly sell stuff at festivals, though we sometimes lend money, too.'

Yui nibbled her lip. Who around here would be borrowing money from the mafia?

She thought of Father and his drinking. No, surely not …

After asking Hiro to let her know right away if Father went anywhere near a loan shark, she went down the hillside to find him. The barn held that smell of sake. She had always hated the scent of alcohol; it reminded her of her mother's drinking, and she couldn't blame Hiro for staying away when he could.

She pushed open the barn door, wondering if Chiyo's wedding had been simple and uncostly. Yui hadn't attended, but she was sure it was already over.

The *kotatsu* table sat in the corner, unused in this warmer weather. Yui moved aside a curtain to find Father lying on Eomma's side of the pile of blankets, his eyes closed and his mouth slightly open. It was over, then.

Yui's foot hit a sake jar, the noise startling him awake. He snorted and looked around, eyes bleary and half closed.

'Good evening, Father,' said Yui.

He had lost weight, almost as much as Eomma had before she'd passed. His hair was thinning, his skin leathery. Yui counted seven jars of sake around him, some tipped over, the sour smell around him strong. Had he been drinking all day?

'How are you affording all this?' she whispered. Perhaps not the most important question, but this was money that could be spent on *anything* else. She understood he drowned his sorrows, but she had sorrows, too.

She tried not to think about what Chiyo was doing right now.

Father grunted, staring sadly into space. Yui moved onto the blanket next to him, not sure what to do to help. Maybe get him some water? Her own mother had always been a ratty drunk, snapping at Yui and Hiro not to disturb her the next day when she was feeling sick and had a headache. But there were no Bufferin painkillers here. Yui couldn't buy a sports drink from a vending machine to take the edge off the dehydration.

So instead, she pulled a blanket up to Father's waist then rose to get water from the well.

'Wait.' Father took her wrist as she rose to leave. His eyes were closed again, his words slurred. 'Please, don't leave me.'

Swallowing, Yui sat on the blanket. To her alarm, Father's thin arms wrapped around her and pulled her down into a lying position.

His breath stank. She could see the stubble growing on his chin, hear his raspy breathing as he held her closer than was comfortable. Yui turned her head away from his sour breath, not sure what to do.

'Mi-Ja,' he murmured, and burst into tears.

Yui patted his shaking shoulder and gently untangled herself from his arms. He fell into a sort-of sleep, snoring and occasionally twitching. Tucking her dishevelled hair behind her ears, Yui stepped outside to head for the well.

She placed the jug beside Father and went to her own space. It was horrible without Chiyo here. But at least Chiyo was still alive.

*

For Chiyo, the day had passed in a blur of congratulations, blessings, gifts, and a thread of nerves.

Grandmother's stern face had watched everything. The Shinto priest's chanting had washed over Chiyo, and she hadn't been able to focus on any of the words as Saburō stood beside her in his simple wedding garb.

She had picked a hangnail on her thumb so much it was dangerously close to bleeding. Now the minimal festivities were over. She hadn't seen Yui anywhere. She hadn't expected to, knew Yui was still angry with her for agreeing to all this, but it wasn't like Chiyo had any choice.

No, she *did* have a choice, and she had made it. All this was worth it if she kept Yui safe.

Now she and Saburō were alone together, in a small room in his house. His parents lived here, too, and they had both warmly accepted her as she had promised to work hard for the family and be a good wife. Even though this house was nice, with heaters for winter and clean, thick bedding, she'd have given anything to be back in the barn with Yui.

They took off their clothes and slipped into their futons. Chiyo lay on her back, staring at the ceiling as her heart galloped. Now there was nothing else to do except wait. Maybe close her eyes and sleep. Maybe Saburō would be tired. Maybe ...

'Chiyo-chan.'

Her heart sank as she turned her head to look at him. Warm brown eyes looked back at her, then a hesitant gaze over the blanket over her body. 'I'll be gentle,' he promised in a whisper.

A tear fell from Chiyo's cheek, dampening the pillow as she slowly nodded.

My duty.

CHAPTER 25

April 1928
5 years after the earthquake

Father stumbled out sometime in the morning. Yui supposed she'd better get up, too, before Grandmother came banging her fist on the barn door. The old bitch just refused to die. Grandfather's health was failing, though he always smiled when he said hello to Yui. Why couldn't the old crone be the one with the failing liver and weak limbs? Was it pure spite keeping her alive?

Another busy day ahead, as usual. Yui closed her eyes, working out her to-do list in her head.

Finish the farm tasks. Sell produce at the market. Go and see Chiyo. Try and avoid Grandmother and her comments about how it was high time Yui got married. Now at twenty-seven, she was practically a shrivelled old spinster.

Yui stepped into the spring sunshine. Four more winters in Hirano had made Yui appreciate food, warmth and sunshine. At least they survived it every year.

New chickens lived in the coop, offspring of the eggs they had saved. Luigi and Momo had died, much to Hiro's devastation, but several new chickens now clucked around their little barn, faithfully laying eggs every day that they ate for breakfast.

Yui completed her tasks with practised skill, letting muscle memory take over while her mind wandered. She always liked spring, a time of fresh beginnings, sowing seeds, and twittering birds.

'Good morning, Yui-chan,' said Saburō brightly. He still came to help at the farm in exchange for fresh produce. Yui smiled back at him. For all of Grandmother's faults, at least she had chosen a kind man to be Chiyo's husband. In four years, she only had good things to say about him.

But that was Chiyo. Her sweet Chiyo.

Yui hurried through her tasks and went to the marketplace, shouting loudly at passersby about their delicious vegetables and eggs for sale, nodding or bowing to people she knew, and tucking away her share of the profits safely in a bag she kept tied on a string around her neck. Hiro might be off becoming a *yakuza* – she was sure he would be showing her his tattoo any day now – but Yui needed to look to a future. A home. Maybe now that Tokyo was rebuilding, she could move back there.

That would be a terrible idea, though.

The highlight of her days was seeing Chiyo. Saburō, after working the farm and bringing home produce as payment, had a second job at the silk factory, and often worked late into the night. Though her muscles ached and she was tired, a smile spread on her face as she headed to Chiyo's house, the day's work behind her.

'Sorry for disturbing,' she called brightly.

'Yui-chan!' Chiyo's excited call whenever she visited, even though it was every day, always made Yui grin. She found her in the bedroom, setting down a book she was reading.

'Not long now.' Yui plopped beside her. With nobody here and the paper *washi* walls concealing them, Yui kissed her lover. Chiyo's tongue slipped into her mouth and along hers, making her shiver with desire. Her hand ran down to her large pregnant belly, giving it a gentle stroke.

'Not long now at all,' Chiyo said happily, her hand landing on Yui's.

Being a wife had been good for Chiyo. Saburō was kind and patient, and never seemed to be suspicious or jealous of all the time she spent with Yui. Grandmother, for all her faults, didn't seem to have had any interest in telling him the nature of their relationship. Sometimes they felt bad about going behind Saburō's back, but Yui figured he owed it to them. Chiyo wouldn't have married him at all otherwise.

Yui would have preferred to be with Chiyo and not have to share her at all. But this was the life she had chosen when she and Hiro had turned their backs to the portal back home. It wasn't such a wretched life. Not when she could hold Chiyo, talk to her about everything, and get excited about the new life growing inside Chiyo with her.

It had taken her a long time to get pregnant, much to Chiyo's despair. Mostly from pressure from her grandmother and from Saburō's parents, who had spent three and a half years loudly wondering why Chiyo had never reported missing her monthlies. But now she was beautiful in blooming motherhood, and though the thought of her having someone else's baby made Yui ache, she still shared her enthusiasm.

Chiyo had already prepared a kettle, and Yui poured them tea while they talked, their fingers entwined. Chiyo always grew sad this time of year, the season Eomma had died. 'She would have loved a grandchild,' Chiyo had sighed when she had first told Yui the news. 'How is Father?' she asked today.

Yui stroked Chiyo's soft hair. 'I reminded him he'll be a grandfather soon and he needs to get his act together.'

Chiyo made a 'hmm' noise. 'And Grandmother? Has she tried to marry you off to any more suitors?'

'A banker from Nagano City, one of the other stallholders, and Mr Takahashi.'

Chiyo wrinkled her nose, lowering her tea. 'The Shinto priest? Are they even allowed to marry?'

'Who cares? He's about three hundred years old.'

Chiyo giggled, then held her stomach. 'Oh, he's kicking.'

They put their hands on her stomach, feeling the strong little kicks. Thinking of children still brought Yui reluctantly to the trauma of the earthquake, the many little legs that would never kick again.

She swallowed and blinked, letting the memory wash away like water.

'I suppose her options are getting limited,' said Yui. 'After all, I'm practically worthless in my old age.'

'Do you want to get married? Have children of your own?'

Yui met her eyes. 'You're the only one I want, Chiyo.'

Chiyo fidgeted, always torn between her desire and love for Yui and her guilt for betraying her husband. As far as he was concerned, the girls were best friends, like sisters, and spent away their free time crocheting, cooking, drinking tea and whatever it was friends did together for hours a day.

Or maybe he knew everything and chose not to mind.

'How is Grandfather?' Chiyo whispered.

'About the same,' Yui said carefully. 'You know, he can still work, though he's a bit slower. At least there's room

263

for Saburō and Hiro to pick up the slack. Don't worry, Grandmother won't let him die yet.'

'Death ...' Chiyo stared at the wall, stroking her belly. 'I'm scared of childbirth, Yui-chan. It's ... a lot of women don't ...' She sighed, a sound full of pain.

'The midwife isn't worried. You shouldn't be, either.' Yui kissed Chiyo's forehead, her tone full of optimism even though she had spent many cold nights alone wide awake, worrying about the same thing. 'You just concentrate on eating well and being strong. We'll all be here: Doctor Tanaka, Saburō's mother, the midwife, and me, too. I'll always be here for you.'

When Yui was on her way back to the farm, she heard raised voices. Father was slumped against the barn, Hiro before him. Hiro, who hardly ever came to the farm anymore.

'What's going on?' She ran to catch up to them. Hiro had on a well-worn Western jacket and trousers. He kept his hair longer these days, and it was tied in a topknot. He had a bruise on his face, near his jaw. The closer she got to him, the worse he looked. There was drying blood on his lip and one of his eyes was swollen.

'Hiro, what happened?' she asked. 'Another fight?'

'You haven't told my sister?' Hiro rounded on Father, who shrank from him. 'You said you'd tell her.'

'Tell me what?' Yui demanded.

'Father has borrowed a lot of money from my boss,' Hiro said, and Yui's stomach plummeted. 'I can't cover for him anymore. They already gave me a beating when I asked for more time.' Hiro indicated the purple-green on his face. He scowled at Father. 'You begged me not to tell Yui! You said you'd tell her yourself. It's been two months, and we haven't had a single sen paid back. Are you going to pay them back or not?'

These days, Father was drunk more often than he was not. Yui could smell it on him: the neglect, the sweat, the old sake. It smelt like wasted money, of a man who had given up. A scent that roiled her stomach.

'How could you, Father?' she asked, even though she knew his dwindling shifts at the silk factory couldn't possibly be paying for his drinking habit. 'No, don't answer that. I know *how* you could. You're pathetic.' Her worry for Chiyo was making her harsher than usual, but right now she didn't care. 'You're going to be a grandfather soon, and this is how you behave?'

'Yui.' Hiro looked desperate. 'I ... I really can't protect him anymore. And they won't just go for him. They'll go for you, too.'

'Me?' Yui asked.

'Because you, er, live together.'

Yui wrinkled her nose. She supposed the limited curtains and boxes that separated Father's ... *habitat* from her sleeping area made them be under the same roof, but it wasn't any choice of hers.

Hiro took her by the elbow and led her gently away from Father, who swayed, trying to lean against the barn wall but slipping down it. 'Can you leave? Go somewhere?'

For a moment, Yui imagined grabbing the little money she had managed to scrape together and boarding a rickshaw to somewhere random. The men Hiro worked for, there weren't enough of them to care about coming to look for her. Father would face the consequences on his own, but maybe that was what he deserved.

'How much does he owe?' Yui asked.

Hiro told her and she swallowed, nodding. 'Well, it isn't that bad.' It was much more than she had, though.

'It is if he can't pay it back,' Hiro said darkly.

For a moment, Yui wanted to admonish her brother for letting it get this far. She had asked him to tell her if Father borrowed from the mafia, and he hadn't. But Hiro had found an income in a world where he felt he didn't belong. And as much as she hated to admit it, he was good at it. Many people in town had heard of Hiro and the thugs he worked with. Thank goodness Chiyo's husband had never been desperate enough to borrow from loan sharks.

Chiyo. If they didn't get paid back, they might go after Chiyo and Saburō. They weren't much better off, earning a modest and comfortable living, but not enough to pay off the angry mafia. And with the new baby coming ...

'I can't leave,' Yui said quietly.

Hiro nodded. 'Then what can we do?'

He followed her gaze to the house. 'There's only one person we can ask.'

*

'I have been cursed with a bad son.'

'Yes. I'm sorry.'

'Pathetic. Useless.'

'I am.'

'You should have died along with that Korean whore of yours.'

'Yes, yes. I should have.'

266

'You should never have come here. Your brother Shigeru was a hundred times the man you are.'

'Yes. I'm sorry.'

Yui clenched her fists to stop them from trembling. Father knelt in the tatami room of Grandmother and Grandfather's house, prostrated on the floor, his forehead pressed against the mat. Grandmother sat before him, glaring down at her only living son.

'I should have died during the earthquake,' he whimpered.

After a cold bath and some tea, Yui had dragged him here to beg his mother for money. She held a paper envelope in her gnarled hand now, and Yui could swear there was a glimmer of glee in her cold brown eyes.

'And you.' The old woman's gaze lifted to Yui, who reluctantly bowed. 'You let it get this far. You let him drink all his money.'

She swallowed the retort that crawled up her throat, something she was getting better at these days. It didn't make it any less bitter.

Finally, Grandmother handed Father the envelope of money. He bowed to his mother, still bowing even as he backed out of the room, almost crashing into Yui.

'No more sake,' she said firmly as Father struggled to put on his sandals, his hands trembling. Hiro, who waited outside, counted out the cash.

'This is enough,' he said, and Yui's shoulders relaxed. She had no idea where the old woman had stashed the money, how she had even got it. It didn't surprise her that she had never offered them help to get a proper home, nor medicine for Eomma. She supposed even Grandmother knew it was better to pay off the *yakuza* than to let things get worse.

'Never let him borrow from the loan sharks again,' she said to him. 'Do you hear me?'

'I won't.' Hiro indicated the bruises on his face. 'And these are just the injuries you can see. You hear that, Father? I'm not taking another beating for you.'

Father muttered something unintelligible as Yui helped him back to the barn. The smell of him and his stumbling, groaning form reminded her of her mother. It had been years now since she had stepped through that passage and found herself here, but sometimes memories of her childhood were bright and stark as though they had happened just days ago.

'You need to stop stressing Chiyo out,' she said when she laid Father onto a blanket. She started clearing away sake jars. 'It isn't good for the baby.'

'I'll do better,' Father sighed into his arm.

'I'll believe that when I see it,' she muttered.

Outside, she felt liquid sloshing in one of the sake jars. She smelled it. The same musk as on Father, except without the body odour. What was it about this that was so great?

She took a sip. It was strong, and she coughed. Then another sip.

She guessed she could understand why people wanted to escape sometimes.

CHAPTER 26

All night, Chiyo's stomach had tightened and relaxed with more and more intensity until the buildup stopped her from moving.

'I think it's time,' she gasped to Saburō in the early hours of the morning when a powerful contraction ended. 'Get the midwife and your mother. Yui-chan, too.'

'All right. Would you like your grandmother, too?'

The distaste must have shown on Chiyo's face, because Saburō chuckled and kissed her damp forehead. 'I'll go and get them. And my mother, she has experience with this.' His eyes, always warm and kind, flicked to her stomach. 'We're going to be parents.'

Chiyo mirrored his excited smile with practised ease. She could not have asked for a kinder, gentler husband. She only wished she could return his love. He still didn't know that when Chiyo lay in her futon, it was Yui she wanted to hold close. It was Yui who made her calm and happy. Yui she thought about when Saburō touched her. Yui who felt like home.

It was Yui she needed right now. 'Quickly!' she gasped as another contraction crashed over her like a wave. Her whole body tensed as her stomach tightened, the sensation washing over her, powerful and crushing, before it descended and washed away like water.

Saburō left the house, leaving Chiyo holding her stomach. So many emotions swept through her at once. Anticipation for the baby, worry for the baby, anxiety about the pain that was surely to come. Saburō's mother and Grandmother had schooled her on what to expect.

'Just breathe,' said the midwife when she arrived. 'Long and slow. Don't waste energy on making noise. Save it for pushing.'

Chiyo immediately stopped the moan that had crawled up her throat. Saburō's mother soon arrived, a quiet, elderly woman who moved with grace.

'Where's Yui?' Chiyo moaned as the nurse moved things and asked Saburō's mother to boil some water.

'She'll be here as soon as she can.'

Chiyo no longer cared who knew of their feelings for each other. They weren't hurting anyone. She lay back, letting the midwife prod and poke her with practised expertise, focusing on breathing.

Every time another strong contraction came, tightening her whole belly and sending her to the edge of oblivion, Chiyo simply sucked in as much air as she could.

If I can fill my lungs, the pain will go away.

'It's coming along nicely.' The midwife sounded pleased as the front door slid open with a scrape. 'Do you have any names in mind?'

Saburō was not here, probably gone off to work and leaving the business of childbirth to the women. But maybe he had come back.

But it was Yui, gorgeous Yui, who stepped into the room, her face drawn with worry.

'Oh, Chiyo-chan, I came as quickly as I could. You know that old crone, she wouldn't let me go until I'd finished planting the potato rows.'

'There's still dirt underneath your fingernails,' scolded the midwife. 'Go and wash before you come near here.'

'Is there anyone around here who isn't annoyed with me?' Yui grumbled and went off to wash.

'Don't go far,' Chiyo called weakly after her. Then she breathed and squeezed her eyes shut against another contraction. This one was the most intense yet.

'Each moment is one closer to the end, Chiyo,' said Saburō's mother. 'You can do it.'

Yui stayed with her, talking to her and feeding her water, as the day progressed. Saburō's mother stroked her hair and talked to her with encouraging, soft words. Chiyo fell asleep between contractions, floating in the clouds, aware of Yui's presence, her voice, the gentle fingers that guided her to sip another mouthful of fresh water.

'Will she give birth today?' Yui asked. 'I won't go to the market, if so, Chiyo-chan. I'll stay here with you.'

'Likely today, yes.' The midwife looked tired. 'I might need your help, anyway. The other midwife is busy.'

'Of course.' Yui rolled up the sleeves of her robe. Chiyo gave a tired smile. That was her Yui. Always ready to step up and do what had to be done.

Hours slipped by, or maybe it was mere minutes. Chiyo focused on breathing, the only thing that was in her control as her womb expanded and contracted. The women kept busy, talking quietly, monitoring her progress. When the sun had passed its zenith and the air was warm with bodies, the midwife took Yui aside and murmured something to her. Yui rushed out of the room.

'Is she coming back?' Chiyo asked in alarm.

'She'll be right back,' said the nurse as she prepared clean sheets. Sure enough, Yui soon came back, and gave Chiyo a smile that didn't quite reach her eyes.

It was in the afternoon when water gushed from Chiyo, and she gasped, 'Oh no! My waters have broken.'

A surge of energy. Encouragement to push. Three tense faces down below. When each contraction hit, the women encouraged her to push as hard as she could. Exhaustion muddled her thoughts, fuzzing over her brain. She had never known such discomfort, but pushing was something to do. She felt more awake now – tired, but free of the half-sleep that had gripped her before.

Another fierce push with all she had, but nothing was happening. Chiyo's head collapsed back into her pillow. 'I can't do it,' she wailed.

'You can!' Yui said. 'We can see the head!'

'Does he … have hair?' she panted.

'Lots!' said Saburō's mother.

'When you feel another contraction, do a nice big push,' said the midwife. 'Ready?'

Breathing hard, Chiyo nodded.

'Keep your eyes open, all right? And no noise. Push when you're ready.'

The nurse's composure calmed her. When she felt the now-familiar rising of a contraction, she pushed as hard as she could.

It all happened so fast. The baby slipped out, a cry of joy rose from the women, then silence stretching on and on as the midwife moved at the speed of light, whispering orders to Yui.

Then a beautiful, perfect wail.

'You did it, Chiyo-chan!' Yui said as the midwife showed them the baby. 'A beautiful little boy. Look at him, he's perfect.'

Chiyo laughed and hugged Yui. The midwife got busy cleaning up.

'Take him,' she said, placing the baby in Yui's arms. Too soon, too fast. Yui's smile faded. The midwife rushed to the door and called into the next room, 'Tanaka-sensei?'

The town doctor came in with a briefcase and bowed to them, his face grave.

*

Yui and Chiyo looked down at the baby. He had Saburō's nose, was little and wrinkly and still covered in Chiyo's blood. Yui couldn't believe a perfect little infant had come out of Chiyo. She was so proud of her.

The nurse and the doctor talked quietly, concern on their faces, as Chiyo birthed the afterbirth. Chiyo was still breathing heavily, her face a mask of pain.

'Are you okay, Chiyo-chan?' Concern rippled through Yui. Wasn't the pain supposed to be over now?

'Here, give him to me. I'll clean him up.' Saburō's mother took the baby from Yui. 'Maybe you should wait outside.'

'But—'

'Go, please, Yui-chan. You're in the way.'

Such direct words from the usually demure woman carried Yui out of the room, to where a flurry of movement and talking could be heard on the other side of the door. Yui stood in the half-darkness of the hallway, numb shock spilling through her. What was the problem? The baby had been born safely.

Saburō showed up just then, startled slightly by Yui standing in the hallway. 'Oh, Yui-chan. What happened? Has the baby been born yet?'

She nodded. 'Yes. A boy. But—' She listened to the voices inside. Chiyo moaned in pain, spiking fear through Yui. 'Something's—'

'Maybe I should go inside.' Saburō ripped off his shoes and made to enter the birthing room.

'Ota-san, your wife is haemorrhaging. You'll need to give us some space.'

'More sheets!' the midwife called.

'She's what?' Yui whispered as Saburō stepped back into the room. He indicated for her to go into the tatami room, but she didn't move.

'We need to help them,' said Chiyo's husband. 'There are more sheets in that room over there.'

Thankful to be given something to do, Yui got to boiling water and getting new sheets, blinking back tears. What did they mean, haemorrhaging? Chiyo had seemed fine. Hadn't she?

'Keep massaging,' the midwife said to Chiyo's mother-in-law as Yui went into the room. Chiyo was pale as death, hardly moving. Yui almost dropped the sheets in shock. She looked awful.

'Chiyo-chan,' she whispered, ice-cold fear gripping her.

'Thank you,' said the midwife. 'Can you set them down here?'

The doctor was still at work. Chiyo's eyes slowly opened and her gaze slid to Yui. She gave her a small smile.

Yui was shooed out of the room. Soon, her mother-in-law stepped through, the baby boy in her arms.

'Let's get this little one cleaned up.'

Using clean sheets, they washed the baby's body, avoiding the delicate belly button and the bloody remnants of the cut cord. He fussed a little, his tiny body wriggling. Love filled Yui from her core and all the way through her body. This might not be her child by blood, but he was the closest thing. So tiny and fragile.

'And wrap him up.' Chiyo's mother-in-law wrapped a clean sheet around the baby's body until only his face was visible, tiny eyes closed, breathing softly. He was so cute Yui choked back more tears. She glanced in the direction of the room. She made to step towards it as the midwife opened the door, looking exhausted.

'Is Chiyo-chan all right?' asked Saburō at once.

'She's resting.'

Finally, they were allowed to go in. Saburō took a turn holding his new son, whose mouth was opening and searching. Chiyo lay on her side, her skin greyer than the sheets. The midwife passed them with a basket full of bloody rags.

'Doctor, what happened?' asked Saburō.

'She was bleeding too much,' said the doctor. 'But she'll be all right. She just needs to rest and eat plenty of red meat. The midwife will check her every couple of hours, and I'll stay close by, just in case.'

Yui almost sagged with relief. 'She's going to be okay?'

'We very much hope so.'

Yui took her hand. Chiyo's eyes flickered open. 'The baby?'

'He's fine.' It hurt to smile, but she did her best as Saburō gently laid their son on the tatami mat in front of Chiyo. The maternal adoration that filled Chiyo's sweat-soaked face almost made Yui break down, but she sniffled and helped off Chiyo's robe so she could feed him. He latched on right away, and all of them watched the tiny miracle. Chiyo stroked his small head with her forefinger, murmuring, 'He *does* have a lot of hair.'

Soon she was falling back asleep, her breathing ragged.

Yui risked a glance between her legs. The midwife had wrapped her in bandages, the futon and mat beneath her bloody. Too bloody.

'Thank goodness they realised what was happening straight away,' said Saburō. 'If they hadn't …'

Yui's stomach tightened. Sickness was something that had concerned her when she had decided to stay here in the twenties. The times when Hiro came back, beaten and bloody from street fights or brawls within the mafia, Yui had had to stitch him up herself when they couldn't afford a doctor.

Eomma might have got the help she needed if she had been in the nineties. And now Chiyo had barely survived childbirth. Eomma aside, they had been lucky so far. Apart from the occasional fever, and that one time Yui had scratched her arm badly on a farming tool, they had been lucky.

But hospitals were miles away, doctors uneducated compared to those seventy years in the future. What if something happened to Chiyo and they couldn't help her next time? Or to Hiro?

'Masao,' Chiyo whispered. 'That's his name.'

'It suits him,' said Saburō.

Baby Masao fell asleep soon after that, and mother and child slumbered together. Yui didn't want to leave her side, and no one protested when she settled nearby, ready to take the baby or to be there for Chiyo when she woke up.

Saburō stayed, too, and after a simple meal of soup, most of which they gave to Chiyo as they insisted she rest, Yui settled herself in a sitting position in a place where she could be there right away if she was needed.

Saburō's snores soon filled the room, but Yui sat awake, cradling Masao in her arms and feeling him breathe against her. His tiny fingernails, his little nose, those delicate soft eyelashes ... Yui wasn't Masao's mother, but she already loved him fiercely.

Chiyo still breathed, too. Yui prayed that wouldn't end.

When Masao fussed, Chiyo was awake enough to feed him. Yui changed the hemp cloth around his waist, slipping outside in the late spring evening to wash it in the well water by starlight. The midwife and Saburō's mother had been well prepared, and Chiyo would be okay after some rest. As Yui looked up at the cloud-strewn sky, finding familiar star constellations, a smile spread on her face. Masao was going to be so loved.

*

When Chiyo felt well enough to walk a few weeks later, she and Yui strolled around the garden. They had fashioned a sling made from a summer *yukata*, though it was Yui who held Masao to her, when Chiyo agreed that Yui was the stronger of the two.

They walked slowly around the garden. Masao was asleep, his little mouth open, so warm and fragile against her chest. Yui walked with her arms around him, gently rubbing his little back. 'I've never been so scared,' Yui admitted. 'I thought you might die.'

'I thought I might, too,' Chiyo said. Yui helped her sit on the grass when Chiyo was out of breath. She was still pale, and grew tired easily, but Doctor Tanaka had assured them she would recover with good food and rest. 'I just felt so sad that our time together had ended, Yui-chan. Most of all, I was sad I wouldn't see my son grow up.' She smiled. 'But I'm okay.'

'You still need to rest as much as you can,' Yui insisted. 'I'll do anything it takes. Household chores for you. You're not doing anything more.' Grandmother could complain until she was blue in the face about farm work; Yui didn't much care.

Chiyo hesitated. 'What else do you know about the future?'

'What?' Yui asked, her heart thumping.

'About medicine. Rest. Things like that.'

'Oh.' Yui relaxed a bit. She told her what she knew, which wasn't much. 'They can do operations on your insides while you're asleep. Give blood transfusions.'

'You mean move blood from one person to another?' Chiyo's eyes were wide. For a moment, Yui saw the glimmer of the innocent girl she met in Tokyo. The pure curiosity.

'Yeah, but you have to know the blood types, I think. Otherwise, the body rejects it. Haemorrhages are dangerous even in my time.' She closed her eyes. 'Just concentrate on resting. The worst is over. I'll help with the baby, too. And Saburō's mother is around.'

Grandmother's usually stern face spread into a smile when she saw Masao. Yui had never seen her eyes crinkle like that, the maternal pride on her wrinkled face. She almost looked kind.

Yui already knew that if the old woman treated Masao harshly, Yui wouldn't be able to hold her tongue. But something about Grandmother's pride told her the old woman already loved Masao nearly as much as Yui and Chiyo did.

CHAPTER 27

Grandfather passed away in late March the following year. Peacefully in his sleep, Grandmother said.

His body was cleaned, given Shinto rites, and cremated. Grandmother and Father solemnly passed the remains, Grandfather's bones, between them with long chopsticks, then they were put in a box in Grandmother's house for the customary forty-nine days. After the mourning period, they buried his ashes in the family tomb alongside Eomma and his son Shigeru.

Father's eyes, red-rimmed, stared hard at the tomb as Grandmother faithfully cleaned the grave. True to his word, he hadn't drunk as much since the day his mother had given him money to pay off the *yakuza*, but he was still skinny and miserable, with sagging skin and dark shadows under his eyes. Where his hair had always been thick and shiny before Eomma's death, he was now visibly balding. He wavered on the spot, but it may have been the staggering weight of grief for his father. He was a shell of the man he had been in Tokyo.

'A good man. Too young to die.' Grandmother glared at Father as though it were his fault.

Chiyo stood with Masao, now a year old, in her arms, tears slipping down her cheeks. It was a windy day, the breeze rippling their clothes. Masao had his head lying on his mother's shoulder, his eyes half closed, not understanding what was happening. Yui stroked his soft head, then reached her arm around Chiyo. Like she was simply comforting a friend.

I wish you *would die, you old bitch*, Yui thought, staring at Grandmother.

Father still drank sake, but only on his own salary and, as Yui had made him promise, never two days in a row. Yui found a half-full bottle in his sleep space that evening and kept it for herself, needing something that would light a fire in her belly and press away the grief of the day.

Most of the time, she would take a few sips and no more, though today she drank the whole thing. She was just pouring the last few drops into her mouth when the barn door opened and Father came in, the familiar sound of clinking jars in his satchel.

'Oh,' he said awkwardly, spotting Yui there. 'I ... didn't know you'd be here.'

Yui rose, staggering a little. She almost fell over, but grabbed the divider just in time. 'Give me some.'

Father clutched his bag, pretend confusion on his face. 'What?'

'Just give me a bottle.' In this moment, she could understand why Father chose to drown his sorrows sometimes.

She accepted an entire jar, at this moment not caring how much it might have cost. They clinked their jars awkwardly together and drank straight from the bottle.

Father's face melted into one of ... not quite happiness, but relief, smacking his lips after the first sip. Yui stared at the wall, drinking with him, the atmosphere between them lingering between awkward and familiar. Yui had never had a father, and since Eomma's death, he wasn't much of one. But he was better than nothing.

They talked about Eomma, about Grandfather, about Masao's future. Mention of the coming years surfaced knowledge Yui had tried hard to bury deep until now. It was the reason she had been so startled by Chiyo's questions about the future, why now she crouched in their dark barn and sipped the pungent sake to dull her thoughts.

She knew what was coming in a couple of years' time. War and more death. A grim future for Japan.

'Goodnight,' she mumbled later, turning to roll over. The alcohol had warmed her belly, her limbs tingling as dizziness rolled over her thoughts. Father's snores soon filled the barn, and even with the alcohol in her system, Yui couldn't sleep. Finally, she couldn't stand it, and she staggered outside to empty her bladder.

Another dry, cool night. Yui rose, tucking the robe she wore for bed back over her legs, then leaned against the wall. She felt calmer, but with an overwhelming need to see Chiyo. To touch her. She missed her so much, and there was nothing at all appealing about going back into the barn among the smell and snores of Father.

She wasn't sure what time it was, but the full moon was high in the sky, illuminating the way to the Ota household. She knew the route through the farm and to the street where Chiyo lived better than she had known even her childhood streets. Cold grass crunched beneath her boots, seeming to whisper Chiyo's name with every step.

She half fell and collapsed against a tree. A drunk giggle burst from her, everything suddenly seeming funnier than usual. Was this how good it felt when her mother had drunk? No wonder Father got steamed at every opportunity. The serious things didn't seem to matter so much right now.

Her mirth bubbled away as she made her way through quiet streets. A cat streaked away, an owl hooted somewhere, and a light breeze washed over her. The wind was still cold, but the weather was marching on towards summer. Soon it would be the season of cockroaches and mosquitos, sunburn and sweat. She liked May. She wished it could be May forever.

Her dry throat prickled as she reached Chiyo's neighbourhood. The lights in people's windows were off, shadows everywhere. But Yui feared nothing as she walked with confidence to Chiyo's front door. Chiyo was always happy to see her.

The front door opened with a rasp and she whispered beneath her breath out of habit, 'Sorry to disturb.'

She slipped off her shoes and was about to enter Chiyo's room when the door slid open. Chiyo jumped violently to see Yui standing there, then covered her mouth with her hand, her eyes wide with shock.

'Sorry,' Yui whispered, ushering her into the hallway and into the empty tatami mat room. 'Are you okay? I didn't mean to frighten you.'

'What is it, Yui-chan? Has something happened? Is it Grandmother?'

'That old bag?' Yui let out a harsh laugh, the thought that Grandmother would have been the reason she'd walked all the way over here in the middle of the night suddenly hilarious for some reason. 'She'll never die. She'll live to be two hundred, Chiiiiyo …' Gravity suddenly lurched, and panic gripped her for a moment as she almost fell. 'Earthquake?' she slurred stupidly.

Chiyo had grabbed her elbow, a firm look on her face. 'Yui-chan, are you drunk?'

'Yeah. Isn't that weird?' She snorted with laughter. Chiyo's alarmed glance darted to the bedroom before she dragged Yui to the main entrance. After slipping her boots onto the wrong feet, Yui followed Chiyo outside.

'What has got into you?' Chiyo demanded.

Yui blinked, teetering on the spot. Chiyo was always happy to see her. What was going on?

'Just had a drink with Father and wanted to see you,' she said. She looked up at the stars, which wheeled overhead, back and forth. Chiyo's strong hand took her arm again and she giggled, leaning against her. 'Isn't the night sky pretty, Chiyo? Chiyooo, my love.' She stroked Chiyo's silk-soft cheek. 'I love you. Can't we run away together?'

'You should drink some water and go to sleep,' Chiyo said firmly. 'Come on. I'll make up a futon for you in the living room.'

'No.' Frustration rippled through Yui. Everything was so obvious now. She had cared far too much before. 'It's you and me, isn't it? Always has been. Hiro's off doing his thing.' She dropped her voice into a whisper, leaning conspiratorially towards Chiyo until she could see the stars reflected in her eyes. 'Saburō doesn't make you happy like I do, does he?'

Chiyo hesitated, glancing back towards her home.

'Seeee,' Yui purred. Chiyo looked so beautiful right now. She wanted to lie on the ground with her in the starlight and peel off all their clothes. Instead, she said, 'Come on, Chiyo-chan. We'll pack a bag, grab Masao, and run away.'

'You need to sober up.' Chiyo disguised her discomfort with a small laugh. 'You'll feel better when you wake up.'

'Chiyo, I feel great.' Yui stepped away from her, spreading her arms. 'It's a perfect night. I feel like doing something crazy, you know?'

'I can't abandon my family, Yui-chan. You know that.' Chiyo tried to take Yui's arm again, but she snatched it away, hurt.

'What about when you abandoned me?' Yui whispered.

Chiyo stared at her, then blinked hard, her eyes shining. 'That's not fair.'

Nausea swirled in Yui's stomach, her good mood evaporated. She felt suddenly tired. 'Knew there wasn't much hope.' She kicked at the dirt like a child. Her head swam. She just wanted to lie down and sleep. 'Sorry I said that. I didn't mean it.'

She turned from Chiyo then, embarrassed, and stumbled back towards the farm. The next thing she knew, her scratchy throat felt drier than a desert and sunlight was on her face. Something hard pressed against her back.

'What the hell?' A boot nudged her foot. 'What are you doing?'

Wiping drool from her chin, Yui squinted upwards to see a man she didn't know glaring down at her. 'You're in my garden,' he snapped as a bird twittered in the tree Yui had passed out against.

Horrified, she staggered to her feet and bowed to the man. She immediately wished she hadn't; nausea washed over her as she rose. 'I'm so sorry.' She moved away before he could scold her again, passed through his gate, and tried to get her bearings.

Her stomach swirled with nausea, the morning sunshine too bright and hurting her already pounding head. No wonder her mother had always snapped at her and Hiro when she was hung-over.

Her mother ... Yui was just like her. Drinking away her problems, making a fool of herself. Shame burned through Yui.

She knew where she was, just a street away from Chiyo's house. She ought to go and apologise, but not yet. Not when she needed a bath and was probably late for the morning farm chores.

How had she cared so little last night? About everything? It all came crashing down on her ten times as hard as before, and anxiety and guilt danced a morbid waltz in her chest as she hurried home, keeping her eyes downcast when someone passed.

Mercifully, Grandmother wasn't stomping around yet. The barn door creaked open, sunshine letting in a slit of gold onto the hay-strewn ground. Father snored in his place, not yet up for work. What time was it?

Yui wanted to lie down and pass out, but she drew water from a well and drank as much as she could until it sloshed in her stomach. Then she washed her face, grimacing as icy droplets soaked her robe. She stared at her reflection in the bucket's remaining water, pieces of last night coming together like fragmented glass. Chiyo must have thought she was such an idiot.

If it was winter, Yui might have passed out in the snow. She could have died. What a stupid, stupid way to go after everything they had survived.

'Never,' she whispered at her reflection. 'Never again.'

She gathered up all the sake bottles around Father, whether they were empty or not. 'These have got to go,' she said firmly. It was Chiyo's face that floated in her mind as she threw all the bottles into a sack and took them down to the lake. She poured the remains into the water, her stomach churning when she caught a whiff of the rice wine.

She would never drink a drop of alcohol again. She would not become her mother.

*

'You've been awfully quiet today,' Saburō remarked as Chiyo sat with him and Masao. They took turns feeding him, his little mouth opening wide for udon noodles. Though it was late spring, nabe hotpot bubbled between them.

'Am I?' Chiyo said vaguely, holding out some food for Masao to eat. He was growing well, her biggest joy in her life. He was a welcome distraction from thinking about the second biggest joy. What had been, anyway.

She was worried. She hadn't heard from Yui since last night when she had walked away from her in the dark.

'How was work?' she asked her husband, eager to listen to him talk so she didn't have to. She didn't want to mention to him what had happened between her and Yui.

She let his idle talk of his job at the factory wash over her, half listening as she hummed and nodded in all the right places, but it was Yui who occupied her thoughts. Saburō never said anything outright about her 'best friend', except to sometimes say how glad he was that Chiyo had her living close by.

'I know how happy she makes you,' he had said once. Then he had hesitated, as though he'd wanted to say more, but had just smiled and planted a warm kiss on her forehead. Chiyo didn't know how much Saburō knew about her and Yui's relationship. If he knew that when he gasped on top of her at night, it was Yui she thought of. Memories of Yui's curvy, supple body that brought her own sighs of pleasure to her lips.

'Kaasan!' Masao cried, snapping her from her thoughts.

Chiyo jumped. 'What?'

Saburō laughed. 'I think he's full.'

Masao had food around his mouth, more on the table around them. Chiyo forced a laugh and went to clean up the table as Saburō piled more cabbage into her bowl.

She couldn't bring herself to be angry with Yui for what had happened last night. She had been hurt at first, but Yui sacrificed a lot to be here with her. She still slept in that barn with Chiyo's father, still worked the farm under Grandmother's ever-scrutinous authority. Apart from Chiyo, Yui didn't have many people in her life. Certainly no one to take care of her like Saburō took care of Chiyo.

'I'm worried about Yui,' she confessed to her husband finally when Masao was asleep.

'Because she hasn't found a husband yet?' Saburō asked from his futon. 'There are a few single men at the factory. I could ask.'

'I'm not sure she'd like that,' Chiyo said. 'But thank you.'

Saburō didn't say much after that, and soon his breathing evened out. Chiyo lay awake for a while, listening to an owl hoot outside. She checked on Masao, lying next to him and gently stroking his head, taking in his chubby, perfect little face. She was lucky. She had a kind husband and a healthy baby.

What did Yui have?

After Saburō left for work the next day, Chiyo strapped Masao to her in the sling, took a bowl of the leftover hotpot stew mixed with rice, and headed to the farm. Masao's big brown eyes took in the spring sights around them, the blooming flowers, the leaves in the trees overhead. Chiyo pointed out everything to him, joy filling her when her son gave her a smile and copied words she said. For a wild moment, she imagined herself and Yui abandoning everything here and boarding a rickshaw, or even a train, to somewhere else in the country. They would raise Masao together.

But it was a dream, nothing more.

Making things right with Yui didn't have to be a dream, though.

The farm floated into view, two figures working on the field. She immediately recognised Yui and Hiro, Hiro the taller of the two, lean and more muscular than before. And there was Yui, who still made butterflies take wing in Chiyo's stomach at the sight of her. Yui rose from her work, wiping her forehead. She said something to her brother, who laughed.

As though feeling her presence, Yui looked in Chiyo's direction. Swallowing, Chiyo walked carefully through the farm paths, a warm breeze washing over her. She glanced at the neatly sowed daikon radishes, spinach, cucumbers and aubergines, a row of edamame beans and another of tomatoes before she had almost reached the siblings.

'Good morning, Chiyo-chan,' said Hiro. His skin was browned by the sun, but even in the warm weather he wore long sleeves. He gave her a lopsided smile she carefully returned. Hiro glanced between her and Yui, then said, 'I'm going to go check on the chickens,' before he sauntered off, whistling.

'Hi, Yui-chan,' said Chiyo shyly. Masao started burbling, wanting to be let out of the sling. 'He wants to walk.'

Masao was a welcome distraction, and Chiyo took her time helping him onto his feet. Yui took his other chubby hand and they slowly walked towards Grandmother's house. Even she wouldn't be disappointed to see her great-grandson if she came to check on them.

'Listen,' said Chiyo at the same time Yui said, 'Chiyo.'

They both grinned. 'You go first,' said Yui.

'All right.' Chiyo carefully helped Masao step over some fallen leaves. 'I'm sorry about the other night.'

'No, no.' Yui stopped. Masao, distracted by the leaves, plopped onto his bottom to play with them as Yui stepped towards Chiyo. 'You have nothing to be sorry for. It was my fault. I just felt so awful, so I had some drinks and ...' She sighed, running her fingers through her hair. 'I was so stupid. It wasn't fair of me to ask that of you. Especially with everything you've sacrificed.'

'What about what *you've* sacrificed?' Chiyo's voice was a hushed whisper, even though they were alone. 'Staying here in that barn, working here, never being with anyone else.'

'I don't want anyone else,' Yui said firmly. 'If I did, I would tell you.' She took Chiyo's hands. Chiyo almost pulled away, worried Grandmother or someone else might see, but she hadn't realised how badly she had craved Yui's touch until now. Yui's hands were rough from farm work, but the pressure of her fingers felt so right. Like home. 'I'm here for you,

Chiyo, and I always will be. It was a moment of weakness. I never want to drink sake again.' Her nose wrinkled. 'My mother … that's all she did. I'm not like her.' She glanced down at Masao, who was waving a leaf around. She scooped him up before he could totter over to the fence separating the path from the potato plants. 'It's you, Chiyo. Always has been, always will be. I can't be your wife, but I can be your friend.'

'More than a friend.' Chiyo hugged them both. Masao blew a raspberry between them, and they both laughed when the leaf in his hand swiped them both on their faces.

'We just need to concentrate on the future,' Yui whispered. 'Hard times are ahead for Japan. But together, we can get through it.'

Chiyo nodded. 'We always do.'

CHAPTER 28

1937
14 years after the earthquake

The years passed more quickly with every season. Grandmother was losing her vitality, though that only seemed to fuel her vitriol. Chiyo and Saburō had two more children, daughters Saeko and Yuiko, the youngest named after Yui. Each birth brought terrible anxiety to Yui, and the midwife always brought Doctor Tanaka during the labour, just in case Chiyo haemorrhaged again. The second birth went well, the third causing only minor bleeding.

'What's wrong with her face?' Chiyo had whispered on a windy night in January 1934, holding baby Saeko to her chest. 'She's beautiful, but ...'

Yui knew, but she wasn't sure how to say it. She opened her mouth, but it was Doctor Tanaka who said, 'It's a hereditary abnormality.'

'What does that mean?'

Grandmother, who had made it to Chiyo's house for this birth, shifted closer to take a close look at her great-granddaughter. 'Will she need to go to a specialised institution?'

'No.' Chiyo held baby Saeko close. 'No, we can't send her away.'

She locked eyes with Yui, who kept her mouth closed until everyone else had left. 'What's wrong with her, Yui-chan?' Chiyo whispered, tears falling down her cheeks. 'Are they going to take her away?'

'Don't listen to her.' Yui put her arm around Chiyo, watching as Saeko fussed for milk. Chiyo fed her, sniffling. 'There's nothing wrong with her. It's called Down's syndrome, I think. It means she might have learning difficulties.' She racked her brain, searching her dwindling memory of the future for what she knew about it. 'There was a boy with it at my school. He got bullied sometimes,' she admitted. 'But he was nice. Saeko needs her mother and father, just like Masao does.'

'She needs her second mother, too.' Chiyo kissed Yui, which made her smile.

Now Chiyo had a third child, a healthy daughter, and time passed so quickly that Yui could feel herself getting older, too. The farm yielded good harvests some years, poor ones others. Father did what work he could, though they couldn't often do more than break even financially. Though no one said it, everyone was thinking it: the barn on the farm was the best they could hope for in this life. The sunny isles of Okinawa, or even getting her own home, was a distant dream now. But when she could see Chiyo every day and raise her children with her, Yui found she didn't mind so much. What good would a big house on the beach be if Chiyo and the children weren't there to share it with her?

She had managed to make her space in the barn somewhat comfortable. She had relative privacy, and once Grandmother was gone, she and Father would have the house instead. Even without Grandfather, the old woman hadn't let her son move into her home. There must have been plenty of space, but the crazy old bat didn't care.

In dark, alone moments, Yui thought of the future. It was now 1937, just a couple years before the Second World War would begin. She hated knowing what would happen. Hated that even though many of her memories of the nineties and what she had learned about history had faded from memory, details of the gruesome war remained stark in her mind as though she had only studied them yesterday. Looking at their rural farm that had been the same for years, it was difficult to believe the country would soon be joining a bloody world war. Japan was already fighting China, some younger men Hiro knew having gone off to fight.

Yui had quite enjoyed her history classes, when she wasn't chasing Hiro around or working or getting into fights. Japan would ally against the United States, and the country would suffer under intense bombing.

That was why she had no desire to return to Tokyo. Only twenty years after the earthquake, the city would be brought to its knees again. Thousands more killed by bombs and fires. She didn't want to be anywhere near all that.

She couldn't keep this to herself. She knew she was being distant when she spent the day at Chiyo's, helping with the children, watching the clock tick ever closer to more darkness and death.

'I've been so blessed to have three children,' Chiyo said. Motherhood looked so good on her. She had a few grey hairs now, and often looked tired, but she was happy and alive. Saburō's job was going well, and good farm food had given her a pleasant figure.

Masao, now nine years old and ready to help with some farm tasks, played with his younger sisters. He was a handsome boy, with the same shape to his eyes as Chiyo. Yui's heart always filled with warmth to see the children, and her love for Chiyo was undying. But now a dark cloud hung over her. Knowledge of an upcoming conflict she could do nothing about. It was the earthquake all over again.

After kissing the children goodbye, Yui decided to go and buy some new farming gear, a lot of their equipment old and rusted by now. Father could have gone, but she needed time away from the farm. To her surprise, Hiro offered to go with her.

'All right, what is it?' he asked her as soon as they were away from the farm. 'You've been quiet for weeks.'

'I haven't *seen* you in weeks.'

Hiro always wore nicer jackets now, typical *yakuza* attire. He seemed to have climbed the ranks, though Yui had decided years ago the less she knew about it all, the better. She knew he still beat people up to get back their debts. True to his word, though, Father hadn't got involved with loan sharks again, and the barn hadn't smelled of sake in years now.

The truth about the war threatened to burst from her, and she didn't want to burden Chiyo with the worry. 'I can tell you, if you don't tell anyone else.'

Hiro raised an eyebrow. 'Well, I'm intrigued.'

They clambered onto a rickshaw that would take them to the larger part of town. Last year, the town of Hirano had ascended to city status and was renamed Okaya. More people lived here now, and the bustling crowds of people reminded her irresistibly of Tokyo during its zenith.

'In a minute,' she murmured, aware of the rickshaw driver who jogged tirelessly before them.

Once they were in a crowded market, looking at wares and it was too noisy for anyone to overhear, Yui said, 'It's about Japan's future.' They hadn't much spoken about time travel, not since they had turned their backs to the portal all those years ago. 'Yeah, it's ... bad.' Her eyes fell on cheap jars of sake. She was tempted only for a moment before she turned back to Hiro. 'Come to the farm later tonight and I'll tell you.'

That evening, Hiro met Yui under the stars. Here, away from Grandmother, from Father's sadness, Yui could breathe and talk freely.

She told Hiro what she knew. Tokyo being peppered with bombs, leaving the city in ruins and tens of thousands dead, maybe more. The sad fates of Hiroshima and Nagasaki. Japan losing the war and thousands of its men, leading to a poor economy and food shortages for years afterwards.

She didn't like the gleam in Hiro's eye when she mentioned the atomic bombs. But she ignored it and kept talking. The worry and burden of the knowledge of the future was easing with every word. It spilled out of her like a river, gushing forth with no dam to stop it.

'When will this happen?' Hiro asked, leaning towards her. 'Do you know?'

She thought about it. 'The war ends in 1945, I'm quite sure,' she said. 'It begins ... um ...' She didn't have all the details in front of her. Her memories of school, so long ago now, were hazy as she tried to focus on the details, and self-doubt nibbled at her. 'I'm not sure. But ...' The thought made her cold. 'They're going to make the men fight. All of them.'

Hiro would be conscripted, especially near the end when things got dire. But even worse was Chiyo's son.

Masao would be a teenager by the 1940s. Not yet eighteen, but maybe that didn't matter. Yui felt her breathing constrict. She put her hand on her chest, feeling her heart fluttering with terror.

'How can I stop this?' she whispered. 'They're going to make Masao fight. And what about you? Will they force you to go to war? You'll both die.'

Hiro came up beside her, putting his arm around her. 'Yui, it's okay,' he said in a surprisingly gentle tone. 'We'll think of a way out of this.'

Yui couldn't help it. Her gaze moved to the tree, the one that so long ago had offered a way out to them. But there was no passage, no whispers on the wind inviting them home. They had lost their chance at returning to the future that night long ago.

Had they made a terrible mistake? Yui had been so focused on the now that she had almost forgotten the difficult years coming up for Japan. The earthquake had been just the beginning.

'So, the war ends in 1945,' said Hiro. 'It must be starting soon, then.'

Yui racked her brain. Her heart rate slowed. Surely the Japanese government didn't make children as young as sixteen go to war? That seemed too young, but ...

'What if Masao becomes a farmer or a doctor?' Hiro suggested. 'There must be ways to not fight, right? Saburō's working in the factory, so they didn't make him fight the Chinese.'

'Well, what about you?' Yui asked, giving him a hard look. 'You're in your late thirties, like me. They might ask you to fight.'

'My boss has ways of making stuff like that not happen,' Hiro assured her. 'He uses bribes and all kinds of things to protect his boys. I'm safe. I think.'

Yui swallowed, wondering if they were being cowardly by trying to work out how not to go to war. But although she didn't know everything about the upcoming conflict, she knew it was the most famous war in the world. Japan was at war right now, Doctor Tanaka's son off to fight in China, but that hadn't entered Yui's mind because her children – she thought of Chiyo's children as hers, too, privately – were still so small.

'Tell me more about this bomb,' said Hiro quietly.

She looked at him. 'I don't know much about it, but I know that thousands died,' she said quietly. She blinked. '*Will* die.'

There were people right now all over the world who would be dead in the next few years. Europe, Tokyo, Nagasaki, Hiroshima. More in China. America, too. And she couldn't do a thing about it.

Why were we sent here? She wondered for the millionth time.

'I wish I didn't know it was coming,' she said, sniffling. 'There's nothing we can do to stop it. I wish I didn't know anything.'

'What we can do is prepare,' said Hiro. 'Let's grow more potatoes, they're always hardy. Store more food, get us prepared for what's coming. That's how we can make a difference, Yui. By making sure the people of Okaya are fed.'

His words bolstered her. He was right. They couldn't stop a war, couldn't stop the carnage, but they could protect their community and family. Could make sure Chiyo and her husband and children, Doctor Tanaka and his family, the midwives who had helped Chiyo over the years, and even the people who lived around here and depended on their agriculture could get through the next tough few years.

Hiro asked about the bombs again, and Yui, disturbed by Hiro's persistence, told him what she could. 'I remember seeing a picture of it in school,' she said, thinking back. As she talked, the memories came back more clearly, and the image floated in her mind's eye. 'They call it a mushroom cloud because of its shape. It looked awful.' Even just the memory of that terrible photograph filled her with emptiness. 'The Americans will drop them on those cities to make Japan surrender. It will work, but ...' She shuddered. 'All those people, dead. Do you think it's worth travelling to Hiroshima and Nagasaki? To try and warn them?'

Could they somehow get people to evacuate? But that hadn't worked when she had tried to warn people about the earthquake. And the only way she'd know about an enemy attack would be ...

'They'd have us tried for spies,' said Hiro, as though he was following her train of thought. 'Imagine if people went to Tokyo, shouting about some upcoming attack from the Chinese. They'd be arrested, even if they were Japanese citizens. And people will die anyway.' He stared off into the distance. 'I want to see this mushroom cloud.'

'What?' She wasn't sure she had heard correctly.

'I just want to get close enough to see it.' There was that gleam again, the same glint of excitement she had seen when Hiro was seeing someone getting beaten up or talking about something violent. She didn't like it.

'That's stupid.' She shifted away from him. 'Why would you want to see thousands of people die, knowing you can't help?'

'I don't want to see, you know, the death. But imagine witnessing a mushroom cloud!' Hiro looked more excited than she had seen him in years. 'I bet it's amazing.'

'I bet it's horrible,' she corrected him. She didn't want to even imagine seeing it. The photograph had been enough.

'1945, right?' he demanded.

'Yeah, but I don't know the exact date.' Fear flashed through Yui. 'You're not seriously thinking of going, are you? It'll be a terrible thing to see. You'll be changed forever.'

'Well, I could go and save some people,' said Hiro. 'You know, make sure they're not in the city that year. With threats or whatever.'

'And what if you're there when the Americans drop the bomb?' Yui demanded. 'You'll die, too. And for a stupid reason.'

Hiro sulked as Yui got to her feet and marched down the hill, almost slipping on the mud from last night's rain. Hiro could be so pig-headed at times. She wished she hadn't said anything.

CHAPTER 29

Yui, Chiyo and Hiro continued to work hard on the farm, Chiyo's husband Saburō helping when he could. Farm work didn't have days off, and cool days with warm sunshine were the best conditions to work in. The adults even encouraged the children to help. Masao ploughed and planted with determined strength, his little sisters mostly playing with pots.

Yui didn't want to burden Chiyo with the knowledge of the future, so she simply told her they needed to store plenty of food, which was common sense anyway. Seeing her or the children go hungry would be worse than anything else so far.

Hiro was playing with the children, pretending to chase them with a rake. Their delighted screams filled the air.

As another long, cold winter began, the barn was full of stored vegetables, rice, potatoes, pickled vegetables, and anything else they had managed to get. It was 1941, when the war was kicking off in Japan and men were being conscripted all over the country. Yui was glad it had taken Chiyo a while to get pregnant the first time. Masao would be sixteen in the last year of the war, and she hoped he would still be considered too young to have to join up. If not ...

'How much can I tell people?' Yui wondered aloud to her brother. It was early spring. They had all made it through the winter without incident, aside from Saeko suffering a brief fever. Hearty stews and medicine from Doctor Tanaka had helped her quickly recover. It would soon be time to till the fields and harvest what they had sown.

Telling Hiro about the war was one thing; he was from the future, like her.

'I don't know,' he said honestly. 'I try not to think about it and focus on the now. The Imperial Army have been through here twice already, and no one who works on a farm or a silk factory is being made to go.'

'Yet,' she muttered.

One small bit of good news came that spring. Hiro's friend, whom he still affectionately referred to as San-ichi, got married to Doctor Tanaka's daughter. She didn't seem to mind the fact he could only hear from one ear.

'He wasn't conscripted either,' Hiro told Yui. 'Because of his ear.'

'From the blacksmith accident?' She thought back to the fire years ago, where a cigarette and coal dust had damaged San-ichi's eardrum.

He nodded. 'Can't have someone half-deaf in the army.'

The couple looked delighted at their wedding, which was a simple, happy affair. Chiyo laughed and clapped next to Yui, the children dressed in their best and playing with other town children.

'Oh, doesn't she look happy?' said Chiyo. 'She's going to be a Sanada. The same surname as you,' said Chiyo in amusement. 'I wonder if you're related?'

Yui watched the couple, talking to relatives and laughing together, in silence. San-ichi wouldn't be drafted because of his injury. The injury Hiro had been there for. Maybe caused. What if …

'Yui-chan, are you all right?' Chiyo looked alarmed.

'Yeah.' Yui took a sip of her drink. 'No, I'm great.'

*

Grandmother, for all her bitterness and seemingly immortal ways, could not live forever. Yui was ashamed to feel gladness at the old woman's deteriorating health, though it was difficult to feel guilty when Grandmother shouted at her to fetch things constantly, while at the same time refusing help.

'Grab my cane, girl. I can walk by myself. I'm not dead yet.'

'Unfortunately,' Yui grumbled under her breath, snatching up Grandmother's stick so she could rise shakily to her feet.

Yui cleaned the kitchen, chopping vegetables and readying a pot for dinner. That was all they ate, potatoes, vegetables, very occasionally some meat if they were lucky. As tired of hotpot as she was, at least they weren't starving. Yui swallowed, thinking of the upcoming years. She didn't know the war's timeline, but she knew people were already dying, being oppressed, being bombed. It was a little easier to hide here at the farm and pretend it wasn't happening, but already news was travelling in from the cities about men being drafted, countries all over the world going to war.

'What are you standing there for, girl? Out of my way.'

Yui shuffled out of the old woman's path, wondering yet again if it was just spite keeping the old woman alive.

Chiyo came by later, caring for her grandmother with dutiful diligence. At least she wasn't as venomous towards her granddaughter. Grandmother had been much nicer to Chiyo since she had her children.

The kids came by later, and though being in Grandmother's house filled Yui with anxiety, she enjoyed the precious time with the children. The youngest girl, Yuiko, deposited herself on Yui's lap, sucking her fingers, and she held her close, hoping she'd never grow out of wanting cuddles.

Grandmother let out a hacking cough, something she did more and more often these days. Yui caught Chiyo's eye, wrinkling her nose at the disgusting noise. Chiyo gave a guilty smile, trying unsuccessfully to hide it behind her hand.

1942
Nineteen years after the earthquake

The war came, though Japan, it seemed, was always at war. As the years went by, it was harder to remember a time of peace, a time of food being plentiful, and winters needing little more than an extra blanket at night. Yui had already passed forty, considered a wasted spinster by the villagers, not that she cared. Chiyo, the children, and Hiro were warm and well, and that was all that really mattered.

Grandmother got worse, her old age catching up to her. Soon she couldn't walk by herself, and to her own disgust, ended up bedridden as her strength failed by the day.

Father was a shell of a man, working his days at the factory as well as he could in his failing body, eating mechanically, passing the days reading by lamplight in the barn and sleeping most of his days off. He didn't drink anymore, but it didn't matter.

'Katsuro,' Grandmother croaked. She was in her futon, the covers up to her chin. An icy wind howled outside, a snowstorm, and Yui was only thinking about the fence outside the farm, its ominous banging whenever the wind blew, and how it would probably be knocked over if nobody went to set it down.

Father looked older than he was. At only sixty-three, he looked older than Grandfather had been when they had reached this farm nearly twenty years ago.

'Yes, *ofukuro*?' Father crouched beside her bed. Grandmother's skin was grey and wrinkled, that constant scowl on her face. Yui brought tea, keeping her eyes averted from the dying woman. Her breath fogged before her even with the kerosine heater. On this dark January day, they had agreed it was worth the expense to switch it on.

Hope shone in Father's tired eyes when his mother called his name. Some last words of encouragement, maybe? Thanks for bringing in some money, however pitiful, and for bringing strong young adults to help with the farm?

Yui hoped Grandmother would find it in her heart to show Father some kindness. Maybe she would simply say 'thank you' before closing her eyes and departing this world.

Father leaned in close to his mother. He looked as though he was going to take her hand but thought the better of it. He knelt on his thin legs, ever a picture of an obedient, attentive son. To Yui, he suddenly seemed younger, not by appearance but by behaviour, a lost little boy hoping for a word of kindness from his mother.

'You've lived in that barn for nineteen years,' croaked Grandmother. 'Never got a house for your family, never

305

aimed for anything more. Just slogged at that silk factory all this time when you weren't drinking yourself into oblivion.'

Yui's heart sank. She had to remain quiet. As much as she disliked Grandmother, she wasn't going to disrespect her by interrupting.

Father's head bowed.

'First you leave us and the farm to marry a Korean, then crawl back to us and use our hospitality without ever a word of repaying us,' Grandmother hissed. 'Your father died disappointed in you. I am disappointed in you.'

Yui let the crazy old bat's words slough off her, as she had always done, but with every rasped word, Father bent lower and lower.

'You are a failure of a son. The only good thing you ever did was bring Chiyo into this world. Maybe in a few generations, the Korean will be bred out of her descendants.'

Yui's hand shook as she held her tea. If she were younger and brasher, she'd want to throw the hot tea in Grandmother's face.

'Then drinking and being useless, leaving the farm tilling to that orphan and her mobster brother.' Grandmother coughed into her fist, a painful sound from deep in her lungs. 'Leave me alone. I don't want yours to be the last face I see.'

Father sloped from the room, hanging his head. Yui wanted to offer some words of encouragement, but what could she say against the flood of abuse?

The wind was indeed howling hard, and the clatter of wood told Yui her fears about the fence were right. She shivered, more sensitive to the cold than she used to be. She wondered if Chiyo was all right, then decided she must be; she wouldn't brave this storm with the children.

After fixing the fence, which wasn't easy while being battered by hail, she headed over to Chiyo's. She didn't want to sit in the barn alone nor look after Grandmother anymore. Let the old *baba* die alone, she thought grimly.

'Yui-chan!' chirped Chiyo's youngest daughter, four-year-old Yuiko. 'Yui-chan's here!'

Yui pulled off her boots, snow falling off her and into the *genkan* entrance hall. The hallway was almost as cold as outside, but Chiyo had gathered the children into one room with a heater and several blankets. With their combined body heat, it was warm and cosy.

'Did you walk all the way here in the snow?' Chiyo asked with sympathy, patting the blanket as an invitation for Yui to slide in.

Masao was there too, though these days he preferred playing with sticks or fishing outdoors with his friends to spending time with his mother. But no one was going outside in this weather. Yui hadn't seen anyone in the white haze of the storm.

'Mother, are you feeling better?' asked Saeko, snuggling up to her mother. She was eight now, a sweet thing, though other children sometimes remarked on her flat nose and short stature.

'Better?' Yui asked sharply. 'Are you sick?'

'Mother had a sore tummy.'

'I'm feeling much better now,' Chiyo reassured her. 'How is my grandmother?' she asked quietly. 'Should I go over there?'

Yui hesitated. It wasn't wise to walk around in the storm, but it didn't seem her grandmother would last much longer.

'I'm not sure. She isn't well,' she said vaguely. 'She was talking to your father.'

Chiyo nodded, convinced that was enough. 'Will you stay tonight?'

Saburō still worked at the factory, once silk and now iron to help fuel the war. His trade had exempted him from conscription for now, but the storm had stopped him from coming home. He sometimes stayed near the factory with other workers. Tonight was such a night.

Once the children were asleep, Yui and Chiyo could have some rare and precious alone time together. Yui nodded, eager, and she almost forgot about the misery of Grandmother's house as they all ate together, Chiyo's potato stew hearty and satisfying, before the children fell asleep one by one, all cuddled up together. Masao, now thirteen, looked younger as he lay with his arm around the slumbering Saeko. It warmed Yui's heart to see them all together and safe, with full bellies. Not to mention with two adults who loved them more than anything.

They might have been past forty, but Chiyo was more beautiful than ever. Every scar on her body from carrying those beautiful children, Yui kissed; Chiyo had matured into a confident woman, her strict but affectionate and loving role as a mother only deepening Yui's affection for her. They held each other as the storm worsened, and when winter morning came, Yui awoke with a smile on her face.

The snow had stopped, the wind having toppled over some more fences and even torn away the wall of a house. People stood outside it, hands on hips and shaking their heads, bandannas tied around the men's heads as they worked out the best way to fix it. Yui gave them a small incline of her head in greeting, shooting them a sympathetic look.

Had the barn survived? Sudden fear spiked in her. Shamefully, she hadn't given Father much thought since last night. She wondered if Grandmother was waiting to scold her about it.

The farm was a mess, things they'd forgotten to pack away strewn across the snowy fields. The barn, thankfully, had survived, though Yui thought she could see a hole in the roof. She half-ran towards it and checked inside. The barn seemed smaller, somehow, than it used to, back when Hiro still stayed here, when Chiyo would hold her at night and Eomma's presence glued the family together.

Father wasn't here.

'Father?' she whispered, wondering if he had got up early and gone to the factory. She wandered over to his side of the barn. His scent lingered, a neat pile of folded clothes and his futon still rolled out. It didn't look like he'd slept in it, but she wasn't sure.

She looked helplessly out at the rough strewn field, tired already at the thought of having to clean it all up by herself. Her body was strong from years of ploughing the field, but often her back hurt. Besides, she had to check on Grandmother.

The old woman was asleep, wheezing slightly as she snored, a frown on her face even in slumber. Sighing, Yui prepared a light meal for her and put it beside her bed, having no desire to wake the woman. Then she got to work.

By evening, she had cleared up a lot of the mess the storm had caused. Arguably, they had been fortunate; the hole in the barn roof could be patched up – she would ask Hiro when she saw him, and Chiyo's husband. And they hadn't lost anything of real value. After checking the supplies in the barn and checking on the chickens – Mario the Third and Momo the Fourth greeted her with their usual peaceful clucks – she took a walk towards the lake.

She wanted to get away from here. To go travelling. But where could they go that was easier than this? Yui had taken on some shifts at the factory, too, every sen essential. Lake Suwa was frozen now, the Nagano winter still frigid and unforgiving. A small smile spread on Yui's lips as she remembered one day, five years ago, when she and Chiyo had sneaked out to skate on the lake. She felt old these days, her youth spent mostly on this farm.

A sad fate, some might think. But Chiyo made it all worth it. Sometimes they disagreed or fought, not speaking to each other for days. But they always made up with tears and kisses, whispers of apologies and chuckled private jokes.

When Yui was growing up and saw how her mother flitted from man to man, faking affection at her work in the hostess club and grumbling about how unreliable people were, Yui had assumed she herself would never find love. She had experimented in high school, sure, but caring for Hiro had always been a much bigger priority than finding a boyfriend. Or a girlfriend. Boys had never appealed much to her. They were too clumsy and rough.

But Chiyo ... ever since fate and magic had brought them together in 1923, Yui hadn't wanted to leave her side. Her love for Chiyo only grew with each passing year, every long winter, and each new challenge. Now the world was at war, and still Yui had that spark of Chiyo-shaped happiness in her life.

She and Chiyo had brought up Masao, Saeko and Yuiko together, teaching them to read, to play and to joke, to work hard and protect each other. Yui may not have birthed them, but she would do anything for the children she privately thought of as her own as well as Chiyo and Saburō's.

She wondered what Hiro was up to today. He didn't tell her much about his life, always redirecting the topic to her, Chiyo's family, or work on the farm, but she knew he was deep in the local mafia now. At least he seemed to be doing well for himself. They certainly didn't complain when he brought things to their house: fresh meat or fish, furniture, clothes.

Yui wandered along the lakeside, not minding the biting cold against her skin. At least there was an end in sight for the war. Maybe when the children were older, she and Chiyo could go and see other parts of Japan. Maybe even different places in the world. She could learn English, maybe go to Okinawa like Chiyo wanted to.

A crowd ahead caught her attention, making her walk faster along the lakeside. Some old men and a few women were clumsily trying to rope off a small area, though many women were crowded around one side.

'Did he drown?' asked one.

'The lake's frozen.'

'He froze to death, look.'

'What a waste.'

'Someone will have to tell his family.'

Her stomach growing cold, Yui slipped past the ropes and pushed through the crowd. A woman scowled, picking up a small child who was trying to rush through to see. Yui didn't know how she knew it was him before she saw the frozen body beside the lake, icicles on his beard, that sad expression even there in death.

Father.

CHAPTER 30

'I'm sorry you lost your father and your grandmother so close together, Chiyo-san,' said a neighbour.

Chiyo felt as numb as the ice around them, the ice that had frozen her father's form as he had sat in the dark. Was it suicide or an accident? Did she want to know the answer?

As though sensing her son's demise, Grandmother had been dead when they'd arrived home. Yui had held Chiyo as she'd cried, then had come the unpleasant business of preparing both bodies. They would be burned and put in the family tomb beside Grandfather.

'We'll put Eomma beside Father,' said Yui, holding the clay jar that held Eomma's ashes. 'No matter what *she* said, she was part of our family.'

'Yes, she was.' Chiyo's heart felt painfully full as Yui moved Eomma's ashes, placed in the corner before, right beside her father. Both her parents, only ash now. Both had died too young.

Masao took her hand, giving her fingers a squeeze. She tried to smile at him, appreciating his comfort.

Grandfather, Grandmother, Father and Eomma. One day, Chiyo's ashes would join her family's. Would Yui's remains be buried here, too?

'When's Grandad coming home, Mother?' asked little Yuiko, not understanding what was going on. Chiyo picked her up as Yui clapped her hands together, praying for the family's departure to the afterlife. Hiro showed up later, wearing a ragged suit. Age had made him handsome, though there was a tired look to him. At least he didn't have bruises and cuts on his face these days. Later, in whispers as Yui and Chiyo cleaned up Grandmother's home, Hiro said that the men in the mafia who hadn't been conscripted into the army were being made to do the most unpleasant jobs.

Chiyo stayed silent. Hiro had spent the last two decades working for a local thug. She didn't approve, but he was Yui's brother. And she knew Yui didn't want him to be conscripted. Yui had whispered to her last night that Japan would lose the war. All they had to do was weather the fallout.

1944
Twenty-one years after the earthquake

Two more years passed, the only change being the children growing bigger and the news of Europe's conflict and Asia's involvement trickling in. Hiro hauled home a radio one day – home being Grandmother's house, now, a vast improvement from the barn – and they all huddled around to listen to the sparse reports.

It was nationalist propaganda, telling people how noble the war effort was and how it was an honour to die in battle.

'Like samurai,' observed Chiyo. Yui snorted. She didn't think there was anything honourable about dying for some lord, any more than it was honourable to deliberately crash your plane into enemy ships or towns.

Even in the mountains of Okaya, the effects of the war were felt. They sold more food now at the market, often desperate people begging to have things for next to nothing. Chiyo often obliged, and Yui had to gently remind her that this was their livelihood, too. 'Think of the children,' she whispered after Chiyo sold a radish to a thin mother with a baby for less than half price.

'How can you be so cold?' Chiyo whispered back.

'I'm being practical. You can't always help people, not if you endanger yourself in the process.'

Hiro still faithfully took care of the chickens. 'This is Yu-Yu,' he said, holding a newborn chick in his hand, to the children's delight. 'This is Chi-Chi.'

'They're funny names, Uncle Hiro,' remarked Masao as he threw seed to the chickens. Yu-Yu flapped out of Hiro's arms with a cluck of excitement.

'They're named after your mothers,' said Hiro. 'See, Yu-Yu is the feisty one.'

Yui raised her eyebrows, but Masao was so absorbed in feeding the flapping chickens he hadn't realised what Hiro had said. Hiro caught her eye and winked.

Hiro sometimes stayed at Yui's house, a rare occurrence that she always treasured. It was one such night, a quiet evening when crickets chirped outside the windows, when Hiro suddenly sat bolt upright.

'Hiro?' Yui whispered from the corner of the room. 'What is it?'

'Shh,' he said. The moonlight touched his face, the silver illuminating his sharp features, tightened in concentration. 'Do you hear that?'

Yui turned her head, listening to the familiar sounds of chirping crickets, the wind in the mountains and … voices. Footsteps outside.

Hiro bolted from his futon, quiet as a cat. Heart thumping, Yui got out, too, and watched from the window as Hiro stepped outside.

Sure enough, dark shadows were moving outside the chicken coop. Another outside the barn. Her heart in her throat, Yui watched as Hiro kept to the shadows, finally jumping out at the man near the barn.

His yells filled the air as Hiro wrestled him into a headlock, both men struggling. The other two ran across the field towards where the pair struggled. Yui yanked on a robe and stepped outside, too, though she wouldn't be much help. 'Hiro!' she called in warning. The men were almost upon him.

Hiro threw away the man he'd been holding, rounding on the other two. In the moonlight, Yui caught sight of them both – thin, pale, ragged clothes hanging from their bodies.

Hiro swung, decades of brawling eradicating his fear. One man backed away in fright as the other darted in. Several punches, though, and the man lay flat on his back.

The second backed away, his hands in the air. 'I'm sorry,' he whimpered. 'I'm sorry. We're just hungry.'

'Please,' sobbed the one on the ground, massaging his bruised neck. 'My family are starving. We didn't think you'd miss a few eggs.'

Yui held her head, pity mingling with anger. Hiro wiped at his chin. 'If I ever catch any of you anywhere near this farm again …'

'You won't! I swear!' The man scrambled to his feet and bolted, leaving his friends behind. The other one on the ground rose, clutching a bloody nose. He bowed in apology to Hiro, then stumbled off with his friend. Hiro spat on the ground in their wake, watching until the men fled into the darkness.

'They're starving, Hiro,' said Yui quietly. If Chiyo were here, she would insist on giving them food. Yui wasn't so generous, but she did feel pity for them.

'Thieves are thieves. Imagine if I hadn't been here.' Hiro wiped his brow. 'If we give away all our food, we'll have none for ourselves. None for Chiyo's family. The kids.'

'I know.' She pulled him into a hug. 'Thank you for protecting the farm.'

'No problem. It's been a while since I was in a good fight.'

1945
Twenty-two years after the earthquake

'It happens this year, doesn't it?'

'What does?'

Hiro looked at her. 'You know. Hiroshima and Nagasaki. The bombs.'

Yui groaned. 'Hiro, that was years ago. You've remembered this whole time?'

'I want to see it.' Hiro shifted closer to her. 'Not get too close, but I want to see this mushroom cloud. It's all I can think about.'

Yui picked at some grass, furious with herself. 'You've always been fascinated with violence, haven't you? Have you never grown out of it?'

She had wrongly thought being a thug would satiate Hiro's strange impulses. She remembered his look when he had beaten up the thief, how easily he had been pulled into the vigilantes in Tokyo as a youth. He didn't only participate, he *enjoyed* it.

'Why would you want to see thousands die?' she asked eventually.

'Come with me.'

She glanced up at him.

'You spend too much time at that factory and working here. It must be lonely.'

Yui shifted. It did get lonely sometimes. And the thought of spending time with Hiro, more than a few hours a week …

'I'd love to go somewhere,' Yui admitted. 'But nowhere like that. It's bad enough knowing it's happening and there's nothing I can do to stop it or to help people.' She added, 'By next year, it'll be over. Can't you wait one more year? The war will be finished. We can save money now and go with Chiyo, maybe the children, too.'

Hiro looked out at the mountains on the horizon. 'I'm going,' he said finally.

Yui remained quiet. She didn't know what she could say to get through to him. 'You'll change,' she said finally. 'Don't you remember the earthquake, how horrible it all was?'

'I know,' he said, though he didn't sound like he meant it. 'You don't understand.'

'No,' she said flatly. 'I don't.'

'You know, don't you?' he asked. 'You know the month it happens.'

Of course she knew. If she didn't tell him, he might go now, before she could convince him otherwise. But if he didn't know and he was there when it happened …

'August,' she said finally. 'August. Don't you dare be there.'

She regretted it as soon as the words left her mouth, but there was no undoing it.

The next day, Hiro was gone.

The days stretched to weeks, and Yui hoped against hope he was out on some bizarre assignment with the *yakuza* and didn't have time to visit them on the farm. He often disappeared for days at a time, though he did come by more frequently now that Grandmother was gone, and often stayed the night.

When the farm work was done and Chiyo was busy with her husband, Yui would sit in the house that was never really hers, trying to read or simply looking out at the farm that had been her home for twenty years, wondering what horrors were unfolding across the water.

A letter came one day, written in Hiro's untidy writing. He had never fully mastered kanji, like her, and when Yui took the letter to Chiyo's, Masao looked over her shoulder and said, 'Uncle Hiro wrote that?'

'Yes,' she said, amused. 'He says he's travelling and having a wonderful time.'

'He isn't getting drafted?' asked Chiyo.

'Hiro's smart.' And probably boasted several mafia tattoos by now. Bribes and threats would help him avoid being drafted. Unless …

'What if he joined voluntarily?' she wondered aloud, ice plummeting in her stomach. Hiro was fascinated with violence. What if he'd joined the army, to see the carnage up close?

'The stamp says he's in Shikoku.' Chiyo pointed out the envelope. 'He's in Japan. Not abroad, fighting.'

Hiro sent more letters, sometimes with gifts and money, all from different parts of Japan. By summer, food was tighter than ever, the cicadas started to buzz from the treetops as the humid season came at full pelt, and the letters stopped coming.

'Hi, Yui-chan,' said Saburō from the entrance of the chicken coop. Yui came in here to check up on the birds and feed them, but mostly because some of her best memories of the farm were watching Hiro name the chickens and hold them close like they were his children.

'Good morning.' Yui always felt a little awkward around Saburō, that spike of guilt prodding her whenever she thought too deeply about the nature of her relationship with Chiyo. But she was always friendly to him.

'Have you heard from Hiro lately?'

The question furrowed her brow; she hadn't had any inclination that he and her brother were close. 'Not for a few months. Why?' A thought occurred to her. 'He doesn't owe you money?' She hesitated, then decided it would be rude to ask if the opposite were true.

Saburō gave a short laugh. 'No, nothing like that. It's … well, let me know if you hear from him, all right?'

'Sure will.' Yui didn't want to be anywhere near a radio when August rolled around. She didn't want to hear about another disaster she had failed to prevent.

The war ended, Tokyo in ruins once again, towns filling with refugees, and doctors and food scarce. For all of Grandmother's sins, she'd been smart to keep the farm where others had sold theirs to go to the cities. The farm had saved their lives. The harvests were not always plentiful or profitable, but there was always food on the table. Saburō's work at the iron factory slowed when the war ended, and he and Chiyo's children helped more. It was like the old crone had said all those years ago: people always needed food.

'It's going to be okay,' Yui said to Chiyo one evening. 'We're safe. The worst is over. Japan will rebuild.'

'And we can go travelling.' Chiyo's eyes shone.

It was something for them to look forward to. Something to distract her from her grief. They hadn't heard from Hiro since his final letter in the spring of '45. Despite her warnings, he had gone to Hiroshima after all, or maybe Nagasaki. He'd got too close and been one of the thousands who'd perished.

Yui spent long nights awake, wondering if she could have saved him if she had kept it to herself. It was only Chiyo who kept her grounded.

'He would have gone anyway, or he would have got himself drafted into the army,' she told her, holding her close as her lips moved against Yui's forehead. 'You did nothing wrong. *Nothing.*'

Yui tried her best to believe that.

'Don't we deserve some happiness?' Chiyo whispered to her. 'Don't we deserve to live without guilt? That passage brought you to me, Yui. There is nothing else you could have done to save anyone, not from the earthquake or from the war. Please don't feel guilty. Hiro made his choice.'

The sound of his name made Yui well up, so she just held Chiyo close as she cried and tried to believe the words.

CHAPTER 31

1953
Thirty years after the earthquake

Yui and Chiyo walked arm in arm through a street in Kagoshima. The children were now grown, Masao had got married, and they and Saburō had encouraged the women to go travelling together with the money they had saved up. Masao was interested in science, and was applying for a scholarship. With his good brains, Yui and Chiyo had no doubt he'd go far.

The past year, though it had come with its own challenges, was the happiest of Yui's life. Nobody batted an eye at two women travelling together, nor getting a single room in an inn. Yui felt her age more these days, but every new place they found, even the places still recovering from the war, was a new adventure.

They would return to Nagano someday, of course they would. But for now, this little Kagoshima street in the summertime was where they needed to be.

'This is where Saigō Takamori was from, isn't it?' said Chiyo. 'Just seventy years ago, the last samurai made their final stand here.'

'The same samurai who's in Ueno Park?' Yui asked, vaguely remembering the statue of the broad-shouldered warrior and his dog. That was where the portal had first appeared, and where she had pinned a note asking Chiyo's family to join them. That was all such a long time ago now.

That thought made her think of Hiro, and her heart squeezed miserably. What a pointless, stupid way to die. She supposed he had died fulfilling his wish. If only his fascination with war and violence hadn't taken him there. If only she hadn't blabbed …

She blinked away the grief as Chiyo said, 'Look! Ramen noodles. I've heard they're delicious here.'

A tantalising savoury smell reached them, and they grinned at each other. Inside, they both feasted on delicious noodles. Yui did; Chiyo claimed she was full after a couple of bites.

'Are you okay?' Yui asked, concerned as Chiyo pulled a face, rubbing her stomach.

'Yes, I'm fine. I suppose I ate too much breakfast.'

They stopped for tea soon after, their stomachs full, Yui still a bit worried about Chiyo. She got full so easily lately.

When Chiyo excused herself to go to the bathroom, Yui looked outside, the hot mug warming her hands. A young man was outside, arguing with an older man. She couldn't tell what they were saying, but the younger of the two looked distressed and annoyed. Finally, he stormed off, entering the teahouse.

He sat by himself at the table opposite, glaring at the window. The older man shook his head, waved his hand as though to say, 'Rid of you, then,' and sloped off.

The man must have sensed her staring, because he glanced up at Yui.

'Good tea here?' he asked. He carried the lilt of the Kagoshima accent that she still wasn't quite used to.

She indicated her cup. 'The wheat tea is very good.'

He ordered some, and she asked him to join them. The young man looked upset, and Yui felt a flash of maternal affection for him as he politely sat beside her. He was about the same age as Masao. Chiyo came back just then, offering the man a curious smile, and they all sipped tea together.

'Are you all right?' Yui asked him. Part of her was curious, but she also was concerned for the man. His hand shook as the held his cup.

'Not really,' he sighed. 'That man outside, he's my uncle. We were having an argument.'

'I could see that.' Yui told Chiyo about witnessing the men's shouting match on the street. She waited, not wanting to push the young man into sharing information he didn't want to.

He looked between the women, seemed to deem it was safe to tell them, and said, 'He disapproves of my choice of partner.'

Chiyo let out a noise from her nose, a mischievous smile on her face. 'Oh, we know exactly what that's like. My paternal grandparents never liked my mother. She was Korean.'

Yui waited for the familiar wrinkle of nose or scowl from the young man, but none came. He said, 'I'm in a similar situation. I went to Scotland a while back and met a wonderful girl.' A dreamy look crossed his face. 'I want to marry her, but my uncle and aunt disapprove. I was only a boy during the war, but my dad fought in it. He was a ... a pilot.' He swallowed for a moment. 'My uncle thinks I'm

323

fraternising with the enemy by wanting to marry a Scottish woman. I explained it was the Americans we were fighting, but they said that the British were their allies so they're the same thing.' He looked down at his tea.

'I think you should follow your heart,' Chiyo declared, and the young man looked up. 'Life is too short to not be with the one you love.' Her eyes met Yui's, and Yui felt a rush of girlish delight.

'Truly?' asked the man. 'I'm not letting down my family? If I go back to Scotland now, I probably won't see my aunt and uncle again. But I'll be with her.'

'That's their problem,' said Yui. 'You can always write, and in a few years, it'll get easier to communicate over long distances, you'll see.'

Chiyo shot her a look of alarm, but the young man just blinked. 'Yeah,' he said. 'I think you're right. I love her, promised I would be back and marry her.'

'You should.' The older women smiled, giving him encouraging nods. 'Otherwise, you might regret it. Better to risk it for love. And I have a feeling you two will be very happy together.'

'My mother told me to be happy in a world that won't accept it,' Chiyo said. 'I did, and I've never looked back.'

'Chiyo,' Yui whispered, feeling tears well up.

The young man drained his tea and rose to his feet. He rifled for some cash, but the women waved his offer away. 'What's your name?' asked Yui, amused by the young man's excitement. Their encouragement seemed to have bolstered him to act.

'Kuroki Yoshitomo,' he said, and bowed low to them. 'Thank you both very much for your advice.'

'Take care,' Yui called after him, and Chiyo gave her a sweet smile.

*

Chiyo's stomach pains were getting worse.

She wanted to visit Okinawa. The white sandy beaches and palm trees and sparkling blue waters Yui had talked about. But her stomach hurt most of the time these days, and she couldn't eat much without feeling bloated.

The trip back to Okaya City was long and hard, but they finally walked upon the familiar farm. Yuiko spotted the women first, waving with enthusiasm, and the children ran across the field to greet them. Masao embraced his mother while the other two hugged Yui. Even in their few weeks of travel, Chiyo felt her kids had grown. Masao was a young man now, so handsome and like his father. Sometimes she felt the children were like Yui, too, maybe not in looks, but in personality. Saeko certainly had her temper.

'Tell us all about your trip,' said Yuiko as they walked home. She was fifteen now, blossoming into a gorgeous young woman many of the village boys already had their eye on. Far too young for a boyfriend for Yui's taste. They had to walk slowly now, not able to keep up with Masao's healthy stride. 'I thought you'd be a gone a couple more weeks.'

'We had to ... postpone Okinawa,' said Yui. Chiyo avoided her gaze.

She was glad to get home and sit down. The children told them of the news while they'd been gone.

'Doctor Tanaka's daughter is in Okaya at the moment with San-ichi,' said Saeko. 'They've had a baby girl.'

Chiyo's brow furrowed at the stricken look on Yui's face. 'Really?' she breathed. Hiro's friend, the one who had hurt his ear and avoided the draft all those years ago, had been trying to have children since they were married, but had always struggled. San-ichi was approaching fifty now, but that didn't seem to have deterred them.

'A baby! How wonderful,' Chiyo exclaimed, pleased. After Doctor Tanaka had helped her so much with her pregnancies, it had always been upsetting for the family that San-ichi and his wife had failed to have any babies. 'We should go and visit, maybe take her a present.'

She made a mental note later to ask Yui what was up. She had gone rather pale. With the chaos of the day, however, and her stomach hurting particularly badly that night, the thought went out of her mind.

*

Yui felt pulled in all directions as they went to visit Doctor Tanaka's granddaughter a few days later. The doctor had reached a ripe old age, for which Yui was glad; he had saved Chiyo's life during her heavy bleeding after giving birth to Masao, as well as helping her with the other births, and she liked the old man. San-ichi, who had grown grey-haired and handsome in his old age, gave her a familiar grin when he saw her. He missed Hiro almost as much as Yui did.

Her heart stopped, though, when a tiny girl waddled behind him, clutching his leg, a fist in her mouth, big midnight eyes looking over the family at their doorstep.

'Oh, isn't she cute,' Chiyo exclaimed. The girl gave a playful yelp and ran into the next room. 'What's her name?'

Yui knew the answer before the doctor responded. 'Her name's Mariko.'

After all, Yui was looking at an infant version of her own mother.

San-ichi had not been drafted into the war because of the accident that caused the deafness in his ear. He had lived instead to marry Doctor Tanaka's daughter. Doctor Tanaka, Yui's own great-grandfather.

She had suspected it during the wedding, when Chiyo had reminded her of their shared surname. Baby Mariko, the little girl toddling about in front of her right now, would grow up to be Yui's mother. How had she gone from a loving family in Nagano Prefecture to being alone on the streets of Tokyo in the seventies, with no relatives to speak of?

It was difficult to know how to feel when she watched Chiyo's children playing with her. She was a baby, not yet grown into the neglectful alcoholic who ignored her own two children. And if it weren't for Hiro injuring Mariko's father, stopping him from getting drafted, she might never have been born. Yui busied herself with preparing tea for everyone, feeling strange.

'Riko!' the toddler shouted. 'Riko!'

'That's all she can say so far,' said her mother. 'Her own name.'

'Riko …' Chiyo whispered, her eyes suddenly glassy. 'I'm sorry, I need to be excused,' she said and rushed out of the door.

Masao gave Yui a questioning look. Abandoning the kettle, she followed her.

Chiyo was outside, vomiting into the grass. 'Chiyo,' said Yui with worry, rubbing her back. 'It's getting worse, isn't it? The pain?'

Chiyo wiped her mouth. Miserably, she nodded. 'I didn't want to worry you.'

Terror flooded Yui. It was as she'd feared, but been too scared to face. Chiyo was sick, just like her mother had been. Medicine wasn't much better now than it had been back then. There were fewer doctors than before, Japan still struggling after the war. There wasn't a hospital for miles, and if Chiyo was throwing up …

'Don't look at it,' Chiyo begged when Yui glanced down.

'Is there blood?' she demanded.

Chiyo hesitated. 'A little bit.'

Yui held her head in her hands. No. She couldn't lose Chiyo. Not after everything they had been through. Was fate so cruel that they had been allowed barely any time together? They were still young. She had already lost Hiro. She wasn't ready to watch Chiyo suffer through illness and leave Yui all alone.

'Yui-chan,' moaned her lover, wrapping her arms around her and pulling her close. 'I'm scared.'

Chiyo trembled in her arms. Yui closed her eyes, trying to find the strength to comfort her. But what could she do? What little funds they'd had had been spent on the trip. And if there was already blood in her vomit, she didn't have much time left.

That night, she raced up the hill where she and Hiro had spent so many evenings talking, looking at the mountains, talking about the past and the future and everything in between. The hill where she had failed to convince her brother to stay. The hill where that one time, a way out had been offered to them.

She looked around in desperation. No passage.

'I need you to open again,' she said. 'I need to save Chiyo. Please. Please.'

She didn't know if anyone or anything was listening, how any of this worked. But she was willing to put her faith in the impossible. After all, it was the impossible that had brought her here.

Chiyo. Chiyo. With every beat of her heart, her soul cried her name.

She stayed awake worrying that night, though she knew if anything happened, Chiyo's husband or one of the children would let her know first. They knew how much Yui meant to Chiyo. How she was as much a part of their family as any blood relative.

She rose early, hoping her plan would work.

*

The children and Saburō were out; Yui told her what she hoped for.

'Go to the future?' Chiyo whispered.

'They'll make you better,' said Yui, determined. She felt like a brash youth, following a plan without thinking about it, but she would do anything to save Chiyo. 'The doctors and hospitals are better in the nineties. Things are easier in every possible way.'

'But what about the children?'

The thought had occurred to Yui too, of course it had. 'We'll take them with us.'

They wouldn't understand. They had never spoken of Yui and Hiro's true origins to the children. But they couldn't leave without telling them, either.

'And what about Saburō?' Chiyo said. 'He doesn't know anything.'

'He doesn't?' Yui asked softly. Saburō was not an idiot. Had he never once suspected, through the years, that Yui and Chiyo were more than friends? Had he never been jealous of their affection for one another? There had been times where they were not so careful.

Chiyo hung her head. 'He knows,' she said finally. 'And he doesn't care because ... because ...' She let out a rattling sigh. 'Because Saburō prefers the company of men.'

Yui blinked. 'He does?'

She nodded. 'All those times he stayed late at the factory ... when he made love to me, he always had his eyes closed. Thinking of ... of others.'

Yui recalled how Saburō had asked if she'd heard from Hiro. Hiro, who had never mentioned a woman. She thought he was being private, but ...

'Saburō loves me and the children.' Chiyo sniffled. 'But he knows that you and I love each other differently.'

'So what do we do?' Yui sighed. She wasn't about to give up a chance to save Chiyo because of Saburō, no matter how much she respected him.

'Let's talk to him.'

That evening, all of them sat together in Chiyo's house. They knelt around the table like they had done a thousand times before, a hotpot bubbling between them.

They made small talk. 'Eriko wants to have four children,' said Masao in amusement as he piled his sister's plate with stew. 'I asked if we could wait for my scholarship first.'

Chiyo was quiet, not eating much as usual. Yui knew what she was thinking. She might not make it long enough to meet her first grandchild.

They finished eating, the children and Saburō growing tense as they sensed there was something Yui and Chiyo wanted to talk about. When the plates were cleared away and everyone was full and sleepy, Yui said, 'Saburō, Chiyo isn't well.'

Her husband sat up as the children looked alarmed. 'Not well? What do you mean?'

The women shared looks. Yui wasn't sure how to explain it. How much to tell. Finally, she said, 'It's the same disease that took away her mother. There's a place I can take her that will make her better, but she won't be able to come back.'

'I don't understand.'

Upset, Saeko crawled onto her mother's lap. She was a teen now, but that didn't stop her cuddling into Chiyo like when she was small. Yui felt a familiar heavy sensation in her chest, and she willed herself not to weep.

'It's a place where medicine is better. If she stays ...'

'I'll die,' said Chiyo simply. Everyone stared at her. She held Saeko to her chest and said, 'I watched my mother waste away. She said the pain was like knives, cutting her from the inside.'

'If there's a way for you to get better, Mother, you should take it,' said Masao. 'But why can't you come back?'

'Maybe we should show them,' said Yui gently.

Yui wasn't sure how she knew it would work. At sunset, when gold and pink coloured the sky, they sat on the hill, inhaling cold, clean mountain air. Yui fixed her gaze on the tree that had offered her and Hiro a way back all those years ago. It hadn't happened since.

She understood now. They had travelled through time to save San-ichi. By rendering him deaf, he had not been drafted into the war, and Mariko had been born. It had ensured Yui and Hiro's existence. But would the passage open again to save one more person?

'What are we waiting for?' Masao paced, anxious. 'Eriko's waiting for me.'

'I'm cold,' Saeko complained.

'Is something supposed to happen?' Yuiko followed the women's gazes to the tree. Saburō stood nearby, looking solemn with his hands behind his back. He had agreed to come out, albeit reluctantly, and Yui got the feeling he was letting the women have their say.

'It will happen.' Yui watched the tree, watched the leaves swaying in the cold breeze. 'Whatever happened that day, it'll happen again. I will save you, Chiyo.'

The sun sank behind the mountains. Yuiko picked at some grass. Saeko made daisy chains. Masao and Saburō quietly talked, casting worried glances at the women. Chiyo remained still beside Yui, whose eyes were watering. The tree was almost a silhouette now in the gathering darkness. In less than an hour, there'd be no more light, and they'd have to blunder back home in the dark.

Then Yui inhaled a breath so sharp it made everyone jump. 'What?' asked Chiyo as Yui struggled to her feet.

Whispers on the air.

A wind whipped up, blowing their hair and clothes. Whispering on the wind, too indistinct to understand, buffeted them.

'You can hear them too, right?' Yui asked, taking Chiyo's wrist. They felt more powerful than ever. Down at the tree, the trunk had widened, and in the centre was ...

'A passage!' Chiyo shouted.

Yui laughed aloud, almost bowled over by the encouraging voices, the wind urging them forward. Saburō and the children stood stunned, holding each other against the sudden strong breeze.

'That is what I meant.' Yui thrust a finger at the tree, where the passage was open to them at last. 'That is the way to my home. My *real* home.'

'I don't see anything,' Saeko shouted.

Her sister Yuiko squinted to where Yui pointed. 'I can't see what you're pointing at.'

Yui's heart sank. The passage was clearly visible. But only she and Chiyo could see it. Only they could go back.

'Listen to me.' Chiyo battled the wind and stepped over to her family. She took Saeko and Yuiko's hands, yelling to be heard over the loud wind. 'Yui and I have to go. Otherwise I'll die here.'

'Go where?' Saeko's voice was full of tears.

'Oh, my darling. I wish you could come with me.' Chiyo took her daughter's cheek in her hand and kissed her on the forehead.

'Chiyo,' Yui called. 'I don't know how much time we have.'

'Come to the Saigō Takamori statue in Tokyo on 22nd July, 1995,' Chiyo shouted at the tops of her lungs. The wind howled around them, whipping their clothes back and forth. The whispers intensified, urging them both onwards. Yui's heart raced. They were running out of time.

'We'll be there, waiting for you. 22nd July, 1995! The statue in Ueno Park!'

'Chiyo!' Yui darted forward and grabbed her hand. The whispers were fading, just like they did that time with Hiro. 'We have to go *now!*'

'Chiyo-chan.' Saburō stared at them both. Their figures were almost lost to the darkness, but Yui could see his eyes were full of tears. 'Go. We'll be there. We will find you.'

Chiyo and Yui ran to the tree, the voices whispering around their heads, the passage wide open and inviting. They stumbled over grass, hand in hand, the wind pushing them on …

Chiyo ran in first, Yui right behind her. Then darkness swallowed them.

CHAPTER 32

Spinning. Churning. A blur of rushing colours and whispers so loud they made Chiyo's head hurt. She held on tightly to Yui's hand, confused. Where was she? Tilling the farm? In bed with a fever? Whose hand was she holding?

She was on her knees, hard ground pressing into her legs. She could hear so much. People. The far-off clanking of machinery. Voices. Rustling tree branches.

'Chiyo?'

Yui, still holding her hand. Had Chiyo fallen over? Her stomach hurt so much. The familiar bloated feeling made her run a hand over her stomach, grimacing as her focus sharpened.

Yui. Yes, there she was. Chiyo must have fallen while helping to maintain the field. But this didn't feel like the field.

It was warm here, like summer. Chiyo looked around as she and Yui rose shakily to their feet. This place felt familiar, like a long-ago memory, but different as well.

The ground was concrete squares. A black fence stood in front of them, low enough to step over. Yui was looking behind them. Her jaw dropped. 'Oh, wow. We're back in Ueno Park.'

'It worked?' asked Chiyo in disbelief. 'We're in the nineties?'

Yui looked around. A building stood close by that said UENO 3153 on it. There were trees, but there was so much concrete and metal and fences.

'No,' she said slowly. 'Something's wrong. Where are the children? They should be waiting for us.'

Masao, Saeko and Yuiko were nowhere to be seen. A little way away, a woman played with a child. Chiyo ogled their clothes. The woman was wearing trousers like a man, and a garment that hung off her shoulders and tight about her arms. Her bag was unlike anything Chiyo had seen. The child, too, wore a backpack and brightly coloured clothes. And they were so *clean*. No dirt or wrinkles or rags, like they were brand new.

'Wow,' Chiyo breathed. So many sounds crashed around her. The rattle of a train, something chiming like a bell, footsteps, voices, wheels on concrete. It sounded like the Tokyo of her childhood, but somehow different, too.

She held her pounding head. This was too much.

Yui gently pulled her forward. 'Come on. We need to get you to a hospital.' She stopped in confusion. 'I can't remember where it is.'

'This is Tokyo?' Chiyo asked. Her eyes were so busy, she didn't know where to look. Some steps – yes, those steps were there when she was a child, she could remember – led down to a packed street. Ueno Station stood there, bigger and grander and with so many lights, and *what was that?*

'What's this box?' She stopped in interest. Bright lights, bottles behind a plastic screen. Three rows of them. Chiyo watched as a young man inserted some coins and pressed a button. Something thumped inside, making her jump. The man had pressed a button under a bottle, and that same bottle came out. He picked it up and walked off, looking at something on his wrist.

And his clothes … they were Western style, not unlike what she'd seen businessmen wear in Tokyo, but different, somehow. All black, neat. And his hair was so neat too, not a strand out of place.

Chiyo felt shabby and dirty next to the tidy, orderly people around them. Some cast them strange looks, though no one stopped to talk to them.

'This isn't the Tokyo I left,' said Yui, sounding more and more worried. 'No, it … excuse me!'

A middle-aged man stopped reluctantly as Yui stepped in his way. 'I'm sorry to disturb you, but could you tell me what that is?'

She pointed to a small, black thing in the man's hand. Chiyo was amazed to see it had its own square of light. She had seen a photo of a television once, and Yui had told her what they were. It was like the man had a television in his hand.

'This? It's my smartphone.' The man looked bewildered as he glanced between the women. 'Do you need help with something?'

'What does it do?' Chiyo asked, bolstered by Yui's boldness.

'What's the date today?' Yui demanded.

The man took a step back as though terrified. 'I, I'm sorry,' he stuttered, and took off, almost running, casting a strange glance back at them both.

Yui sighed. 'Everything feels wrong here.'

'Yui-chan,' said Chiyo slowly. 'What if time kept moving?'

'What?'

'What if this isn't the moment you left, but time continued flowing while you were there?'

Sudden pain flared, burning across her stomach. Chiyo gasped, clutching her belly. The pain brought her to her knees.

'Chiyo-chan,' Yui knelt beside her, panic in her voice. 'Please, someone help us!'

'I'm all right.' Chiyo breathed through it like she always did.

'You're not. We need a doctor.'

She breathed hard through the stabbing pain in her abdomen. People were rushing forward, some holding their strange television-boxes to their ears and asking for help. Chiyo's vision swam, but she focused on Yui's hand. A strange flush of embarrassment swept through her at all the attention.

She ended up sitting somewhere. A woman brought her some water in a plastic bottle. She looked at it in confusion before taking a tentative sip. It tasted so ... clean and cold.

'Thank you.' She inclined her head. She was so thirsty she wanted to gulp down the whole thing.

What came next left Chiyo so stupefied she almost forgot about her pain. It was an ambulance, like ones she had seen as a child, but far more sophisticated and advanced. Paramedics came with machines she didn't recognise, speaking swiftly and professionally to her as they encouraged her to lie down.

'Let me in with her. I'm her sister,' said Yui.

Amusement rippled vaguely through Chiyo as she breathed slowly through a strange plastic mask they pressed over her mouth. Her eyelids grew heavy, but she focused on the Yui-shaped shadow and her echoing voice assuring her everything was going to be fine.

*

Yui didn't know if it was safe to ask a paramedic the year. This definitely wasn't 1995. She had spotted an enormous tower, much taller even than Tokyo Tower, that hadn't been there before, so tall it made her dizzy. Maybe Chiyo was right, and time had continued passing.

That possibility hadn't occurred to her. She had assumed she would step back to the Tokyo she had left, the summer of 1995 during the festival, only at her current age.

Her stomach dropped. That meant Chiyo's children would have waited for them in 1995, hoping to see them at Ueno Park. If her theory was correct, that was thirty years ago. She had to know for sure.

A paramedic gave her a sympathetic look. 'It's 2025, remember?' He gave her a small smile. 'The fifth of October.'

So the day was the same, though it was as she'd feared. 'My ... sister has stomach cancer, I think,' she said to the paramedic. 'You need to give her a scan and ... and whatever else you can do for that.' *Has medicine advanced in thirty years?* Surely it had. 'Can you help her?'

'We'll make sure a doctor sees her right away,' promised the man. 'Does she have her medical insurance card with her?'

Ah.

'Um, not right now. But I can get it for you.' Yui wondered if they would treat Chiyo without any form of ID. Neither of them had any that would be valid; it hadn't been needed on their little farm. Part of her suddenly missed the calm quiet of the place. It was chaotic here. 'Just make sure she gets the care she needs. I can cover it.'

She was guided out of the way once Chiyo was in the hospital, and Yui paced the waiting room, glancing at people who had the funny little *smartphones* in their hands. Their clothes were different from what she had even seen in her childhood. More formal, neutral colours. She felt out of place with her grubby robe. Make-up was a distant memory.

After what felt like a lifetime, a staff member came out and said, 'Sanada-san?'

Yui jumped from her seat. No one had sat near her, and she supposed next to their clean and spotless clothes, she must smell. The nurse gave her a strange look that she immediately smoothed to professionalism.

'How is she?' Yui asked as they walked.

'She's had a scan. We'll have to keep her here for a few days. Were you able to get her medical insurance card yet?'

Yui chewed the inside of her cheek. 'Um, not yet. But I can fill out some forms if you need me to.'

The paperwork was long and complicated, and Yui was ashamed to realise she couldn't read all of the kanji. Most of her high school education had been looking after Hiro – thoughts of him still brought on a lonely pang – and she hadn't mastered all of the characters. Working on the farm for thirty years meant she hadn't needed reading skills, and she had almost forgotten how to read anything beyond the simplest.

A kind staff member noticed her struggle and politely helped her. 'I can pay towards some of the bill now,' Yui said, pulling out the old wallet she had kept with her for the past thirty years. Still inside was the handful of ten-thousand-yen notes withdrawn to pay her mother's rent. Emotion welled up inside her as she held them in her fingers.

'Oh,' said the older staff member in surprise as Yui placed the notes on the little blue tray at reception. 'I haven't seen those notes in a long time.'

'You'll accept them, right?' Yui asked, a jolt of desperation running through her. She could still remember the prices of things in her youth in the 1990s; the money she had was enough to put a dent in the bill, surely?

The worker confirmed it with a manager, who gave Yui a strange look before they took the notes from the tray to count them. 'Yes, we can accept them.'

Yui sighed with relief, sitting on a nearby chair. According to the medical bill, bringing Chiyo in and her initial tests were paid for now, so at least they wouldn't be kicking them out anytime soon. What were they going to do without any medical insurance, though?

Yui decided that wasn't important right now. All that mattered was that Chiyo got better.

After what seemed like several decades of waiting, Yui was finally allowed to see Chiyo.

'You're going to be all right,' she said fiercely, taking Chiyo's hand. Her lover lay in the bed, staring sadly at the ceiling.

'Is it the pain?' Yui asked anxiously.

Chiyo shook her head. 'They gave me medicine. Put this in my arm.' She raised her hand, showing Yui an IV drip. 'The future is … I'm still trying to get my head around it.' She turned to look at Yui. 'A man told me it's 2025. Will the children even still be alive?'

Masao would be over ninety, probably with children and grandchildren of his own. 'We'll find them,' Yui promised, though she wasn't sure how. Would Chiyo's son and two daughters still be in Nagano Prefecture? Masao had talked of a scholarship; had that brought him to the capital?

But even if it had, he would be long finished with that now.

Chiyo was taken somewhere for more treatment, and Yui found herself with a lot of time on her hands. She didn't have a phone – it still amazed her that if she did have one, someone could call her wherever she was – and she had nowhere to go anyway. She wandered the hospital, watching people talk, catching snippets of their lives. She sipped some of the free water from a cooler, and watched someone get an iced coffee from a vending machine.

Everything was so different here. But Chiyo was getting the treatment she needed, and that was the most important thing.

She sat in a waiting room, stretching out her legs and rotating her ankles. She wished she could take a bath. Everyone here seemed so clean, their clothes immaculate. The occasional person glanced at her too long, but mostly people ignored her. She was fine with this.

She ended up sitting near a group of young adults who were all looking at a smartphone. They erupted into stifled giggles and shushes, one girl casting an apologetic glance at the people quietly waiting. An amused smile spread on Yui's face at the kids' antics.

'Are you watching something funny?' she asked with interest.

'Just a silly video.' The young woman holding the phone showed it to her. Yui tried to get her mind around the fact that she was looking at someone through a screen, someone who wasn't really there, and politely laughed at the video that had amused the youngsters so much, a sequence of people falling over.

'What else can you do on a smartphone?' she asked them. 'I'm not very good with, er, modern technology.'

The young adults glanced at each other. 'Lots of things,' said the girl eventually, coming to sit beside Yui so she could show her. 'Watch videos, message your friends, search for information.'

'Really?' said Yui with interest. 'You mean you could find someone you're looking for on there?'

'Well, sure, if they have Facebook or Instagram or …' The girl trailed off at the confusion on Yui's face. 'Well, I can give it a try if you want. Who are you looking for?'

Yui tried not to let the excitement show on her face. Could this magic little box help her find Chiyo's children? 'Could you search for Ota Yuiko?' The youngest would be a good place to start. 'She'd probably be in Nagano Prefecture.'

The girl tapped her smartphone for a good while, finally coming up with several results. But the pictures that came up were either the wrong age or in the wrong place. Besides, none of them looked like her.

'Try Ota Masao.'

Yui clutched her grubby robe in her fingers, her heart thumping. The girl obediently checked her phone, the screen light reflecting in her large eyes as she searched. 'Hmm. I can only find information about the physicist.'

'Can I see?' Yui scooted over to peer at an information page detailing a Professor Ota. He was retired now, but the page said he had worked in Nagano University and Toyo University in Tokyo. A jolt of excitement ran through her.

'That's him!' she exclaimed when the photo of him came up. He was older, yes, his hair white and his face wrinkled, but it was undoubtedly him.

'You found him?' The young woman looked delighted. 'That's so cool. Look, there's a phone number here. It might work.'

Yui hesitated, but the girl smiled at her and said, 'You can use my phone to call him, if you want.'

Yui thanked her profusely, then clumsily took the phone when the girl showed her how to put the phone number in. To think Masao had used those good brains of his and achieved that scholarship after all.

The phone number led to the university, not to Masao himself. They told her he was retired. 'Can I have his personal number?' she asked, her heart pounding so hard it hurt.

'Please hold for a moment.'

Blaring music blasted from the phone. Yui held it away from her ear, nose wrinkling in distaste.

'Will they give you his number?' The young woman and all her friends were standing and staring at her in anticipation, apparently all invested in her search for Masao.

'Don't worry,' said Yui. 'I have some experience in tracking down university professors.'

CHAPTER 33

M asao, it turned out, had retired in Kanagawa Prefecture, just a train ride away from Tokyo. He was already in his nineties, but he had remembered Yui. He had even made an excited squeak down the phone when he'd realised who she was.

'You're back! Oh, you're back!' A rustling of papers in the background. 'I always knew you would one day … oh, my, where is my cane? You're at Eiju General Hospital? I can be there in an hour. Oh, you've no idea how happy I am to hear your voice.'

Yui was tearful by the time she handed back the phone to the kind stranger. 'He's on his way,' she said. One of the young men handed her a box of tissues, and she thanked him as she wiped her nose.

The group of young people received news about their friend just then, and she waved goodbye to them before they could ask too many questions. She was grateful for their help, but the less they knew, the better.

In a little over an hour, a man in his nineties hobbled into the waiting area, looking around. His eyes lit up when Yui stood, and she moved to embrace him, laughing into his shoulder. He may have aged, but he was still strong, still held that spark of life she had loved about him as a boy.

'You're here,' he said again, looking her up and down. 'Oh, you haven't changed one bit since I last saw you.'

They managed to find a quiet waiting area, where they sat together. Masao struggled to sink into a sitting position, and Yui grasped his elbow, his other hand holding his cane.

'Tell me everything,' said Yui, so many emotions welling up inside her. 'First of all, I'm so sorry we didn't come back in 1995. I thought that was where we'd go. It brought us to 2025 instead … time moved on without us.'

'I'm going to get the others straight away,' said Masao. 'Everyone. Where is my mother? Is she here?'

'Getting treatment.' Yui supposed 'the others' were his sisters, Saeko and Yuiko. Happiness ballooned inside her. It had been less than a day since she'd seen them, but for them, it had been decades.

'I have a son now. Yusuke,' said Masao. 'And he has two children of his own. And Yuiko, she has a daughter. Her name's Mayumi.'

'How about Saeko?' asked Yui eagerly. The sweet little girl had always envied her younger sister's good looks. 'Is she married? What is she up to these days? Are they all in Nagano?'

Masao's wrinkled face creased in sadness. 'Oh. Saeko. She … she died. In 1964.'

Yui's joy dissipated. She swallowed, fresh tears pinpricking her eyes. 'Oh … oh my.'

Masao's hand found her shoulder, gave it a gentle squeeze. 'She got sick easily. One day she got a fever and … there wasn't much we could do.'

Yui nodded in silence, leaning against Masao. Chiyo would be crushed.

*

Chiyo looked around at all her family. Her son, Masao, sat nearby, holding his cane. His son, a handsome man in his middle years, was standing behind him, wearing a suit. Chiyo's youngest daughter Yuiko was there, too, with her daughter Mayumi.

Chiyo had wept for Saeko. For Masao and Yuiko, it had been many years ago, but the news had been a shock to Chiyo and Yui. But at least her other two children were here.

'How difficult was it to believe your father?' Yui asked Masao's son, Yusuke. Chiyo couldn't believe that her own grandson was a few years older than she was.

'He first told me when I was a child,' said Yusuke. 'We went to Ueno Park to wait for you in 1995.'

Masao nodded. Despite his age, he dressed well and there was a sharp gleam in his eyes that told Chiyo age had not dulled him. His career in physics had allowed him to explore the possibilities of time travel, and the research, he said, had kept him young. 'We hoped to see you, back then,' he said. 'But you didn't come.'

Chiyo's heart bled at that. 'I'm sorry. We thought we would emerge in 1995.'

'I didn't count on time moving forward without us,' Yui said. 'It must have been awful, waiting around that day.'

'I'm just glad I lived long enough to see you again.' Masao's hand, the skin translucent, blue veins visible, reached for his mother's. Chiyo squeezed back, emotion welling up in your eyes. 'If you had stayed there on the farm, you'd have died.'

'This is just so strange,' said Yuiko. 'You're here, but you're the same age as you were in 1953. And we've all grown older, have children of our own, and now you're younger ...' Her face screwed up in confusion, and Chiyo couldn't help laughing.

The treatment was doing its work. It had taken operations, scans, and a close call that had left them terrified, but Chiyo was on the mend. The magic these doctors had performed would never have been possible on the little farm in Nagano. It made her sad that her mother had suffered through so much pain, when in the future she could have been healed.

She thought she saw a flutter of curtain on the other side of the room, but she couldn't be sure. Nobody else seemed to have noticed it.

'I suppose you'll need some ID,' said Yusuke.

'And medical insurance,' added Yuiko.

Yui chewed her lip. 'Um, yes. I don't know how we'll go about getting those.'

'First thing is paying the medical bills,' said Yusuke. 'We can help cover those.'

Chiyo wanted to hug them all.

When the relatives left, squeezing Chiyo's hand one by one, a handsome doctor in his middle years approached them. 'Excuse me.' He hesitated. 'I couldn't help overhearing what you were saying before. Something about 1953?'

Yui and Chiyo glanced at each other. Chiyo didn't know what to do, so she stayed quiet. Yui cleared her throat. 'Yes, we were talking about it.'

The doctor's gaze flicked between the two of them. 'And I also heard you don't have any medical insurance or identification?'

'The medical bills are taken care of,' said Yui, an edge to her voice.

'It's not that,' said the doctor. 'Let me explain. I'm Maeda Keisuke.' He swallowed, his Adam's apple bobbing. 'Twenty years ago, a woman from Scotland went missing in Kagoshima Prefecture. She came back again nine months later, claiming she had been to 1877.'

Chiyo's insides froze with shock. 'And, had she?'

Doctor Maeda nodded. 'I'm the only one who believed her, because she met one of my ancestors. A samurai. I saw everything through his eyes.'

'A dream?' asked Yui.

'Memories,' corrected the doctor. 'Whenever I slept, I saw life through Maeda Keiichirō's eyes. I saw her. Isla. And when she came back to the present – back to 2005 – I found her.'

'So other people *can* time travel,' said Yui, looking awed. 'How many other people have done it?'

'You went to 1953?' The doctor sat where Masao had been sitting. 'And then came back?'

They quickly explained. 'So people can come forward through time as well,' the doctor confirmed, looking amazed. 'Well, it's no wonder you don't have insurance or ID. What year were you born, Ota-san?'

'1902,' said Chiyo meekly.

'I still have this ID,' said Yui, pulling out a worn and battered card. 'It's from the nineties. I was born in 1973.'

'Then your address should still be registered here,' said Doctor Maeda, looking at her ID. 'Though I'm not sure what we can do about you, Ota-san,' he added to Chiyo.

'A problem for another day,' said Yui. 'I'm just glad you're going to be all right.' She kissed Chiyo's forehead.

'Leave it to me. I'll help,' said Doctor Maeda, gaining his feet. He bowed to them and stepped out, giving them privacy.

'To think there are more time travellers out there,' Chiyo whispered. 'How many people walking among us are from a different time, do you think?'

'It could be hundreds.'

Yui climbed carefully onto the bed beside Chiyo. Their foreheads touched, their breathing in sync, as they inhaled clean, fresh air, listening to the city sounds outside. Chiyo couldn't remember the last time she had felt so peaceful. Her stomach didn't hurt. Yui was here. Two of her children were still alive, and she had a beautiful big family to look forward to getting to know.

'There are other time travellers,' she whispered to Yui.

'Hundreds, maybe.' Yui's voice was sleepy. A gentle hand tucked some hair behind Chiyo's ear. 'I love you.'

*

Mayumi, Yuiko's daughter, offered Yui a place to stay while Chiyo was in hospital. She apologised for the lack of space in her small Tokyo apartment, but after living in the barn and then Grandmother's old creaky house, this warm, clean little flat was a luxury.

It was on the fourth floor, and from here Yui could see so many tall skyscrapers. In thirty years, the Tokyo of her childhood had changed so much. It was busier, the loud noises bothered her, but it was also cleaner, brighter, neater. Yui had no doubt Chiyo would recover in the hospital, especially with the children's help.

'It's so strange, being the same age as my own grandmother,' said Mayumi.

'It must all be strange,' said Yui. For her and Chiyo, going from 1953 to 2025 had happened in moments. But for Chiyo's family, the story of Chiyo and Yui stepping into the portal, never to return and promising to emerge again in the future, had happened a lifetime ago. Three generations.

'Uncle Masao always told us about it, since we were kids. His kids, too,' said Mayumi. 'I always thought it was a family legend or something, or a bedtime story. But now here you are.'

Mayumi beamed at her, no hint of doubt on her face. Then her eyes widened. 'Have you seen your missing person's report yet?'

'My what?' Yui asked as Mayumi pulled out her smartphone. Yui watched in awe as Chiyo's granddaughter tapped the screen, making different colours and shapes appear. She would never get tired of looking at it.

'Here.' Mayumi handed her the smartphone. Yui held it clumsily, frowning at the screen. It was a report from 1995, a blurry photo of her twenty-two-year-old self shortly before she went missing. She was scowling, thick eyeliner smudged beneath her eyes. And there – Yui's heart gave a sad squeeze – was twelve-year-old Hiro, an expression on his face that said he'd been asked to smile but didn't want to.

It made sense that their mother, however useless she had been, had reported her children missing. Yui read old news reports from that time, dozens of them, eventually saying the trail had gone cold after lengthy interrogations of their mother. So, she had been a suspect.

'We saw you that day, in Ueno Park,' said Mayumi. 'We knew we mustn't talk to you or stop you, because it might have undone everything if something happened and you couldn't go to the portal. Uncle Masao smiled at you, and you looked annoyed about it.'

Yui nodded, recalling seeing the mother and daughter at Sensō-ji Temple that day, purchasing fortune papers. The old man who had waved to her at the festival.

'Hiro ran past us, then you went to the statue. We wondered if you might emerge right after that with Grandma, older, but you didn't.'

'Because time moved forward here as well,' said Yui. 'The portal acted as a … bridge through time, I suppose, but the timelines move simultaneously.'

She told Mayumi about the portal opening once for her, years ago. 'It was after our ancestor was injured,' she said. 'So he could marry and have my mother, Mariko. We had ensured our own existence, so we were offered a way back.'

'But why did the portal open a second time?' asked Mayumi.

'So I could save Chiyo.' It made sense to her now. 'The portal, or gate, presents itself when a life has to be saved or preserved. The first time, it opened because we'd saved an ancestor and secured our own existence. That's what I think, anyway.'

'I think you're right.' Mayumi slowly exhaled. 'So what happens if you *don't* go through the portal the first time?'

Yui frowned at that. 'You wouldn't save your ancestor, which means you wouldn't exist.'

'But if you didn't go back, you wouldn't exist anyway.'

'A time paradox.' Yui laughed. 'It hurts my brain to think about it.'

'So Sanada Mariko is your mother?' asked Mayumi in interest. 'I remember Uncle Masao talking about it. She disappeared, you know.' Seeing Yui's shocked face, she added, 'When she was a baby. They never found her. It was really awful.'

'But she ended up in Tokyo,' said Yui. 'Working as a hostess, where she had me and Hiro.'

'How did she end up there from Nagano?'

They puzzled over it. 'The Mariko I know was by herself. She said she didn't have much memory of a family, but she didn't like talking about it,' said Yui. 'I barely knew anything about my father. She said he was half-American. Whenever I asked about her own parents, she just drank more.'

'The Sanadas were devastated. She went missing near the farm, I think. She was only two or three.'

'But she ended up in Tokyo,' Yui repeated.

'What if … ?'

The women stared at each other, frozen as the same thought hit them both.

CHAPTER 34

Tracking down Sanada Mariko wasn't as difficult as Yui had expected. An inspection of obituaries told her that her mother was still alive, and Mayumi, who had worked in elderly care in the past, helped her find a care service for the elderly with Yui's mother's name listed on it. She lived in a tiny apartment in East Tokyo, not far from Asakusa.

'How did you do that?' Yui asked in amazement. 'Find out all that information so quickly?'

Mayumi blushed, and for a delightful moment she looked just like Chiyo. 'Well, it's not that difficult,' she said. 'There's a database I still had access to.'

Yui didn't know what a database was, but she decided it didn't matter. She felt suddenly nervous.

Mayumi managed to pull some strings to have Yui hired as a temporary cleaner to cover for an absence. 'How are you feeling?' Chiyo's granddaughter asked one breezy morning as Yui stood before her, wearing an apron and clutching a mop and bucket in one hand, a box of cleaning supplies in the other.

Yui had no idea how to answer that, so she defaulted to, 'Fine.'

'I'll call you later,' Mayumi promised. Yui still couldn't get used to the little flip phone Chiyo's granddaughter had given to her. It sat in her pocket now.

Yui nodded and headed for the flat. The stairs were rickety, the cold air dry and smelling faintly of something cooking. 'Excuse me,' she called, letting herself in like the trainer at the care facility had taught her to do. 'The cleaning service is here.'

'Come in,' croaked an old lady's voice.

Before they had left the farm, Yui had seen her mother as a one-year-old girl. Chubby and healthy and innocent, all her mistakes ahead of her. The woman Yui beheld now was over seventy, though she looked as old as Masao. Her hair had thinned so much Yui could see her scalp, and her gnarled hands were wrapped around a cane.

The older woman blinked in confusion. 'You're not Chizu.'

'I'm working with you today, Sanada-san, as Chizu-san is off sick.' Yui stepped into the home, a cramped, cluttered little one-bedroom apartment. She wondered whether their old building, the place from her childhood, had been torn down yet. Maybe. This one was newer than theirs had been, but it was still overcrowded with things, with not much space to move. She supposed that was just the way her mother had lived.

My mother. Was this really her?

Ms Sanada sat on a worn cushion on the tatami mat, watching as Yui performed her cleaning duties. 'What's your name?'

'I'm Aoki Yui.' It felt natural to use Chiyo's maiden name as her own. Chiyo's parents, after all, had been like the mother and father she'd never had.

'Yui.' Ms Sanada's eyes glazed over, and Yui looked at her. 'I used to have a daughter called Yui.'

Used to.

She wondered whether to say anything, whether to open those old wounds. Despite how she felt about her mother, she didn't want to cause her any pain. She was a pathetic thing now, living by herself with carers attending to her needs. Yui couldn't bring herself to be angry about such a long time ago.

'Really?' she said, keeping her voice light as she busied herself tidying up the kitchen table.

'Yes. She ran away. I was a terrible mother.'

Yui put down the papers she was holding and peered into the living room. Ms Sanada was staring at the wall, lost in thought.

'If you could see her again,' said Yui, 'what would you say to her?'

Ms Sanada didn't respond at first. Yui deposited some old rubbish into the bin and started wiping down the kitchen's side cabinets.

'I would tell her and her brother I'm sorry. And that I hope wherever they are, they're happy.' Ms Sanada let out a slow breath. 'I never told her everything. About my childhood in Tokyo. A Tokyo that doesn't exist anymore. About meeting a girl who gave me the name Yui. There was an earthquake, lots of fire, and I stepped onto a path that took me ... here. They told me it was all a dream.'

Yui closed her eyes for a moment. A time traveller, like her. The portal had sent her to Tokyo.

Yui carried on cleaning, not letting her mother see her tears fall.

*

Chiyo was released from hospital in remission, which Doctor Maeda said meant all the signs and symptoms of cancer had gone. 'It's good you brought her back when you did,' he said to her. 'Another couple of weeks and it would've been inoperable.'

Chiyo left the hospital with her family around her, her arm linked with Yui's. Yui herself was a picture of health and happiness. More easily accessible food, nice clothes, and Chiyo's good health had healed her, too.

'Let's take a trip,' Chiyo said happily as an autumn wind blew over her.

'To Okinawa,' Yui said. 'Chiyo's always wanted to go.'

'I want to go to karaoke,' said Chiyo, her eyes shining. 'We can sing that song you taught me all those years ago, Yui-chan.'

Masao had joined them, holding his mother's other arm. To anyone else, it might look like Masao was Chiyo's parent, not the other way round.

Yui couldn't believe it had all come to this. She only wished Hiro had survived, but his knuckle-headedness was always going to get him into the worst kind of trouble. There was no point in blaming herself or wondering if she could have done more. She could accept that now.

'Let's go somewhere to eat,' said Mayumi, to general cheers and nods of agreement. 'Are you hungry, Grandmother?'

'Famished,' said Chiyo.

She looked so happy. Yui beamed back, squeezing her thin arm in hers. Things were going to be okay. She had made the right decision both times when she had seen the portals open to her. The first to stay, the next to go back.

She didn't understand what forces controlled opening gates and time travel, but she had saved her own legacy and

Chiyo's, too. Love filled her heart as they headed for the metro, Chiyo exclaiming in delight at every modern feature she saw. Mayumi chatted excitedly about what she wanted to eat while Masao listened to his niece with delight, nodding along to all her suggestions.

They could make a good life here. One free of war and fire, cold winters and empty bellies. Life here would have its own challenges, but as long as Chiyo was by her side, Yui knew everything would be all right.

ACKNOWLEDGEMENTS

The writing of this book happened during a tumultuous time of my life: a marriage separation, a surprise pregnancy, moving to a different country and even as I write this, a long, expensive and painful custody battle. It seems fitting, then, that the contents of the book are also so tumultuous and focus on the themes of found family and finding love and peace amid chaos.

Writing a second book is no easier than writing the first, but it is just as wonderfully rewarding. I wouldn't be where I am today without the support of some very special people in my life. Declan, you saved me. I was just starting to write *Passage to Tokyo* when we met, and you provided so much inspiration for Yui and Chiyo's blossoming romance. Jack Valentine, my son, whom I miss more than words can say, I love you and think about you every minute of the day. I hope things work out and you can join me in England. Mammy is doing everything she can to make it happen.

My friends and family who never gave up on me and continue to offer their love and support, even when it seems like all I do is make mistakes. And to the people in my life who have only ever put me down and abused me: you made me stronger and more resilient.

A huge thank-you to Jenny Parrott. Even though you're no longer my editor at Oneworld Publications, I'll never forget our chats and your enthusiasm throughout the production of Book 1. And to my new editor at Oneworld, Wayne Brookes, who couldn't have been a better choice to take over from Jenny.

A huge thank-you to my editor at HarperCollins US, Sara Nelson, who guided me greatly along edits and suggestions with *Passage to Tokyo*. And an extra-huge thank you to my wonderful agent, Edwina de Charnace, who made all this happen in the first place when I humbly approached her at MMB Creative to give my debut novel a shot.

Thank you to the wonderful team at Oneworld Publications, HarperCollins, and foreign language publishers as well: Sperling & Kupfer (Italy), Planeta (Portugal), Eksmo (Russia), and the rest!

Thank you especially to you, the reader, who decided to give the Ancestor Memories series a chance. I humbly thank you from the bottom of my heart.

© Oktavianti Nila

POPPY KUROKI was born in Scotland and grew up in England. She lived in Japan for eleven years, where the country's history and culture inspired her to pen the Ancestor Memories series. Poppy now lives in a beautiful city in Yorkshire and likes reading, singing and playing video games.